THE
REAPER

THE
REAPER
JACKSON P. BROWN

DEL REY

UK | USA | Canada | Ireland | Australia
India | New Zealand | South Africa

Del Rey is part of the Penguin Random House group of companies
whose addresses can be found at global.penguinrandomhouse.com

Penguin Random House UK,
One Embassy Gardens, 8 Viaduct Gardens, London SW11 7BW

penguin.co.uk

First published 2025
001

Copyright © Abigail Jackson, 2025

The moral right of the author has been asserted

Penguin Random House values and supports copyright. Copyright fuels creativity, encourages diverse voices, promotes freedom of expression and supports a vibrant culture. Thank you for purchasing an authorised edition of this book and for respecting intellectual property laws by not reproducing, scanning or distributing any part of it by any means without permission. You are supporting authors and enabling Penguin Random House to continue to publish books for everyone. No part of this book may be used or reproduced in any manner for the purpose of training artificial intelligence technologies or systems. In accordance with Article 4(3) of the DSM Directive 2019/790, Penguin Random House expressly reserves this work from the text and data mining exception.

Set in 13.5/16pt Garamond MT Std
Typeset by Jouve (UK), Milton Keynes

Printed and bound in Great Britain by Clays Ltd, Elcograf S.p.A.

The authorised representative in the EEA is Penguin Random House Ireland,
Morrison Chambers, 32 Nassau Street, Dublin D02 YH68

A CIP catalogue record for this book is available from the British Library

ISBN: 978–1–529–90719–3 (hardback)
ISBN: 978–1–529–90720–9 (trade paperback)

Penguin Random House is committed to a sustainable future
for our business, our readers and our planet. This book is made
from Forest Stewardship Council® certified paper.

To Ms Mary Matthews — thank you
for telling me to keep writing.

In memory of Verona.

Please note

This book includes depictions of domestic abuse, sexual assault and grooming.

The Awakening

It was the wrong night to come to Camden Town.

Thanks to his own misjudgement, the man was forced to hide in an end-of-terrace alley just as he was assaulted by the amorphous essence of his Awakening. It was a physical manifestation that only he could see. Unfocused shapes reached towards him from the sky as membranes of pale star-matter, and he pressed his back against the cold brick wall, his breath becoming haggard and raw in his throat.

The membranes thickened, pulsing and growing until the deluge surrounded him, congealing over his body, making it difficult to move. He inhaled deeply, letting the air out in quick, measured gasps. When he was covered completely, the outside world faded to nothing, and his Awakening began.

His ancestors brushed against him, their touch filled with understanding and tender warmth. When they offered their energy and power, he grasped it firmly. As it seeped into his flesh, every fibre of his body began to change. Their power caressed his skin, his bones, his marrow and joints, and as it sank deeper and deeper into his flesh, it pushed him across the border of his previous existence.

When he finally opened his eyes, the entrails of the galaxy had vanished, leaving the horizon clear once more. He let out a deep breath, revelling in the feel of his new self. Now he could finally step into his rightful place as heir. Now he could finally be who he was destined to be.

But the stars maintained their watch.

A pulsing void opened from among them, darker than the night sky. It split the constellations in half. Dumbfounded, he stared as the opening expanded. Its magnitude grew so wide, he felt it had swallowed him whole.

And then it spoke, the sound so potent it troubled the water in his skull. This was not an ancestor; this was someone else. Something else. His toes twitched with the instinct to run, but his limbs were cement, and his mind lost between those contradictions. The mythical language sounded at first like song, then a whispered requiem, and then finally a warning.

When it was over, the void in the sky knitted itself closed and was healed, collapsing into the surrounding universe. But his body still bore the fingerprints of that voice, that malicious anomaly called Great Father. Progenitor. Dark Man. Harbinger. Death King Armageddon. The warning had been burned into him, and heat coursed down his neck, enveloping him. He was in flashover.

As the world returned, he peered at it through new eyes granted to him by his Awakening. Millions of silken threads floated before him, brushing against his face and glinting in the moonlight. These were the human lives that populated not just Camden, but all of London, the city of bodies, and he marvelled at his new ability to see them. To touch them. The threads danced and swirled like seaweed, before drifting away on the air. They were weak and thin, insignificant cilia compared to the thick ribbons that had hung from the stars previously – as was to be expected of humanity.

If he wanted to, he could snatch these threads and break them. A scarlet flame pulsed and swelled in his body as he reached a gloved hand towards one, feeling it dance and struggle against the tight leather encasing his fingers. He stroked it with a beckoning embrace. Only he could see it; could touch this web of human inferiority. He contemplated what it would feel like to sever it – the small snap, and the resultant squelch of fresh blood.

'Shit,' he whispered, and he sunk to his knees.

But before he could regain his composure, a quiet noise alerted him to his surroundings. He glanced across the street towards it, searching for the source. There was nothing to see, but his ears were well seasoned to the sound of caution: the leathery grind of numbed toes in boots, the small, dull thuds of rubber soles against the ground, and how these combined to carve a wound in the air.

They were gone now, but someone had been there.

PART ONE
Downstairs

Haunted Creatures # 1: Vampires

Definition: Humans that are revived with *lichid noir* at the brink of death.

Strengths: Ageless, extraordinary strength, regenerative powers, no need for food or sleep.

Weaknesses: Require human blood to retain strength. Can be killed by a stake to the heart (the aortic valve specifically) or by exposure to extreme light.

Notes:
- Vampires often derive pleasure and strength by drinking blood from other vampires. Usually from the jugular, saphenous or radial veins
- Vampires appear to be culturally or otherwise prohibited from killing their prey. They are expected to exert self-control when drinking from humans.

CHAPTER ONE

Amy

The clock shifted to midnight as Amy sat at the downstairs bar of Dishoom. Drunken customers stumbled down the walnut stairs and were quickly escorted to their booths by a strained yet friendly waiter. The constant chatter, chorus of happy birthdays and resulting cheers engulfed her in a tide of cocktail-infused madness.

She loved it here: the polished furniture adorning the vintage tile floor, the large booths finished with velvet and stained glass, the Victorian street lanterns, and the walls papered with colonial news items and artwork from Asia. In recent years, Dishoom had cemented itself as a lauded venue among the yuppie classes, and oftentimes an impossibly long queue would snake its way out of the venue and down the adjacent street, accompanied by a waiter serving milky chai from a modernised tuk-tuk. But with the décor so quaint, the lighting so dim, and the crowds so thick, it had also become a popular destination for vampires.

Amy was now an expert in detecting them. When a vampire drew near, the air around her would grow thin, as if the world had turned to mist and vapour. And as they drew closer, cold would lance through her body, the glacial ridges of goosebumps appearing on her brown skin. They also tended to ensure their eyes were covered, a fact revealed after a chance encounter with an impossibly thirsty vampire outside Ministry in Elephant and Castle. His tinted shades had slipped, and Amy had glimpsed two black coals with no sclera or iris, just an endless gaze of shadow. It was a far cry from the beauty myths that were so prevalent in popular media.

Tonight, hours had passed, and not a single vampire had appeared. She paid for the last of her drinks and reluctantly stowed her notebook away in her forlorn bag. It didn't seem like there would be any new observations tonight. When she moved to push back her chair, a line of cold water trickled down her spine. She repressed the urge to flinch at the sensation.

Breathe, she told herself, lowering her shoulders, and settling once more. Through long lashes she saw a pale white couple emerge from the gloom of the stairs, both with stunning bone structure and angular features. One was blond, the other black-haired. Both male and female had thick fringes that flopped over the bridge of their noses, shrouding the top half of their faces in shadow. They glided past where Amy sat at the bar before taking a seat somewhere behind her.

For twenty minutes, Amy waited, her breaths slow and controlled. It was late and she should go home. Vampires were dangerous, and it wasn't safe to be around them with anything less than her full wits.

Despite the risk, she moved to another stool to watch them.

They whispered to each other behind their menus and pretended to sip white wine. When their waiter reappeared, the couple quickly ordered and then received a mountain of food – a platter of pilau rice, naan, saag aloo, a spiced lamb dish, what looked like a chicken curry, a bowl of spiced okra chips, and several miniature plates of meat and vegetables – which they promptly ignored. They spoke close to one another's faces, lips brushing against nose tips, fingers circling the backs of hands. The female would laugh with a shrill, whistling noise, coquettishly covering her mouth to hide her canines. All things considered, the vampire couple looked unassuming and delicate. Amy was captivated, as she always was, by their measured, human feint.

Her notebook returned to the table as she observed the pair, and she wrote the day's date before scribbling her customary *Dear Nan*. Tonight, she wrote about their clothes, their actions, and the fold of their expressions behind the curtains of their hair. Sadly, there was little else to write. She had been hoping for more excitement this evening; some new discovery to add to her field notes. At home, she had countless notebooks, all colour-coded to indicate the various creatures she had identified over the past five years: blue for mages, green for witches, grey for warlocks, black for vampires, and yellow for the unknown. She touched a fingertip to the page, running her hand over her grandmother's name, hoping that in some way her notes were being read, that in the strange world of the beyond, she was commending her work and noting her keen observations.

She moved her attention back to the couple as a young woman rose from the table opposite and headed towards the toilets. As she did, the female vampire straightened in her seat, smile faltering, and Amy's heart began to race. The female's nails dug into the table and her breathing deepened, thin shoulders rising and falling in a hypnotising rhythm. The male ran his fingers down her exposed shoulders, his grin hungry and awestruck. Then she stood, and languidly followed the unsuspecting woman.

With every step the vampire took, an ecstatic, pleasurable feeling pulsed in Amy's stomach, rippled down her thighs, and twinged sparks of euphoria on her skin. The vampire was going to feed, and it *had* to be from that woman. No one else in the restaurant was suitable.

This was an oddity that Amy had observed many times, but one that she could not quite find an answer for: vampires would often frequent busy places, but despite a mass of bodies to choose from, they were always waiting for one specific person. It was as if they had previously marked the person in some way. Regardless, the feed always ended the same: a vulnerable, dazed human stumbling uncertainly from a darkened alley or a tinted car, the heat of their body dimmed with fatigue.

Amy sucked in a haggard breath and headed to the toilets herself, purposely not looking at the male vampire or anyone else. But her confidence drained with every step. Why was she doing this? Despite all her observations, so far, her skirmishes with the supernatural had been infrequent and accidental. She much preferred the self-assumed researcher role: armed with notebook and pen, watching them as if unseen behind reinforced glass, scribbling notes like a scientist of the underworld. She'd actively avoided vampires until recently for just this reason. They possessed unfathomable speed and were inhumanly strong. They were immortal. They could bewitch humans to volunteer their blood and forget the whole affair a moment later, and they were cunning, with some having already lived for centuries. This vampire would be no different. But the pulse of her hunger echoed in Amy's stomach, and she just couldn't sit back and do nothing while the human was in danger.

With a final burst of courage, she shoved the toilet door

open so forcefully, it banged on the nearby wall and echoed off the tiles in the room.

Three mahogany cubicles faced a bank of ivory washbasins. Amy steadied herself, fighting against the wave of biting cold that coursed through her body. She loudly walked to the nearest sink, pumped copious amounts of soap into her palms, and splashed her hands with water. Hot, then cold, then hot, until they were soft and wrinkly. All the while, she could sense the vampire standing motionless on the other side of the locked cubicle directly behind her.

The faint, fleeting warmth of a human body pulsed beneath the vampire, wilting further as the moments passed. The woman was helpless – structured with inferior biology that rendered her vulnerable against the insatiate thirst of a supernatural predator.

It appeared that the female had only just started drinking when Amy had entered the room. She'd likely used an enchantment to render the human unconscious, then dragged her into the cubicle for the feed. Amy closed her eyes in concentration, reading the scene behind the door from the tension in the atmosphere. Alongside the typical vampire iciness, a burning anger prickled Amy's scalp. *Dangerous,* she thought. The vampire was trapped, waiting, mouth poised over the vulnerable neck she was aching for, as her thirst grew to a critical, desperate pitch.

Amy quickly dried her hands, and retreated. In her fear, she had mistaken the female's hunger for violence, and her presence had only made the situation more volatile. She couldn't risk the vampire losing control and accidentally draining the woman of all her blood.

With limbs numbed by disappointment, she opened the door of the bathroom as exaggeratedly as she had entered, making sure the vampire knew she had left. Then walked directly into what felt like a wall of ice. Amy rubbed her arms instinctively, ridding her skin of the coldness, before staring up at the male vampire in horror.

'This is the ladies,' she said quickly.

'Oh, so it is. Apologies.'

He shot her a wary frown, his eyes shrouded dangerously, before disappearing into the male toilets.

Amy sighed as her body finally decompressed. With trembling hands, she hurried to gather her belongings from the bar, and finally left Dishoom behind.

She wandered aimlessly along the streets of north London until she heard the distant hustle and bustle of Camden Town. When she closed her eyes and focused her senses further, she was rewarded with the pulsing susurrations of human drunkenness, and the blaring melody of a gig at Electric Ballroom. She made her way towards the main concourse of the town, hoping to experience something a little more inviting than a vampire feed.

As she crested the horizon, she witnessed Camden Town at its best. The late hour had no meaning for this community of rebels. Brightly coloured shops boasted elaborate façades. She saw the shadows of giant Doc Martens and vintage Vans jutting from first-floor balconies. Startling adverts for the latest New Rock boots hung from gothic clothing emporiums. Neon lights marked nightclubs, and the bass of house music tremored through the pavement. Languid queues of intoxicated patrons snaked beside late-night tattoo parlours. The people wore leather jackets and denim studded with rhinestones, and tattered skirts and scuffed tracksuits, and their bodies tinkered and jangled with the sound of metal piercings.

The air swelled with shouts from food vendors desperate to receive drunken money, and laughter from merry partygoers sauntering down the busy street in PVC leggings, fishnet shirts, and muddy Converses. Many wore the bright uniform from Cyberdog, all pink and green and blue and yellow, phosphorescent beneath the street lights. All the while, car horns blared and buses hummed and women cackled as they piled into waiting Hackney cabs. As always, the pulse and prickle of Otherworldlies accompanied the human auras. They loved Camden for obvious reasons: it was where a ghoul or a monster could be most open, pretending that they were simply showcasing local fashion.

Amy weaved through the crowds, politely refusing a hooded man who approached to offer drugs. Surrounded by this many bodies, the swell of auras was quickly growing unbearable. She usually avoided big crowds, but tonight the risk of overwhelm had felt more tempting than going home to her empty house to spend another evening alone. She looked for somewhere quieter to go, but the as the pressure continued to build in her skull, she staggered slightly with a sudden dizziness.

She bowed her head and rushed through the throng, pressing against the tide of humans and auras, until the Underground station came into view. She paused outside the entrance, breathless and thankful the immediate concourse was empty and clear. Leaning against the red-tiled walls, she sighed, pressing her fingertips against her temples. What a useless night. She had learned nothing new, she had failed to save the human woman from harm, and even worse, her involvement had almost caused the evening in Dishoom to end in both the woman's death and her own.

Her power – empathy – was supposed to be a gift, but it

was not one she had ever truly wanted. It had awakened when she was only five years old, knocked her to her knees in the garden by an overwhelming sadness not her own. She had staggered to her podgy feet, not understanding what was happening, and went to look for the source of the anguish. It had grown stronger the closer she walked to her parents' room, and when she flung the doors open in a panic, her mother was silently crying, a handkerchief stuffed in her mouth. Amy appeared, arms wide, clutching desperately at the air to offer an embrace, but an expression of inexplicable horror had veiled her mother's face – a silent, censorious rejection.

For the next few weeks, the young Amy had felt a distance swell between them, and the air had grown thick with unspoken questions.

But all the prevaricating came to a halt when her father returned home from an overseas work conference, shrouded in a feeling Amy didn't recognise, but now knew was lust. Her mother had made herself busy fixing lunch, not looking at him as he walked over to hug Amy, and Amy had recoiled, confused.

'What woman is that?' she had asked the room, parsing her father's aura, pondering the bright redness of it, the heat of it.

In her parents' shared embarrassment, they had eventually sent her to live with her grandmother, her predecessor in empathy. The ability had skipped a generation. She still remembered the morning they finally rid themselves of her – her mother's slight frame cast in the shadow of her husband, her eyes vacant and wary and betrayed. The stench of their auras had assaulted Amy's senses – a miasma of hateful effluvia she could not understand. Now she was grown, she could parse the contradictory webbing of her mother's feelings — her determination to stay with a man who did not love her properly, and her need to condemn anyone who tried to deglove the absurdity of her self-hatred, even if that person was her own daughter. Her father had been equally stubborn, clinging to the woman who had modelled herself as human furniture, and rejecting the child who couldn't help but hold up a paranormal magnifying glass to his guilt.

In her new home Amy was not an aberration. Nan understood what was happening to her, and walked her through the brilliant paths of their shared ability. Despite this, throughout the years they lived together, Amy had never once felt a single Otherworldly presence, and so had assumed strained tolerance whenever Nan began her long, rambling speeches about the witch who sold herbs on Electric Avenue or the mage who worked at their local Pizza Express, but never truly believed her fanciful lessons about the hidden supernatural world.

She knew better now, but it was too late. Her Nan had died five years ago and Amy still mourned the questions she never asked.

Dragging her thoughts back to the present, Amy plotted her route home. As she turned back towards the station, her body was disarmed by a raging Otherworldly emotion. Stunned, she staggered against the pressure, grasping at the wall of the station for support. Her eyes scanned the surrounding streets, but it had not come from the retreating crowds of Electric Ballroom – all humans there. The Underworld Pub was equally nondescript, and so were the nearby bus stops and corner shops. She closed her eyes and steadied her breathing, as she pilfered through the layers and threads in the air. An aura felt from such distance could only belong to an Otherworldly of tremendous power, most likely from a class she had not felt before. Its force burrowed deep into the concrete of Camden, coursing through the layers of gravel and mud and bones she currently trembled upon.

The aura was devoid of vampire chill, prickly werewolf heat or drowsy and nonsensical mage presence. Every pulse filled her with longing and awe, and her body instinctively moved towards it, her feet following the trail of sensation around the other side of the station, past several bus stops, and down a quiet residential street.

It was dark here, and everything was still. Despite the inherent power in the aura, she was unafraid. Her instincts were sure the power would not hurt her.

On the other side of the street, just out of sight from the road, she finally found its source: a slender man pressed against a wall, shrouded by the unfathomability of himself. He wore a simple black cloak that dragged on the ground and a ream of dark fabric hung in loops around his neck. His head was flung backwards and his eyes were cloaked in shadow. Full lips, currently parted, contrasted with his gaunt cheeks. Amy saw him grip the wall behind him, and as she watched, he slid down to the ground, struggling for breath. His legs twitched before him and he drew them close to his chest, curling in on himself. Despite the power rolling off him, he looked like a fragile rock – just an onyx injury within the alley.

She stared, transfixed and unable to move, as a wave of euphoria washed over her body. Submerged within the unknown man's aura, she tried to piece together how someone who looked so slight could contain so much power. She had no idea why he was in the alleyway alone, wrestling internally with a tsunami of magic, and her presence felt invasive, but she remained transfixed. She watched from her place across the road, tucked into the shadows.

Since her grandmother's death, she had stalked the streets of London, assuring herself that non-human creatures existed, confirming that Nan's tales had not been lies. It was a secret she shared only with her piles of notebooks, all addressed to the woman who had taught her so much: a one-way conversation that would never end. But this man was something Amy had never encountered, and something her Nan had never mentioned, even in her wildest stories. Watching him felt like delving into the aura of a god. The thought was terrifying.

She had to know what he was.

At last, the pressure in the atmosphere ebbed away, and the man seemed to regain his senses, refolding the black scarves around his head. As he rested against the wall, Amy could see his shoulders heaving and he gasped, trying to regain his composure. Before he could notice her, she quietly moved away.

She knew what his aura felt like now. It was burned into her cells. She would come back to Camden and find him again.

CHAPTER TWO

Amy

It was still early when Amy woke the next day. She had barely slept since taking the night bus home from Camden to her humble dwellings in Streatham. Instead, she had spent several hours trawling through the notebooks she had accumulated over the past five years, all stacked into neat little piles beneath her bed. The only person she could have confided in about all this was buried in West Norwood Cemetery. It was painful to think about.

Amy remembered bending over the fresh grave after the funeral, how the magnolias and lilies gleamed in the deep sun, how the glares of her estranged parents burned her back. They had both carried auras of suspicion so deep it was as if they feared she could raise the dead. After that day, Amy had visited the grave daily, talking to the surrounding air, trying to feel the presence of the only woman who understood her. And on one of those days, in the depths of her grief, she had felt a spark of hot lightning in the base of her back.

Amy had spun around, examining the vestiges of sorrow floating between the graves, and then she stopped, staring at the source of frantic heat. The cemetery's caretaker roved down the winding path beside her, his grey overalls scuffed. He stared straight ahead, two nutmeg eyes set in a peaceful brown face, lightly lined like the veins on the underside of a leaf. *He's not human,* Amy had realised, a fresh wave of grief engulfing her. All those years doubting the existence of supernatural creatures, all those stories that she had discarded so carelessly. Her tears fell and, filled with both gratitude and guilt, she decided to buy a notebook.

Her guilt was not so potent these days. She had come to love the feeling of discovery, and yearn to know as much about these hidden people as possible. Her notes had dwindled of late and her observations had proved fruitless, but the mysterious man in the alley had given her a new spark of inspiration.

Nostalgia made her attempt cornmeal porridge for breakfast. She got the battered wooden spoon from the drawer, rinsed out the milk pan, boiled the kettle with fresh water, and placed the Dunn's River bag of cornmeal polenta beside the stove.

A rickety kitchen table faced double windows that looked out onto an overgrown garden and a weather-beaten patio. Two plastic garden chairs had been warped by the sun and stained by half a decade of rain. A rusted barbecue from Argos was stowed away in a rotten and mottled cardboard box, still hopeful that one day, it would be used.

Inside the house, the brown lino was tacky beneath Amy's slippers, and occasionally, she felt the crunch of a biscuit crumb, some scattered stale cornflakes, or a grain of rice. The countertops were crammed with junk: bread tins with no bread, biscuit tins with stale biscuits inside, broken tea leaves, cans of baked beans, butter beans, chickpeas, bags of red kidney beans, gungo peas, lentils, and sea moss. A fruit bowl spilled over like radioactive waste: rivulets of sagging bananas, deformed tangerines, a mango that was shiny and wet with mould, and plums that were slowly turning into prunes.

She found a bowl and placed it on the only island of solitude – one patch of peach faux marble among a sea of wreckage – and set about making the porridge.

Amy made cornmeal like her grandmother had taught her because her mother's way was prone to lumps. Nan had instructed her on cornmeal artistry when she was fifteen ('Your mother used to make good cornmeal, you know? Good, good cornmeal. But after she got a black heart, the gift leff 'ar. Now she cyaan mek it!') and she always made sure to keep a bag in the cupboard for days when she wanted to feel close to her again.

She boiled the water in a pot, then mixed the cornmeal in a separate bowl with milk before adding it to the water. Afterwards, she poured in nutmeg, a generous helping of condensed milk, some brown sugar, and a bay leaf, and stirred it slowly with her wooden spoon. The quiet bubble of the porridge and the monotonous turning of the spoon sent her into a fitful trance. She thought about the man in the alleyway and the powerful aura that surrounded him; the awe he had triggered within her. He had appeared as both an injured animal and a force of nature. She needed to know more.

Amy returned to the porridge, gave it one last stir, and poured it into her bowl. The pot was left on the stove, where the cornmeal residue would slowly cake at the bottom and cause her more stress when washing up.

She scrolled through her phone unthinkingly, hot spoon hovering beside her mouth as she read the news and her favourite gossip pages. Her mind was split between the mundane and the paranormal. One painful gulp of cornmeal, another minute scrolling, an endless reverie about the Camden man. She did this until her breakfast was finished and her tongue was swollen and stinging, then she looked around the kitchen deflated.

Her bonnet was still on. The dressing gown haphazardly wrapped around her body was worn and threadbare. The entire house was windswept and battered, with coats hanging from door frames, newspapers spilling out of bins, and beauty products – Nivea cream, shea butter, black elastic bands, Eco-Styler gel – strewn across coffee tables. The army of plants, once so pregnant with moisture, was shockingly skeletal as they desperately clung to the indoor trellis around the living room windows or fell in brownish vines over bookshelves. This was no way to treat her grandmother's house. She was embarrassed.

She looked around the kitchen, the hallway and the living room with new eyes. As she wandered through the house, glancing a finger across the various picture frames on the mantlepiece, a petite woman with a neat bun and mischievous eyes was present in every photograph. Oftentimes, she had her arms around Amy: a teenaged Amy with a scowl and acne; an older Amy with some confidence, beaming under the mortar board of a former-polytechnic university; Amy as a child, the confusion of her parents' abandonment evident in her wide, questioning eyes. And when the warm pad of Amy's fingertips connected with the cool glass of the picture frames, she could feel it: the spark of Nan, the aura that refused to disappear. It was a small imprint, slowly fading into the air, but Amy craved it like oxygen. The aura told her that things would be okay.

'Right,' she said to the room. 'Fix up.'

And slowly, she began to clean the house.

CHAPTER THREE
Amy

Amy finished cleaning by the late afternoon. Then after finally washing and putting on some decent clothes, she flopped on the sofa that overlooked the darkening landscape of her droll and tired neighbourhood. The past five years had changed everyone, and the world outside was dull and listless. In the weeks following Nan's death, neighbours stopped by with Dutch pots of pea soup and little containers of ackee and saltfish, the contents barely visible beneath a violent sheen of orange grease from an ancient Chinese takeaway or a Nigerian birthday party. But second-hand grief waned easily, and soon the stream of visitors and well-wishers seeped away to rejoin their old lives, and Amy was left hollow once more.

At least Nan's spirit was more pronounced in a clean house, her mark on its foundations evident and easily discernible. The settees were all entombed in the plastic casings they had arrived in, almost melting into new creations after years of being untouched until it was impossible to know where the plastic ended and the faux silk began. A varnished cabinet guarded the head of the dining-room table, its glass façade gleaming proudly beneath the chandeliers purchased at East Street Market aeons ago. Inside the cabinet, glass figurines of dogs and horses, gold-rimmed china plates, and crystal glasses stood frozen in time, having never been used despite patiently waiting for the day when special guests would arrive for dinner.

The mantelpiece that guarded the electric fireplace boasted a problematic display of figurines with tar-black skins that were shiny and garish, and facial expressions that were obscenely exaggerated as they blew on dull saxophones, slapped steel pans, and smoked oversized spliffs over watermelon slices. All were acquired from a market stall in Clark's Town, Jamaica, by Amy's father as a crude joke, and Nan, too wise to cuss him out to his face, left them there for everyone to see, making great pains to inform visitors that her British-born son-in-law, a small-island Kittitian, had bought them after being swindled and hoodwinked by Jamaican craft sellers in true Trelawny style.

Amy frowned as she looked at them now, the pale white eyes of the figurines appearing to stare back at her. She could feel the vestiges of a maelstrom imprinted on them: disgruntled factory workers forced to craft them for white tourists to the Caribbean, the many tired hands they had passed through to arrive at the Clark's Town market, and the damp print of her father. It was as obtrusive as an ever-spreading grease stain on a satin dress, seeping into the underside and clinging to soft flesh beneath, impossible to remove. With a decided grunt, Amy vowed to throw the figurines in the bin – Nan always hated them, anyway.

Stretching, she gathered her notebooks and scanned the scribbles of field notes she had made. She saw the blank expanse at the end of her most recent entry, a space that exemplified the vastness of the man she had witnessed in the early hours of the morning in Camden Town. His endlessness both frightened and intrigued her. Finding him was the only way to know who – or what – he was.

The impossibly long bus journey from Streatham to Camden Town had been fraught with anxiety – so much so that Amy found herself slipping into the auras of her fellow passengers just to distract herself from her mounting nerves. It was the end of the working day for some, and the atmosphere bubbled with the airiness of relief and anticipation for a relaxing evening at home. End-of-weekend jitters surrounded others – a roiling grey mass of dread and fatigue. These auras were peppered with stress from teenagers who were about to enter the end game: the penultimate term before their final exams. Everything was normal. It all reminded Amy of just how strange she was.

She disembarked at Camden Town with new purpose, heading straight to the residential street from earlier, not stopping until she arrived at the opening of the alley: an end-of-terrace walkway that cut through to houses on the other side. A few wheelie bins awaited Monday morning collection, their lids open and overflowing with black bags. The ground was cobbled and cracked. It was all quiet, save for the startling aura that smothered the area.

The epicentre was between the two bins. A perfect sphere of bottomless energy hung above the ground to mark where the man had crouched against the wall, and then, like a bomb blast, streams of his presence shot outwards, imprinting a star-shaped fault on the air. She reached out a hand to the atmosphere before her, where nothing could be seen with the naked eye, but as her fingers glanced against the place where the streams hovered, a coldness stabbed into her. It snaked up her arm, rattling the marrow in her bones. Amy snatched her hand away and gathered herself. She closed her eyes to visualise the aura more properly, examining every layer of it until she knew she could identify it elsewhere. She immersed herself until it felt like it had become a part of her, moistening her skin like sweat.

'My days.' Amy stepped back with a sigh, staring around the alleyway in wonder. 'What the fuck is he?'

Before her thoughts slipped away, she quickly scribbled her findings in her new book, shivering in the wake of what she had just felt. Not wanting to waste any more time, she all but jogged to the main streets of Camden, parsing the air to identify where the man had travelled to next, his distinctive aura trailing on the wind like a sweet scent. She must have looked ridiculous, aimlessly traversing the busy street at such a slow pace, her eyes wandering and unfocused, mouth set into a deep frown. She was only dimly aware of being barged into a few times by passers-by, but she had no time to care.

Eventually, his aura seeped away on the cusp of Tottenham Court Road, and Amy was bombarded with the usual kaleidoscope of auras, smells, noises, and traffic of central London. She forced herself to go further, pilfering through the layers in the air until a vestige of the man's aura remained, but it was difficult to determine his location. Instead, a barrage of supernatural presences floated back to her, mainly coming from Covent Garden. No vampires were out at this time as it was still too light. By this point, the muted rays of the sun crested over the tops of buildings like blankets of frost. With a growing confidence, she made her way to Covent Garden in the hopes of getting clues from the Otherworldlies in the area.

The cobbled streets of Covent Garden teemed with tourists and travellers. The pavements were lined with vintage wooden carts that were filled with fresh flowers and hanging leaves. The Punch and Judy pub overlooked the main square, where a magician made several attempts to juggle pirate swords before an increasingly anxious crowd of onlookers. Amy ignored the magician's garbled curses from the tinny microphone pinned to his shirt, and she politely pushed past the queues outside The Ivy, and the Apple Store, and the new ice cream parlour that served candy floss cones. She immersed herself in the earthy warmth of the many witches that pottered around the area, looking just like normal humans as they wandered into the Godiva chocolatier or clutched paper coffee cups or leaned against walls to gawk and laugh at the human performer in the square. She could feel the cool ambience of warlocks, the witches' counterparts, taking photos of the statuesque street performers with bemused expressions.

None of these creatures carried the alley man's aura with them, and she feared he was a lone traveller, totally unrelated to the magic community in London.

Until she caught it.

Amy's heart fluttered as she made her way to Penhaligon's, the famous perfumery that looked out onto the illustrious view of the main square. It was near closing time, but shoppers still crowded around the entrance, staring at the jewelled glass decanters of expensive perfumes as they shone amber, ruby, emerald, indigo.

''Scuse me,' she muttered as she squeezed through the crowd. Inside, the shop was brightly lit, adorned with walnut and oak fixtures, and primarily illuminated with walls of perfumes. The backlit shelves shone through the glass bottles, subsequently casting a stained-glass mural on the floor and the faces of everyone who ambled around inside. It smelt beautiful, like cloves and roasted sage and caramelised chestnuts and rosewater, but the most distinctive presence of all was the aura of her alley man.

She knew he wasn't here in the shop with her; he was far too powerful for his aura to feel so dim, but it was imprinted on some of the bottles and the main service desk.

'May I help you?'

Amy had been so lost in her parsing that the aura of the shop assistant took her by surprise. She turned to face the man more fully. He was tall and unmistakably beautiful. His honey-brown skin glowed beneath the lighting. He obviously knew the effect he had on people as he casually shot overly friendly smiles at the shoppers as they brushed past, a startling expression marked by the subtle parting of his lips, offering a glimpse of chalk-white teeth, and a narrowing of the eyes which almost made them glint. He was also a mage, and Amy was overcome with the power that clung to his body, flowing from the base of his spine. It was hot with frenzied chaos. She stepped back instinctively and tried to match his smile.

'Ah, I was just looking,' she said.

'Sure. Well, if you need anything—'

'Oh, actually . . .' Amy drew in a shaky breath. She was doing something stupid, but it was worth a try. 'I'm supposed to be meeting a friend here, I dunno if you've seen him . . . ? Maybe we missed each other. Um, he's kind of my height, maybe a little taller. Dark-skinned. He's probably wearing all black? Like a cloak? And, sometimes a little bit of cloth around his face, like a veil or something. Has he come here yet?'

The mage tilted his head in thought. 'Hmm. No, haven't seen anyone looking like that, sadly. Well, maybe stick around? If he comes, I'll point him in your direction.'

The mage promptly turned to help another customer, and Amy's heart turned to lead. She felt her blood pulsing through her body frantically as she watched the mage glide around the shop. His facial expression had been deceptively calm, but at the mention of a face veil, a storm had rocked his aura, almost freezing the air around him until he was nothing but a wall of panic, anger, and deep suspicion. Amy pretended to read the labels of the display bottles, but a blizzard of concern fell upon the cramped space of Penhaligon's, making the air insufferable, and it all emanated from the mage.

Move, she thought to herself. *Get the fuck out of here.* And with all the strength she could muster, she put one foot in front of the other, failing to appear nonchalant and distracted by the ambience of Covent Garden. A wave of heat almost knocked her over as she passed the threshold of the door. The mage was frantic now, as if trying to decide how to get her to stay. She was in trouble. So much trouble. She scanned the faces of the crowd, almost expecting her mystery Otherworldly to emerge from the throng, signalled by his friend in Penhaligon's, and whisk her away — but for what? To devour her? Cut her throat? Was he an ancient vampire with an insatiable bloodlust?

'Oh fuck, oh fuck,' she whispered, picking up the pace towards the performance square. The magician had given up and packed away his trade for the day, leaving behind a tattered bowler hat, his worn barrier tape, and some scraps of cloth that wilted away in the wind. The aura of the surrounding crowd was damp with quiet embarrassment. Amy dived into it, trying to calm herself and breathing through her mouth to quell her panic. She broke into a jog when she was clear of Penhaligon's, far on the other side of Covent Garden and hidden within the craft markets, where the smell of crêpes, Nutella, incense and old leather shielded her from the mage's inferno.

When Amy finally arrived home, she slumped against the front door and slid to the ground. *Stupid, so stupid,* she thought. She desperately hoped that the mage would forget about her, but she knew it was too late: she was a marked woman now. What that actually meant she could only imagine.

CHAPTER FOUR

Amy

Normally, her job at Camden Town Library provided a rare space of peace. It was generally more tranquil than most places in London, and like all libraries, gave her a chance to think and relax. But since waking, Amy was tense with fear. She could not articulate the mounting dread that threatened to swell and crash over her all day. But as her shift groaned on, and the same customers she always saw flitted in and out of the library, offering little bits of gossip and small talk, she started to relax again. By the time she headed home, she felt more like herself. No Otherworldlies had used the library. Nothing untoward had happened. She had only roused the mage's suspicions, nothing else. She was safe.

After work, she bought a beef and cheese patty from the Caribbean shop and nibbled away at it as she walked. It was her first meal of the day, and as her anxiety sunk into the soles of her feet, her appetite steadily returned. After her patty, she bought a carton of mango Rubicon from the shop a few yards down, finishing it soon afterwards.

The auras around her started to shift as they always did. New thoughts, an exchange of people going to and from bus stops, and as she neared the Underground station, she felt the growing and ebbing swell of passengers from the trains, struggling through the ticket barriers, running to slip through the train doors even though another would arrive only a minute later. And then there was the gentle increase of Otherworldly auras. It was all rather comforting and normal. With new-found confidence, she trailed back to the alleyway: the fated spot that had become a pilgrimage.

'Where are you?' she whispered to the air around her, the space now free from wheelie bins after that morning's collection. She hovered her hand over the fault in the atmosphere, her skin rippling into goosebumps when her fingers touched the cool, jagged arms of the star-shaped blast. It was mesmerising. Auras just didn't *do* this.

Tentatively, she crouched until she was level with the epicentre, that sphere of origin. It was just empty air and cobbled streets and a few tufts of weak grass springing from the gaps of cracked paving cement, but a devastating imprint rested here. Her mystery man had crouched here, distressed by waves of euphoria and power, and then melted into the surrounding shadow. It was a vision from a dream, but the aura was proof he existed.

She wandered around Camden Town for a long time, desperately hungering after the traces he had left behind, suppressing the urge to go into Covent Garden in case the mage from Penhaligon's spotted her again.

Her aimless journey proved fruitful: a stronger vestige of the supernatural mystery descended on the atmosphere like an autumn mist, emerging from the swell of the various Otherworldly auras that floated around the area. The presence overwhelmed them, and they were submerged within its stronger current.

She stood now in the midst of the busy London streets near King's Cross and St Pancras, where every aura, both human and Otherworldly, dissipated like swirls of cigarette smoke to make way for the alley man. She saw the red brick peaks of the British Library and the glowing frenzy of King's Cross station, the dark cloisters of St Pancras International, and as she strolled along the winding concourse of the restaurants and cafés and boutiques of Pancras Square, she felt the surge of the inexplicable presence.

Amy froze, sensing him in every layer of the air, every stone on the ground, smeared against the side of every black cab as they awaited customers leaving the train stations. The layers of his aura were complex in their intensity, denoting the long time that he had traversed this district, circling over themselves like a never-ending helix.

She rested against a nearby bus stop, immediately gathered her notebook, and scribbled her findings. Her alley man was here, somewhere, and the calming pulse of his aura was comforting, a reassurance that she was on the right track. She just needed to search a little further.

It would take a while, but at least she had a more promising lead than Penhaligon's. She had to strategize and gather evidence. After such a long time of stalking around her empty house like a ghostly apparition, contemplating loss in all its traumatising forms, she had been given something to look forward to. This man was her new obsession. It would be worth it. After finishing the last of her observations, she got on the bus back home with a sense of purpose.

Amy arrived back in Streatham in the late hours. For the first time in a long while, she didn't feel so alone.

By the evening, the mantlepiece had been cleared of the unfortunate emblems of her father. In their place was a neat pile of notebooks, boasting Amy's half-decade of Otherworldly musings. She rested the latest addition, with her growing pages of information on the alley man, at the end of the row. Then she turned on the heater below, ordered a seafood platter from Soul Kitchen and caught up on *EastEnders*. This was all finished with a rum and coke, before she headed to bed.

The night grew cold as she slept. March had now ended and the season had begun to change, but the remnants of winter proved powerful. Though Amy had warmed the house with the electric heater from the living room, it soon faded away, leaking into the cold concrete walls, heralding an uncharacteristic chill that made her shiver even in the midst of sleep. Her dreams were erratic, influenced by the auras she had encountered during her waking moments, with all their intricacies and the ways they made her feel.

A sharp iciness jolted her awake. Amy's eyes fell on the window that overlooked the dark road outside. It was closed and frosted with condensation. In her tiredness, she frowned. She normally left it ajar.

She turned in the bed, scanning the room as she did so, taking note of the sharp edges of the dresser, the gleam of her mirror reflecting the orange glare of the street lights outside, the roundness of her rug on the ground, and her coat stand propped behind her door. As her eyelids grew heavy, she considered the coat stand again. As far as she was aware, she had never owned one.

Her eyes flew open, fully awake. A man stood beside her door, staring at her.

She had no time to react. She wanted to get up, to fling the duvet in the air and run for her life. Before the thought could materialise properly, a weight of iron pressed her back into the bed, and the man, a dark slip of a shadow, was upon her. A pair of raven-like eyes stared into hers, marked with a ring of scarlet around the outer iris. The rest of his face was hidden in a veil, and his form was shrouded in a dark cloak. Amy's breath became lodged in her throat as she locked eyes with him. He had no presence, no aura. It was like a hole had been gouged out of the air, allowing him to occupy the resulting nothingness. But she was positive: it was the alley man.

'You're not who I thought you were,' he said. His voice was quiet, with a lilting accent saturated with aristocratic politeness.

Amy exhaled as his weight shifted, and he rested on his knees, still regarding her shrewdly.

'So, who are you?' he asked.

Amy swallowed. Her tongue felt heavy. She swallowed again, and it was like trying to dislodge a lump of cement from her throat.

'Who are *you*?' she tried. Her heart was beating so hard she could feel it in her temples. The room swam as a fearful dizziness overcame her. Had she misread his aura? Had she antagonised the most dangerous Otherworldly in London? Cursing her own stupidity, she thought back to that fateful conversation in Penhaligon's. The mage had appeared so calm and ordinary, perfectly masking the ferocious spike in his aura the entire time. Perhaps this man and the mage were part of something Amy had had no business trying to investigate.

'I believe I asked first,' the man said.

'But *you* broke into my house,' Amy said. She wanted so desperately to believe that he meant her no harm. His lack of aura was frightening her, but she could not forget the glow of inspiration that had called out to her that night, propelling her forward, assuring her that she would be okay, enabling her to witness something that she still struggled to articulate. All alone in that alley, the man had seemed so devastatingly powerful. She refused to see him any differently.

'But you've been following me,' he countered after a stunned pause. He then slid off the bed. Amy saw his eyes wander to a space on the ground, where he appeared to kick something that she couldn't see. 'I happened to find some notebooks downstairs. You've been writing about us. Vampires. Witches. Warlocks. Werewolves. And lots more. Then I found an entire notebook dedicated to me. An acquaintance informed me of your visit to Covent Garden. So I searched around and found you. I've been tracking you since you left the library in Camden Town.'

'Doesn't that mean you've been following *me*?'

'You seem quite nonchalant.'

'I'm not trying to be.' She almost whispered it. If this continued, her heart was sure to burst out of her chest. He stood unnaturally still, guarding himself, so she was unable to read his aura or his body language. It was unsettling.

'Who are you?' he repeated.

'Amethyst – Amy. I'm Amy. Who are you?'

'Why are you making these notes?' He kicked the notebooks again.

'Because I know you all exist. It's just something I'm interested in. I'm not trying to cause trouble.'

'I watched you for several hours. You walked with a purpose, correctly identifying places I've been to. Who are you working with?'

'No one!' She shook her head for emphasis, clinging to the duvet, pulling it close to her chest in self-defence. 'I swear I'm not. I'm just a normal human. Well . . . I'm an empath. That's how I know about you lot. That's it.'

He rested his hands on his hips, sighing deeply. 'An empath,' he said, his voice small and contemplative. 'Why are you searching for me?'

The anger had left his voice now, giving way to a sense of trepidation and mild curiosity. Amy took this as a good sign.

'Because I saw you late Friday night. In Camden Town. And it was like . . . nothing I've ever felt before. I just wanted to find you again.'

'That was you. And what did you feel?'

'A god.'

The alley man leaned against the dresser, his face impenetrable from behind his veil. 'I'm not one.'

'Yeah, I guessed that. I doubt a god can . . . well, you know.'

'Know what?'

'You . . . you, well I saw you come. You came, didn't you?'

The man blinked. Then his body trembled, and she saw his eyes narrow into bemused crescents. A light, wheezing laugh escaped the folds of his veil. Amy smiled despite herself, watching as he struggled to contain his mirth, feeling slightly vindicated that he didn't appear to be as frightening as before.

'That was very blunt. And inaccurate, by the way.'

'Sorry. I didn't know how else to say it.'

His joyful demeanour vanished again. She saw his shoulders tense, and his brows furrowed as he assessed her. 'You say you can feel people who aren't human. That you know we exist. I've read your notes. Some of them are very thorough. But everything you've written about me is scanty. I'm impressed by what you've done so far, but I haven't seen a name or a category. What do you think I am?'

'I don't know,' she said. 'I haven't felt anything like you before.'

He seemed satisfied by this. His body relaxed and he pushed himself away from the dresser. Two hands held the veil, and he hesitated. During the pause, his aura re-emerged. It was like the outer wall of some illustrious fortress had slowly assembled itself, then fortified its defences, until she was wandering around in the maze of this man, feeling dizzy by the endless walls and long winding corridors to nothing. As he paused, his hands still gripping his veil, he watched her with such intensity that she looked away from him.

'So you felt all that? That's . . . pretty outstanding.'

'Thank you.'

The man nodded, then pulled away the veil and unwrapped the reams of fabric from his head, revealing a handsome face, dark skin, and a fade with a high top of thick brown curls. There was an auburn tinge to the tips of his hair. He looked young and playful. To emphasise this, he smiled at her kindly. 'I'm Gerald.'

'Nice to meet you, Gerald. Your name's a bit plain.'

'We can't have it all, I suppose.'

Silence descended on the room. Amy tried to make sense of what was happening – how she had fallen asleep in such mundane circumstances only to be awoken by an Otherworldly breaking into her home. She was dimly aware of the vanishing coldness that had alerted her to his presence. The icy ambience appeared to withdraw into his surrounding aura, like an ebbing tide, replacing the frosty atmosphere with a mild warmth. Gerald approached her cautiously, surrounded by a cloud of self-consciousness.

He flexed his fingers. He wore leather gloves that crunched quietly with his movement. Amy faltered. There was something strange there, an aberrant mist hovering around his lower arms. 'So you can feel that too? How frightening.'

Amy stared, waiting for an explanation, but he said nothing else. He promptly stuffed his hands in his pockets.

'You saw my big Awakening, then,' Gerald said. 'It was my twenty-seventh birthday.'

Amy nodded to herself in comprehension. 'So . . . you started wanking in the alleyway?'

'What? No.'

Against her will, Amy laughed. It was a fragile, trembling sound. 'My bad.'

Gerald sighed, but he relaxed his posture, and the waves of his aura grew hesitantly warm. 'This is really odd.'

'You're telling me.'

He was suddenly distracted by Amy's bedroom. 'Can I apologise for breaking in here and causing you concern? I thought you were a spy.'

'I appreciate that. It's cool.'

She stared at him again because he had focused his gaze on the window. It was a wistful, lingering look, as if he was considering taking flight. Amy shifted in the bed and leaned forward. The movement alerted Gerald, and his aura thrummed with an intense wariness. His body returned to emphatic vigilance. It seemed like he was going to leave her. Amy didn't want him to; she felt something cold grow within her – a pathetic loneliness. This man was supposed to give her purpose.

'Can you stay?' she asked, instantly feeling like an idiot.

At last, Gerald returned his attention to her. He frowned, incredulously. His aura sputtered with confusion, and the suspicion returned. 'Why?'

Amy shrugged. She had no sensible way to describe her reasons. 'Can you tell me more about what you are?'

Gerald folded his arms, still staring. His aura had settled

now, and the smoke of curiosity returned. His brows furrowed as he pondered something, and Amy was lost in her own head, trying to imagine the thoughts that unfurled within this man, and what secrets he clung to so tightly. After a frozen moment, Gerald nodded. He offered a tentative smile.

CHAPTER FIVE
Gerald

He waited outside the bedroom door as the human Amy changed into some house clothes. The landing was narrow, and photographs lined the walls, depicting several instances of a younger Amy, often accompanied by a much older woman whose eyes twinkled with mirth and cunning and mischief from the other side of the glass. He used the time to recover from his embarrassment; he had watched the human for several hours as she scanned the alleyway of his Awakening, and then wandered around King's Cross with an air of determination that unsettled him. He was a man people often avoided, but he had many enemies – it was not unusual for someone to try their hand at revenge. He had been so sure of this human's dubiousness he had made a great show of himself only to harass a totally innocent woman – even breaking into her bedroom. How uncouth.

When Amy emerged in jogging bottoms and a T-shirt, with a silk bonnet still on her head, he smiled tightly, stepping aside so she could lead him downstairs. She was strangely inquisitive, and as they walked, he could feel her parsing through his aura with unnerving precision. She had an absolutely frightening ability. He observed her hesitant footsteps and the way she loosely clenched her hands by her sides as she walked. She was nervous, and he more so. He had made a reckless decision to stay here, but her expression had been mournful at the thought of his departure, and her curiosity made no sense for a human. Her probing ability was rare: she had felt the presence around his hands and she appeared to sense when his aura was concealed. He did not know empaths could do this. *Perhaps,* he thought, *she's the one.*

'You work very far from here,' he said.

'Mmhmm. I do a lot of travelling around these days. Since my grandma died, I don't like staying at home for too long. I'm the only one here. Gets lonely.'

'I'm sorry to hear that,' said Gerald.

Amy shrugged. He could see her starting to relax, for which he was grateful. 'It's been five years since she left me,' she continued, 'but I'm not used to it. This house was hers, and she basically raised me since I was five. She was from St Thomas originally – in Jamaica. A Windrush baby. I got my powers from her.'

'I see. So she's the Nan in your notebooks?'

'Yep.'

'They read like letters to her,' said Gerald.

Amy nodded, her smile sad and wistful. 'She'd be happy to see me learning all these things, feeling the same things she could feel. I want her to be a part of it.'

Gerald considered this. Her reckless acceptance of his existence made sense. 'No parents?'

'Might as well not have any.'

It took him a few moments to realise she was referring to estrangement. It was something he could never relate to. The relationship he shared with his parents was like his attachment to his arms and legs: it felt like they were one person, totally in sync, functioning to complement each other even though they no longer lived in the same place. Sometimes, he missed them so much it hurt, and the emptiness of his own home was like a death – there was just vacancy and spaces where other people should have been. When he slept, he dreamt of his old life, and sometimes he would slip into the melodic language of his ancestors. Then his memories and dreams became incoherent and abstract as everything melded into one desperate need for his people.

'Do they live near you, at least?' he asked.

'Yeah, they're from Norbury. Not too far, but far enough. I like it that way.'

He decided not to pry further. 'Is that how you found out about us? From your grandmother?'

'You mean Otherworldlies?'

'I beg your pardon?'

She smiled at him. 'It's what she always called you lot.'

Amy gestured for him to sit down at a rickety kitchen table. The room was tidy and visibly occupied, with mangoes and bananas and a massive pineapple in a fruit bowl near the stove, along with sealed packets of various dried beans. A white cloth hung above the kitchen door, fashioned with two wooden borders, like a scroll. A poem was printed on the cloth in black stencilled letters:

> REMEMBER THIS
> *When you come here*
> *What you do here*
> *What you see here*
> *What you hear here*
> *When you leave here*
> *Let it stay here*
> *Or don't come back here*
> *JAMAICA*

He read it several times in utter confusion before turning away to examine the rest of the kitchen. When Amy opened the cupboard, he saw that they were packed with rice, biscuits, spices, canned food, and sweets.

'D'you want tea?'

'Yes please.'

'What one?'

'Erm, what do you have?'

'Mint.'

'Is that it?'

'Yeah.'

'Mint will do, then.'

The kettle whistled loudly as it boiled, and Amy busied herself around the room, shuffling an assortment of biscuits into a bowl and snatching a half-eaten bag of Butterkist toffee popcorn off the counter. They were soon seated opposite each other, using the tea and the snacks as a comforting hedge to fidget with or stare upon in case things grew too awkward or they ran out of words.

In the meantime, he felt Amy setting to work, hammering into his aura again. Gerald raised his teacup to his lips, watching her, wondering how far her parsing would take her. The empath surprised him; she dug so deep that she finally hit his inner core. He hissed in surprise before setting the teacup onto the table.

'What was that?' said Amy.

Gerald glanced at her, then looked away. 'What was what?'

'That.'

'Describe it to me.'

His eyes met hers, and she frowned at him again. She was both suspicious and curious, but it was clear her curiosity was stronger than her sense of self-preservation. How bored and lonely she must have been to entertain him in her house after he had scared her so terribly. He watched as she hesitated to describe what she felt, and he was anxious to hear it explained in her human tongue.

'It feels like a wall,' she said at last. 'Your aura is very strong. The strongest I've ever encountered. That's what made me try to find you in the first place. It was like this overwhelming power was calling out to me, telling me I'd be okay if I looked for it. I still get that feeling when I parse you. But then it gets thicker and thicker, and a bit colder, and then *wham*. I hit a wall. I just hit it a second ago. It literally feels like walking into a block of ice. It's so ... powerful.'

'That's ... scary,' said Gerald. He could think of nothing else to say. His Wall was one of his final astral defences, and this human empath had discovered it in a matter of minutes. Not thinking, he took a sip of the tea again, appraised it, then took a heartier helping. 'Are you sure you're human?'

Amy regarded him pointedly. 'I'm sure. So what are you?'

Her demeanour was so abruptly insolent that he almost laughed, but not to be taken off guard again, he swallowed it down and assumed a placidity that was more fitting for one of his stature. This human made no sense, and she had a dangerous ability. His intuition tugged at him, and he resolved to listen to it.

'I don't mind telling you what I am, but I think you'd need to see it to believe it.'

'And how will I do that?'

'Can we ... exchange numbers? Let's meet tomorrow evening.' Gerald glanced at the clock above the fridge, mentally calculating a good time. 'We can meet where there are more people about so we'll both feel safer. And I'll tell you more about me and what I am, and all these Otherworldlies, as you call them.'

Amy also took a small sip of her tea. 'Okay, cool. You give me your number first.'

She pulled a phone from out of her trouser pocket and pushed it across the table. Afterwards, she fiddled with the back of her bonnet and did not look at him. Her expression was painfully honest – she tried and failed to remain passive, to appear in control, but he could see the upwards tilt of her mouth, and how the flesh at the base of her throat fluttered with the strain of a pounding heart. She had an impressive power, but she was still human, still intimidated by him. There was something endearing about her attempts to hide it all.

At last, Gerald complied, quickly tapping in his number. His own phone rattled in his pocket as she subsequently called him, and he showed her the flashing screen to confirm.

'This has been interesting,' he said.

'Yeah, it has,' Amy said. 'Can't you give me a hint? Do you have to be so extra?'

He smiled at her before standing. 'It's getting late, Amy. Let's meet tomorrow.'

She was clearly unimpressed, but the pride returned to her demeanour, and she said nothing else. Gerald laughed quietly at the plain stubbornness of it. She smiled in turn, looking genuinely relieved. He was glad their meeting had ended so amicably.

'I am sorry,' he said as he followed her through the passageway towards the front door. 'For scaring you.'

'It's fine. I'm sorry for freaking you out. You know, following your aura all around London and that.'

As they paused at the threshold, Gerald felt Amy parsing

his Wall again. She would never be able to penetrate it, and he fortified its defences by making it colder and encrusting it with black ice, making its atmosphere so hostile and foreboding that she finally backed away, her face a mask of concern.

'What a frightening ability you have,' he said to the door, but she heard him and snorted. 'I'll see you tomorrow.'

Once outside, he inhaled deeply. The night was dark and quiet, and even though he couldn't see any movement behind the windows of the neighbouring houses, he covered his face with the veil.

'Make sure you call me,' Amy said from behind him. He turned to regard her. Her expression was both doubtful and pleading.

'I will,' he said. 'I promise.'

'Oh, and . . . happy belated.' Amy smiled before closing the door.

He saw her shadow wavering behind the stained glass. A few moments passed before she finally stepped away, disappearing into the shadow of her house.

He waited until he saw the soft glow of the master bedroom appear, casting a peach blanket of light on the ground on which he stood. He was curious to know if she would appear by the window, or how long she would stay awake with the light on, or whether he had frightened her enough to keep her awake for the rest of the night.

Eventually, he knew it was time for him to go. He turned on his heel and disappeared soundlessly into the night.

CHAPTER SIX
Gerald

In the cacophony of North London, a cloistered neo-Gothic palace observed the concourse at King's Cross St Pancras. The Renaissance Hotel contained a top-floor apartment in its clocktower, delicately furnished with mahogany and leather, wrought-iron staircases, and oak bookshelves stacked with leather-bound tomes. A Chesterfield suite in the ornate living room encircled a stack of newspapers: *The Times, The Guardian,* and *The Independent.* A study table rested against the clocktower windows through which Gerald could watch time pass.

The desk was where he kept all his ink pots and quills, and right in the middle of the mess was his Book: red moleskin, tattered spine. On the night of his Awakening, the creamy pages of his Book had been blank but this morning, two names glistened in scarlet ink. His phone rang as if on cue.

'Good morning, Father.'

A pause.

'Now that's the voice of an Awakened man. I'm happy for you, son.'

'I do wish you had given me just a little more information about what it would entail, Dad.'

A raspy chuckle hissed down the phone. 'What's the fun in a *warning*, boy? I'm just glad you're all well and in one piece.'

'I guess so.' Gerald hooked the phone between his

shoulder and ear and made his way to the next room. In the kitchen, the floor had black and white checked tiles. The massive ivory sink was clean, and a set of gold-rimmed plates rested in a brass drying rack. The marble worktops were empty, save for a few mason jars of homemade jam, pickled fruit, and brined peppers. A walk-in fireplace stood opposite the island, replete with a hanging rack of brass kitchenware and gingham wiping cloths. All the cupboards were painted matte black, and the chandelier was a glossy iron fixture with industrial bulbs that cast a warm orange glow over the room. Gerald opened the Aga doors and found a tray of fresh granola made by Zis, glistening with maple syrup and jewelled sultanas.

'But Gerald,' said Father, his voice solemn, 'Gerald, what did the stars tell you?'

Gerald froze before the Aga, closing his eyes to remember that crucial moment when his ancestors' powers invaded his body. He had thrown himself against the brick wall in desperation, seeing the threads of humanity swim before his eyes, and the universe came down on him and whispered things in his ear.

Then the voice had appeared through a fault in the galaxy and said something that Gerald was still trying to make sense of, but the magnitude of its implication made him conceal its words. He was wary to withhold information from Father, but it felt like the best course of action for now.

'They told me everything, Dad,' he said eventually, which wasn't a lie.

'Wonderful. Phenomenal. I'm so proud of you, son.'

'Thank you.'

He spooned the granola into a bowl, patted the stove plates affectionately, and then found stewed fruit and Greek yoghurt in the fridge, which he added to his breakfast. He returned to the living room and sat before the open Book on his desk.

The crackle of a breeze interrupted the silence on the phone, along with the pattering song of water falling on porcelain. Gerald heard the distant tinkling of wind chimes. He closed his eyes and he could see it: green tea, golden-rimmed cups and saucers, a midnight blue tablecloth spread over a great mahogany chest, the soft sheepskin rugs, and the light scarlet fabric of the family tent. He saw the opening of the tent flutter in the desert wind, and beyond it – the pure golden sea of the Sahara, his ancestral land. He saw the camels and the merchants, men and women and children of all sizes enshrouded in black cloaks. He could smell the incense and the cinnamon sticks his mum kept on the dresser. Opening his eyes again, he was confronted with darkness and shadow.

'How is Mum, by the way?'

'Oh, she's fine. She's sitting right next to me. Empress, come and greet your son.'

A whisper of silk fabric. The chatter of metal. His mother had a weakness for the old, homemade jewellery that the Malian girls offered to her as thanks for helping them bake cakes for a wedding, or for donating her expensive fabric to a party, or for braiding their hair in the elaborate way that was her signature. She also adorned the hem of her robes with cowrie shells and gold-plated medallions engraved with the Tribe insignia.

'Gerald, baby.'

He allowed himself to collapse in his study chair and rested his chin in his free palm. Her voice sounded like the peaceful crash and foam of the sea. He could feel her sunny warmth down the phone.

'Ma.'

'Did you pick up your perfume?'

'Yes, thank you for the birthday gift.'

'You must send us a picture. I'm so happy you've Awakened, my love. And please be careful with those names – you can always say no if it's too much.'

'I understand. But who requested these?' He tapped his Book for emphasis.

'Oh dear, I couldn't possibly get into it all with you. I think your dad is best at explaining it. Just thinking it all over gets me so stressed.'

'Don't get stressed, Mother. Go back to the spa.'

She cackled at that. What a sweet, ridiculously joyful sound it was. The gruffness of his father's voice was an almost unpleasant return.

'Dad, what's happening with these names?' Feeling more at ease, he tucked his legs beneath him on the chair and spooned the granola into his mouth. Zis had made an exceptional breakfast.

'The mayor asked for them. Your mayor in Downey.'

'Well *that's* something.'

'I know. Gerald, these names are serious. They've been doing all sorts of things, as I'm sure you know. We all know. They threaten to blow Downey's cover. You can say no. It's not our usual fare, but I accepted because I thought it was the right thing to do.'

'If you think that way, then why are you offering me the chance to decline?'

'I just want you to be safe. Enjoy your Awakening.'

'If you think it's important, then I won't refuse, either. Are you scared that I'll die?'

'No.'

'You're scared that I'll go too far.'

'Gerald,' Father said after a pause, 'when I Awakened, I was young and foolish. I was given the name of a well-known serial killer, and this was the seventies in America. A lot of those killers that roamed the streets back then were unknown, but this guy . . . someone knew him, and they knew he was different. A human had made the request, you know, but the killer apparently revealed that he was a vampire. To save herself, she delved deeper into our world, and there you go: a request. Everything was set up. It was my first kill since the Awakening, and I was so excited. Imagine, getting a notorious vampire that's been terrorising his city!

'But I wiped out an entire family that lived next door by mistake. I was so embarrassed, I fled for a month. I kept asking the stars, "You gave me this power, but what's the point? Refine me, make me elegant." I came all the way back here and hid in the desert. It was the lowest moment of my life.'

'Dad . . .' Just the thought of his stalwart father hiding from anyone was a shock, but to hear that he had made such a grave error was unbelievable. He placed his bowl on the desk.

'How did you overcome it?' he asked.

'I just . . . did the cleansing. Then I got back to work. I don't want you to go through that, Gerald.'

'I understand. I won't let it happen.'

'Hmm.' A forlorn silence descended on the conversation. Gerald waited for Father to stop thinking, ruminating over a past he could not change or control.

'You know these two are in hiding as well?' Father asked at last.

'They're humans now?'

'The warlock is. I hear he uses wonderful disguises. It's as if he's skinned a few humans alive and walks around at night with the skins on like coats.'

'Can you curb your hyperbole please?'

'This is serious.'

'I know, but talking about coats made from human skin really won't help me here. Downers are tricky. And they all know who I am.' He closed the Book and his eyes wandered to the mezzanine floor that overlooked the living room and the vast shelves of leather books detailing history, family scriptures, and notes on the unknown and bizarre. He had thought about Amy all night, and now, as he considered the names in his Book, his mind dwelt on her powers. He remembered the words the voice had spoken, and he felt a chill in the base of his spine.

'I met a strange woman yesterday,' he said at last. He mounted the spiral staircase and browsed the shelves. 'She's a human, but she's an empath.' He found the book he needed and flicked through the pages until he arrived at an entry regarding the gift of empathy in humans: a rare inherited phenomenon devolved to mythical status, signified by the ability to read the emotions of others through the sensations and colours that auras emitted. They used this information to build rapport, affinity, and understanding with the aura-bearer.

He frowned, expecting to read more, but there was none – and nothing to explain why the woman he met yesterday had been able to follow the traces of his aura imprinted on the air, detect the nature of his hands, feel his Awakening from across the road, or notice when his aura was concealed, much less the very process of it re-emerging. She even seemed to identify the subtle changes in his attitude. 'She's not a normal one, Dad. She's . . . extraordinary.'

'Oh?' He listened as Father stirred his tea. 'How extraordinary?'

'She felt my Wall.'

'*What?* Are you sure she's not a Downer?'

'No, I'm sure she's human. But she says the gift was passed down from her Jamaican grandmother, so she appears to come from one of those old spiritual families that were prominent in the new world. The power is potent. I threw up the Wall twice, and both times she noticed it. The second time, she tried to probe it, wondering what it was, but her fear stopped her. I felt her retreat from it. Her power is rather brilliant.

'I think . . . I think I might use the human for this job, seeing as it's the first time I'm required to *search* for a target. She can follow auras through the air and locate people that way. I wish I had met her sooner, to be honest.'

'Be careful, Gerald. Remember Andrew. These work partnerships with humans don't always turn out well.'

'Of course. But Uncle Andrew lied about who he was at first, and then he tried to marry the woman. I'm going to be absolutely honest with her. She already knows about us, too. Not *us*, I mean Downers in general. She's written notes about us; she appears to search for Downers as a hobby.'

'What's her surname?'

'I'm not sure. I'll have to find out.'

'I suppose it makes things easier that she's one of those humans who knows about our kind. But being an empath complicates things. She could prove dangerous.'

'How so?'

A pause. 'Remember your upbringing. Your training.'

Gerald halted as all around him memories piled up and then collapsed like skeins of old papyrus, trembling under the weight of his years. He recalled the sandstorms of the desert smothering him as a child, flanked by Father and Grandfather. That day, they had marched across harsh terrain until they reached the outer borders of Kenya, where once verdant land had turned brown and cracked with famine. The trio donned disguises, pretended to be humanitarian healthcare workers, and slipped through the plastic, clinical folds of a mobile hospital tent. It was hot inside and quiet with death; the acrid stench of the dying stained the air. Occupants of a row of beds stirred silently, but the staff was frantic, cacophonous, pushing past Gerald and his two patriarchs and then ordering them to be useful. Father gestured to the bed nearest to Gerald, where a child half-lived in emaciated terror. Gerald held the child's hand.

And what do you feel? Grandfather had asked.

Gerald shrugged. *Nothing.*

'And what does that have to do with anything?' Gerald asked Father.

'Empaths feel. You don't.'

'There's nothing wrong with me talking to one, is there?'

The silence was long. It clogged the phone. Gerald thought again to the night of his Awakening, and the words Armageddon had gifted him. He parted his mouth to explain it to Father after all, but he feared the time had passed.

'I'm the heir,' he said eventually. 'I'm not stupid.'

'I didn't say you were, son.'

'You can trust me to make reasonable decisions. And even if there are risks involved, you know I'm smart enough to get myself out of danger.'

Father sighed, defeated. 'What a strange son I have.' The humour returned to his words. 'You always manage to get yourself into something unbelievable.'

'I think I got that trait from you. If I'm not mistaken, Mother and her frivolous ways are already a big enough risk for the whole Tribe.'

Father wheezed down the phone, his laugh contagious. Conflict averted. 'Well, just get this done quickly, either way. I would hate for you to waste your new powers on such people.'

'Why not get me something more worthy then? Been a while since an aristocrat's crossed my path.'

'Ha! Don't ask for something you'll regret.'

Gerald laughed. A swollen silence followed, with both men undoubtedly watching their respective phones. Gerald gripped his own, training his ears to steal an audible glimpse of the desert and the strange town that had been his home for the first eighteen years of his life. It was April now, and London was starting to grow brighter, a little warmer, and the smoggy air that hung over the city was tinged with the hopefulness of a new season. It was one of the best times to be a Londoner. But it wasn't home.

'I'll visit soon, Gerald,' his father said at last.

'Thank you. I'd like that a lot.'

'I'll bring your mother. Have you spoken to Gamaliel lately?'

Gerald bit his lip. 'Not for a while. I'll do it soon, though.'

'Hmm.'

'Are . . . are you going now?'

'I'm afraid so. There's a very long list of requests I need to sort through and send to your other relatives. We might be in for a wild year.'

'Well, it's what you're paid to do. Have to earn your keep.'

'It's not as easy as it sounds. You'll see one day. At least you work alone. I can barely get things done with your mother chewing my ear off. I do *not* want to know who is pregnant and who is getting a divorce – it's not funny, Gerald!'

'Right, right, I'm sure.'

They ended the call in high spirits, but Gerald still felt lonely. Rather than get lost in his thoughts, he called Amy, his latest distraction. She answered on the fourth ring.

'Who is this?' she said.

'Now that's a lovely welcome.'

'Well.' She sighed. But there was a smile in her voice afterwards. 'Well, I was just checking. You never know, you might've set me up and given your phone to someone else. Something told me it was you, though. You feel honest.'

'I'm sure your intuition's never failed you.'

'Can't say it has.'

'What are you doing now?'

'Working.'

'You went to work? You were so busy doing other things yesterday.'

'And whose fault is that?'

'And you're a public librarian, yes?' asked Gerald, recalling the building he had seen her exiting yesterday evening.

'That's right. I'm at the Camden Town Library. We finish late today.'

'Oh, how wonderful. That's a great career to have.'

'Hmm. And what do you do, Gerald?'

He smiled and chose not to answer. 'When will you be free?'

'Seven-thirty.'

'Okay, good, fine. Meet me outside the British Library at eight, then. I would like to talk to you about something.'

She hid her elation well. 'Okay, good. Fine.'

In the early hours of 31 March, Gerald had Awakened.

It unleashed a new range of powers that he would spend a lifetime perfecting, and one of these was the ability to commune with the Death King Armageddon. When the stars descended upon Gerald's shoulders, that voice had advised him to beware of a major disruption coming his way, and to welcome it. Then he met Amy, and felt the remarkable nature of her power, and their unprecedented meeting had felt like the foretold interference. He wanted to trust his instincts and discover the truth of his Progenitor's promise.

Tonight, he would tell Amy, the human outlier, what he was. And if all went well, he would recruit her.

CHAPTER SEVEN

Gerald

Gerald sat on the cool stone steps of the British Library with a can of KA grape soda warming between his leather gloves. A calm wind swept the courtyard, ruffling his clothes. The crowds forced him to abandon his full night-time gear, so tonight he donned a black face mask with accompanying baseball cap instead of his turban and veil. Some students shot him furtive looks, quickly scanning the dark eyes behind all the cloth before skipping down the steps away from him, retreating into Pizza Express, Five Guys, or any local café they could find. The sky was still rapidly darkening at this time of year, but as it rolled deeper into April, it was easy for Gerald to anticipate the later evenings, brighter mornings, and shorter nights in which he had to work. Now that he had Awakened, he knew the job would be easier, but the lists were longer. There was always so much vengeance in the summer.

   He saw Amy at the iron gates of the courtyard, watching him behind a pair of oversized glasses. She had bunched her afro into pigtails. They clouded around her head in a celestial fashion. Oversized jeans hung from a full waist, and a long woollen cardigan enshrouded her in cream-coloured serenity. Her eyes were a different matter. She didn't move. She stared at him, her expression openly fearful. He saw her scan the area around him, the steps, the crown of his head. She was searching for something. Somehow, she had detected the Book he was carrying today, and was desperately trying to find it.

'Amazing,' whispered Gerald. 'That is *scary*.'

From her obvious hostility, he knew Amy would go no further than the gate, so he sighed inwardly and made his way towards her – slowly, arms swinging amiably by his sides. He almost floated along the steps, bouncing on the balls of his feet, grinning widely and hoping that the expression was maniacal enough to show through his mask. At the gate, he threw the soda can in a nearby bin and regarded her.

'Good evening, Amy.'

Amy blinked rapidly, as if she was surprised to hear Gerald's voice, and not that of some unknown monster.

'Are you well?' he pressed, placing a hand on his hips. He rocked back and forth, head tilted to one side. Amy took a step backwards.

'Not sure,' she said. 'What's wrong with you?'

'Hmm?'

'Something's *wrong*.'

Gerald stopped, mid-rock. He watched her, trying to figure out where to start. First, he lifted a hand towards her. He held it there expectantly, eyes locked with hers, wondering if she would shake it. The sight of his hand made her flinch, and she stepped back again. He examined her expression and how the rainbow of emotions – from concern, to fear, to awe, to confusion, to disgust – flickered across her face like a film reel. Gerald shrugged, letting his hand fall back to his side.

'What are you?' asked Amy. She was angry now.

'Can we go somewhere private?'

'Private like how?' She looked around them. The courtyard

was clearing as the library got ready to close to the public. Soon enough, they would be the only people there.

'Inside,' said Gerald, jerking a thumb at the library entrance.

'It's closing.'

'Not for me. Not for us.'

He turned on his heel and wandered towards the vacant building, knowing she would follow. When the light patter of her Converses joined his heavier leather soles in song, he smiled, but it was hard for him not to feel disappointed. Their first meeting had been so bizarre, and he knew that anyone else would never have agreed to a second. Looking back on the bedroom introduction, he admired just how impulsive she had been. Today, her reactions were all too human. For some reason, it made him feel lonely.

At the door of the British Library, he nodded to a security guard. The Downer was pale and muscular and remained silent as the pair crept through the open doors. On the other side, there was no security station and no extra guards to check bags. The lighting was dimmer to signal the darkening evening outside, and the polished floor echoed across the wide foyer as they disturbed it. Directly in front of them, ancient leather books towered on top of each other in a polished glass cage. Escalators ran alongside the structure, spiralling to higher floors where cafés, reading rooms and exhibitions boasted the history of British literary achievement. Every now and then, a dark-clothed guard would wander across the foyer, or along the escalators, regard them briefly, and then continue a seemingly aimless journey around the empty building. Gerald walked up to the mezzanine floor without thinking. He stopped and whirled around.

'What the fuck are you?' asked Amy behind him. She

glanced around, catching sight of another guard, and flinched. 'And who the fuck are they?' she whispered.

'Amy, you won't indulge me? You're a lover of books, aren't you? We're in the biggest library in the city here. I thought you would appreciate it if I took you somewhere comforting.'

'I'm *not* comforted, not when this place is crawling with Otherworldlies!'

'You've given us such a whimsical name.'

'I think I need to go.'

'Okay, okay, enough jokes, I'm sorry.' Gerald rushed towards her, lightly touching her arm. She stopped, albeit reluctantly. Facing her properly, he sighed, and as a courtesy, removed the coverings from his face and crown. 'I'm sorry, Amy. I agree I'm being a dick.'

'Right.'

'Can you sit with me?'

He gestured for her to follow as he took his seat on the marble steps. Amy complied, pointedly crossing her legs and folding her arms. She watched the door and the shadowy guard. As time passed, her large brown eyes would flicker elsewhere, apparently noticing another non-human entity. Gerald counted fourteen flickers. Somehow, she had identified fourteen individual Downers through the brick and plaster and marble of the foyer. Her ability would never not be unnerving.

'First of all,' Gerald continued, 'the elephant in the room.'

He straightened, and then placed a leathered hand on his abdomen. His hand sunk into the fabric and the flesh on the other side. He heard Amy gasp beside him, as he expected her to. From where she sat, it would have looked as if he had no real body, just a black cloud draped in cloth. It was cold inside. He rummaged through a few shelves, accidentally knocking over some empty glass phials. An ink pot threatened to spill over, but he caught it just in time. He frowned, annoyed that he had left the object of his desire so far away. It would only make this whole interaction stranger and more uncomfortable. When he finally found the Book and presented it to the light of the foyer, he found Amy had turned a dull grey colour, the brown hue of her cheeks awash with sickness.

'Okay, well, let me explain that first, quickly.' Gerald placed the Book on his other side, away from her glare, as he noticed she had caught its aura again and had retreated to that fearful, bewildered expression from before. 'That's called Hammerspace. Just how cartoon characters always gather items out of thin air, us Otherworldlies – I don't think I can get used to that name, I'm afraid – do the same. It's an invisible space of our choosing where we can store our personal inventory. We use it to travel to different places too. I retain my Hammerspace on my person because it's easier, but most people prefer to utilise the folds in the air in their immediate surroundings. So, um. Yes, that's Hammerspace. Anyway—'

He held the scarlet Book before her, not waiting for a response. Amy recoiled. Gerald could hear the pounding of her heart.

'Tell me what you feel when you parse this.'

'I don't need to parse too much,' said Amy, her voice barely a whisper. 'As soon as I walked into the courtyard outside, I could feel it. It feels like hatred. There's a *lot* of hate in that Book. A lot of anger. And death. Maybe it's what Hell feels like, I don't know.'

Gerald rested the Book on his knees.

'I can imagine so,' he said. 'A lot of hatred created it, I suppose.'

He ran his hands along the smooth, cool cover. It was nondescript and unassuming. Inside were crêped wrinkled pages that would never crumble, tattooed with hundreds of thousands of names: names that belonged to murderers and thieves and backstabbers and womanisers and man-eaters and careless teachers and irksome parents and betraying cousins and adulterous spouses, as well as just the general annoyances that took things a step too far. Only hatred – an irrational, potent desire, could create a Grim Book. And the immersion within it was what kept him alive. The Grim Book was the cornerstone of his family, a dynasty that went back through millennia and affected every country and continent on the planet. Wherever humans existed, a Grim Book would be there, and with every Grim Book, there was a member of his family.

'Amy,' said Gerald, turning towards her. 'I'm Gethsemane Phoenix Sekou Reaper. I'm the *Grim* Reaper, in fact.'

CHAPTER EIGHT

Amy

She listened in a patient stupor as Gerald explained his life. She also felt the presences of more Otherworldlies entering the library. Some came through the front entrance, nodding quickly at Gerald before swanning off elsewhere. Others she could feel coming in from the roof or a series of unknown passageways underground. She was accustomed to some of the auras: untransformed werewolves were in attendance, and more witches beside that. The rest was a mystery, and the knowledge of the unknown was daunting to her. They possessed a pleasant ambience as they browsed shelves, sat in contemplative studiousness in the research rooms, and cradled cups of coffee and herbal teas in the cafés that were now closed to humans. It was monotonous and extraordinary.

Returning to Gerald, she was taken aback at how easily he revealed his identity. He leaned back, resting on his hands, stretching his legs to kick his feet in the air. His expression was serene, his eyes wandering. He told her that he came from the ancient Grim Tribe, a nomadic people that travelled around the Sahara. They were cursed with the ability to kill by a single touch, subsequently marking them as perfect assassins. For millennia, politicians, cuckolded lovers, jilted friends, and confidants made requests to the Tribe to assassinate their enemies for a fee. As time wore on, their activity created the legend of the Grim Reaper – a cloaked entity that stole away earthly souls.

'The Grim Book,' he said, flicking through the pages of the red tome, 'lists all our assassination requests. People come to us in many different forms. If people know about us, then they contact the Tribe directly. Other times they rely on someone else who's in the know. It's mostly rich people, elites and the like; they're the ones who can afford us. My Father is the current head of the Tribe, so he's the one who assigns the requests to our Books, all depending on our personal skill. My people are stationed all over the world, tasked with observing the humans in different cities – mainly the cities in which a lot of hatred can thrive.

'It's a curious thing, being a Reaper. My whole life's work depends on negative feelings. There are some individuals that have so much hatred directed towards them that a request is automatically made in the Book, triggered at random. That's why it makes you feel so bad, Amy. There's very little good in it.' He glanced towards her, but Amy looked away. 'Do I make sense?'

'Yeah, you do,' she said, eyes fixed on the ground. What could she say to all of that? The Grim Book was shrouded in a thick grey cloud and sitting next to it felt like she was inhaling soot. When she met Gerald at the library gates, its aura saturated his otherwise sanguine, appealing air. She was relieved to know that he hadn't suddenly turned evil on her, and that the Book was the real culprit behind the sensation.

'So, you're the Reaper for London?'

'London is my turf. I've been here for a few years. And I'll stay in London until my retirement, when I'll go back to the Tribe and take over as the head.'

It was hard to believe. His face was childlike and earnest,

and his thick, curly hair made him look so innocent. And yet, she flushed cold whenever she remembered his Awakening, when the whole world emanated from his body, and she felt the presence of a god. She probed his aura, confirming that he told her the truth. As she went deeper into his presence, she hit a blockage. That thick Wall. It was more impenetrable than before, and this time, it was accompanied by a layer of frost that pushed her away. She could not get past it. She wondered if she would ever know his true nature.

As if sensing what she was trying to do, Gerald's eyes swivelled in her direction, and he grinned at her. 'Any questions, Amy?'

She observed him, trying to see the Hammerspace in which he had held the Book, but only his black clothes remained.

'Can you do magic, then? Like the Hammerspace thing. Can you do other things?'

'Plenty of other things. But I won't tell you. It would spoil the mystery.'

'Is that how you kill people? With magic?'

'No, the curse isn't a spell and it doesn't abide by any laws like magic does. It's something I'll never be able to hide from. Not all members of the Tribe have the ability, mind you. There are many branches of the Grims, and we have several sister tribes. The Reaper family is the only one with the curse, and our branch leads the Tribe.'

He straightened and placed his hands in his lap, staring at them with a blank expression. Amy followed suit. There was a discomforting aura around them that was distinct from the rest of his body, as if they belonged to someone else. Within the splendour of all his other emotions, the whirlwind of his presence, those hands were like hazardous debris picked up along the way, splicing gaps between the gales that comprised him, reminding her to be wary of his appearance.

'Your hands are cursed?' she prompted.

To answer, Gerald unsheathed their leather coverings. What remained were two polished skeletal entities, devoid of skin and muscle and blood and tendons. It was as if someone had cut off his real hands and affixed a stage prop to his arms in their place. The brown skin of his wrist turned thin and grey, and then white, melding into the bone. Gerald steepled his fingers, his expression wary. Amy felt a wave of apprehension, as if he was scared that she would run and reject him. She straightened her back, looking at him squarely.

The Reaper stood. 'I'd like to show you something,' he said, and turned towards the entrance, slipping into the gift shop immediately beside the security booth. A six-month exhibition was currently running at the library: *Tombs: Discovering the Dark Underbelly of London*. As was customary, the shop was stacked with themed books, coffin key rings, chocolate skeleton lollipops, and shelves of maps from all around the city detailing ancient tombs which were said to be haunted. Amy had spent much of her time travelling around London and she was certain the maps were factual. Oftentimes, she would feel the echo of a wail, a scream of fear on the wind, and a vision would flash in her mind, piercing and dreadful: grey bones, blood, a dark cavern, an executioner's axe, a martyr's pyre. It made her shudder to think about it.

A potted money plant cast a pretty green shade on the pay counter, illuminated by the spotlights from the shop's ceiling. Gerald touched a fingertip to one of the bulbous leaves. In response, the plant wilted, shrivelled into a dark brown stump, and disintegrated until only grey, dry soil remained. Gerald danced his fingers along the topsoil, subsequently evaporating whatever life forms had dwelt within it. The soil became ash, and the terracotta pot dimmed to grey and cracked. The rocky, ashen soil spilled out onto the floor, leaving a dark shadow of the plump green plant from before.

'Shit,' Amy hissed as she backed away, resting on the adjacent wall for support. 'You have no control over that?'

'No. I can't turn it off. If I touch anything, it dies. The gloves aren't for show.'

'Shit.'

'Are you scared?'

His quiet tone caught her attention. He was staring at her with unwavering focus, his eyes boring deeply into hers. Beneath the dim light of the library, the red ring around his black irises seemed to glow. There was something awfully comforting about his face, but it contradicted the magnitude of his power. The icy wall within him was a concern. He was still hiding so much from her.

'I'm not sure,' she said.

Gerald nodded. 'Smart.'

She scanned the pages of his aura, reeling beneath the contradictions that formed him. A sanguine air and an amiable countenance, the smooth face of innocence: all a potential façade. He did not look like a murderer.

'But could you ever say no to all the killing?' she said. 'Like, "I don't want to do what other Reapers do. I'd like to open a bakery."'

His eyes twinkled with humour when he answered, 'I could still open a bakery.'

'And kill on the side?'

'And kill on the side.'

'*Why?*'

'Because we're cursed.'

She paused because his aura grew thick. A heaviness descended upon him – a monsoon of emotions. She could feel the weight of his thoughts pressing against his shoulders, carving indents in the air.

'Who cursed you?' she asked, worried about the answer.

Gerald smiled. 'You make it sound so sinister, but it wasn't done out of malice. It was more a process of nature. We have a Progenitor. He goes by many names, but His most common is the Death King Armageddon. You say when you met me, it felt like a god. Well, He is the closest thing we have. He is cognizant. A living creature. But He is so powerful that the only way to prevent cataclysms across the universe is for Him to separate the worst of His energy and mould it into a Spirit outside of His body, called an Excess. Death's Excess is Vengeance and the Reapers have all been issued a portion of this Spirit. In a way, we protect the world from Armageddon. The Grim Tribe as a whole, therefore, protects the world from the Reapers.

'Reapers were born from the Spirit of Vengeance – *the desire to kill*. If we don't use the curse, we would be consumed by it, obsessed with death like vampires starved of blood. We are born engorged with bloodlust, and so to avoid turning mad with the thrill of it, we regulate ourselves through codified killing. Assassination abates our bloodlust and prevents the worst of our temptation. We can pick and choose when to kill, but eventually, a killing must happen. My limit is two months exactly. I grow aggravated otherwise, and that's a dangerous thing.'

She knew he was telling the truth. His aura was without deceit, and the deluge of power that leaked from his body on the night of his Awakening had stunned her to silence. Despite his innocence, she could feel the magic that swirled within him, that pull of the unfathomable. Yet, she felt something else in him now. He was concealing some thoughts, and whenever he mentioned Armageddon, some acerbic jolt assaulted him. It was a tremor of something that subdued his entire body and diminished him with its power. This Death King was far greater than Gerald Reaper, and together they nursed some private knowledge.

'Explain your Awakening to me,' she said. 'You say you're not a god, but there's a lot going on with you anyway. It's not like you're normal, is it?'

'Very much abnormal. The Awakening means I can kill from a distance now. And I can use omnipresence to see people from far away. I can look through walls, and I can freeze the air around me. I can control people with my speech. None of these things are unassailable, and if people know to expect me, they can counter. But it makes me very powerful – even more powerful than the other Reapers before me. My Awakening was a bit different.'

'And why was that?'

'Various reasons.'

Amy laughed. She felt the heat of irritation burn her temples. 'That's it?'

'Well,' Gerald folded his arms, his skeletal fingers resting on his biceps, and his aura bubbling with mischief. 'It wouldn't be fun if you knew everything, would it? I thought you were an *Otherworldly* investigator. Wouldn't you feel more satisfied with your field notes if you'd made the discoveries yourself? I'm sure your grandmother would approve.'

'Swear? It's like that?'

'It's like that.'

'Challenge accepted.'

'Good,' he said. 'That's really good. You know, I brought

the Grim Book with me because I've been assigned some new cases to handle. These aren't humans, so they'll be tricky to kill. Even worse, they're currently in hiding.' He turned away from her, walking back to the stone steps. 'Now, empathy is one of the few gifts that we Grims have *not* been blessed with. It would be great if I had a partner who could accompany me on this task, or any task, really. Perhaps a partner who had an extraordinary ability that could help me track targets, that can feel auras in the air and follow them. It's the type of empathy that most non-humans would kill for. I think that partner could help me find these criminals.'

'Are you . . . you're not joking?'

Her mind unravelled at the fantasy before her. Amy's life was one of isolation – she was an empathetic oddity too obscene for the conventions of maternal attention, and for the past five years, a self-imposed wall had separated her from the truth once offered by the only person who had given her love. Regret was written between the spaces of her notebooks; white spaces born from a granddaughter unanchored from her mentor. Now, she was being invited into a world that she had tried so hard to understand. She wanted to see the truth according to Nan, to live in it, and offer a posthumous vindication.

'Amy, I would love to have your help on this case,' said Gerald, and his voice rang in her head. 'I think we would make a fantastic team.'

'So do I,' she said. The words were quiet. They rested as condensation on her lips. She worried about looking too enthusiastic and turning him away.

'Good. First, I think I'll take you Downstairs. Some things need to be seen before they are believed. Afterwards, let's get to work.'

Gerald escorted her out of the library. The streets were dark and busy. London turned as late commuters went home, and buses chugged in traffic, and people had sex, and dealers exchanged gear, and the sky seeped into night-time. Everything appeared normal, but Amy's vision was altered. She would never look at her city in the same way again.

CHAPTER NINE

Amy

There was a block of flats on the road behind the library. They were plain and shabby, and could have been home to council tenants, students on visas, or bohemian professionals on a desperate quest to hide their wealth. Gerald donned his face mask and cap. Two shrewd eyes examined the night amid all that gloom. With a gloved finger, he tapped a code on the intercom of the building, and with a low buzz, the door opened and gave them way.

'So ... Downstairs is someone's house?' asked Amy. Inside, the building was lit with white panel lights. The floor was sticky linoleum. A metal cage of a lift awaited them straight ahead. She stifled a laugh when Gerald punched the call button and escorted her inside.

'Not quite,' he said.

She stared him over. His aura was totally serene. It reminded her of the stoicism that surrounded a bus stop, and beneath that cloud of indifference, she could sense a mild excitement. She delved deeper into this feeling, immediately understanding that her presence was an enjoyable novelty for him. She almost got lost in his aura, and instinctively pushed herself until she was surrounded by it – that warm buzz of someone happy to have a companion to talk to. But further still, and her body turned to marble. The cold Wall appeared as if on command. Encrusted with a film of ice. She edged away from the Wall and retreated from his aura. When she looked at Gerald's face, she found him staring at her.

'Having fun?' he asked.

'No.'

The Reaper pressed the button for the fourth floor. The lift jolted to life. The doors opened on a silent passageway lined with apartment doors that were chipped and cracked and flaking with old paint. Amy heard muffled music from behind some doors and smelt the remains of a roast dinner behind others. Gerald waited, watching the nothingness ahead, before calling for the second floor instead. When the doors opened once more, he watched the empty second-floor corridor before them, with its unbothered entrances, and the little signs of life seeping through the door jambs. Before the lift motioned to close, he pressed for the sixth floor. Once there, he opted for the second floor again.

'Are you taking the piss?' asked Amy. 'Where is this place?'

'Almost there.'

He continued riding the lift to various floors. His aura never changed, but Amy's did. It was out of stubborn curiosity that she didn't just get out and leave him there to play with himself, but before she had a chance to really give him a piece of her mind, the lift doors flung open with a creaking groan. They were on the fifth floor.

The corridor was the same. The pale walls and the dim lights that flickered onto sticky flooring. A row of doors, leading to different flats, lined the walls. The only difference was the girl facing them.

She wore a hooded cloak that covered her eyes, but the chin that emerged from the shadow was brown and rounded with the baby fat of adolescence. She nodded at Gerald without a word, and the doors closed behind her. When she turned to Amy, her hood flew backwards on its own, revealing a pair of purple serpentine eyes. She hissed at Amy, and a forked tongue slithered from between jagged teeth. Amy screamed and jumped backwards on the wall behind. The girl's foreboding aura filled the small space so suddenly, she found it hard to breathe.

'Oopsie, Carole!' said Gerald. He placed an amicable hand on the girl's shoulder. 'Amy's with me.'

All at once, the monstrous visage evaporated. What remained was the rounded, sickly innocent face of a Black child. Her dark, doe-like eyes watched Amy inquisitively. Amy felt the pressure seep away into the walls of the lift. It was replaced by a calming lull of an aura, one in which she drifted against her will.

'Your friend?' asked Carole, not taking her eyes off Amy.

'Yes.'

'But you're a human.'

'And?' said Amy. She shrugged Carole's deceitful aura away and squirmed as far into the corner of the lift as she could go. 'Who are you?'

'Now, now ladies, let's be nice.' Gerald beckoned Carole closer. 'Amy, Carole's family guards the passages in and out of Downey. The Warden family is almost as old as the Reapers. They're all very useful and we're grateful for them.'

Seemingly satisfied, Carole extracted a key from her pocket, which she pressed into the lift panel to halt it. They were now stuck on the fifth floor.

'I didn't mean no harm,' she said. She knelt beside Amy. A silvery line, like fishing wire, appeared in the air beside her. Carole tugged at the wire, unzipping the seam as if it was a handbag. She pulled apart the opening and extracted various items from within its contents: a cauldron, a sage smudge stick, some tea leaves, and a portable stove. Amy watched in wonder as Carole boiled the tea leaves on the stove. She lit the sage stick and paced the small space of the lift, paying close attention to wave it around Amy's head and shoulders.

'This is because you're a human,' she said to Amy. 'There are some creatures in Downey who'd love to get a piece of you. This ain't strong, but it will help to mask your scent a bit and ward them off. Tea's done.'

She produced a teacup from her Hammerspace and spooned a generous helping for Amy to drink. Amy sniffed the dark brown liquid and frowned.

'You know how humans are,' said Carole, 'always getting into stuff. Always finding things out. You heard of the lift game?' When Amy shook her head, she continued. 'Some humans found out how to get to the *other world*, as in, *our* world. The lift sequence to get to Downey used to be so simple, but we had to keep changing it. Kids dare each other to use the sequence and find us. So I have to come in and scare them, like I did with you, and then take them back to the ground floor. One look at me and they never try it again. Drink up now.'

Amy took one sip of the tea and politely let it dribble back into the cup.

'*Cerasee tea?*' she spat. She felt the bile rise in her throat. All those times that Nan forced her to drink cerasee tea for health, or for strength, or for strong bones – whatever the Jamaican folktales said. It was a punishment for West Indian kids: an elixir so bitter it made her eyes run. She handed the teacup back to Carole. 'I can't drink this.'

'You will drink this,' said Carole. An icy aura encircled Amy, snaking around her ankles until she felt frozen. She shivered and drank under duress, gulping huge mouthfuls that burned her throat. When she was done, she almost smashed the cup on the ground. She was dimly aware of Gerald's husky, quiet laugh at her expense in the background.

'Thank you,' said Carole. She stowed the rest of the paraphernalia into her Hammerspace, zipped it closed, and returned to the lift console. Turning the key halfway, a new button materialised marked *SSB*. When Carole pressed it, the lift dropped, and Amy swayed dangerously on her feet.

'Are you Jamaican?' Carole asked, turning to watch her.

'Yeah. Why?'

'Your reaction to the tea. It really is good for you. You should listen to your elders. Which part of Jamaica are you from? Do you know?'

'My grandma's from St Thomas.'

'Hmm. What's her surname?'

'St Clair.'

'I don't know the St Clairs.'

'She was a human too, though.'

'I'm sure she was, but there's something unusual about you. And if your family hails from St Thomas, then . . . well who knows.'

'Yeah . . .' Amy looked away, but she could still feel Carole's eyes watching her. She knew that St Thomas was a parish known for its supposed magical activity, but she had assumed that her family's ability had been born from a necessity of the environment.

'And how have you been anyway, Carole?' asked Gerald.

Carole turned to him. 'Oh, wonderful, Mr Gerald. Um, I do hope you can visit us for tea and biscuits soon. My mum's always asking . . .'

As she rabbited on, Amy felt a sudden warmth on her

shoulder. It felt like someone had placed their palm there to reassure her. She looked at Gerald and turned away again. As he distracted Carole by promising all sorts of pastries to gift to her family, the warmth never left her.

At long last, the lift halted. The pressure on Amy's body was unmistakable. It felt like the world, with all its soil and cement, was pressing dangerously against the walls of the lift as an obvious chill entered the space. When the door opened, the area outside was pitch black. The only light came from a series of bulbous street lights that lined a silent, cobbled road. They emitted a dim glow around their immediate area only. Everything else was cast in shadow. The darkness was frightening, and as she trained her senses, Amy could feel the vampiric chill at the base of her spine, and the heat of witches, and the wild thrill that could only be the aura of masses of werewolves, all in human form during moonless nights. She could see none of them, and she wondered where they were hiding.

'See what I mean about Carole? So dependable,' said Gerald.

Carole tipped her head, blushing.

'What do you mean?' Amy asked once they were outside the lift. Carole did not follow. The doors closed with her still inside, and her hood returned to enshroud her face. All at once, the door and the lift melted into the blackness, and once again, Amy was entombed in the unknown.

'Well, I didn't need to tell her where I wanted to go,' said Gerald. 'Other than Downey. The Wardens control all entrances and exits, and they can make the lift go to whatever part of the city they want. I'm here to meet a friend and discuss some important matters, and Carole obviously knew this without my saying so; she's fantastic at cold reading. Such an intelligent child. Ah, are you cold? I have some cardigans in my Hammerspace.'

'Erm, no thanks.' Amy rubbed her arms anyway. 'It's not that it's cold. I mean, it *is* cold, but this is a different kind of chill. It's the blackness, and the things I can't see. Nothing will jump out and get me, will it?'

'No. Come.'

They walked silently down the cobbled street. As they walked, Amy's eyes adjusted to the darkness, and soon the area brightened with every new step, revealing the extraordinarily high ceiling that enclosed the area, covered mostly in thick shadow. They were currently traversing a beautifully sleepy avenue lined by black-leaved cypress trees. The street lights were made of gold. An eccentric mansion of indescribable size appeared every few yards, each one guarded by a black gate. The homes were finished with green ponds, stables, carriages of varying sophistication, and immaculately dressed skeletons that were busying themselves with house fixtures, the lawns, and polishing the finish of expensive supercars. Amy halted.

'Am I imagining that?' she asked, parsing the auras instinctively. She could feel nothing. Even dead bodies left an aura behind.

'Nope. Skeletons are a race down here. They're literally born that way. I can't explain it, I'm afraid.'

Amy tried to stop staring, but it was impossible, especially considering the mansions the skeletons maintained. Each building grew obscener in its display of luxury. One was made of a glossy midnight blue slab that reflected all the other houses around it. Bright orange water trickled from the mouth of a dancing stone elf.

'What the hell,' she said, losing her train of thought.

'Ah, Bear Gecko's house. He's famous down here as well. He's the inventor of Gecko tea – wonderful stuff. Just don't drink the red one, otherwise you'll be confessing to sins you don't even know you've committed. The Downey Met really need to stop using it in their interrogations; it's been proven to be unreliable countless times.'

'So this is like, you lot's version of Belgravia or Hampstead and whatnot.'

'You could say that. We're here.'

A great house, made from obsidian brick, waited ominously at the end of the avenue. It was larger than all the others, and the quietest. The only signs of life came from red velvet curtains that glowed with soft lighting and the distant patter of horses' hooves signified carriages and footmen. When they reached the intercom, Gerald pressed a code on the keypad. A crackle later, and a raspy, irritated voice hissed '*What?*' down the speaker.

'Important news, friend.'

There was no verbal response, but the gates opened, and Gerald all but dragged Amy towards the polished scarlet door.

'Wait, wait, wait,' she said, eyes darting around, half-expecting some unwelcome interference, 'you never told me who this is!'

'You should have asked sooner.'

'Are you serious?'

'He's nothing to be frightened of. But I need to discuss the names in my Grim Book with him. He knows more about what's been going on and I would like his opinion on the case.'

He hesitated, his posture uncertain as he considered an unspoken thought. 'I should say . . . he can be antsy.'

'Define antsy.'

'My friend is suspicious of those he doesn't know, and he's often harsh with his words. But he's harmless ... I think. He's been a bit of a caretaker for me in London, seeing as all my family is elsewhere.'

'Right. Not exactly reassuring, but we'll see.' Amy calmed herself. 'And ain't you got special friends?' she muttered afterwards, shooting an indignant glare at the pomp of the mansion before her.

'You forget that I'm special too.'

Before she could answer, the front door swung inwards and a skeleton butler greeted them into a lavish foyer.

'Good evening, Archer,' said Gerald to the skeleton.

'Master Reaper.'

'This is my friend, Amy St Clair.'

'Hi,' said Amy.

'Lovely to meet you, Ms St Clair.'

Gerald smiled at the door opposite. 'He's in there I suppose?' he asked Archer.

'You know him well.'

'If we could have a pot of jasmine, Archer, I would be so grateful.'

The skeleton bowed quickly and disappeared down an adjacent corridor. Afterwards, Gerald opened a door, leading them both into a shadowy office that was overcrowded with bookshelves and furniture. It smelt of leather and rose, but much of the room was saturated with thick, sooty cigar smoke. A cold, hostile aura penetrated the fog from behind the only desk, and two scarlet eyes glared at them through a cloud of newly puffed tar. Gerald dragged a leather-backed chair in front of the desk, helping Amy to sit down before getting one for himself. He sat lightly in his seat, one leg crossed over the other, waiting with a wide, patient expression for the owner of the red eyes to speak.

Amy could not determine a figure because the smoke was so thick, but alongside the anger and loathing was a cold, supernatural air that made her skin prickle. It reminded her of the aura that lingered over cemeteries: ghostly, an imprint of a life once lived, and the presence of something that was missing. It was always a strange sensation, to feel an absence and the personal significance it once held, but unable to feel the thing itself. Sometimes the vacancy was so wide and so deep and so strong, she was left with the impossible sadness of a life cut too short, severed before having a chance to realise their massive dreams. She parsed the air around the tarry smoke before her and felt the loss of many dreams, as if the entity was made entirely of obsolescence. It was an unsettling and incomprehensible sensation.

She knew that the person was not a ghost or revenant, so she flicked through the pages of notebooks in her mind. Many of her notes were seemingly nonsensical scratchings, oftentimes written as a daisy chain of dribbling thoughts as they popped into her head. But most had sense to them, informed by web searches, the perusal of old books, and the lengthy tales of various self-proclaimed mystics that she had crossed paths with. There was talk of a species of ghost people with scarlet eyes and the ability to disappear, phase through objects, and manipulate air. Urban myths persisted in tropical countries of the ghost people creating tornadoes and storms. Amy deduced that the third person in the room was a wraith.

One last puff of smoke, and the wraith with the hostile aura stubbed the cigar into a metal ashtray. He made a quick slicing motion in the air with his hands, and a wide incision appeared in the curtain of smoke, clearing the view completely. The cut grew wider until the smoke dissipated, revealing the beautifully cosy room they sat in. Long elaborate tapestries donned violet walls and velvet curtains covered the sash windows behind a polished maple desk adorned with intricate hand carvings. The desk was also littered with parchment paper, quills, leather-bound books, and an open case of fresh cigars. The case itself was gold-plated.

The wraith was a male of small stature and youthful appearance, but the slight wrinkles in the corners of his wide, protuberant eyes gave his years away. Thick brown hair was styled in wide coils, clouding around a face that was round with a pointed chin. His skin was a deep walnut brown, which only emphasised the stunning intensity of his eyes. Full lips were cast in a frown. His gaze fell upon Amy, and she cringed.

'And who are you?' he asked with a voice that was high-pitched and raspy, barely above a whisper.

'This is Amy,' said Gerald, 'my . . . partner.'

The wraith acknowledged Gerald for the first time. His frown deepened. 'You have a partner. Really?'

'Yes, really. She's a human, but she's an empath. The best empath I've ever met. Honestly, her ability is phenomenal.'

Amy's face burned. She wouldn't admit it, but she was honoured, even more so that her gift was useful enough to make her the working partner of the Grim Reaper. The wraith expressed his scepticism through his aura. She met his gaze evenly.

'Oh?' he said with a sneer. 'Looks like she felt that.'

'Blythe,' said Gerald, 'Amy didn't come here to be insulted, and neither did I.'

'And why did you come, Reaper?' Blythe's eyes didn't leave Amy's, and Amy's didn't leave Blythe's.

'Tyrell Bane, Melanie Lavender,' said Gerald.

Blythe turned to Gerald at last. 'And why do you have *those* names?' he wheezed, and a spark of indignation ruptured the room's atmosphere.

Gerald sighed, plunging his hands into his abdomen again to retrieve the Grim Book from his Hammerspace. He flicked to the most recent page and placed the Book on the table for Blythe to see. Amy peered over the desk, identifying the two names scrawled in red, slanted font.

'Who made this request?' asked Blythe.

Amy caught a sense of trepidation from Gerald. He grimaced before lifting the Book from the table. 'A direct request from Lex Crow.'

'Oh. Oh ho-ho. I see. I see how it is.' Blythe pushed himself backwards, snatched a cigar from its case, and scrambled out of his chair, pacing the floor with one hand in his pocket while the other clutched onto the freshly lit cigar. Now that he was on the ground, Amy could see just how short he was. The wraith barely reached over the height of his own desk, and he wore dungarees that were so big they bunched around his ankles and threatened to trip him over. His sweatshirt was just as ridiculously oversized; the sleeves slid down his arm as he smoked.

'Well, there goes *his* sponsorship,' Blythe said to no one. 'Let's see him win the next election without the Mason purse.'

'That's a bit mean-spirited, Blythe,' said Gerald, turning in his seat to watch the wraith pace around, his curls askew.

'What's mean-spirited is our mayor using me and my organisation to do all the dirty work and clean up the mess that Downey leaves Upstairs, never thanking me by name while he gallivants to human meetings with the mayor of

London. But when things get a little too difficult, he goes behind my back and makes a request to the Reapers? *I* was working on this case. If you kill any of those Downers, I'll kill you, Gerald.'

'Oh, I wouldn't want that.'

Blythe halted. He looked at Gerald askance. 'Shut it. Shut your mouth and get out of my house.'

'Blythe, Blythe, Blythe. Come on, sit down.'

They were interrupted by a light knock on the door. Archer the skeleton appeared with a silver tray of biscuits, cheese, a willow pattern tea set, and a decanter of whisky. He poured the tea – pale pink in colour – into two cups and tipped the alcohol over a whisky ball in a glass. Blythe nodded his thanks to Archer as he handed the glass over to his boss, while Gerald made a great show of thanking the butler, sharing out tea and biscuits to Amy. She took the snacks quickly, wanting to do anything to take her mind off the worsening atmosphere in the room. Blythe's anger rolled off his body in thick, stony waves. It was like trying to breathe in cement. She inhaled the sweet, flowery smell of the jasmine tea and sipped without cooling it, burning her tongue in the process. When Archer was gone, Gerald turned to her, smiling lightly.

'Perhaps some backstory?' he asked as Blythe returned to the desk. 'Lex Crow is our mayor, the mayor of Downstairs, and as Blythe says, he's known by the mayor of London and a few senior civil servants. He's the one who made the request to my family to kill these two individuals.' He patted his stomach to indicate the hidden Grim Book. 'They're both Downers: Tyrell Bane is a warlock. Melanie Lavender is a witch. You know the differences between the two?'

'Witches feel earthy,' she mused. 'Like never-ending forests.

Warlocks are a bit different. They're male-identified, and their auras are metallic. Industrial.'

Gerald considered this. 'That's a great way to put it. They both draw on the natural magic from the earth. The main difference is that witches conjure spells out of thin air, but warlocks store theirs in special phials. They're normally lower-level than mages – mages have a much vaster range of abilities.

'Melanie and Tyrell are exceptional practitioners, with magic abilities that do, in fact, rival mages. They once led the Downey Gang together, which gave us Downers a lot of problems, as they tend to work with humans. I have no doubt that some of these members are aware that their bosses aren't human, which isn't a good thing. They had a schism and the gang is split now: Bane's faction is Darkhouse and Lavender's is called Lads.'

He nodded to the wraith before him, who stubbornly ignored his guests. 'Blythe here has a secret agency called *Gardien*. They're a team of specialists akin to your intelligence services Upstairs, and are mostly unknown by the Downstairs community. I can only assume that something really bad must have happened for Mr Crow to ask for my family's help.'

'Something did happen,' said Blythe, puffing on his cigar and slicing away the residual smoke again. He rummaged in a nearby drawer and tossed an open folder across the desk, which Gerald promptly examined. He shuffled the contents until they spilled over the desktop.

Amy peered over, frowning at the grainy photographs of shipping containers from some unknown location. The photos increased in detail, showing various openings and hidden doors between the containers. In the final photograph, a dozen children in lifejackets stared at the camera with haunted expressions, their eyes eclipsed by black circles as the camera flash brightened their pupils to white pinpricks of fear. In the shadows of the flash, the pile of gaunt, dead bodies of their parents and fellow refugees provided a startling backdrop.

Gerald passed a tentative finger over the last photograph with an unreadable expression. Amy averted her gaze. A wave of nausea disturbed her stomach.

'They've mentioned this on the news,' she said to Blythe. 'It's a massive scandal right now.'

Blythe regarded her stiffly. He took a decisive sip of whisky before drawing from his cigar. 'Bane's faction was behind this,' he said to Gerald. 'The government Upstairs has closed the English Channel against migrants and refugees, creating opportunities for people smugglers. Darkhouse took up the helm and was found out.'

'And all supernatural involvement was just blotted out of the news, I suppose,' said Amy.

Blythe glared at her — astonished, it seemed, that she had spoken to him so freely for a second time. A deep, black loathing peeled off his skin and fluttered towards her in clumps of ash. She held his gaze. He snorted at her response, rolled his eyes, and focused on Gerald instead.

'Incidents of this nature get covered up normally,' Gerald said to Amy, clearly ignoring the tension. 'There's a whole host of tragedies that happen Upstairs all the time because of Downers, but the Concealment Act is there for a reason: a law of secrecy between Downstairs and Upstairs, maintained by a select few civil servants, the mayor of London, and the royal family. When Downers cause trouble or threaten to break the Act, it's our responsibility down here to do what we can to mitigate the problem. That normally means NDAs, memory-altering spells, and lots of money. So, while this refugee tragedy would have made the news, the supernatural involvement would have been quickly hidden.'

'Nan was right about you lot,' Amy concluded.

'I'm sure,' said Blythe, stubbing his cigar in the ashtray. 'I do find it hilarious, Gerald, that you've picked this human up off the street and made her your partner. What credentials does she actually have?'

'She can sense my Wall,' Gerald said, hand raised to stop Amy from responding.

This was the first time he had mentioned the mysterious defence within his aura. Glancing at Blythe, she found an incredulous expression on his face. The wraith looked at her again, more intently this time, but without anger. A tinge of curiosity rode the waves of his hostility like a paper boat in the sea. The waves within Blythe were troubled and erratic, and now that his anger had cleared, Amy could feel a roaring anguish that threatened the surface of his façade – anguish and jealousy.

'Are you sure?' asked Blythe, not taking his eyes off her.
'Yes. She probes it all the time.'
'I'm here,' said Amy. 'I'm right here.'
Blythe frowned. 'What did you say your surname was?'
'St Clair.'
'There are no St Clairs down here.'
'Glad to hear.'
'Yes, so am I.'
'Well anyway!' said Gerald. He poured himself another cup of tea and picked a lemon and white chocolate biscuit from the tray. 'As you can imagine, Amy, Bane's people-smuggling

exercise has put him at the top of our law enforcement's hit list, and I suppose Mr Crow no longer wants to wait for *Gardien* to conclude its investigations. He wants both Bane and Lavender gone.'

'I don't care what he wants. I'm still working on this.'

'I've already accepted the job.'

Blythe stiffened and his hands balled into petulant fists on the maple desk. Whereas the air around the Reaper remained pleasant, Blythe's grew wary and despondent. A silent agreement was being woven in the space between them.

'What happens when you accept the job?' Amy asked. She reached forward to touch Gerald's forearm to get his attention and baulked, considering her proximity to his gloves. His skeletal hands remained hidden, enclosed in shadow.

Gerald appeared to notice her hesitation and raised a subtle brow. He smiled faintly before continuing. 'It's my personal principle. Once I accept a request, I always see it to its end. I quite like sticking to consistency so targets and requestors take me seriously.'

'It's all very stupid,' said Blythe.

'And you can't compromise, like ever?' asked Amy. At her words, she felt Blythe's aura simmer once more, maintained by mild anticipation. Beside her, Gerald weighed her words in thought.

'Compromise how?'

'Like . . . I dunno. Push it back or something? Do it another time?'

'Hmm. I can. Yes, in a way. Blythe, how about we work together a bit? I will delay this request. During that time, you can get to the bottom of whatever gang activity you and your team are investigating, and afterwards I can do the deed.'

'We have no choice.'

'Good good!' Gerald downed his tea, packed his and Amy's cups away, and rose to his feet, stretching afterwards.

Amy followed suit, taking another look around the room. Blythe was clearly a busy wraith – his shelves were stuffed with folders, binders, and endless documents. The cleanest part of the office was the smallest set of shelves beside his desk. They were home to a few photographs and medals of service, most likely awarded to him for his crime work. Gerald came to stand beside her, observing the shelf with much interest.

'Blythe! You framed it!'

He pointed to the only golden frame on the shelf, showing Amy a photograph of Blythe, in black dungarees, looking absolutely hateful beside a birthday cake with *Happy 30th!* written in the icing by a clear amateur. Beside him, with one arm around his shoulders, and grinning maniacally, was Gerald. He waved at the camera, and with its slanted selfie angle, his bony hand was exposed, leather glove clasped firmly between his white, vampiric teeth.

A blade of ice shot down Amy's spine. She flinched away from the shelf, rubbing her lower back responsively. Gerald watched her, frowning. Afterwards, both Gerald and Amy turned to Blythe. He seemed momentarily perturbed by Amy, but recovered quickly enough to raise his free hand before closing it tightly in a fist. A sharp gust of wind blew past Amy and Gerald, and the photo slammed face down on the shelf. Blythe met Amy's eyes. She felt his anxiety towards her and her ability to sense his use of magic before it even happened.

'Just get out of my house. You've been here long enough. Get *out*, Gerald.'

'Of course, let me not disturb you any further.'

Amy could feel Gerald's elation so intensely, it made her smile. The photograph had been a pleasant discovery for him.

Just as they were at the office door, Gerald turned to Blythe again. 'One quick question. What *is* your group trying to uncover with the Downey Gang?'

Blythe sipped his drink once more. 'A gang such as theirs shouldn't be so elusive. We should have caught them far sooner. Long before they had gained enough power to pull this Channel business. They're being protected, and I want to know how.' His eyes narrowed from behind the glass. 'And by whom.'

CHAPTER TEN
Gerald

The pair walked in silence down the slumbering cobbled avenue. Gerald's head was full of thoughts – mainly how much work the capture and killing of Melanie Lavender and Tyrell Bane would entail. These types of assassinations were always the most arduous, and he normally avoided them to economise his time, but the challenge also provided a thrill that was undeniably alluring.

When the target was human, a Reaper's job was mostly quick and routine; their power was so great and efficient, there was rarely a need for major operations. Targets were killed before they had a chance to react. Whenever a Downer request was made, it provided him with some variety. But anything relating to the Downey Gang would be complicated: both leaders' political relationships with Upstairs made them difficult foes to catch, and their numerous human followers would always provide a collateral foil to the Concealment Act. He could only hope that teaming up with Blythe's *Gardien* would help ease the mounting political fallout, and that the inevitable deaths would provide a satisfactory pay-off.

He turned to Amy, who stared at the mansions as they journeyed down the avenue.

'Are you currently free?' he asked. 'I have an assassination that I would like to do tonight as well. It should be a quick one, but I'll need to get my timings right on it, and we have time to kill . . .'

'Time to kill? Honestly.'

He laughed at that, then, 'Are you okay with all this? I'm sure it must be overwhelming.'

'It is a bit,' she said. 'Not a bit. A lot. Fucking crazy, actually. I'm excited to see all this, but I think I was being naïve before.'

'How so?'

They stopped at the end of the avenue. It was quiet, but he could see from her body language that Amy was unnerved by it. She sighed, eyes quickly scanning the darkness of the area.

'I didn't realise how political this all was,' she said. 'I heard about those refugee kids in the news. When you and that Blythe guy were talking about a Downey Gang, it sounded a bit cute, like something off *Emmerdale*. But this is some really heavy stuff. If I get involved in this, I'll be all up in government business.'

'Is it too much?'

She looked at him and her expression was unreadable. They hadn't even started working together, but he wondered if he had shown her too much, too soon. He wanted to know what was going through her head, wistful that her potent empath abilities were not part of the Awakening package.

'It's not too much,' she said at last. 'It's complicated. Am I even making sense?'

'A little bit. This world is all I know, and by comparison, yours isn't half as exciting.'

'I hear that.'

'Should we hold off on the assassination today, then? We can do it tomorrow night. Let's just get something to eat. Upstairs. There'll always be time to show you all of this.'

Amy was clearly disappointed, but she nodded, more to herself than to Gerald. He was sure that she also realised how overwhelming it would be to see so much of London's supernatural community on the same day as learning about the Reapers, feeling the aura of the Grim Book, and visiting Blythe's house. He held out his arm and smiled to challenge her previous reticence. Amy inhaled, meeting his gaze evenly, and hooked her own around his.

'So,' Gerald said, feeling relieved, 'what do you think of Blythe?'

'He's an arrogant prick.'

'Ha! He can be difficult, but he means well.'

'He does mean well.'

The thoughtful tone of her voice made Gerald pause, and he waited as she stared out at nothing, her eyes searching the discordant layers of the air around them.

'All that rudeness is hiding something. Beneath it all, he feels quite lonely. It's like grief, almost. You attract outcasts, Gerald.'

The Reaper shivered in the wake of her words, dumbfounded that she could read Blythe so easily. The wraith carried many sorrows, but his self-imposed isolation from the world was one he nursed with territorial obsession, and the Reaper felt it would be improper to expose those secrets to Amy. He only nodded in silence and determined to visit Blythe more often. There was only so much Archer could do.

'And why's he so rich?' Amy glanced back at the mansion, now succumbed to the shadows behind them. 'That massive house can't help if he's just living in it all by himself.'

'It's just one of those things. The Masons are another one of our old Downstairs families. They own that avenue, and a lot of the land down here. Like many wealthy families, they have close ties to politics, and they often donate large sums of money to Lex Crow's election campaigns. Lex has been the mayor of Downey for ten years now; he's the most popular leader we've had for a long time.'

'Doesn't seem smart, then, if he wants to piss off his biggest sponsor.'

'Not his best decision, no.' Gerald frowned inwardly. In a way, he could understand why Mr Crow felt apprehensive towards the Masons. A relationship so dependent on money and popularity would never end well, and Blythe had already exploited it by getting permission to establish *Gardien*. Crow had a right to divert from the Mason script, regardless of its risk. As he explained this to Amy, she rolled her eyes, clearly sympathising with the mayor.

'What does *Gardien* even do? You telling me they've been investigating this gang for two years and nothing's happened?'

'Well, I wouldn't say nothing,' Gerald said in defence of his friend's efforts. 'Most of our intelligence on the gang has come from *Gardien* in the first place, and the Downey Gang isn't the only thing they investigate, it's just taken up much of their time now that things have become so flagrant. I downplayed their skill before, but they really are specialised and totally independent from the Downey Met, most of whom know nothing about them. A lot of their cases are bespoke, like the type of crimes that could breach the Concealment Act or ones that involve high-profile individuals: politicians, Upstairs elites, and the like.'

'Are there a lot of them?'

'No,' Gerald frowned. 'I think there are eight, excluding Blythe. And maybe some part-timers.'

'That's a bit small!'

'As I said, they're elite. No doubt we'll meet them the more into this Downey Gang case we get.'

'Any vampires on the team?'

'I believe so, yes.'

He led them to the lift. To Amy, it would have looked like a wall of empty blackness, but Gerald, like all Downers, could sense where the nearest lift was. Soon enough, a sliver of light appeared, and a pair of doors slid open, revealing an alert Carole on the other side.

'Back home, Mr Gerald?' she asked.

'Yes please. Same flats.'

She clicked her key in the console again, and the lift shuddered to life.

'Did you enjoy your time Downstairs?' To Gerald's surprise, Carole had asked the question to Amy.

'I did, thanks.'

'And . . . will you be coming again?' Gerald asked.

'Yeah. Of course I will,' Amy smiled, folding her arms. 'You won't get rid of me that easily.'

Gerald mirrored her pose. 'Well, I'm glad to hear it.'

They both thanked Carole once they were back Upstairs. King's Cross and St Pancras was as busy as always: the traffic was at a standstill, and the pavements were littered with people.

Gerald hooked his arm around Amy's again. 'Let's get some dinner and you can ask me any other questions you have.'

'Oh great. I have loads. It might get on your nerves.'

He laughed lightly, mentally preparing himself at the same time. The next few weeks – maybe months – were sure to be laborious, but he was prepared. At least he had company this time.

CHAPTER ELEVEN

Amy

They met the next evening after Amy's library shift. The pale blue lights of Chancery Lane Underground station waned in the distance, almost smothered by the litter of street lights, Hackney cab squadrons, and masses of people flurrying between cafés, restaurants, and theatres. The London streets burst aflame as the city's nightlife began. There were some parts of London that Amy simply never visited, and as they wandered further away from the major intersection and onto a quieter street, she felt a sense of unease. The street was wide enough, lined with shops on either side of it. She could imagine how busy it would have been during the day at lunch time when the workers would rush to get Marks and Spencer's sandwiches and salads from Sainsbury's.

'You've never been to Chancery Lane?' asked Gerald, noting her demeanour.

'No.'

Gerald looked at her askance. Confusion rolled off his body in waves.

'I'm not a tourist, Gerald,' she said. 'I don't walk around these parts because I don't need to.'

'Well, it's just so close to the Four Inns, that's all. A lot of things happen here.'

Amy frowned. She watched her surroundings. There were

a few pubs here and there and a bistro or two. None of them looked special enough to receive a title like the Four Inns.

'You're planning to kill off a drunk man?' she asked.

At that, Gerald stopped to watch her fully. The confusion switched to a deep incredulity. She couldn't see his face as it was covered by his veil, but his dark eyes were wide. He tilted his head to one side, seemingly expecting an explanation.

'All right, man about town,' said Amy, 'just tell me where we're actually going. Act like I'm an alien and this is my first time ever coming to London.' She stepped away from him then, feigning whimsy as she sauntered down the road. 'I don't know what an Inn is, don't know what the Four Inns is . . . or are,' she called over her shoulder as he followed her with uncertainty. She smiled at his trepidation, then continued, 'I'm just a lowly commoner. Don't know any British history . . . not that I care for it. So explain, Mr London.'

'Okay, okay,' Gerald said. He stopped outside an austere building, tall with red bricks, a pristine courtyard, and ostensibly gated. 'Here we are, but shuffle beside me a little bit, yes, that's far enough.'

Amy followed his gaze to observe the building. Few lights were on. Out of habit, she read the auras coming from within, and even extended her search to the bricks and what she could gather from the polished wood and marble inside. She knew he was watching her, and she almost felt compelled to put on a performance, but the monotony of the place siphoned away her enthusiasm.

'Law and order,' she said flatly, then turned to him. He was immediately surrounded by feelings of awe. Somehow, she had impressed him anyway.

'Right, right,' said Gerald. 'The Inns of Court. They're special offices for barristers and judges and the like. Lincoln's Inn, Inner Temple, Middle Temple, and here, Gray's Inn.'

'Sounds masonic.'

'Quite.' A light eye-roll from between the folds of Gerald's veil. 'They're very old and prestigious. A barrister will die tonight because he found out about his manager's affair.'

'So why does *he* have to die? Kill the cheater!'

'The adulterer isn't in the Book, Amy.' With a sleight of hand, the Grim Book appeared from out of Gerald's Hammerspace. Amy held her composure, steeling herself against the malicious smog in the air. She stared at the red leather cover as Gerald flicked through its pages, stopping at the most recent entry. 'Stephen Walters's name is here, but no request for his boss, Owain. If there was, then I would probably accept that one, too.'

'But just out of a moral thing, why can't you kill them both?'

'That's not how it works. Being a Reaper isn't about justice. Not all the time, anyway.'

Amy watched him in silence until he relented.

'Amy'—Gerald stowed the Book away—'I'm an assassin first and foremost, not a crime fighter. Not a mediator. Sometimes the job requires me to do things that are unsavoury, and it's my choice whether or not to take it on. But my principle remains: I've accepted this job, so I will finish it.'

He turned away from her then and began walking closer to the black gates of Gray's Inn. He spoke over his shoulder in the same way Amy had done prior. 'It's not all killing indiscriminately. You'll see; sometimes there's morals involved, and sometimes there's compassion. And just like with this Downey Gang case, some mystery here and there. But please remember that my curse is just that – a curse. My family never chose this ability. Curses aren't good things, you know?'

She didn't need to read him to know he was getting annoyed. She followed him without judgement. 'I hear you.'

'Good. We're going inside.'

He splayed his hands towards the ground and the silvery outline of a door flashed on the pavement. It contained a cool ambience, and reverberated with a broad, indescribable magic. Amy now knew this sensation belonged to Hammerspace, and she edged away from its magnetic power.

'I've just transferred my Hammerspace from here,' Gerald said in response to her wariness. He then patted his abdomen for emphasis, showing that his hand could not sink inside.

Amy crouched beside the silver door. She shot a look at their surroundings, satisfied that they were alone and that the only other human auras were entombed in the velvet and marble of the Inn before her. Waving a hand above the door did nothing, but when Gerald touched it with his own gloved hand, the door swung open. He turned to her, his eyes sparkling with a knowing glee, and his aura warm with anticipation, waiting for her to respond.

'Can you go first?' asked Amy. It was only darkness inside, and a nervous chill pebbled her arms.

'Of course.'

The Reaper slipped inside his Hammerspace, leaving her to follow in her own time. The empath chewed her lip as she did so, poking the descending staircase that emerged with an intrepid foot, her Converses melting into the folds of subterranean darkness. Once inside, she stopped in wonder. The door sealed her in from above, and she stood in an upholstered room of emerald walls and oak floor, a crackling fireplace, and a round table which was host to the Grim Book and a belt of lockpicks. The shelves were stacked with phials of unknown contents, and one far wall displayed a collection of lethal scythes and sickles. As Gerald gestured ahead, the room narrowed and stretched forward to accommodate his movements to form a winding corridor. Amy clasped her hands together and followed, her tongue stunned into silence. She was desperate to make note of this event, and her phone was near enough to do so, but her limbs grew solid with her hesitation. At last, the ground sloped upwards and another opening appeared in the distance. A rush of wind swirled in her ears, and she was soon outside Gerald's Hammerspace. The Reaper faced her with his brows raised, waiting for a verdict.

'What happens now?' asked Amy, as she could think of nothing else to say.

Gerald gestured to the door on the ground, and it flashed and disappeared. This time, Amy felt the ripple in the air: a shunt of frost, spiced with icy magic, that flocked to Gerald's abdomen with desperation. Amy reached a tentative hand towards him, following the magic's trail, then baulked at the keen intensity of his eyes.

'Are you . . . okay?' he asked.

'Maybe.' She examined her new surroundings. They were now in a dreary and lonesome corridor, their surroundings covered in oak from ceiling to floor. The quietness was unsettling. When they had been outside, she was sure she had heard the distant mutterings of human life. Now that they were so close to Stephen Walters's room, it felt like the upcoming death had enshrouded his workspace. Amy could feel an unearthly chill from Gerald's body, and the sudden change in his aura had affected the atmosphere around him.

'I underestimated this a bit,' she said. 'I can feel other humans all around us. People. And you'll kill one of them, just like that. Wouldn't that make me an accomplice?'

'Not really.'

She frowned inwardly at the cold peace he emanated, a perfect equilibrium of emotions that betrayed nothing of the task at hand. If Gerald could read auras instead of Amy, he would feel a roaring dread from within her, along with guilt and nausea. The excitement of their first meeting was now a source of childish embarrassment for her, and she turned away, reeling from the vibrant auras that calmly navigated the building.

'I feel like one now,' she said. 'I think I need to see what you do, and then I can make a proper decision about our partnership.'

'That's fair,' he said with a shrug. It was the motion of one who was lightly considering a business venture.

'Is the man in there?' She nodded to a nearby office door.

'No.' Gerald leaned against the door, took his phone out of a hidden pocket, and flicked through messages that Amy couldn't read. 'I spoke to my dad earlier about this case, and I was able to do some reconnaissance beforehand. Stephen Walters and Owain Chambers are in a meeting right now. Stephen will come here alone, and Owain will go to his private office where he can speak to his mistress in peace. I was hoping to intercept him out here, but we've arrived a little early. We're going to meet Stephen in his office and kill him there instead.'

He splayed his hands towards the office door, enclosing the entrance within his Hammerspace, and they stepped through together. On the other side of the door, Amy scanned the plain office, with its metal filing cabinets and untidy shelves, the remnants of a sandwich in the bin, a crumpled tie hanging from the coat rack, and coffee rings on the desk. She found evidence of the human that occupied this space: a polystyrene cup beside the water cooler that had been bitten to breaking point, the Warhammer figurines on the windowsill, and the odd collection of holiday romance novels on the bottom shelves, their spines near to shredding. Against her will, she searched for photos of a family and found none – something for which she was grateful.

Gerald also scanned the room, touching shelves and peering over court notes, his expression mild and disinterested. It was the demeanour of a spectator at an oft-visited museum. She wondered how he had felt when he killed for the first time. Had he been scared? What did it mean to be so constantly surrounded by death, holding death within your fingertips, always separating yourself from others due to the risk you posed to them?

'Do you have any questions for me?' he asked, not looking at her.

Amy sat on the nearest available seat beside the desk. 'Do you like your job?'

He paused, then, 'It's not a matter of like or dislike. I just do it.'

'But does it make you feel guilty?'

'Not really.'

He paid attention to her silence and paused his perusing of Walters's belongings to look at her. Whatever he found in her expression troubled him, and he leaned against the table, meeting her eyes directly, and folded his arms tightly across his chest. 'Should I feel guilty?'

'Maybe. Lots of normal people would feel guilty.'

'I'm not normal.'

'Yeah, I get that. But you still have feelings, no?'

'I have feelings . . .' His brows furrowed in thought, and his gaze wandered to the window, where the distant lights of central London glared against the thinly paned glass. A trail of confusion emerged from him, wafting through his usually settled ambience as untethered smoke. 'I . . . was just trained against feeling too deeply,' he said eventually. 'I was trained quite thoroughly. A Reaper who feels too much will become reluctant to kill, certainly. And a Reaper who doesn't kill in the reasonable, codified way that has been our practice for millennia will end up killing indiscriminately, violently, and uncontrollably. I would feel bad about *that*.'

Amy considered this. 'Why would you feel bad?'

He examined her expression with sincere focus. His gaze unclothed her, but she stood firm against it. They both knew where her question was leading. He sighed and the exhalation billowed his veil. 'Because it would go against the methods of the Tribe. Reapers are renowned for our clinical elegance. We're not supposed to be emotional killing beasts. No, Amy, I wouldn't feel bad about the bloodshed itself.'

He tugged at the veil, as if contemplating whether to remove it, but he opted to fidget with his gloved hands instead. They rested in his lap and twitched erratically, and the leather crunched in the silence. 'And I'm . . . sorry about that.'

'Not really,' she said. His aura was now a churning conflict of emotions, swirls of smoke and gas that layered upon themselves, but guilt did not emerge from the miasma. 'You're uncomfortable. But not sorry.' She raised a conciliatory hand as his shoulders tensed at her words. 'And I'm not judging you about it. This is your thing. You've been doing it for ages – much longer than you've known me. I was just curious about it. We're both feeling different things in this room.'

'And . . . what do you feel?'

'Sad. I don't know this man, but I'm sad he'll die tonight. Do you have to complete this job just because you accepted it?'

'Yes. It's a principle I simply don't break. I like keeping to my word, even if it's just a word I've spoken to myself. I'm sorry.'

Amy nodded before saying, 'How do people even know to contact you guys to do all this killing?'

Gerald visibly relaxed at the change of question. The glinting mischief returned to his eyes. 'Humans use what you would call dark magic to contact us. It's another reason why so many of our clients are elites and aristocrats: if you want to lead this world, you have no choice but to meddle with the unseen. No person in charge of the human world doesn't have some paranormal secret, and the Grim Tribe is chief of them. Either way, their dark arts bring them into communion with my father, who then assigns the requests, and we individually choose whether or not to accept them. We mostly do.'

'You told me you can last two months without killing. How often have you gone that long?'

'Once. I only tried it the one time. It was unpleasant.'

'Can you . . . do you mind telling me about it?'

Gerald nodded, but he said nothing at first. He left the desk and dragged the other chair along the ground until he was beside her. He leaned his forearms across his knees and watched his hands as they hung limply between his legs: a mess of spider limbs, hauntingly dangerous. Their air was opaque and unrelenting.

'Before I do, there is something I hid from you when we

spoke last time. I told you about the Progenitor of the Grim Tribe, but I did not tell you that He had spoken to me.'

Amy's stomach quivered. 'When?'

'On the night of my Awakening. That was the first time I ever heard His voice. But He's appeared before: apparently, when I was born, a light hovered over my head, and such a showing hasn't been seen in the Tribe for several centuries. Armageddon was choosing me as his latest Medium.'

A pause. That same sharp anxiety from their first conversation flared in Gerald's aura. Amy waited, hoping he would explain what this meant.

'A Reaper Medium is a rare honour. Something that only happens every few hundred years. Their role is to balance the supernatural threat posed by Conquest.'

'Conquest? Conquest,' said Amy. She snorted involuntarily, and Gerald watched her, not unkindly. He nodded, encouraging her to continue her train of thought. 'When you say Conquest, you mean like the Four Horsemen? Death, Conquest . . . and the other two.'

'Famine and War, yes. In my world, the supernatural world, they're simply the *Apocalypsis*, or the Disaster Quartet. Death is the leader and strongest of the Four. The other three are His offspring. They don't normally bother with this world, but they all have Excesses, like Armageddon does. These spirits can have adverse effects on humans anyway. Death's Excess is Vengeance, which has been transformed into the Reaper curse, while Conquest has Vanity. It's an overindulgence, in essence. One such overindulgence could be life itself: the pride of it, and the yearning for longevity. People are consistently conquered by this greed.

'Our Tribe scriptures state that Death and Conquest aren't on good terms, and they haven't been for several thousand years. None of us know the reason why, but every so often, Conquest's Excess accumulates in power, seeking to possess an unsuspecting vessel – normally human, but it's been known to take control of animals and nature. It causes issues for the Quartet and unbalances their already fragile collaboration.

'As Death's Medium, I will one day be called upon to confront Vanity in some way – to drive it out of whomever it's possessed and banish it back to its parent body. It could be anything, and no one knows when and how it will manifest, not even Death Himself. Either way, I've been given stronger powers than other Reapers. He gifted them to me.'

In the silence, Amy glanced at the bookshelf, at the romance novels and the white stretchmarks on their spines. Their frivolity was in conflict to the austere setting, and their obsessive overuse was evidence of the need to escape: a means to focus on simplicity, on comfort, on things that made sense. The universe was concealed within Gerald's cloak, a startling figure of complications. She knew about the Four Horsemen and had relegated them to religious myth, but the Reaper was proof of their existence. If their collaboration was as fragile as he suggested, it implied a catastrophe for the human world if things went wrong. 'It sounds like you're the main guy preventing a major disaster.'

Gerald shrugged. The narrowing of his eyes suggested a smile. 'In a way. They are distant, stubborn entities, and the only one I have a relationship with is Death, and even that's only just started. I have a long way to go, but it's a heavy burden. No one wants the Horsemen to start a war with each other. The whole reason for my existence is to *mitigate* Conquest's Vanity, not destroy it. Just goes to show how important the four-fold balance is – they cannot function if one of them is totally eradicated.

'And as such, when I'm at my limit, I can be arrogant and careless, and full of bloodlust. My power is just that dangerous. It was my father I snapped at the last time that happened. I was cruel to him. We were in an argument over the phone and I told him I would murder him in his sleep. I love my father, and he's never brought it up again, but it's not a nice memory.'

'I'm sorry to hear that,' said Amy, and she frowned at the sorrow that flushed his aura. This was genuine guilt, a stark contrast to his former hazy ambivalence. 'He's obviously forgiven you.'

'Of course he has. He loves me too much, I fear.' He sighed as he watched her, and Amy grew self-conscious beneath his gaze.

'So *that's* what an empath is,' he said, his voice quiet. 'It feels like therapy.'

'So I've been told.'

'By whom?'

'Nan. And a couple of her friends. My parents thought it was prying, though. And people at school used to come to me with their problems all the time. It was always "Amy, you're so easy to talk to," but that's all it ever amounted to. I never had proper friends. They left me alone after they got their venting done.'

'Why's that?'

'My abilities are strong, and people started picking up on me being weird, I guess.' Amy shrugged. 'It was hard. When you're a teenager, you're anxious anyway, and then you feel everyone else's anxiety and mental health issues weighing on you. It feels like a physical pressure and it's exhausting. And sometimes I could sense what people felt about me and it made me feel funny and paranoid. I couldn't tell them about my powers, obviously. So they all left me alone.'

'Sounds lonely.'

'It was. Sometimes I get that vibe from you too, Gerald.'

'Because I often *am* lonely. There's only one Grim Reaper like me in the world, and even among my own Tribe, I'm treated differently. Preciously. It's not good ground for friendship. Only veneration.'

'Do you want friends?'

He flinched at her question. She watched as he clasped his hands together, as his brows furrowed in confusion, and as his aura bubbled and spat incoherently, overwhelming him with horrified surprise. She leaned forward to console him, amused by his ill-fitted innocence, but a third person joined them. Amy paused, feeling the dampness of a stranger on her skin, a human stalking towards the office door. She scrambled to her feet, her heart pounding inside her body, and she looked around the office for a place to hide.

Gerald sprang to life, gesturing for Amy to follow him behind the door. She squashed against the wall, hiding in the space she knew would conceal her once the door opened. Gerald stood in front. He unsheathed his gloves, and the deathly aura wafted from his exposed, skeletal hands. As they waited, she could no longer hear him breathe, or see the gentle rise and fall of a living person in his shoulders. He stood still, mirroring the coat rack that watched over them. It was predatory.

The door opened, and a white man entered the office. He had cropped strawberry blond hair, and the blotchy redness of excessive wine bloomed in uneven patches on the back of his neck. He glanced at the chairs that they had carelessly left in the middle of the room before turning to make his way to the desk. Before he'd taken more than one step, Gerald soundlessly moved to within breathing distance of Stephen Walters, and touched his neck.

It happened so unceremoniously. Walters never even had the chance to exhale. Gerald caught him before he fell to the floor, cradling him expertly, and dragged him behind the desk. He then propped the body in the leather chair that once belonged to a living man.

Amy stared at the piles of binders and files around his desk that would now remain forever unfinished, and the half-painted Warhammer figurines that would collect dust, to be swiped away into boxes, and discarded as nerd junk unless a kind loved one decided to take them in. And then she felt it: the aura that wasn't an aura, the absence of something that enshrouded Walters's body. It was as if someone had gouged out a piece of the air and left behind an ashen imprint. The emptiness that remained was pitiful. It spoke volumes about the banality of life and how quickly one could be snuffed away mid-thought and roughly handled like a mannequin immediately afterwards. The body that remained was soulless, and the unassuming face of Stephen Walters went slack, its expression calm as if he was asleep. But no one was there.

Gerald plonked himself on Walters's desk and proceeded to write notes in his Grim Book, his brows furrowed as he fiddled with a fountain pen snatched from his Hammerspace. The body slouched in its seat behind him, its glassy eyes staring at Gerald's back.

'Right, all done,' he said, making a definitive line across the name, then stowing the fountain pen and Book away in his abdomen again.

'You're so calm,' Amy muttered. 'Can you not see that body behind you? Nan always told me it's better to respect a dead man than a live one.'

'Why on earth is *that* the case?'

'Because . . . they can linger. If someone's left this world with regrets, their spirit can't rest.'

Gerald watched her, his eyes unreadable.

'What?' asked Amy, pushing away her embarrassment.

'Nothing. I just . . . don't believe spirits can do anything to me unless it's Vanity. I've been killing people for a while, and no spirit has chased me around yet.'

'Yet.'

Gerald glanced over his shoulder at the lifeless form of Stephen Walters. 'But what's your answer?' He crossed his legs until they were tucked beneath him. All the while, the body languished. It was a ghastly image. The Reaper concealed his aura from her until he was hidden by a thick, impenetrable fog.

'I've only ever seen one dead body in my life,' Amy said. 'Nan was sick for a while, with Parkinson's, and sometimes her immune system just went haywire and made her prone to illnesses. She had good days and bad days. When I went to work on *that* day, she was having a good one, but she'd had a cold for a little while, and I think she was starting to get an infection. She even had a fever, but I didn't think it was that bad . . . neither did she. I left her when she was in the kitchen, making up some breakfast. I came home and the breakfast stuff was still in the sink, and there was a pot on the stove, but it was empty.'

Amy found solace in the street lights outside the window, and how they were stitched together in a blanket of urban stars. They lulled her into a trance, and even though her tongue was dry and thick, she found she could talk to them instead of Gerald.

'There was, like, half a sweet potato on the counter. Some yam. An unpeeled green banana,' she continued. 'The beginnings of soup. The knife was on the floor. I ran up the stairs, and she was there in bed, looking blue, eyes rolled back. I basically yanked her up by the dressing gown, and can you believe she gasped? Like, she was still alive. And her eyes flung open and she stared at me. It felt like she'd looked right into my soul, deep inside my chest, my heart. And her body was *hot*. She was on fire. They rushed her to hospital, but she never got better. I stayed around her bed all night, just obsessed, never even got to call my parents. And it's because I could feel her slipping away. I could *feel* it. And I just held her hand and let her pass.'

Gerald slid off the desk. He glanced at the man behind him, but Amy could see the coolness of his body language; how he had stood to attention because it was expected of him to do so. He was not soulless, but he was in need of something. An emptiness existed within the Reaper, one carved from the tireless, worryingly vague training he had mentioned before. It was unnatural, and his loneliness and isolation were evidence of it.

The Hammerspace door appeared between them and they left the office in silence. Stephen Walters oversaw their departure, and his lifeless expression bruised Amy's skin.

Outside, Gerald returned to a leisurely walk. He never looked back at Gray's Inn, but Amy did. As the building receded into the distance behind them, she tried to locate the floor they had been on, scanning the opulent windows for signs of anything untoward. She expected to feel the frantic auras of barristers running down the hallways, perhaps hear the dissonant ring of a fire alarm as someone panicked to get everyone's attention, but the Inn was morosely quiet. No one had yet noticed the death. With pity, she worried that he would be left in the office to slowly rot away until morning, only to be found by a cleaner on the early shift – a disconnected stranger. Did he have anyone at home who missed him? Would his body ever rattle with the vibration of a dozen unread messages and missed calls? Would there be business emails expecting urgent responses? She could only hope so; the other options were too sad to dwell on.

Gerald slowed his pace once they were back on the main road. He had removed his scarf and veil and now donned a black surgical mask instead. 'Are you okay, Amy?'

'I'm fine.'

Holborn buzzed around them and the night was warm, but she walked with her arms folded. Gerald shifted closer to her as they journeyed down the streets, staring at her for longer than was necessary.

'You don't look fine,' he said. 'I can't read your aura, but I'm at least smart enough to know when someone's uncomfortable.'

She said nothing, and Gerald responded to her silence by encircling her closest wrist with his hand, undoing her folded limbs in the process. The leather was cold, and beneath the fabric were the hard ridges of his bones. He held her loosely, uncertainly, and the furrowed brow returned, and all the while he withheld his aura from her.

He eventually nodded towards a nearby Soho Coffee, and all but coaxed her towards the entrance, only allowing himself to touch her wrist in his fragile way, his eyes focused on everything but Amy. His movements were stiff, battling against the rigor mortis of her bleakness, but Amy was not sorry for it.

'Can I get you something to drink? A hot chocolate?'

Amy nodded. Gerald paused at her wordlessness. He appeared to decide something before promptly dipping inside and returned moments later with two cups of hot chocolate and a pair of cookies. They journeyed through central London and Gerald explained the need to find a good lift to get Downstairs. His voice was muffled against the noise of the streets and the din inside Amy's head, but she deciphered through the cotton that he wanted to investigate his two main targets as soon as possible – if it was all okay with her.

Amy allowed herself to drift in and out of the surrounding auras to take her mind off Stephen Walters's assassination. There was a strong sense of relief in the air as everyone left work to go home, or left home to start socialising with their friends.

'I'm staying with you,' she said.

Gerald froze. As the time stretched between them, he uncovered his aura, swamping her in his sense of relief. In the distance, the ebb of anxiety lapped around the edges of this emotion, but it soon dispersed and was lost to the greater tide. The Reaper exhaled and nodded, his eyes fixed upon her.

'Thank you,' he said.

'Why are you thanking me?'

'Because I wanted you to stay. And I'm grateful for it.'

'Do you get why I was freaked out earlier?'

Gerald focused his gaze on the people around them. 'I know why. But I don't understand it, not in the same way you do. I don't have the capacity to.'

'Mmhmm. I know. And that's okay.'

'I would never be intentionally flippant.'

'I know, I know.'

He narrowed his eyes, and Amy saw him search her face. In all the while they walked, his hot chocolate and cookie remained untouched, and as they resumed their stilted journey, he threw them in a street bin.

'It's not natural to not understand, though,' said Amy. She took a bite of her own snack, and promptly finished it. 'A lot of people would. And I think the fact you were trained not to empathise means that at some point, you could. Isn't that right?'

Gerald did not respond, but a surge of panic flashed through his aura before he had a chance to conceal it. The concealing arrived a moment too late, and the electric thrum of his emotions left a vibrating imprint on the air. Nothing in his body language gave him away – ever the perfect assassin. It was obvious that Amy had touched on something he had no intention of discussing, but she was glad that something existed for her to touch. This was her mission now, she realised. It went beyond writing letters to Nan. The Reaper needed to resolve his emptiness because he did not know what it meant to be whole.

Over on the South Bank, the lights of the National Theatre blared at the sky, its walls thrumming with the anticipation that preceded an evening show. On the sprawling concourse that moated it, masses of people weaved between food stalls and neon-painted restaurants; drunken frivolity swirled around massive carousels as adult children rode plastic unicorns. Street performers, pianists, breakdancers, violinists, and indie singers assembled in regular formations along the river, conjuring clouds of serenity and awe and mirth.

Amy perused these auras, reading further, beyond Holborn and South Bank, where she felt the peak and dip of audiences in West End haunts on the Strand, responding to crescendos of numerous musicals. She often did this during some of the lower moments of her teen years, just walking around Streatham and Brixton and Norbury, standing outside Creams, pretending to be indecisive about an order of waffles just to sink into the pleasant auras inside. When she was older and fully understood the depth of her abilities, she went to more sensual locations, strolling through Soho and Covent Garden, drinking in the heated swell of lust and pleasure.

She glanced at Gerald as he ventured to the Old Building of the London School of Economics. On his birthday, he had been encased in a vastly appealing aura. She had wanted so badly to share what he had felt more deeply. She sipped her hot chocolate as they crossed the threshold of the building, trying to hide her smirk. If Gerald knew that she could share sexual arousal, he would probably be mortified.

It was quiet inside. Amy expected the university to be teeming with the pressure of deadline stress and student anxiety – the jostle of late workers trying to finish papers and assignments before their heads exploded with the nonsense of it all. Instead, they were met with the calming silence of a reception area and a single security guard behind a glassy booth.

The aura of the guard emitted the sensation of something moist and sticky. There was a humidity to it: the swell of heated bodies, skin frosted with sweat. The man was white and rosy, with dark eyes that unclothed her. He smiled at the pair as Gerald pulled away his mask, and the curl of his lips was both lecherous and tantalising. He straightened in his chair when he regarded Gerald, almost on instinct.

'Mr Reaper,' he said in a silk-soft voice. 'Good evening. Lift?'

'Yes please, Rowan.'

Rowan smiled again, inclining his head at Amy, and unlocked the gate to his desk. Once they were on the other side, they followed him down a corridor that was restricted to staff only, after which he used a key to open the private lift at the other end.

'I'm the only one on duty for now, so you came at a good time. Safe travels.'

'Thank you, Rowan.'

'Um. Thanks,' said Amy as she quickly shuffled behind him. She flung her empty cup in the adjacent waste bin and used the moment to glance over her shoulder. Unsurprisingly, Rowan stared at her with a ravenous expression. An oily tongue slithered from the dark opening of his mouth, and he wetted his lips intentionally slowly. Rowan turned away before Gerald noticed, and the lift closed without incident.

'I take it you know that that's a fucking incubus,' Amy said.

'Yes.'

Gerald clicked through the sequence to Downstairs, driving them up and down several floors until the hooded Carole appeared on the other side. This time she only offered Amy a tight smile before immediately gathering the cauldron and paraphernalia from her Hammerspace.

'Good evening, Mr Gerald,' she said pleasantly as the tea boiled.

'Hello, Carole. Didn't expect you to be manning this shift.'

'Oh yeah, they're working me extra hard. Drink up,

Amethyst.' She all but shoved the hot mug of tea at Amy's chest, and Amy had to stumble backwards for her own safety. Blocking her nose, she gulped the cerasee tea down, eyes streaming in horror as she did so, and shoved the teacup back at Carole's earnest, unassuming face.

'Do you have a problem with incubi?' Gerald asked as the lift moved again.

'I avoid them if I feel one nearby. Their auras are heavy and deceitful. At least vampires have finesse. But with incubi, I heard some of them only have to say one word and then your knickers are down around your ankles.'

'Well, they kind of need to be that way, don't they? Their life force depends on it, and it's not as if they have the option to reveal their nature to the humans they prey on. Although, I wouldn't be surprised if at least *some* of them did. Always better to exercise consent in those matters, after all.'

'Did you see how he looked at me?'

Gerald smirked. 'Sadly not.'

'It's not funny.'

'I didn't say it was. But I'd protect you.'

'You better.'

When the lift halted and the doors opened, they were thrown into a wild cacophonous city centre. It was a warped replica of Piccadilly Circus. Amy steadied herself as she was totally engulfed in a tsunami of auras. They all melted into one paranormal mass, and for the first time, she was unable to detect what any of it was. Sensing her shock, Gerald took her arm, slowly escorting her out of the lift and closer to the throng of hundreds of Downers going about their subterranean business. They brandished shopping bags, and they rode on the back of rickshaws and carriages, while some women hovered overhead on broomsticks and others flew.

If she concentrated, she could feel the icy sharpness of vampires, the prickle of werewolves, the vacant emptiness of wraiths, and other auras she recognised as belonging to warlocks, mages, and succubae. Individually, they were already formidable, but all together, it was horrifying. She wondered if Carole's cerasee tea would ward off so many strong presences.

The only thing that consoled her was Gerald. He walked purposefully, eyes ahead, back straight, almost haughty. It was a new demeanour for her, and his aura dominated everything else. The further they walked into the city centre, the more Amy noticed that the nearby Downers would see Gerald and offer a strained greeting before withering away. Despite the hectic nature of Downstairs, everyone in the vicinity noticed the Reaper. Their behaviour was not unpleasant, but there was a clear boundary they set between themselves and Gerald, and by extension, Amy. It was an isolating experience. Gerald appeared unbothered by it, but Amy wondered if situations like these were what led to his feelings of loneliness.

They arrived at a ramshackle skyscraper with storeys that piled on top of one another like old cardboard boxes. The LED screens that snaked around the building were older than the others in the area, with blackened pixels that would occasionally spark the red-green chevron of an electrical fault. The bass of house music and garage and drill rumbled through the building and into the ground, and the auras that wafted from within it were thick with the frenzy of illicit drugs, the saltiness of sweat, and the prickling heat of alcohol-induced arousal.

The ground floor was different from the rest of the building. It was unusually quiet in the sea of noise and was home to a single pizza restaurant called Voodoo Rays. Amy frowned at the sign that was so similar to the real Voodoo Rays that she had seen Upstairs in her world, but so different, somehow tainted with the otherworldly flavour of Downstairs. Inside was dead empty. A bored warlock rested against the till. He had nose studs and an afro that had been combed out until it fell in thick curls by his shoulders. His expression became dutiful when he saw Gerald and he fumbled around for a menu in response.

'No need, thank you,' said Gerald. He led himself to the booth nearest the door, beckoned for Amy to follow, and smiled at the warlock. 'Please, I would like to speak with Megan.'

The warlock frowned, nodded, then went behind the till and through a back door.

'Megan?' said Amy, eyeing the menus by the till.

'Melanie Lavender's older sister,' said Gerald. 'They're estranged, so she's always been cooperative with law enforcement when it comes to Downey Gang matters. I can imagine it must be annoying to keep getting contacted, though. This is her restaurant.'

'Yeah, I'm sure. Can't you talk to the parents instead?'

'Dead. Melanie killed them just over two years ago.'

'Ah. Okay. Wow.'

'The Lavenders are a dysfunctional family.'

'You're telling me,' Amy muttered. 'Can we at least get some drinks?'

Gerald frowned. 'Oh, of course.'

As they waited for the warlock to arrive with Megan, Amy reclined in her seat, thinking. 'Why did she kill her parents?'

Gerald sighed. 'Melanie's much younger than Bane. She's eighteen, and he's thirty – Blythe's contemporary and former school friend. They used to go out, even when she was still underaged. I can only assume her parents had a problem with the relationship, especially as it resulted in Melanie getting involved with an Upstairs gang. Most people Downstairs thinks she did it to prove her loyalty to him. It's a reasonable assumption.'

The menu proved a poor distraction, and as Amy stared around the restaurant owned by the elder Lavender sister, she considered how life's options appeared so limited when they were tainted by infatuation.

'She's really young,' she said. 'That kind of behaviour isn't normal at all. He's groomed her.'

'Right. Even among Downers, such things are met with disapproval.'

'You said there was a schism – so they're not together anymore?'

'Unlikely,' said Gerald, shaking his head. 'It took a while for *Gardien* to realise the gang had been split in two, but thanks to extensive interviews, things grew much clearer. We have Megan to thank for it, really – she alerted the Downey Met as soon as she spotted strange activity from the old Lavender family bank account. It gave the authorities enough to trace it back to Melanie, but the trail soon went cold again. These days, Megan doesn't keep up to date with things, but I'm sure she can grant us some access.'

'Reaper.'

Their attention was taken by a very pretty witch who had dyed her hair platinum blonde. Her soft brown skin glowed with some shimmering contour make-up that dusted her cheekbones. Gerald nodded towards her as she slid into the seat opposite. Immediately, Amy was entranced by the holistic earthiness of a witch's aura. When Megan's eyes met

Amy's, they narrowed, and she slid further along the bench to sit more closely to Gerald. The witch's demeanour was similar to Blythe's: a mix of guarded suspicion, and soon, the ambivalent aura became heavy with curds of disdain.

'Hello, Megan, this is Amy, my new partner. She's an exceptional empath.'

'Hmm. Hello. I've heard rumours floating around about a human partner. Interesting.'

Amy shifted in her seat. 'Is it that big a deal?'

'That a human's with the Reaper?' Megan's eyes were wide with incredulity. 'Of course it's a big deal! Have you any idea how many Downers would kill for that opportunity? The Reaper's *apprentice*? None of us even knew Reapers *had* partners. If you were in need of one, Mr Reaper, you could have sent an advert round. You would've got loads of applications from actual Downers.'

'I'm good with Amy, thanks.'

'If you say so . . .' Megan beckoned to the warlock. 'Jen, can you get us some – what drinks are you lot having?'

'Just a coke,' said Amy. She leaned against the backrest of her seat as far as it would allow.

'Some blue Gecko tea, please,' said Gerald.

'Any food?' asked Megan with a frown. 'I mean, you can hear the noise up there, right? We've been open for a month and no one comes here. I thought this would be a prime location. People love going to Voodoo Rays Upstairs, so I thought bringing it down here would be a hit. I even added Downer stuff to the pizzas!'

'Downer stuff?' asked Amy, her curiosity temporarily overriding her annoyance.

'Yeah. Braised cockroach gorgonzola, fried hemp and mugwort, that kind of thing. Give it a go?'

'No thanks,' Gerald and Amy said in unison.

Megan rolled her eyes, then folded her arms once Jen the warlock presented their tray of drinks. 'The family curse strikes again, right? What was the point of trying with this thing, anyway? No one wants food from the *other* Lavender. What d'you need from me this time, Reaper?'

Gerald appeared taken aback by Megan's brazenness, and Amy felt a cooling sobriety surround him, a contrast to Megan's heated indignation. She glanced outside and noticed the Downers that passed the glossy windows with a determined effort to look anywhere but the restaurant, and the same suspicion that plagued Megan was reflected in the surrounding crowds. The elder Lavender was a pariah.

'I'm sure someone wants your food,' said Gerald. 'Are your neighbours aware of this place?'

Megan quirked a brow. 'They're aware. What do you need from me, Reaper?'

'Well . . . some access to your old house, if that's okay. It's to gather Melanie's aura for Amy to read.'

Megan focused her attention on Amy, and the empath met her gaze evenly, overcoming the soot of the witch's ire to do so.

'And how will you do that?' she asked.

Amy exhaled. She prepared a polite tone, hoping to appear professional as Gerald's work partner. 'I can feel auras long after someone has left a place. They normally leave vestiges on the rooms, their objects, and those vestiges are unique to them. No two are the same. I've never met your sister before, but once I get a read on her aura, I'd be able to spot her in a crowd, or know if she ever walked past me in disguise.'

'That's . . . empath abilities don't normally work like that.'

Megan watched both Amy and Gerald with incensed incredulity. 'It's just about feeling moods.'

'Mine work like that. I get it, you don't want a human in your business. Do you lot – do Downers think humans are inferior?'

Gerald froze beside her, his countenance a wall of warning. Megan watched the Reaper's defensive posture and how he appeared ready to guard Amy from insult.

'No,' said Megan. The word was truth, but it was threatened by an undercurrent of deceit. Amy chose not to press further. Her motivation to engage with a stranger on such matters was exceedingly low, and she could not forget her own previous wariness towards Downers, a suspicion that was only assuaged by meeting Gerald. Megan would have to overcome her issues in her own time.

'Are we okay?' asked Gerald.

'Not really.' Megan rested her elbows on the table, her eyes boring intensely into Gerald's. 'You're trying to find Melanie *in a crowd*. For what reason?'

When the witch was only met with silence, she flopped back in her seat, and a frown curdled her features. 'Who made the request?'

'Lex Crow.'

'That bastard.'

This took Amy by surprise. She parsed the air around Megan, and was lost in the thickened brambles of guilt, and rage, and sorrow, but they were unrooted, and she could not place to whom the emotions were directed. 'You don't want her dead?'

Megan ran an agitated hand through her hair. She shot Amy a surly look, but resigned herself to the conversation. 'No. I don't. I want her to be arrested. She could still suffer that way. I would've visited her all the time to gloat. Death is a weak punishment. I don't ... what am I supposed to do after she's dead? When do I get to confront her again? Where's my justice? It's rich that Crow just all of a sudden asks you to kill her when she's been at large for two years and he hasn't caught her yet. It's like he's not even trying. He doesn't care. I hate how things work down here. If our surname was Mason or Gecko, Mel would've been found in a second, and she would've had a trial.'

'Well, now that I've been tasked to kill her, she'll definitely be found. But I've already accepted the request, so I'll be following it through.'

Megan's eyes narrowed. She stared at Gerald in silence. Her aura changed, simmered calmly. It was the atmospheric shift of a calculation. Amy could only imagine the mass of thoughts swarming in the witch's head.

'And that's definite. No wiggle room?'

'I've already accepted the request.'

Megan unfixed her gaze from the Reaper and turned to the window, where the crowds continued to ignore her. Amy nudged Gerald, hoping to get his attention but he only offered her a glancing look.

'I've already accepted,' he said, apparently talking to both of them. Megan stood, and her attention was focused on the back door behind the counter, as if it was the only presence that made sense in the room.

'I'll get the house key.'

'Thank you very much.'

Amy and Gerald waited in thoughtful silence until Megan returned with a small, beaten fireman's key attached to a frayed rope. She looped it over Gerald's outstretched arm and leaned against the back of her seat afterwards.

'Just get it done quickly,' she said. Her voice was clear and firm, but Amy felt the wavering resistance in Megan's aura. She had never experienced such a fluctuating presence – it was as if Megan's entire being altered with every new thought. It was a great wheel of emotion, one thread spooling into dozens of others, at once singular and many.

'We'll try our best,' she said eventually. 'Hopefully it can bring you some closure.'

Megan crossed her arms again. This time the hold was so tight, she looked like she was struggling to breathe. 'I doubt it will.'

'I get you. I'm just saying. I know family stuff can be the worst.'

Megan sighed. 'It can be. And it's so tiring that *everyone* knows our business. Not fun being thrust in the spotlight so much, or seeing how everyone looks at me like I'm the same as her, or the same as *them* . . .' Her expression wandered as her thoughts tumbled around her. 'I was the only normal one in that family. The only one that had something to give—' Her expression soured abruptly as she stared at Amy. 'No empath stuff in here, human! Can you two leave now?'

Jen jolted into action at Megan's flustered tone, kindly escorting the pair out of the shop and back into the noisy din of the city.

'I think that went well,' Gerald said. Amy saw him frowning, peering through the crowd.

'What?' she asked.

'I'd like to get a rickshaw to the house. It's not far from here, but I thought you would like to see some sights.'

'Yes! Yes I would.'

Gerald snorted, promptly hailed a rickshaw driven by a werewolf shifter in human form, and helped Amy onto the seat in the back. Afterwards, she stared wide-eyed at the city as Gerald showed her the different roads and districts. She played the part of the tourist well, and momentarily forgot that she was assisting in an investigation to execute an eighteen-year-old girl.

CHAPTER TWELVE
Gerald

It was enthralling to see Downstairs from the eyes of a human visitor. Sometimes Gerald forgot how bizarre the underground city was. Outside the major centres that often replicated Upstairs – Piccadilly Circus, Leicester Square, Covent Garden – in all its ghoulish wonder, the streets slipped into quiet, cosy avenues, quaint villages with butchers and sweet shops and pubs, or descended into something else completely, like a red-light district or an illegal werewolf fighting pit. Amy had appeared suitably entertained by it all, and he was mutually intrigued by her empath abilities. Her demeanour would change dramatically whenever she felt a new aura and experienced an alien sensation. Often, her eyes would glaze over in concentration, and she would clasp her hands together, or tap an absent foot on the floor of the rickshaw. Sometimes she would bite her lip in discomfort or concern. He could not read auras, but as an assassin, observing body language was an important skill. He realised he could learn more about Amy from the things she did not allow herself to say.

They soon arrived at Willow Drive, a small neighbourhood characterised by thick bushes that enshrouded the cottages in a pungent mist. Witches were known for their potions, and the area was a treasure trove for ingredients. Even now, witches trekked through the neighbourhood with woven baskets and gardener's gloves, fingering petals as they passed, sniffing leaves from the trees overhead, and carefully plucking what they wanted from the surroundings. It was a serene and tranquil environment, and the residents included a small population of warlocks and wraiths. Everyone protected the terrain, and the clipped hedges and manicured lawns spoke of aspirational affluence.

The cottage at the northernmost part of the neighbourhood was ignored by all and devoid of any plant life. It was cloaked in darkness. The paint around the sash windows was chipped and flaking. The crazy paving path that led to the front door was overgrown with moss and weeds that swelled between the slabs like green foam. The thatched roof was in disrepair, and when Gerald pushed open the rusted gate, he could smell the residue of old blood.

Melanie Lavender had stabbed her parents multiple times after serving them a deep sleeping potion. It was testament to her skill as a witch that neither had noticed the potion beforehand. After haphazardly wrapping the bodies in a bedsheet and clearing away most of the blood, Melanie had gathered her belongings, hands still wet and sticky, and left. It had been a crude and shocking operation, one that made front page news Downstairs for a few weeks, then slowly disappeared from the papers once it was clear she would be difficult to catch. Not long after her escape to Upstairs, the Downstairs mayoral elections started with much political excitement. After Lex Crow's reappointment, no one cared about the trials of the Lavender family.

The hinges of the front door were equally rusty as Gerald unlocked it and pushed it open. He was plunged into the dank darkness of a sparse living room. He fumbled around on the nearby wall until he found a light switch, which only showed a decrepit home. Amy inhaled sharply, and Gerald watched her with concern.

'What is it?' he asked.

'I don't know if I can stay here for long. The death is everywhere. It's like I can taste the blood in my mouth.'

'Okay, if it's that strong, perhaps you can stay by the door and wait. I'll look for a few things, some items from the rooms, and then we can examine them another time so you can get a feel of her aura.'

'Yeah. Go on then.' Amy's voice wavered with nausea.

He worked quickly, pilfering through the rooms and easily ignoring the old blood smell. The house was frozen in that fateful night in the past. Every corner and every room told the story of the murders, from the crusted knives in the sink, to the slightly darkened carpet in the master bedroom, to the discoloured wallpaper in the hallways. When he opened the door to Melanie's room, he found it fixed in the post-school glow of a typical adolescent: walls tattooed with the posters of boy bands and cartoon characters, and a metal-framed bed that had wigs, hat boxes, and discarded foundation brushes stowed beneath it. Gerald opted for the small cauldron on the windowsill, its bottom crusted with the residue of a practice potion, and stowed it away in his Hammerspace before rejoining Amy.

She was outside on the path this time, quietly observing Willow Drive and the coquettish pairs of witches that strolled around the neighbourhood so carelessly, swinging their baskets, chewing on leaves before deciding on them, talking loudly about people from work or school, and cackling without inhibition. When he came to stand beside Amy, he noticed that her expression was wistful.

'I'm done here, I think,' he said. 'I might come back, but for now, I have a good item.'

Amy nodded before saying, 'This Melanie girl could have been like them. Just being a kid. Because she is one. D'you have to kill her?'

'Yes. I don't waver in my decisions.'

Amy still looked thoughtful. 'I hope Bane was worth it,' she said quietly, talking to no one.

Gerald placed an uncertain hand on her shoulder, then pulled it away. He balled his hand into a fist, feeling the cold leather creaking against his bones. 'Shall we leave? We can sort this all out later. I need to discuss the events with my dad.'

'Sure. I can already feel the aura anyway.'

'What?'

'Your aura is very distinct. Extremely so. It's why I was so uncomfortable when you had the Grim Book for the first time. So if there's something else on you that's not *you*, I can feel it. And right now, there's a glimmer of a witch's aura on you. Or not so much her aura, but the imprint of her aura. Still, I'd like to do an accurate reading of it later, but I think I could sense her in a crowd Upstairs now.'

Gerald was speechless.

'Okay,' he said at last. 'Well, that's helpful to know.'

Amy smirked at him.

When they left Willow Drive, Gerald was lost in his thoughts. He couldn't help but wonder how the confrontation with the witch would transpire. His chest flared with the excitement of the prospect of a real chase, a satisfying kill. He looked forward to erasing her name from the Grim Book, but he said none of this to Amy, and he concealed his aura. A Reaper's bloodlust was something she would not understand.

CHAPTER THIRTEEN

Amy

The following evening, Amy met Gerald outside St Pancras station. She felt his presence behind her before she saw him, and was surprised to see his casual clothes. Black fitted jeans, a dark top that hung to his knees, and his customary leather gloves. She quirked a brow at his pensive expression. It was clear that civilian attire made him feel naked at night.

'We have a meeting with the Downey mayor, but that won't be until well after midnight, so we have plenty of time beforehand for me to give you a bit more of a debrief of this case,' Gerald said. 'I thought it best if you came to my home instead. We can have dinner?'

'Oh, sure.' Amy looked around. 'Bit of a late meeting, ain't it? Good thing I took tomorrow off.'

'Sorry about that. I should have warned you – most of our business in Downey will be during the later hours. Time moves differently underground.'

'I'm sure,' said Amy, then, 'So whereabouts do you live?'

Gerald smiled and pointed upwards. Amy watched the clock tower that loomed over St Pancras station – at the gleaming façade of the Renaissance Hotel. Before she could ask any questions, he had already turned, beckoning her to follow with a playful nod. She was still in disbelief when they passed the hotel entrance, crossed the marble foyer, entered the gilded lift, and disembarked directly in front of an engraved door. Gerald unlocked it, allowing her entrance to an opulent apartment assembled with mahogany, oak, oxblood Chesterfields, cast-iron chandeliers, and the dry sweetness of parchment paper, leather-bound books, and cinnamon tea.

In the left corner of the living room, an open door led to what must have been a kitchen. Amy immediately felt the strong presence of another person within it.

'Make yourself at home,' said Gerald, gesturing to a nearby sofa. 'Dinner will be ready soon.'

'I knew you had money, but I didn't know you were moving like this.'

'Assassination is a lucrative business, Amy.'

'You don't say.'

At that moment, Gerald's mobile rang from his office desk. He rushed over to it, and his face broke into a smile when he saw the name on the screen.

'Dad,' he said, 'good evening,' and Amy was overtaken by his sense of joy. It was such a pure feeling that she looked away from him for fear of being intrusive. Gerald gestured to her quickly, then took the stairs to the mezzanine landing above. She took note of the innumerable books up there, encased in black leather, and reeled at the crêped layers of ancient auras that clung to the pages. Gerald sat before them, his own aura mirroring their vast power. She was curious about their contents. The Reaper no longer noticed her in the midst of his own splendour and the pleasure of speaking to his father.

She felt lonely, and a distant memory of her own parents gave her a pang in her stomach. It was irritating how often their loss affected her; how her daily life was littered with constant reminders of their abandonment. Not wanting to get too depressed, she went to the kitchen, hoping to chat to the person in there.

The kitchen was just as grand as the living room. The massive Aga nursed various simmering pots. Wooden spoons stirred the contents of each one, moved by an invisible hand. Amy froze, watching as the fridge opened by itself, and a jug of cream floated out of it, tipped a generous amount into one of the pots, and then returned from where it came. The presence of the third person was all over the kitchen: she could feel them beside the fridge, hovering around the island, watching over the Aga, and tinkering within the cupboards. She didn't notice Gerald until he was standing beside her, and his sudden appearance made her flinch.

'Ah! I see you've met Zis,' he said. He went over to the Aga and gently patted the only unoccupied plate. 'My Cast Iron Stove, without whom this house would be in the gutter. Zis, this is Amy, the new partner I told you about.'

In response, Zis flared the oven, and a wave of warmth washed over Amy.

'Hi,' she said. And nothing more was said on the matter.

Gerald clattered around the kitchen, getting plates and cutlery from cupboards and drawers. He spooned basmati rice, curry goat, and steamed vegetables onto plates and placed them on the island. Amy sat on one of the bar stools, mildly impressed.

'Zis is Jamaican?'

'Zis can cook anything. I told them your heritage.'

'Oh? Thanks a lot, Zis.'

The oven flared proudly again.

'So,' said Gerald, cutting into a generous helping of curry, 'Lexton Crow. He's the person we're meeting tonight. Quite a humble man, I would say, but he's obviously desperate. Mr

Crow has been excellent these past ten years; it's difficult to maintain the Concealment Act, but he's kept everyone in check for the most part. I'm sure this Downey Gang business is incredibly stressful for him. It's very rare for the mayor to directly ask anything from the Reapers. We work independently.'

'And that's why Blythe was so upset, right?' asked Amy.

'Um, yes . . .' Gerald rubbed the back of his neck absently. 'I mean . . . well, politicians need money, and the Mason family is extremely wealthy. They've always donated to Mr Crow's office and helped fund his election campaigns. When one family has been so instrumental to your success, it won't be long until things get a bit too entwined, I suppose. If I'm being honest, I think Blythe's *Gardien* gets a few too many privileges for an intelligence service.'

'Well maybe if Blythe and his little *Gardien* did their job properly, Lex Crow wouldn't have had to ask you for help. This food tastes *so* good.'

'Yes, it's delicious, Zis. But to be honest, this is the first time a criminal, or criminals, have evaded *Gardien*'s capture for so long. I think it's a sore spot mainly because one of the leaders is Blythe's former schoolmate.'

Amy paused. 'I was gonna ask you about that. Were they that close?'

'Very, from what I hear. But Bane went down a devious path a long time ago. When rumours arose about Lavender's involvement with him, people started to pay closer attention to his movements.'

'So who started the gang in the first place?'

'Oh, Bane. Back then it was a silly thing. Petty crimes, postcode wars, that kind of stuff. But he's powerful and managed to lead a fully organised unit in just three years. He soon moved Upstairs permanently, and Lavender followed shortly afterwards – she never completed her schooling at Greymalkin's Academy. Then there were more rumours: human men mysteriously dying, apparently enchanted and extorted by her. But there was never enough evidence to do anything. And because she associated herself with poor, destitute humans, the investigations never went anywhere Upstairs, either.'

'And she was doing all this by *what* age?'

'Well, around fifteen, really. And then you know what happened with her parents a year later . . .'

Amy frowned, pushing the rest of her food around the plate. 'That's a lot going on for someone so young. Living rough at fifteen, killing her parents at sixteen, then leading her own gang faction at eighteen. Did Megan ever say anything about their home life?'

Gerald shook his head. 'She doesn't talk about it often. I know what you're getting at, and I've come to the same conclusion. I don't think their situation was good at all. And as Megan herself alluded to – her family's dysfunction is part of the reason why the murders slipped away from the news in the first place.'

'Melanie got groomed by a man twelve years older than her. Sounds like she's in danger too.'

'Perhaps she is.'

After an uncomfortable pause, Gerald said, 'According to the most recent *Gardien* intelligence, only Bane's faction has senior executives who know what he is. This provides all the ingredients for a major breach of the Concealment Act. If any of those executives defect, they could go public about this. The gang's activities cause problems for the millions of Downers who are trying to live peacefully in secret. When I spoke to Mr Crow about it, he seemed beyond stressed. It looks like there's been a recent development that's almost sent him over the edge. How he manages to keep such a calm composure to the public is beyond me.'

'Does he know I'm coming? I wouldn't want to cause him more hassle if he's worried about humans getting all up in his business already.'

'He knows.' Gerald smiled at her. 'And you're not exactly a normal human, are you?'

Amy shrugged.

'Let's get to work, then.' Gerald's hand sunk into his stomach, disappearing up to the elbow. He placed Melanie Lavender's cauldron on the table. Amy shivered at the sight, still bewildered by the Hammerspace mechanics, and equally disconcerted by the aura that surrounded the cauldron.

She put her cutlery on the island and ran a pensive finger along the blackened rim. She inhaled the dusky scent of crushed cinnamon and ground pimento, and the sting of raw, unfiltered rum, unearthing the aura nestled deep inside the cauldron. It told her a little bit about Melanie Lavender: a young, confident witch with an arctic aura that was grey with ambivalence. She could sense the essence of betrayal, but the sensation was complicated – Melanie had betrayed people, she had been betrayed, she had witnessed countless instances of fake friends and false feelings. The final scent was of love, but it was a wavering feeling, almost non-existent. It felt like the soft vapour from a menthol cigarette, something that would easily dissipate on the wind.

'I've got all I can from this,' she said quietly, returning the cauldron.

'Would it be enough to detect her in a crowd?'

'Most likely. Depends how close she is at the time.'

'Well, it's a start, thank you. As always, I'm impressed by your ability.'

'Ha. Thanks.'

They chatted for so long over dinner that midnight almost passed them by. Gerald donned his outdoor cloak and veil and ushered Amy out the door. They hastily journeyed to the block of nearby flats, and Gerald went through the ritual with the lift until Carole Warden met them on the fifth floor.

'Mr Gerald,' Carole said, turning to the Reaper, 'you really need to give me a date. My mum's getting a bit annoying now.'

'Oh, goodness. I'm sorry! Tomorrow afternoon? I have a few assassinations to do in the morning, but I should be available after three.'

'Great, she will be so happy.'

'I'm glad to hear it.'

Before long, the lift doors opened, and they were back in the busy city centre of Downstairs, only this time, it was reminiscent of Whitehall. Hundreds of witches, warlocks, vampires, werewolves, and a host of other magical creatures jostled against each other as they flitted in and out of austere buildings. Some were in formal attire, and others donned the casual wear of revellers, shoppers, and Downers about town.

Gerald led the way to the largest building on the street. Just like before, his fellow Downers parted for him, and this time many of them noticed Amy, her infamy as the Reaper's human partner apparently spreading quickly through the city.

The Downey version of City Hall was as busy as if it were

midday. Downers in office wear bustled down marble corridors, hissed into earpieces, tapped rapidly on tablets. Gerald approached the main reception desk, behind which sat a woman in a long elaborate cloak. She straightened immediately when she saw Gerald, then quickly scrambled to her feet, talking breathlessly about the honour of meeting him – that it was her first week on the job and she was aware he was coming but she didn't realise he was so *young* and so *handsome* (Gerald was still wearing his veil), and that Mr Crow was so anxious to meet with him.

Amy noted the long staff that the receptionist had strapped to her back, and she allowed herself a moment to parse its aura. A mass of energy clung tightly to the cedar wood, reverberating in synergy with the nonsensical whimsy that buzzed near the base of the woman's spine. It was this energy that Amy recognised as belonging to mages, but the magic staff was new to her. She made a mental note to write it all down. Next time she was out and about in the city Upstairs, she would be sure to check for hidden staffs, wands, or bracelets.

'Thank you very much,' said Gerald once he was outside Mr Crow's office door. The receptionist flitted down the corridor again, glancing back at Gerald every few steps or so until she was out of sight.

Gerald tapped on the door. It flung open almost immediately. A tall man with rich russet skin and an aura of absolute anxiety hovered on the other side. Leaning against his desk was a polished staff of magic energy that far surpassed the receptionist's. His mage's robes were emerald and too big for him, for the hem dragged on the floor like a wedding train and swamped his thin, gangly arms.

'Mr Reaper! And Amethyst, was it?'

'Nice to meet you,' said Amy.

'Please, do come in. I'm beside myself. Some Gecko tea?'

A gold embossed table appeared in an explosion of smoke. An expensive-looking tea set, along with a tray of cheese and biscuits, rested upon it.

'Thank you, Mr Crow.'

'I'll get right to it, Mr Reaper.'

The mayor slid an envelope across the desk. Then he sighed, a great, heaving exhale, and pleaded with the ceiling in silence as Gerald read the letter inside the envelope.

Amy poured herself a cup of tea, did the same for Gerald, and nibbled on a digestive, waiting until he was finished. After hearing so much about Bear Gecko and his tea, she was excited to try it for herself. A steaming purple liquid filled her cup, smelling strongly like rosewater. Out of habit, she parsed the air around it, pilfering through the layers of steam as it rose. It was a pleasant feeling. She could almost hear the notes of a distant lullaby resting on the atmosphere. When she sipped the slightly medicinal tea, it gave her a buzz of warmth in her stomach. She would have to take a few sachets home with her.

'Oh dear,' said Gerald after he had finished reading. 'And you're sure this is legitimate?'

'Yes. One hundred per cent.'

'Okay. Is Blythe aware of this?' Gerald passed the letter to Amy.

'Yes. Now I'm sure we can all agree that this whole thing needs to be wrapped up much more quickly than it is currently, sir. But now I need an escort for Peaches . . .'

Amy frowned as she read, slipping away from the room's discussion.

Weekly Timetable for Peaches Crow
  Monday – Downstairs all day
  Tuesday – Morning classes, Fitness First Gym on Tooley Street (Upstairs) at 3 p.m.
  Wednesday – Morning Pythagory, Lunch Upstairs at Peggy Porschen. Evening with Mother (South Kensington. Heavy security, house enchanted with trespasser spells)
  Thursday – Morning classes. Afternoon Upstairs (South Kensington)
  Friday – Home study with housekeeper Martha (house enchanted with trespasser spells)
  Repeat ad nauseam. Target is lost to the nonsense inside her head. Easily followed.
  I don't think I need to explain the purpose of this letter, sir.

What an eloquent threat, she thought, and was quickly snapped out of her reverie by Gerald.

'I'm busy, Mr Crow. I can only sacrifice one or two days. Amy also works full time. If escorting your daughter garners a lead on this case, then I'm prepared to accept. If we are unable to locate the gang leaders . . . or members, even, by the end of that week, then I'm afraid you'll have to let me investigate normally, and you'll need to transfer that task over to *Gardien*, or at least the Met.'

'Of course, of course.' Mr Crow's voice was jovial, but his expression and aura were apprehensive.

'Sorry, can you let me know what we're doing? And what I'll apparently need to take annual leave for?' asked Amy.

'We're going to be official escorts for Lady Crow. We start at Greymalkin's Academy next week.'

Amy looked from Gerald to Lex Crow and back again for an explanation. 'I'm sorry?'

'It's okay if you can't do it,' said Gerald. 'But it might help the investigation ... if that letter is anything to go by, Tyrell Bane is back on the prowl, and is stalking Peaches Crow for his comeback. I'm assuming he wants money from you, Mr Crow? I'm sure his latest failed operation has set him back a bit.'

'I think so ... or maybe he knows about the assassination request. If that's the case, I'm in a lot of trouble.'

Gerald flashed the mayor a kind smile. 'You have nothing to worry about, sir.'

Amy flopped back in her chair, still mulling over the tiresome operation she had been dragged into. She weighed up which task sounded more interesting – library work or escorting a mage politician's daughter to her magic underground school. The latter was obviously more appealing, but her schedule had been erratic lately, and she did not want to seem unreliable. The library had been her refuge for years to the point where she barely took annual leave – perhaps she could afford a change of routine for once.

'I can help,' she said.

'Oh, I really appreciate this,' said Mr Crow. He sighed in relief, rose to his feet, and shuffled towards the nearby bookshelf. The shelves were neater than Blythe's, but were lower in quality and indulgence. The mayor fiddled with a diary on the middle shelf immediately below an emerald amulet shaped with the unmistakable curve of a paisley tear. Beside the amulet was the photograph of a plump white woman holding a baby with a buttery complexion. Deep notes of love and sensuality emanated from the photograph, and Amy was overcome with sympathy for Lex Crow's predicament.

'Here,' the mayor said, handing the diary over to her, 'this is Peaches' schedule. Seeing as though you can only do a few days, perhaps starting on Tuesday would be best? She's going

Upstairs for a dress fitting after school in preparation for prom on Friday.'

Amy glanced at Gerald for a second opinion.

'I guess it's up to you as you'll be taking the time off work,' he said with a shrug, 'but we'll discuss, Mr Crow. Thank you.'

'No, thank you both.'

When they were outside, Gerald hailed a rickshaw.

'Where we going?' asked Amy.

'Well now that Bane's shot himself to the top of my list, I guess we should snoop around *his* old haunts. He used to frequent one of the warlock dens. We'll see what we find.'

What began as a pleasant journey through the hustle and bustle of central Downstairs quickly descended into unsettled, dangerous adventuring. They entered a slum of a neighbourhood, primarily occupied by prefabs, grubby tower blocks and vacant spaces of wild, overgrown black grass. It reminded Amy of her own ends, where comfortable, homely terraces were never too far from towering flats and neglected council estates. This neighbourhood, aptly named Bloodwood, was so far removed from Blythe's illustrious avenue that she almost laughed at the stupidity of it. Even underground, London was a mess of inequality.

She followed Gerald to a one-storey building with blacked-out windows and a crumbling slated roof. One sharp knock at the door caused a peephole to slide open, then two bleary eyes widened in fear, and the slate was slapped shut again. Behind the door came the noise of breaking glass, shattering wood, the rumble of panicked feet, and the gruff yell of dozens of male voices. The aura surrounding the building was both sultry and ripe with the stench of opium and weed, and the tang of brandy.

'Hi all,' Gerald called to the door. At once, the noise ceased. 'I'm not here to kill anyone, I promise. I would never come through the front door to do that. Just need to look at a few things.'

'*What* things?' was the muffled, acerbic response.

'I'd like to look at Tyrell Bane's old room.'

The clattering and panic continued. Gerald sighed loudly.

'Maybe tell them they're not in trouble,' said Amy with a smirk. Gerald raised a brow, but did so anyway. The clattering only grew louder.

'Okay, I'm coming in now,' Gerald said. He gave the door a firm kick, and it fell inside into a cloud of dust. The stench that Amy had felt within the aura enveloped her now. Breathing through her mouth, she entered the den closely behind Gerald, squinting to see the lumpy shadows of anonymous warlocks as they clambered out a window on the opposite end of the room. The den was lit by a dark green bulb, and most of the view was obscured by thick cigarette smoke. Bongs, blackened spoons, powdered glass, and slick, tarry puddles marred the ground. Squashy beanbags, ripped open and leaking white filling, were riddled with patches of spilled alcohol. Amy waved a hand in front of her face to clear the air, worried about the stench attaching to her hair and clothes.

'Oh my God, let's get out of here quickly, please,' she said. 'It stinks so bad.'

'Sure,' said Gerald. He pulled the veil away from his face with a gasp and quickly fanned himself. 'I can barely breathe right now.'

They shuffled around the dirty space, Amy reluctantly following behind Gerald, hoping that he would hurry to wherever Bane's old room was.

'Did he seriously live here?' she asked.

'Afraid so,' said Gerald as he continued down a brightly lit corridor that was painted a garish bubble gum pink. One open door revealed a toilet that was destroyed by yellow and black stains, and a bathtub beside it that had been used as storage for mouldy cardboard boxes, piles of moth-eaten clothes, and dirty plates. Amy gasped and turned away from it.

'For fuck's sake!' she whimpered. 'Where's the room?'

Clearly not wanting to touch anything, Gerald kicked open the nearest door, shook his head, then tried two more times until he arrived at one that was empty and surprisingly clean. The pale wooden floors were swept and mopped. A single wash basin was without rust or grime. A mattress was pushed against the far wall, sick with the pockmarks of worn fabric. Metal bedsprings jutted out of the holes. A chest of drawers was the only other furniture. When Gerald neared it, he appeared to notice something, for he nodded and turned to Amy.

'Locked,' he said, before using one of his lockpicks to release it. 'Would you like to come a bit closer? You can parse these items from a distance, right?'

'Yeah, sure.' Amy crept towards the open chest. The first drawer contained one afro comb and a rusted tin of original Vaseline. The second was empty save a black scrunchie that held the faint essence of Melanie Lavender. The third and fourth were littered with cigarette roaches stained with tobacco and the green crumbs of cannabis. When Amy parsed them, she experienced a smoky, aggressive aura that was mirrored in the empty mattress on the wall. Unlike the ambiguous presence that clung to Melanie's cauldron, Bane's items were a revelation. They were saturated with cunning, with anger, with a hostile desperation. What was he desperate for?

Amy glanced around at his impoverished dwellings and considered how the warlock had clambered up to high society through gang activity Upstairs. His new-found power had placed him in surroundings formerly reserved for the innately privileged.

'What's his family history?' she asked.

'That's something I don't know.' Gerald fiddled with the veil as it bunched around his neck. 'I'll have to ask Blythe. I've only ever known Bane to be a man from the slums that had enough talent to impress Blythe and pretty much everyone else he went to school with. He had far too much potential for where he ended up.'

'Easy for you to say. You're basically royalty. People make stupid decisions when they're living like this.'

Gerald regarded her evenly. He nodded, but said nothing else.

'Let's get out of here, then,' Amy said. 'My skin's crawling.'

'Right, of course. Hopefully the other warlocks return soon. I don't want them to think I ran them out of their home.'

'That's the life of a Reaper, I guess. People running from you every minute.'

'Well, that's certainly true.'

Gerald breathed deeply once they were outside, and Amy did the same, her lungs expanding to a capacity that had been restricted when she was inside the den. She gulped in the fresh air, but to her dismay, she could still smell the smoke and grime on her clothes. She was desperate to get home and have a hot bath.

'It's late,' said Gerald. 'I'll escort you back Upstairs? Let's meet at a more reasonable time tomorrow so we can discuss our plans next week.'

'Yeah, sure.' She knew she would not sleep that night. Her mind was already imprisoned with excitement and apprehension for the week that lay ahead.

INTERLUDE: THE WITCH

It was midnight and the witch listened to the rustling trees overhanging the Duck Island Cottage at St James's Park. The cottage was a small, flower-embossed artefact that overlooked a vast pond where a stone island broke the surface of the water to provide sanctuary for gulls, ducks, and a startling pink pelican. At this time, the park was almost empty, and so the witch was alone in her thoughts, staring out at the pond now washed grey with night-time, the window crusted over with old cobwebs and dust. In the day, she liked to watch the humans as they sauntered along the decked pathway of the cottage and wandered around the surrounding flower garden. They took pictures outside the permanently locked door, and they peered through windows that revealed nothing. She didn't worry about being seen because a spell clouded their vision.

She glanced around the small space, smiling smugly. If not for her spell, they would witness signs of the paranormal: brown phials holding potions and unnamed elixirs; dried tropical plants hanging in vines touching the ground; a black clay jar revealing nothing from the outside, but filled to the brim with parricidal blood.

The witch was in hiding. Her phone was in a state of shock, assaulted by dozens of messages from her executives, all enquiring where she had vanished to, but she wanted to talk to no one. They all saw her as a vociferous young woman with an enchanting charisma, someone they followed willingly. She knew they were glad that they had chosen her side over Darkhouse now that the smuggling ring had forced Tyrell Bane back into the shadows of petty hustler life, but the witch was far from happy. When the news broke, she turned cold and hid herself away in this private cottage, thinking of what to do next, and confused as to her feelings of foreboding.

The newspapers on a nearby chair were crispy and tattered from overuse. She could see the marks of her reading in different stages of distress: greasy splodges from when she binge-ate cheap crisps and studied the words written in terse blackness, rough tears during times of anger, scars of folding and unfolding to mark key pages, little highlighted paragraphs when searching for clues. Tyrell was in big trouble. In all their work together, he had never ventured into something so depraved, so extreme, and she could not understand his thought process.

She snatched *The Mirror* from the top of the pile, frowning again at the photos of gaunt, frightened children on the front page and the political debate on the second page, and on the third page, the threats of upcoming protests from those who wanted the Channel reopened, and for the refugees and migrants fleeing war and distress in other lands to find solace in England. And then the Home Secretary's address on the page after – diverting, distracting, obfuscating nonsense, but the message was clear: fortify the island and let the inconveniences drown in the water.

'You want attention, is that it?' she said to the newspaper before chucking it on the floor. Petty, petty Tyrell.

She rummaged beneath the table for her best cauldron,

and then poured in the last of her bottled water. It filled halfway. The witch sighed and waved her hands over the tremulous surface, hoping, waiting, until an image appeared. It was faint and obscure, with white outlines shimmering against the black base of the cauldron, but she knew where this was: a mossy puddle in the corner of his lair, the angle of which permitted her only a view of the ceiling and bricks of the room.

Soon, a shadow glanced across the puddle to enter her field of vision, a shadow she recognised, a shadow that had often loomed over her, blocked her sight, pressed against her body, clung to her skin, burrowed in her hair, tugged at her scalp. Tyrell had a presence that cowed her, made her feel cold and hot and ambient. His eyes stole her speech. The shadow, swimming in and out of her cauldron, appeared to call out to her in its loneliness.

'No,' she whispered. She blinked, and the cauldron was on the floor, rolling against the flagstones with an empty groan, spilling its contents over her feet. She did not recall pushing it off the table, but she was glad for it. The Lads was all hers now. If she was smart, she could even overtake Darkhouse – swallow everything Tyrell had. She would show him she was just as powerful as he was, make him grovel, force him to beg. She imagined his arrogance shrinking into itself, his body folding over like rose petals until the face that had bewitched her emerged again: innocent and childish and charming and beautiful, doe-eyed. That was the face he wore when they had first met. She missed it. *Mel*, he would say, *A little help?* And like the fool she was, Melanie would help him.

An unhealed scar snaked around her neck. It told the story of the first time his mask slipped. Nail grooves in her back was the second time. Little leopard prints of Tyrell Bane's anger mapped her body. But she yearned for his old expression, the one that made her feel loved.

Melanie knelt on the ground, patting the cold wetness, feeling a hot warmth run down her cheeks. Why did she knock the cauldron over?

She wanted to see him again. She wanted to run from him. She wanted everything. She wanted nothing.

PART TWO
Vanished

Miscellaneous Powers #1: Hammerspace

An invisible storage pocket in the atmosphere. It requires a high level of magic. Some creatures, usually those who were once human, like werewolves and vampires, cannot use it. There are different layers of Hammerspace – not all magic creatures have access to the same one.

Hammerspace manipulation is the ability to warp Hammerspace into different shapes and purposes. Examples include curtains to hide people, tunnels to create passages to other places, and realms, which can be for imprisonment or to repurpose the interior of a building.

Hammerspace inventories can sometimes continue to exist after death, depending on the magic prowess of the caster.

CHAPTER ONE
Gerald

It was early when a new name appeared in the Book, so Gerald phoned his father.

'So you've seen the request, then?'

'Yes. This is a heavy name.'

'Indeed.'

'And who did it come from?'

'Imogen Carrington.'

Gerald nodded, running an ungloved finger across the page. The Carrington family was an elite dynasty in human circles, and this wasn't the first request he had fulfilled for them. Their power was invasive and ubiquitous, occupying unlikely spaces between industries, and oftentimes of dubious origin. It was no surprise they had enemies to eliminate.

There was laughter in the background, and the rapid flapping of the tent.

'Who's that?' asked Gerald.

'Your Aunt Huldah. I'm visiting her for a day or two. You heard about her recent assassination?'

'Father, we all heard. It was on BBC Africa. An NGO director *and* a diplomat in one day?'

'Well, don't sell her up too much.' Father slurped down the phone. He was probably drinking some of Aunt Huldah's favourite rooibos. She always ran out of green tea, his father's preference, too quickly. 'You're stepping straight into a political scandal yourself. We've all been so interested. We have five televisions on in the main house right now. Watching British news, Russian news, Malian news. Even French news.'

'Oh? I missed this one. What happened in France?'

'Prima ballerina. Dead just after opening night. Your cousin Marcus did that one.'

'Oh gosh—'

'*What a cursed family*,' they said together. In the background, Gerald heard Aunt Huldah's satisfied laugh.

'Well, I just got word from Tobias. He'll meet you outside the station now.'

'Thank you. Have a wonderful day, Dad.'

'Not yet. Are you not planning to tell me anything about the empath?'

Gerald's hand froze over the Grim Book. He examined the inflections of his father's voice and searched for answers among the layers of crêpe before him. There was much to say, but like with Armageddon's message, he did not want to share such words right now. He had pondered Amy's admonition in Stephen Walters's room, still unable to process the depth of her feeling, and the empathy she felt towards the living and the dead. The dead meant nothing to him, and yet, he felt her judgement against his stoicism.

Worse still was the observation she had made as they walked through Holborn, where she had excavated a shameful experience from within him without knowing, and for a breath of a moment, Amy had transported him back to the desert. There, he was encircled by Father and the Tribe elders, indignant and horrified against the blank fear in their eyes. It was a fear triggered by something he had done, a manifestation of his true power as Death's Medium. That day had conjured legends across the supernatural world beyond mere knowledge of the Grim Reapers; it had forever branded him as a danger to others, and everyone was warned against the abject violence that lay dormant beneath his assumed benevolence. As Gerald thought of all this now, he reinforced the Wall that protected the world from himself. Today's assassination required the use of his Awakened powers. He needed to be sober and prepared.

It was still a new quarter, and Armageddon already confirmed He would only visit at the end of three months, which left Gerald no choice but to hope that the empath was the interruption Armageddon had alluded to.

'There's not much to say,' he said at last. 'We did our first assassination together. She was very helpful, and she now knows my targets' auras, which is useful. It's been good so far.'

'Has it, now?'

'Yes, I think so.'

Father grumbled beneath his breath, and his voice was smothered by the crackle of sand. The voice of Aunt Huldah interrupted them, and Father sighed loudly. 'Business calls. I will find out more about your empath later.'

'I'm sure you will, Father. Enjoy your business.'

'Humph! I certainly won't. This family is picking up lazy habits. The Tribe is in a bad way!'

Gerald snorted, not unpleasantly, relieved at the lighter timbre of Father's exasperation. When they parted, it was in good spirits.

He snatched a slice of blueberry jam toast from the kitchen counter and dashed outside. Tobias of the Sharan – sister tribe of the Grims – was serene inside the bustling interior of King's Cross station. Tobias was tall and willowy, with copper skin and deep-set eyes. The signature silver hair of his tribe was on full display. He cropped the sides and allowed the top to flow over his shoulders in thick, bouncing curls. His appearance caught the eye of many a commuter, and he clearly enjoyed the attention.

'King,' he said, firmly grasping Gerald's wrist.

'Stop that, Tobias,' said Gerald, but he humoured him with a smile.

'Oh, so humble!' Tobias handed him a leather satchel. 'You'll be Daniel Yeboah this evening, a cyber security engineer from the Cabinet Office. I've got an outfit here with a pass. Make sure you wear the accompanying cap this time.'

'You can't blame me for wanting to take the last one off. I hope you made a handsome alias today.'

'Oh come *on*,' said Tobias, but he was grinning. The pair left the station together. To avoid arousing suspicion, Gerald kept off his hood and veil, but retained his black mask for casual wear. He stayed close beside Tobias as the Sharan enchanted the security cameras so that they could remain undetected.

'You've been busy, haven't you?' Tobias said. 'With the Downey Gang shit.'

'I have. And I doubt this new job will go down quietly. Actually, I anticipate some retaliatory requests. It's sure to be a lot of headache, but I've accepted the request so I'll see it to its end.'

'You keep going on like that and everyone on Whitehall will be dead.'

'It is what it is.'

'My days.' Tobias rummaged in his pocket for a cigarette packet. Once found, he bit one out of the open top and lit it with a sigh. 'Truly a cursed family.'

Gerald grinned. 'Not that bad. We're rich too.'

'So are we. Rich and sexy and innocent. You be careful out there.'

'I will be. Thank you, Tobias.'

'No probs. See you at the next council meeting, I guess. Whenever that will be.'

Gerald watched as Tobias disappeared in the rush hour crowds. He spent the rest of the day preparing for carnage.

It was seven p.m. and the crowds at the Civil Service Club dwindled and swelled with each passing hour. Gerald was dressed in a dark emerald suit with a vest, his gloves loosened around the wrists. He was in disguise as Daniel Yeboah, and the enchanted trilby hat magicked by Tobias upheld the illusion: as Daniel, Gerald was now over six feet tall, slightly lighter in complexion, and sporting neat stubble on his jawline. His forged membership card peeked from behind a pocket square. A mystery of Sharan magic was its ability to enchant the memories of surrounding onlookers. If anyone else from Daniel Yeboah's department happened to visit the Club this evening, they would have recollections of seeing him in their office. At some point, the memories would fade, and the face of Daniel Yeboah would grow hazy, but everyone would remember that someone had once occupied that space.

Gerald observed the iron gates that surrounded the beer garden outside the bar. He trained his ears, picking up on hushed conversations from the surrounding civil servants who knew Stephen Walters and had attended the memorial service earlier that day. Many more knew about Owain Chambers' affair and were highly suspicious of Walters's untimely death. Gerald always found it fascinating how quickly news spread around elite circles; the members of the Inns were not civil servants, but they worked so closely with the civil service that they may as well have been.

A portly man entered the beer garden through the iron gates and began pushing his way through the assorted tables and chairs. It was a mild evening, and the days were longer. Above them, the sky was pre-summer turquoise. Gerald smiled at the sight. The man was several tables away now. He would see someone he knew, nod his head at them, then continue pushing through the din. Gerald saw the beads of sweat on the man's forehead. He panted, not from exhaustion, but fear.

The man was Sir Alastair Duke-Fitzgerald of the Cabinet Office. Minutes before arriving at the Civil Service Club, Gerald had watched with admiration as Sir Alastair posted a dossier which detailed illicit Friday night parties held at a Dolphin Square flat attended by several senior ministers, particularly one Henry Butler, a precocious and influential frontbencher. Sometime about now, a sprightly journalist from *The Times* was opening the manila envelope that would elevate their name to legendary status. Gerald could only imagine the doors that would fly open, both above and below the journalist's feet.

Gerald had contemplated whether to wait until after the dossier was posted before carrying out the assassination, but he decided the information was of public interest. Amy's morals must have rubbed off on him.

He sipped his beer. He watched Sir Alastair. He rested the grooves of his lips against his pint glass. He released his inhibitions and mentally beckoned the powers he kept hidden. In response, a moist warmth swelled behind his navel. The sound of shattering glass echoed in his head, and he felt the deathly weeping of ice: the arctic climate fortifying his Wall had weakened. A sensitivity not felt since his Awakening rested on his skin. With a cold confidence, Gerald tracked Sir Alastair now, waiting for the right moment to reduce the human to nothing more than flesh and blood and tendons.

'*Laanah morthexis*,' he said.

It was a phrase from *loquella universalis*, known among the tribespeople of the supernatural world, but only used by Reaper Mediums, of which Gerald was the first in over four hundred years. The manifestation of the spell was instant. A glinting wire emerged from the air, swaying in the breeze. It was silver and thin, and flowed freely from the centre of Sir Alastair's shoulder blades. The end of it landed delicately on the table before Gerald, almost dancing between the knots of the worn wooden panels. The Reaper smiled, watching its pitiful inelegance – how pointless a human life could be. He still remembered the great pearlescent membranes that had draped from the sky on his birthday, caressing him, imbuing him with powers beyond description. This wisp of thread truly meant nothing.

'*Sever*,' said Gerald.

Sir Alastair shivered, looked over his shoulder, and instinctively met Gerald's gaze.

Then he fell to the ground, clutching his chest.

Several people darted towards Sir Alastair. Someone yelled for someone else to call an ambulance. Gerald rose to his feet, looking the part, ensuring his expression was as shocked and as horrified as everyone else's. After it was clear the man was dead, the Reaper left. Not long after, the bar was cordoned off by police tape and the area was besieged by the press. He observed the flashes from the crowd, saw the hundreds of little spider eyes of mobile phone cameras, and flitted away with superspeed, completely unseen.

This was the first time Gerald had used his Awakened ability. He had been unable to kill from a distance before, and even though it was valuable in public assassinations like this, it came with its risks. As he removed his disguise, thus triggering the Sharan memory-obscuration in the eyewitnesses of the Club, he felt the heat behind his navel intensify. He flitted towards home, but at some point, his legs became loose and unstable, and he had to stow away among the bins behind a restaurant. He clutched his stomach, tried to steady his breathing, and dabbed at the sweat on his forehead.

It had felt good. Killing Sir Alastair felt good. The man's body returned to him now as camera flashes, spreadeagled on the floor of the beer garden, pale skin and purple tongue lolling out of a wet, petrified mouth. Gerald's blood coursed through his body with aching fervour. Why did that feel so good? He rested against the cool brick wall behind him; clenched his jaw to focus. The stench of rotting food smothered him. He forced himself to focus on the smell, on the innocent, unsuspecting humans in the restaurant behind him, of the school children travelling home after their extra-curricular activities, of the parents and families hopping on the nearby buses. He had to control himself. These powers were dangerous, and only to be used when necessary.

'What messy business,' he said when he was at home, looking over the crossed-out name in the Grim Book.

His phone rang. He smiled.

'Amy,' he said, padding over to the kitchen to see what Zis had made this evening: beef Wellington and the fattest homemade chips he had ever seen.

Amy paused on the other end of the line.

'Feels like you've just killed someone. I *was* wondering if you were behind all this madness I'm seeing on the news.'

'You never told me you can parse over the phone.'

'I can't. But even if I couldn't, I wouldn't need to right now. Your voice sounds different after a kill.'

He halted. 'How so?'

In the lengthening silence, he concealed his aura, suddenly wary of her. He recounted the aftermath of the previous assassination and how her body became a wall of rejection. He was still grateful that Amy had decided to stay with him, to satisfy her curiosity and observe the world as told by her grandmother, but now he couldn't help but ponder the extent of her abilities, and whether her keen senses could be detrimental to his work.

She snickered down the phone and the noise distracted him. 'You don't sound as friendly.'

Gerald was still unconvinced, but he knew she would say nothing more, so he bit down his suspicion to continue the conversation with some dignity. 'Makes sense. Have you had dinner?'

'Yeah. Well, I say yeah. Just a crisp sandwich.'

'A . . . a *what* sandwich?'

'You've never had one?'

Gerald frowned. He was in shock. 'No? Would you like to come to mine? There's a lot of beef Wellington here.'

'Okay,' said Amy. Her tone was light. 'Can you also ask Zis to make some Black people food?'

This time he laughed. 'I can do that, no problem.'

When they hung up, he stared at the phone for a long time. After an evening of such a high-profile assassination, it felt good to return to some normality, no matter how small.

CHAPTER TWO
Gerald

Blythe Mason's office was sooty again. His scarlet eyes pierced Gerald from behind a curtain of grey mist. As always, Blythe kept his lamps dim, and black shadows stretched across bookshelves, over furniture, and imprinted onto walls. As Gerald started to discuss the contents of Bane's letter, he noticed Blythe's eyes widen, then narrow into slits, and they continued to grow smaller until they were almost totally closed. He stopped abruptly when Blythe slammed his fists on the table.

'Erm. Blythe? Did you not know about the ransom letter?'
'No.'
'Mr Crow told me he informed you.'
'He didn't.'
'Oh.'

Gerald poured himself a cup of yellow Gecko tea and nibbled on a lemon madeleine.

'What is he playing at?' Blythe reclined. 'First, he makes the assassination request without telling me. Then, he gets a whole ransom note from Bane and asks you and that bloody human to escort his daughter? That's a *Gardien*-level job!'

'Why did he tell me he told you about this?' asked Gerald to the room.

'Oh, isn't it obvious? He's been avoiding me ever since he made the request. He doesn't want to answer to me. He doesn't want to face a confrontation. If it was up to him, he would bypass me completely and have this all done on his own merit.'

'Well' – Gerald waved some of the fog away so he could look at the wraith properly – 'can you blame him? Your family is virtually holding him to ransom too, don't you think? Every single election he's won was primarily funded by the Masons. Your family is all over City Hall, owns half of Downey. I think you're all a bit too powerful. He must be looking for more sponsors, and perhaps he might try to disband *Gardien*. You and your organisation answer to no one. Not even the mayor. That's scary.'

'He's being corrupt.'

'He's a politician.'

Blythe folded his arms, scrutinising Gerald properly. 'How is the human? Did she feel anything strange about Crow?'

'Not that I'm aware of. Amy's quite good at those kinds of things. We've already visited Lavender and Bane's houses so she can take a mental note of their auras. She'd definitely be able to tell if Mr Crow harboured ill will towards you.'

'Isn't that lovely?'

'I think so.'

'Gerald. Let some of my people help you with this escort.'

Gerald grimaced. It was getting convoluted now. He had no desire to get in the middle of a political conflict. As a Reaper, he was impartial.

'I don't want to cause trouble,' he said at last. 'Can't Amy and I just get on with it?'

'No.'

'Why not?'

'Because *Gardien* knows more about the Downey Gang

than you do. We have profiles of several members. We also have a witch on the team with years of experience that far outranks Lavender. Believe me, you need us.'

Gerald shrugged. 'I suppose so. But do it in a way where Mr Crow won't find out, otherwise I'll be roped into your . . . dramas.'

'I honestly don't care if he finds out—'

'—Blythe—'

'Why do you act like you don't know who you are?' Blythe poured some whisky into his tumbler. 'You say that the Masons are too powerful, but that's nothing compared to the Reapers, is it? You *know* that out of the two of us, Crow is more scared of you, as well as your friendship with me.'

Gerald stared at Blythe, open-mouthed. He placed his madeleine on the table beside him. 'Friendship? You consider me a friend for real?'

Blythe's disgusted expression was his only response.

'Well anyway,' said Gerald, bouncing on the chair as he spoke, feeling giddy. It was hard to concentrate after that admission. 'It's that reason why I'm so careful around everyone. You know how people are – they act like I'm just itching to kill them. That's why we Reapers are impartial. We just preside over things here and there. It's not my place to take sides. Or at least look like I'm taking sides.'

'But we both know you're on *my* side.'

'The jury's still out on that, Blythe. I take my position very seriously.'

Blythe rolled his eyes. 'Whatever,' he said. 'And how on earth does your human come into this? Isn't she a liability as an empath? And doesn't allowing a human down here break several rules?'

'You know the rule for humans with special abilities as much as I do.'

'Well I can't wait to see how useful she is.'

'You'll see next week at Greymalkin's. Who from *Gardien* will be accompanying us?'

'I'll think of someone.'

'Perhaps have them follow us from the sidelines. Neither me nor Amy need to know.'

'Fine by me.'

Gerald stirred his tea, remembering the visit to the warlock den two days ago. 'Is Bane an orphan?'

'No.' Blythe raised a brow. 'Why do you ask?'

'Well, I mentioned it earlier, but Amy and I went to Bloodwood the other day to investigate any belongings he might have left behind. He had pretty much cleaned out his room, as expected, but there were a few things. I was just surprised at the state of it.'

'Oh.' Blythe swirled his whisky absently. 'He lived there for ages, even when we were in school.'

'Gosh, really?'

'His parents are crack addicts. They're all from Cruickstown originally.'

'Cruickstown,' Gerald repeated. 'That's in the south-east? Near Regalia Park?'

'Yes, that place.'

Cruickstown was even more dilapidated than Bloodwood. Known as the scourge of Downstairs, it was a maze of grey interlocking tower blocks that housed thousands of Downers for three miles of land. It was a city within a city, a deformed Vatican of a fortress that seemed to repel any social service that should have assisted it. Cruickstown hoarded the vulnerable and the poor within its cold cement walls. It was a forgotten place, a hovel that Gerald had had no reason to visit before, and he planned to keep it that way. He glanced at Blythe and noticed the wraith's discomfort.

'Is there much point interviewing them?' Gerald said.

'No. They're in a rehab facility anyway, and they don't like visitors. The last time someone went there, they tried to smuggle in drugs, so the staff have been extra strict since then. All sorts of enchantments guard the place. And it's best not to distress them. They hate talking about Bane because they think they failed him. But . . . these things just happen sometimes.'

'May I ask what facility?'

'St Olave's.'

Gerald blinked in shock. 'That's a private hospital,' he said. Situated on the outskirts of the neighbouring Regalia Park, St Olave's was known to have treated local Downey celebrities. Gerald stared at Blythe, waiting for an explanation. The wraith sighed in frustration, taking a mirthless swig from his tumbler.

'I'm paying for it,' he snapped.

'I see.' A stilted silence, then, 'Did you ever visit him in his den? When you were schoolboys.'

'Yes.'

'Must have been strange for you.'

'A little, but I got used to it.'

'Have you ever tried—'

'I'm not discussing him with you anymore, Gerald.'

'Fine, sure. Would you like me to leave?'

'Yes.'

'I'll take some of these madeleines home with me, if that's okay with you.'

'Whatever.'

'Well, see you later, friend,' said Gerald.

'Get out of my house.'

Gerald promptly left the office, making sure to confirm that the photo of Blythe's thirtieth birthday party was still in its special place on the shelf. When he finally got home, he checked over his new assassination requests and spent the day completing them, then he phoned his parents to let them know of the recent developments. He shuffled off to bed well after the witching hour. He stared at the dark ceiling above him, thinking about Bane and Lavender and the thousands, probably millions of Downers like them, and the environments that created them.

He succumbed to a fitful sleep. The lives of the disenfranchised – the existences of such Downers – had not registered with him before. Amy had already exposed that aspect of his ignorance, and to his shock, Blythe had intensified it. His dreams were peppered with his sense of embarrassment, but he found he had no real desire to lessen the gaps in his knowledge.

CHAPTER THREE

Amy

Greymalkin's Academy, est. 1804, was nestled in between a ring of muddy fells in the north of Downstairs. It was a haunting cathedral made of pewter-coated stone with a trio of spires that overlooked the fells. A lawn of black grass surrounded the school and a moat fortified its illustrious grounds. Pupils from eleven to eighteen flocked to the building on Tuesday morning and wore a notable uniform: a violet tunic over leather trousers, with sturdy black boots to match. Gerald came in his full Grim best: turban and fresh veil wrapped tightly around his face. Beside him, Amy wore a plain black outfit. As they mounted the steps, the Downers gave them a wide berth. Peaches Crow marched in front.

They had picked her up from the mayoral residence in the city centre, and she complained at the standard horse and cart Gerald had rented for transport. A shrill, incessant whine escaped her mouth, and grew increasingly louder until Lex Crow caved into her demands and hired an enchanted vehicle instead. The trio journeyed to north Downey in a sleek pumpkin-style carriage that moved by itself.

Peaches Crow was everything that Amy had expected of a mayor's daughter. She keened and moaned and spent the forty minutes of travel talking about all the teachers that were unfair to her, and all the boys that apparently loved her, and all the girls that were jealous of her. Mrs Crow was white, matching the image of the woman Amy had seen in the emerald frame in the mayor's City Hall office, and so Peaches was of a tanned complexion, like the ridges of a conch shell. She had watched them with protuberant, hazel eyes. It looked like she was accusing them of something, but her aura fluttered with the fragile noise of teenage angst. She had regarded Gerald with a poor attempt at condescension, as if she was unaccustomed to not being the most important person in the room, and all the while, the keen reverence that dominated every Downers' aura whenever they encountered the Reaper filled the carriage. Of all those Amy had met, only Blythe remained internally unmoved by the Reaper. She admired his commitment to indifference.

'So, for how long will you be looking after me?'

'Just today,' Gerald had said.

'Just today? And you think you'll nab this Downey crew in that time, do you?'

'We hope so.'

'You *hope* so? But what about Friday, Mr Grim?'

'It's Reaper—'

'Prom is Friday. I'm happy for you to escort me around today and let's keep it that way, assuming that you find my daddy's enemies. Otherwise, I hope you don't think you'll be hovering around me while I'm trying to have fun with my friends. It might prove difficult—'

She blushed then, as if anticipating the humiliation of Gerald watching her dance and bear witness to her acting like the teenager that she was.

'Erm, well . . . ?' Gerald looked at Amy.

'Maybe you won't be going to prom in the end,' Amy said. 'It might not be safe. Let's just say that it's cancelled for now?'

The thunderous aura that rocked the carriage was

impressive for someone so young. It had been worth a little discomfort to shut her up for a few minutes, so Amy bit her lip so as not to laugh and watched the city from the open carriage window, trying her best to get accustomed to all the auras around her.

Now, as they stalked around the school, Peaches was still inconsolable.

'Why did you say that?' Gerald muttered beside her.

'You telling me that wasn't funny? She's bloody annoying.'

'Well now what? We need her to cooperate with us.'

'She will. Especially if she thinks her prom is at stake!'

Peaches was popular, but she maintained a frosted distance. No pupil approached her or raised any childish conversation; there was no gaggle of girls moaning about first period or fretting for the upcoming prom. Peaches all but glided along the mosaic ground, waited outside her first class – Dynamics of Levitation 1 – and found her seat at the back of the classroom beside a floor-length window that looked out onto a football pitch. She acknowledged no one. Her expression was conceited.

'Lots of confidence,' said Gerald as he took a seat towards the rear of the room.

'Hmm. Nan used to call that Light Skin Syndrome,' said Amy.

Gerald stared at her. Amy returned his gaze innocently. Then she grinned, which made him burst into laughter. It was a self-conscious hissing sound. She watched with amusement as he tried to conceal his noise.

'Your grandmother was a funny woman,' he managed at last. He cleared his throat and straightened his veil.

'I'd say so.'

As the rest of the class flittered in, they barely registered

Peaches. From their auras, Amy knew they were all mages, and all carried long rowan wood staffs strapped on their backs. Each mage looked directly at Gerald sitting behind Peaches on a wooden stool in all his cloaked mystery, and a fissure of fear would radiate from their auras before they scrambled to a seat. Amy glanced at Gerald every time this happened, but he only stared straight ahead at the blackboard, pleasantly peaceful.

The teacher was Mistress Abercrombie, a stout woman who drowned in her mage's cloak. She waved a pensive hand towards Gerald, frowned at Amy, and then attempted to teach the theory of levitating spells to her class, but the distractions overwhelmed everyone in the room. Amy too began to feel exhausted, battling against the tumult of feelings of the class. She observed the typical movements of anxious teens: fidgeting hands beneath desks, sweaty foreheads, a furtive finger tucking an unruly strand of hair behind a reddening ear, the confused glances at Amy. Her presence was known by most of Downstairs, and even though her status as a gifted empath allowed her entrance to the city, it was her position as Gerald's partner that had caused a Downey sensation. Even now, Peaches appeared to cool down, her former hostility towards the Reaper dissipating to something akin to jealousy. It wasn't long before she also looked his way, as if desperately trying to catch his attention.

The rest of the day continued without incident. For Amy, it was the most exciting school day she had ever experienced. Six thousand pupils attended classes she never would have imagined, from flying lessons to blood sciences to enchantments, all alongside conventional maths and English. She saw skeleton caretakers cleaning the exterior stained-glass windows, and wraiths serving lunch, and vampires cajoling each other on the playgrounds.

Much later, the Greymalkin's pupils spent their free period planning for prom. On the ground floor, Peaches led Amy and Gerald to a grand hall that was doused in kaleidoscopic light from the windows. An indigo mosaic floor told the story of the school's founding from the first brick that was laid at the site all the way to the impressive cathedral that stood between the muddy fells of Downstairs. Above them, cast iron chandeliers draped from stone pillars and wooden beams.

The pupils darted every which way. A massive fern tree with black leaves grew from the centre of the grand hall by magic. At the top, a group of young witches on broomsticks added decorations. By the feature stained-glass wall, a line of mages waved their staffs in synchronised motions and soap suds bubbled out of the panels to clean the windows to gleaming perfection. A group of vampires, all pale skin and black eyes, directed a gang of warlocks on how to hang ivy fixtures from the ceiling. When Peaches entered, all purposeful and important, the noise dimmed, and several of her classmates shot her hopeful glances as if awaiting her approval.

For the next hour, Amy and Gerald stood sentinel as fifty pupils argued over punch flavours, band orders, and colour schemes. Peaches sat at the head of the table, observing while looking mightily important, and then offering a terse word or light suggestion, which would then sway the direction of the meeting.

'Maybe Upstairs ain't so bad,' she muttered to Gerald, wrinkling her nose at the familiar auras. 'All this angst. For what?'

'Oh come on. Didn't you have a prom? I'm sure you behaved the same way.'

'I did have a prom, but I didn't go. I wasn't popular like that.'

She felt Gerald staring at her, but she didn't want to talk about it, so she kept her mouth shut. During the day, she had tried to figure out why Peaches annoyed her so much. Of course, she was annoying by herself, but something about her self-assuredness reminded Amy of everything she hadn't been at her age. She had been shy and anxious, and always kept herself at a distance to protect herself from the deluge of auras she could not control. The worst was feeling the sense of wariness that constantly wafted towards her from girls she admired or boys she liked. It thrust her into the shattered memories of her parents. No, she did not attend any proms. No one had asked her to go.

Once everything was finished, Peaches said, 'I suppose you'll be coming along to my dress fitting then?' She walked ahead of them to a waiting carriage. 'It would make sense, wouldn't it? The atelier is Upstairs so I'm sure I'm in more danger up there than down here.'

Amy shot Gerald her most foreboding look. He pretended not to see her.

'Of course, Peaches. Harrods, isn't it? I have business there, anyway.'

'Oh my God,' Amy muttered. She succumbed to an irritated silence, and only vaguely listened to the conversation as it flowed with stilted pressure. Their carriage eventually stopped at a black wall, far away from the busy city centre. A single lift door awaited them.

Inside stood a tall hooded Warden that was not Carole. When the trio entered, her hood immediately flew backwards, and she advanced upon Amy before anyone could react. Gerald quickly stood between the two.

'Clover,' he said brightly, 'this is Amy.'

'The human.'

Amy frowned at the brazen hostility of the Warden. Clover had spat the words, as if she was repulsed that a human was inside the lift. Amy shuffled closer to the wall, grateful for Gerald's intervention.

'We're going to be late,' Peaches said to Clover, tapping her staff on the ground. The doors of the lift closed. It did not move, however.

'Explain this, Mr Gerald,' Clover said without taking her eyes off Amy.

'I can explain this myself,' said Amy. 'I'm an empath. I'm Gerald's partner.'

Clover looked from Amy to Gerald, and back again. She shifted ever so slightly, but her contempt for Amy filled the lift like smoke. Amy tried to appear nonchalant, but the pressure of Clover's aura was stifling. It was hot and sparked with a biting energy that made her feel sick.

'How's the family, Clover?' asked Gerald. He removed his turban and veil and swapped them for his daytime face mask.

Clover immediately turned her attention to Gerald. 'Fine. Thank you so much for the biscuits.'

'You're very welcome. Now, we're a bit busy today. I'm going to need you to start this lift.'

Clover shot a wary look at Amy but complied. It was extraordinary how much the Warden's demeanour changed when speaking to Gerald. He continued to watch her, his face and body language pleasant and relaxed, but there was a foreboding authority that overpowered Clover's anti-human sentiment and Peaches' impatience. Amy watched as both women shot nervous glances to Gerald as the moments passed. Peaches made a big fuss of stowing her staff away in her Hammerspace, which, in true Peaches fashion, took on the form of a Louis Vuitton dresser.

Perhaps it was her lack of knowledge of how things worked Downstairs, but Amy found it difficult to fear Gerald like everyone else seemed to. Yes, she had glimpsed the breathtaking depth of his power on that night in Camden Town, and she felt the sickening aura of the Grim Book, and she was aware that he was a walking killing machine, burdened with a curse she would never understand, but their first meeting had ended with them amicably drinking tea in the comfort of her kitchen beneath the calming atmosphere of her grandmother's remnant aura.

Gerald turned to her unexpectedly, his expression playful. 'Yes, Amy?'

'Don't *yes* me, I didn't say anything.'

Peaches snapped her head in Amy's direction, brows furrowed. Clover wheeled around. The shadow of that serpentine visage she had witnessed with Carole crossed the Warden's features.

'We're good, Clover,' said Gerald.

She looked at Gerald pleadingly. A whimpering sound rumbled in the back of her throat, and she swivelled around again.

At long last, the lift shuddered to a halt. The doors opened into a foyer of an anonymous building in a Knightsbridge back alley, fronted by red brick and pale stone. On either side of the alley was a main road. Car horns blared, bicycles chimed, and hundreds of leather-soled shoes slapped against some of the cleanest pavements in London. Out on the streets, the gleaming façade of luxury hotels reflected the waning April sun, and supercars were parked with violent inconsideration, half propped against curbs, spilling onto pedestrian areas. Women in flowing abayas meandered outside designer outlets, international students balanced an overabundance of shopping bags, and the sky was polluted by glaring adverts for priceless junk.

'Thank you, Clover,' said Gerald as he exited first.

'Yeah, thanks,' said Peaches.

Amy was the last to leave. As she turned to thank Clover, she faltered. Clover's face had completely disappeared, and beneath her hood was a grey scaled reptilian creature with jagged teeth and haunting purple eyes. As Amy stumbled away from the lift, she vowed to never upset a single member of the Warden family again.

Amy did not have Harrods money, so it was a place she had never visited. It was hard not to feel some resentment at the row of expensive shops leading up to the department store. An oleaginous avarice seeped from the miles of gleaming glass all around her. The aura of swollen, rotting money papered the ground. Peaches led the way once more, a haughty spring to her step, and Gerald obliged with good humour. Once inside Harrods, everything was loud. Flowers and sandalwood wafted from the perfume booths. Tall ceilings of gilded gold and soft marble floors and the quiet patter of leather soles surrounded Amy. She felt the sustained unctuousness hovering over her shoulders, but the air was thin. Many of the shoppers were existing on fragile glass. She soon ambled down a corridor lined with Louboutin's and expensive jewellery.

'Did you see those earrings?' Amy hissed, slapping Gerald in the side.

'The Tiffany's?'

'I don't know what they are. But they cost six grand!'

Gerald frowned. 'Remind me to return there. It's been a while since I bought something for Mother.'

'Fuck you!'

Gerald smiled and his eyes flashed with a familiar mischief. 'I did say assassination was lucrative.'

They soon arrived at the Egyptian escalator. The gold stairway elevated them to an indigo ceiling adorned by constellations. Sphinxes, pharaohs, and engraved marble pillars lined the floors and walls. They had been transported to an ancient tomb.

Gerald and Peaches were unperturbed, so Amy kept silent to preserve her own dignity. When they finally arrived on their floor, Peaches flocked to the atelier which specialised in elegant, yet garish, dresses.

The young mage immediately proceeded to ignore them, floating off elsewhere with a sycophantic shop assistant, and left Amy and Gerald on the outer shop floor.

The world disappeared when Peaches left. Amy plummeted into a vat of cotton, and the senses she used to parse the air vanished, dispersing in the atmosphere. She froze, desperately clinging onto the vapours that had just surrounded her, and felt nothing. She exhaled; calmed herself. She could still feel some things, namely, the humans of Upstairs. A swathe of understandable emotions and temperaments were there, but all signs of the supernatural were gone.

'Is everything okay?' prompted Gerald.

'No. I can't feel you lot.'

'What do you—'

'Other – Downers are everywhere. Look, you and Peaches are right here. So many of you are able to come Upstairs, I meet loads of Downers just going about my day-to-day business, and I can *always* feel them. Right now, I can't feel *anything*, not even you two. It's like when you conceal your aura, but this time it's covered every possible Downer in here.'

'That's . . . not good.'

'How's it even possible?'

Gerald scanned their surroundings. His expression was shrewd. 'There are techniques out there, certain spells or amulets that can hide auras. But it's strange it would happen now. Have you encountered anything like this before?'

Amy shook her head. A cold fear flooded her insides. She had been doing this for five years and had never felt the sudden loss of supernatural life from the atmosphere. This was a spell someone had suddenly cast, perfectly timed for a moment when she was on an observational exercise to identify a fugitive from a crowd.

'You don't think . . .' she started.

'We're being watched.'

'Oh God.'

'I'll protect you.' He smiled at her.

'That's not the point!'

'*Well?*' Peaches reappeared with the shop assistant in tow. The latter held a silk hanger above her head and an ivory gown was draped around it. The dress was gaudy and dated, something that an elderly woman would wear for her fifth wedding, but Peaches beamed at it, and so did her shop assistant.

'Well what?' asked Amy, averting her eyes from the dress. She was unsettled, suffocating beneath the sickly polite cloud that surrounded the shop assistant, and blind to the irritable spice of Peaches Crow.

'Isn't it pretty?'

'Wonderful!' said Gerald.

'Thank you, Mr *Reaper*. One can always trust you with fashion.'

'Since when?' asked Amy.

'Please wrap that up, and my housekeeper will collect it tomorrow.' Peaches waved the assistant away.

Gerald rummaged in his robes, checked the time on his phone, and stowed it away again.

'We have some time for cakes, don't we?' he said to Peaches, but not Amy.

'Oh? Will you be treating me?' Peaches' eyes grew wide with delight.

'Of course, Peaches. I'm sure it hasn't been easy having us accompany you everywhere like a convict.'

'Oh, gosh, don't worry about that!'

Amy tried and failed to read Peaches' aura, and her sense of unease increased. She scanned the shop floor, looking for anything untoward between the clothes racks and displays, but everyone around her acted normally, absently browsing shelves, hissing demands into mobile phones, clinging onto the arms of aged men while nursing plasticised expressions welded from cosmetic surgery. Whoever was watching them had made themselves invisible both physically and on the paranormal level, and Amy was left to the impenetrable darkness. She wanted to read the room.

'Do we really have time for sweets?' she asked.

'Yes,' said Gerald. He then turned to Peaches. 'Let's go to the top floor, shall we?'

Amy trailed behind the pair. She didn't follow them into the Godiva café. She waited outside for what felt like ages until they finally returned with two cardboard bags filled to the brim with chocolates and cakes. Peaches loitered beside

Gerald, surreptitiously nibbling on a truffle. He flashed her an amiable smile and she beamed in response. The doting, pleadingly jealous Peaches was a much more annoying companion than the Peaches from the morning, and Amy desperately yearned for her.

'We going now?' she asked.

'Yes,' said Gerald. 'Peaches, would you like to lead the way? Ah, let's go *that* way.' He nodded straight ahead towards an exit that was further than necessary.

Amy was about to ask why, but something about the Reaper's body language made her hesitate. Gerald made no indication that anything untoward had happened, but his eyes were set on something far ahead in the distance. Amy darted her eyes around the shop floor, examining the faces of the various shoppers, loiterers, and tourists. Everything appeared normal.

'What, did you see a member of the gang?' she asked.

Gerald ignored her.

They passed a group of shoppers that chatted excitedly beside a navy-dyed mink coat on a display. Despite the missing auras around her, a coldness of unease rested on her shoulders. Her intuition told her something was wrong, and she was reminded of the predatory demeanour Gerald had assumed in Gray's Inn. She turned to Gerald instinctively, wanting an answer, but he refused to look at her. His mask was still on. She saw it billow above his mouth, as if he had whispered something within its confines that he had not wanted her to hear.

'Keep going,' he said more audibly. His tone was austere.

When they arrived at the other end of the shop floor, one of the men in the mink coat coterie collapsed. The women around him screamed. Security guards ran towards the commotion, and shop assistants pushed through the growing crowd. Peaches turned to look, and Gerald, his aura still untraceable, feigned surprise as he also watched the events unfold.

'Oh *yuck*, he *died*,' said Peaches. 'Let's go. The scent of death is *everywhere*. I hope it doesn't attach itself to my gown.' She spun on her heel and departed.

Gerald sighed, and his body visibly relaxed. He stared at Amy. 'I'm an assassin, Amy.'

'Yeah. Yeah . . . I know.'

He promptly accompanied Peaches. It took a while for Amy to unglue her feet from the floor, but she eventually followed him. Gerald had showed her something new, and for the first time, she felt the nudge of fear in the pit of her stomach. She already knew he could kill from a distance, but she hadn't anticipated the shimmering glow that eclipsed his face in the aftermath. A dreaminess had enshrouded his expression – it was a countenance she associated with sex. The auras of the humans around her remained visible, and she could feel the shocking loss of life beside the coat racks. An emptiness pressed against the air. There was nothing pleasurable about it.

Their final stop was South Kensington where Mrs Crow was holding an evening tea party at which Peaches was expected. The journey happened in sightless silence. Amy could not feel the presence of any Downer, no matter how intensely she grasped for them.

'We're still being watched,' she said.

'Noted,' said Gerald.

They escorted Peaches to an ivory townhouse situated away from the main road. Two suited men stood watch outside. Unable to read their auras, Amy could only guess what the guards could be. They both nodded at Peaches and opened the emerald-painted front door. Inside, additional guards calmly patrolled the elegant corridors. Mrs Crow met them from the other side of the door, her face bright and hopeful.

'Peachy!'

'Mother!'

Gerald stepped forward quickly, cutting the reunion short. His expression was hardened and calculated.

'Hello Mrs Crow. I'm awfully sorry, but Amy and I need to do some patrolling of our own. I know this is impolite of me.'

'Oh, no worries at all.' Mrs Crow failed to hide her disappointment.

'You won't be coming to tea?' asked Peaches.

'Unfortunately not,' said Gerald.

Amy could tell from his body language that he had sensed something she couldn't. Her heart raced. She tried to take a subtle look around their surroundings, but there was nothing out of the ordinary. Just a calm orange sunset, a pristine road, expensive cars, and the delicate smell of artisan coffee in the air.

'Mr Reaper!' Peaches whined.

'Oh don't bother the man, Peachy. You must come next time, Mr Reaper.'

'Absolutely.'

Reluctantly, Mrs Crow closed the door. Neither mother nor daughter acknowledged Amy. She was happy to leave them.

Gerald stalked towards the main road again with Amy in tow.

'Who is it?' she asked.

'I think it's one of Blythe's—'

An explosion. The shocking, biting chill of a hundred vampire presences in the base of her back, the prickle of a pack of werewolves, the spiced rumble of innumerable witches, and the cool nothingness that she had come to identify with wraiths. The presences of countless other Downers, including the warlocks and mages in the Crow house, were made alive again. Amy staggered to the ground, and Gerald grabbed her by the elbow. Despite the cacophony of noise, something else reached out to her. It was markedly different from the rest. A presence that was previously hidden had miraculously appeared along with the Downers. Its authoritative nature gave itself away as the culprit.

'Amy?'

'Human! Over *there*,' she gasped. Before she could say anything else, the auras disappeared again.

Just as she gestured in the direction of Cromwell Road, a figure dark as shadow flitted across the street. Their movements were clumsy, but their speed, gait, and overall demeanour was without the power and formidability that Amy attributed to Downers. They disappeared quickly, slipping behind a row of parked cars.

Gerald grabbed Amy's arm, and she was thrown into a wind tunnel. Her feet left the ground as Gerald dragged her along with him, running at a speed that reduced South Kensington to smears of brown and grey. The streets melted into car headlights and street lamps and stone and brick. They finally stopped beside the Science Museum. Amy leaned against the wall to catch her breath.

'I can't sense them now, Gerald,' she panted. The journey had winded her. 'I'm not sure where—'

'It's okay, I saw them.'

He dropped his gaze to the cobbled ground. She saw a rim of scarlet flash around his irises.

'*Below,*' he whispered. He splayed his hand outwards and a faint silvery line appeared on the ground. Gerald gripped Amy by the waist and stepped above the outline on the pavement. The busy South Kensington streets rose to meet them, then covered their heads. They returned to the leather and mahogany room with its rich emerald wallpaper and dark tapestries on the walls. Amy saw the Grim Book, the lockpicks and low-burning fireplace. They phased through Gerald's Hammerspace quickly, and the room shuddered up and above them before disappearing into blackness. When their journey was over, they were standing in the putrid ankle-deep waters of a sewage tunnel.

Amy felt the human again, and then in a flash, the sensation was gone.

'Straight ahead!' she said. 'But please drag me and let me fly like last time – I can't be standing in this shit water!'

Gerald complied, flitting down the tunnel and spraying the shit water into the air instead. Amy screamed in horror, clamping her mouth and eyes shut, and wishing there was a way to cover her hair. She made a mental note to pack a disposable bonnet next time Gerald had the audacity to take her into the sewer.

When they stopped, the ground was damp but without stagnant water. It still stank, and above them, Amy could hear the rumble of cars and the disgruntled clatter of a sewer hole cover. The little light from above ground pierced the dark tunnel with bullet holes of white. Shafts streaked across their faces. Amy tried to parse again, but the person had vanished completely. Gerald's soft aura enshrouded the tunnel immediately after the unknown human's departure.

'Missed 'em. But your aura's back,' she said. She covered her nose with the back of her hand. 'How was a human doing all that?'

'A talisman, I reckon,' said someone who was not Gerald.

Amy spun towards the voice. The Reaper stood beside her, but he did not feel worried.

'Is that . . . Joshua?' he said to the darkness.

An abnormally pale man with an athletic build slinked towards them. Coming into the light properly, he lifted his Ray-Bans and flashed them a smile. His eyes were scarlet.

'Ah, Amy, this is Joshua; Joshua—'

'Josh is fine,' the man said to Amy. 'You're the empath I keep hearing about? Lovely to meet you.'

'Thanks,' said Amy. Around him was the friendliest aura she had ever felt from a Downer.

'So I'm guessing you're the one Blythe sent to watch over us?' asked Gerald. 'I caught a glimpse of you just as we got to Peaches' house.'

'Of course. Gah!' said Josh, running skeletal fingers through thick black hair. 'I almost got that guy just now! Was literally just about to slip through that wall over there and nab him! But *someone* opened a Hammerspace door for him and he disappeared.'

'It sounds like you know who did it,' said Gerald.

'I wish I did. But let's just assume Bane, seeing as though he sent that awful letter to Lex.' Josh patted his leather jacket absently. 'Can I vape down here?'

'No, I think you might blow us up,' said Gerald.

'Ah well. Let's get back up there. I'll give Blythe the wonderful news.'

Amy and Gerald waited on the steps of the Victoria and Albert Museum, watching as Josh paced up and down, grimacing, then frowning, then mouthing obscenities at his mobile. His glasses were back on so his eyes were hidden, and with the obnoxious smoke of his vape pen, he looked deliciously cool.

'So what we saying about this human?' Amy asked Gerald.

He reclined in thought. 'I think Josh is right about the talisman. There are ways for Downers to imbibe their magic into items for humans to use for certain periods of time. I can imagine such a spell to conceal auras would be useful for the gang – after all, some witches can read auras, though not as precisely as you. This human must be one of Bane's top executives. They're the only ones who would know how to use something like that, and I've already confirmed that Lavender's people don't know about magic.'

'And what happened earlier? All those auras came flooding back for, like, three seconds? Why would the human randomly allow *that*?'

'That was a mistake,' said Josh. He had finished his conversation with Blythe. 'That's what Blythe thinks, anyway. Still a human – they can only handle so much. He probably dropped it while he was following you, and then ran away into the sewers in a panic once he realised what he'd done. I don't claim to have the same level of abilities as you, Amy, but we wraiths can feel general presences to a point. Out of nowhere, I felt my ears pop. They *popped*! That was a big booboo from our human stalker.'

'Did Blythe tell you off?' Gerald asked.

'When isn't he telling someone off?'

'Josh is part of Blythe's *Gardien*,' Gerald told Amy. 'Normally he's with his partner . . . where's Ulrich?'

'PTS. So I'm out here alone.'

'Oh, fair enough.'

'Um, what's PTS?' asked Amy.

'Pre-transformation sickness,' said Josh. 'Ulrich's a werewolf shifter.'

She couldn't help but laugh at that.

'It's a real thing!' said Josh, but he was grinning. 'They're a sensitive lot, can't handle silver, all crying at the moon. And then they get sick before *and* after transformation week. It's a real mess living with him. But I do love his fur when he transforms' – his smile grew wistful – 'like a L'Oréal ad.'

'I'll have to meet him one day.'

'Oh, definitely!'

Gerald stretched and stood. Amy did the same. It was dark now. Behind them, the museum slept in its splendour. The brick and glass and iron melted into one hulking shadow. The streets were noisy at this time. Hackney cabs blared their horns at Uber drivers. Tourists with designer suitcases said their greetings to hotel door attendants, the latter tipping the rims of their top hats as they allowed their guests entry. Many of these people were Downers, like Peaches and Mrs Crow, and to some extent, Gerald and Josh – the ones who passed for human. It was both amazing and terrifying.

'Would you two like to come Downstairs for tea?' asked Josh. 'We could talk this over.'

'I would love to,' said Amy, 'but I think I need to get home before it gets too late. I'm a bit worried about people following me and I've been out after midnight pretty much every night since meeting this guy.'

'Of course. You get your rest,' said Josh. 'I'll see you both later and we can discuss this some other time. Shame we never caught the guy.'

'It's been an evening of false starts, I fear,' said Gerald. 'The upside is, Peaches is staying with her mother in their

Upstairs house for the rest of the evening; that building is highly protected, so we're relieved of our duties. Let's reconvene with some better news.'

'Definitely, definitely.' Josh waved, then turned on his heel as if he was about to walk in the opposite direction, but by the time his back was towards them, his body had vanished.

'Oh, that's cool,' said Amy. 'I think if I was a Downer, I'd be a wraith.'

'Not a Reaper?'

'You're literally a walking curse.'

'Fair enough.' Gerald smiled, then looked uncomfortable. 'I think, after the events of this evening, it's best if I took you home. Now that we know we're being watched, I would rather know you were safe.'

'I definitely agree. I've already been stalked by one Downer. Don't need another.'

Gerald tugged at his mask. 'Oh. We're bringing that up.'

'Bringing *what* up? How you broke into my house and pinned me down—'

'Let's get you home, Amy.'

He all but dragged her away, concealing his aura as he did so, but it was no use; Amy could sense his mortification through the tightly wound cords in his body.

Gerald dashed across West London with Amy on his back, but she made him get on the 333 to Streatham. They had to buy him an Oyster card, and it had been hilarious watching Gerald slap the card against the reader on the bus in wonder, then trying to spark up conversation with the driver, who promptly pretended he didn't exist. The journey had been long, but when they finally disembarked at Streatham Hill station, she felt rested.

Streatham was just as alive as central London; years of steady gentrification had produced a new type of nightlife for young white professionals looking for their first homes in the area. Yoga studios, cafés, nightclubs, and fine dining restaurants made up Streatham Common and Streatham Hill, while the residents of the Vale, and Streatham proper, dwelt in an endangered land of increasingly narrowing communities with tremulous foundations – sprawling and unkempt council estates left to decay beneath the threatening shadow of property developers. Amy observed her hometown a bit more closely this evening. It was exceptionally busy and what she had mistaken for barbecue smoke soon began to singe the lining of her throat. The roads were clotted with traffic. Everything was at a standstill.

'I think something's happened,' she said. 'Probably an accident up the way.'

It wasn't until they arrived at her neighbourhood that Amy felt the cooling charge of a warlock's aura and realised something much worse had happened.

'Gerald, something's wrong.'

He stared at her quizzically. He said something to her, but she only heard silence. As they rounded the corner to her road, she saw the fire engines, and the source of the tarry smoke that clung to the area. Neighbours stood around in turmoil, some dressed in nightwear, watching the events unfold.

Her house was on fire.

Amy darted towards number eighteen Shadwell Avenue on numb legs. Neighbours tried to flag her down hysterically, but they all melted into the darkness. She felt firm arms drag her backwards; it could have been Gerald, a firefighter, or someone else.

In all the furore, she could feel a multitude of auras that

did not belong in her neighbourhood, inappropriately gleeful, tainted with the presence she felt in South Kensington. She had no desire to seek them out. The orange flames of the house cruelly siphoned whatever energy she had left.

Her grandmother's home. Amy's refuge. The living room where she was first told that there was nothing wrong with her and that she came from a proud line of St Thomas empaths; the pimento-scented kitchen in which all the stories from Jamaica had been told to her in the soft, lilting voice of a woman who refused to allow her accent to conform to British expectations; the great master bed that had nurtured Nan during her final months, quickly turning into a shrine of knowledge as she continued to teach the last of what she knew to her most treasured grandchild. Amy thought about the bowls of nutmeg-spiced cornmeal porridge she had wolfed down during the winter months. She recalled all the time spent in the garden, honing her skills, learning about Otherworldlies and the hidden world within her world. She envisioned the countless photographs currently curling into black feathers, and the vintage Windrush-battered clothes burned to dust in the attic.

What good were memories? All tangible evidence of Diamond St Clair was gone.

CHAPTER FOUR

Gerald

Blythe Mason had taken an uncharacteristic journey into town. Gerald waited for him at his front door, his anxiety dissipating with the shock of it, and was doubly surprised to see the wraith struggling with a heavy paper bag of food shopping upon his return. Blythe paused on his own doorstep, his frown deepening when he saw Gerald.

'Hello, Blythe,' said Gerald. 'Would you like some help?'

'No.'

He fished his keys from one of his oversized pockets, jangled them in the door lock, and promptly dropped two buffalo tomatoes on the stone steps. He brushed over them as if nothing had happened, and immediately dumped the shopping bag into Archer's expectant arms on the other side of the door. Gerald retrieved the tomatoes and popped them in the bag.

'Any reason for his little excursion, Archer?'

'He said he wanted to walk.'

'Well, well.'

'Are you just here to loiter?' Blythe asked from his open office. 'If so, you may leave.'

'Thank you, Archer.' Gerald entered the office swiftly. By the time he got comfortable, Blythe had already lit a cigar. 'I'm sure I don't need to go into detail about what happened two days ago.'

'The arson attack.'

'Amy said she felt people in the area as it happened,' said Gerald. 'One was Bane . . . we believe the others are associated with the person who was following us around South Kensington.'

'Bane's executives.'

Gerald frowned. 'I thought so.'

'He has a team of senior-ranking humans, all aware of Downstairs and the nature of our world. Didn't take long to track them down.'

'You . . . wait. Pardon?'

Blythe offered him a twitching mouth in lieu of a smile.

'Blythe!' Gerald drew closer to the desk. 'You've caught them?'

'Don't sound so surprised. That ransom note was Bane coming out of hiding, so I moved as soon as he did. He became so focused on you that he failed to consider *Gardien*, which made it easy for my men to track down his executives. Six lumbering idiots. Currently in custody. We haven't located Bane's whereabouts yet, but we will in time.'

'Blythe. Thank you.'

'Of course. I suppose you could extend some gratitude to Dani and Felix as well. They're the ones who did the chasing.'

'I'll remember that. So, can I see them now? Perhaps it will make it easier to find the rest of them, like Lavender and her associates.'

'That's the plan. They're tight-lipped. You know I don't do torture.'

Gerald scrutinised Blythe. He was worried about following where his train of thought was leading him, but he had no choice.

'They're not in the Downey Gaol,' he said. 'When you say custody, you mean your private prison Upstairs.'

'Correct.'

'So it was more than a little walk you were doing this afternoon. Blythe, are you that mad at Mr Crow?'

'I *told* you. I've been putting a lot of effort into destroying the Downey Gang. If the mayor found out I had captured six key members, I would never get the answers I want. He would take over.'

'Okay, fine. But remember, I did say I wouldn't kill either Bane or Lavender until your investigation was done. To a certain extent, anyway.'

'I remember.'

Blythe stubbed his cigar in the nearby ashtray and slid off his chair.

'Let's go then. It's not far.'

They took the lift to London Bridge on a street behind the Underground station. Workers from The London Bridge Experience, all powdered up and imprisoned behind melting prosthetics, frowned at the arrogant-looking man with his impenetrable sunglasses, and his taller companion, swaddled in black and hidden by a surgical mask. Neither Gerald nor Blythe received a brochure for the exhibition, and across the road, tourists queued up to learn about the bloody history of London Bridge and its subterranean tombs.

Inside the Underground station, some disused railway arches were used as a shopping concourse. Blythe ducked beneath one of the arches and slipped into a hidden door. Gerald was plunged into darkness on the other side as he followed. The passage led them to a humid cavern. The grooves in the stone walls told an ancient history of catacombs, and the six men kneeling on the floor, all tied by their ankles and wrists, seemed to understand this too. They cast wild looks at the cavern, and at the two Downers that kept watch over them.

'Gerald!' said Josh with a frantic wave.

'Oh, Mr Reaper,' said the second Downer, a witch with long braided hair and skin the colour of burned umber. She automatically rose from her chair, looking at the room's latest additions.

'Hello, Dani,' said Gerald. 'Thank you for tracking these down for us.'

'Oh, please. Don't mention it.'

'And who's this then?' One of Bane's executives wriggled in frustration against his restraints.

Although Blythe was against torture, it was obvious he had authorised a thorough beating of his prisoners. The humans bore an overfamiliarity around Downers most likely due to their proximity to Bane. Gerald unbuttoned his cloak. He wore black jeans, a black sweatshirt, and Doc Martens, and kept his face mask on. He ran a gloved hand through his thick curls, then examined each of Blythe's charges. They may have been well acquainted with Downers and the truths of their world, but they had never met a Reaper.

He crouched before the one in the middle. 'Do you mind telling me where Tyrell Bane is?'

The six prisoners looked gobsmacked, then incredulous at Gerald's earnest questioning. They turned to each other and smirked, clearly believing him to be an amateur, their supernatural torture hardening them against the Reaper's deceptively affable demeanour. Gerald undid his gloves while they were distracted. He slapped his bare hand on the middle prisoner's face, and he fell backwards, dead. Behind him, Dani and Josh gasped, and the remaining five prisoners scuttled backwards.

'The fuck you do to him?' asked one.

'I killed him. Let's try again. Where is he?'

They were on guard now. Their companion's body was already beginning to pale, and his eyes were open and glassy. They shifted their attention to the body, then back to Gerald. At last, they noticed the horror of his hands.

'We're not snitching,' said a brave one. 'I don't know who you are, but lemme tell you something—'

He died mid-sentence, slumped against the wall.

'I'm low on patience today,' said Gerald as he turned to the others. 'Where's your boss?'

The group scrambled around on the floor.

'Allrightallrightallright!' One volunteered to speak first. 'We don't know right now. Boss always keeps his location hidden, even from us.'

'Do you know where he *might* be?' asked Josh, his voice dripping with false politeness.

'Not . . . not really.'

'Not good enough,' said Gerald. He lightly touched the speaker on the forehead and turned to the remaining three once the body fell backwards. Behind him, Josh and Dani whispered curses.

'You can't kill them all,' snapped Blythe.

'Tell me,' Gerald said to the now pale white trembling gang members. 'Who was running around South Kensington the other day following us?'

It was either fear or defiance, but the gang members only stared at Gerald in silence. When he shifted his position, one of the men scuttled backwards, gesturing wildly at his furthest companion with his bound feet.

'Himhimhim! It was Gary!'

'Shit!'

The accused rolled onto his stomach. He fought against his restraints, scrummaging to nowhere. Gerald crouched directly in front of him, watched the pitiful display, then felt the bile of anger rise in his throat. The executive known as Gary stiffened, forcing himself to look at Gerald before baulking and averting his gaze to the pocked wall behind.

'Are you the one who started the fire?' Gerald asked quietly.

'We all did it!' Gary turned his head and spat at his other two companions. 'All of us here. We *all* did it.'

'Why?'

'He told us to.'

'So that's it?' asked Dani, her eyes narrowing. 'You would destroy an innocent woman's home just because your boss tells you to?'

'Why wouldn't we?'

'Self-respect, maybe?' asked Josh.

The prisoner laughed. 'We've got plenty, don't you worry about that one, mate.'

'We won't,' said Gerald. He pressed his palm against Gary's face before turning to the other two. They screamed in unison, shifting backwards until they were pressed against the wall. Gerald saw the shimmer of tears in their eyes, the wetness of their foreheads and the beads of sweat that bloomed from their skin. They stank of fear and piss. He ignored Blythe's complaints and Josh and Dani's mutterings of discomfort as he rose to stand, his eyes never leaving the two prisoners.

'Tell me again that you don't know Bane's whereabouts,' he said.

'Okay, okay. We literally don't know everything,' said one. 'There's an order to these things, and with you lot running about, it's not even safe for everyone to know his proper office. He's in loads of places, I dunno—'

'For goodness' sake, just give us a location,' Blythe sighed, staring at the ceiling. 'Value your life a little.'

The two prisoners exchanged a glance before the second one said, 'Okay, well . . . he has a few safehouses. There's this place in Clapham, a hidden office in the old gents toilets. Then we got the basement in that old shop next to Voodoo Rays in Dalston . . . it's closed up, but there's a hidden door on the side. Um. Sitton Road, in Dalston again, there's a house there.'

'House number for Sitton Road?' Josh asked, frantically tapping the locations into his phone.

'Erm, forty-nine. Yeah, forty-nine.'

'Anywhere else?' asked Josh.

'I think he has a little flat in Hackney? He's got a few hideouts, but just let me think a bit and I'll tell you, I swear.'

'And what about Melanie Lavender?' asked Dani.

They both stared at Gerald pleadingly. 'We don't know where she is. Seriously.'

'Some gang,' said Josh as he saved the notes to his phone. 'You lot ain't that scary at all.'

'I'll need you two to send word to the others that they are to get on that immediately,' said Blythe, pointing to Josh's phone. 'You'll all have to search those locations. This is the best lead we have so far on Bane's whereabouts. Work on the other places this afternoon and wring out every safehouse from these cretins.'

As Gerald turned to leave, he glanced at the prisoners. 'Why? Why do all this? Why did you burn her house down?'

After a pause, one spoke. 'He said he'd give us powers.'

Gerald shook his head at the stupidity of it, and then followed Blythe back up the stairs.

'That was unexpected,' Blythe said once they were on the high street outside. 'I thought you took assassinations more seriously than that. That's the first time I've seen you kill someone outside of an official request. Is that even allowed?'

'I do take it seriously,' said Gerald. 'But you should have seen her. The house burned all around her. Nothing was salvaged. Not one thing.' When he blinked, he could see the scarlet and blue flash of emergency vehicles as they blocked Amy's road. Since their first meeting, the empath had been refreshingly easy-going, and he found that he enjoyed her company. The woman on the charred road in Streatham had been someone else, a vapour of a person. The image wrenched at his innards and he felt guilty for partially causing it.

'Well, at least you've avenged her somewhat. And she's living with you now, isn't it? I'm sure there are worse places to end up after losing a house.'

They journeyed to the same abandoned building behind the station that they had used to travel to London Bridge. In the rapidly changing landscape of London, the space only had a short time left before it was knocked down and made into something better. The Wardens would have to find another building in the meantime. All around them, new complexes rose to the sky with phallic defiance, all glass and metal, with tighter security that would make it difficult for Downers to just walk inside and use the lifts. Absently, Gerald considered the human-passing Downers that would apply as doorkeepers and receptionists around the city to allow their fellow underground citizens free access around London.

Claudia Warden, five years old and new on the job, greeted them on the fifth floor from beneath a hood that was too big for her.

'Good afternoon.'

'Good afternoon!' said Gerald. Blythe stared at her sceptically.

'Goinggg Dowwwn!' said Claudia. She jabbed at the buttons, whispering the sequence to herself to make sure she got it right.

'Well done, thank you!' said Gerald once their journey ended. The pair had been taken to Downey city centre.

'This isn't where we wanted to go,' snapped Blythe. Gerald looked back at the lift. Claudia waved at them, a massive arch of a motion that made her whole body sway with it. The hood flopped over her eyes.

'Oh, aren't they just extraordinary. What a lovely family. She's adorable,' said Gerald as he waved back at her.

'Where are you off to now?'

Gerald adjusted his coat. 'I did need to speak to Mr Crow. He sent me a message to ask if we could accompany Peaches to prom, considering what happened in South Kensington. Amy said she'd be up for it. I think she's just desperate to get out of the house before she gets too depressed.'

'Quite. Well, he won't be in his office for a while. You can join me for lunch at mine if you want.'

'Oh? You're inviting me to lunch.'

'If you want.'

'How kind, Blythe.'

'If you want.'

'I would love to.'

'Ugh.' Blythe rolled his eyes, hailed a carriage, and hosted Gerald for lunch.

As Gerald made his way to City Hall, he felt a sharp tremor in his Hammerspace that signalled a new name in his Grim

Book. He slid onto one of the benches that ran the length of Downey's version of Whitehall. Normally he would wait until he was home, but the afternoon's events had left him jittery and in need of the relief of an assassination. Regretfully, he agreed with Blythe. His senseless killing on Amy's behalf now made him feel uncomfortable in the sobriety of passing time. Even worse, he knew Amy would be horrified to hear about what he had done. A legitimate assassination would calm him down a little. Flicking open the Book, he frowned at the name scrawled in the customary red.

'Nadine Samson?' he said. He phoned his father.

'Son.'

'Hi Dad.'

A pause. 'What's the matter?'

'Hasn't been a good day.' Gerald leaned back on the bench, pinching the bridge of his nose to ward off the incoming headache he could feel swelling behind his eyes. 'Amy's in a bad way. I did something just now that I regret. You know, I just wanted some justice after the house burning.'

'You murdered someone.'

'Yes. Four.'

'Son . . .'

'I know. I'll be better.'

'You're Awakened now. You know that puts you in a fragile state of mind. You'll be quicker to anger and more emotional than you were before. It's like a puberty that never resolves itself. You'll be constantly swaying between emotions, sometimes reacting in ways that seem alien. It's because you're sharing your body with hundreds – thousands of powers. You cannot afford to be irresponsible. You're not like the rest of us, and I shouldn't have to explain why.'

'I know. I know.'

'I'm worried about your liaisons with this human.'

'Please, Father. Don't start.'

'Gethsemane.'

At the sound of his real name, Gerald straightened his posture. His father then admonished him in the Grimtongue, and he felt much worse than before.

'I apologise,' he said.

'You know I love you, Gerald. You are the best of us, so I want the best for you.'

'Understood.'

'Please do the cleansing after this.'

'I will.'

'Now' – Father's tone relaxed instantly – 'what did you call me for? I doubt it was to vent.'

'No . . . no, it was about this new name, actually.'

'Ah yes, Nadine.'

'Who is this?'

There was another pause as his father clinked glasses around in the background. Gerald heard the tinkering *plop* as a sugar cube was dropped into hot water. A breeze made the phone crackle lightly, and Gerald could almost feel the light sprinkling of sand that inevitably came with it. The main house was right in the middle of the desert in the hottest region. They were surrounded by miles of golden sand. It was a volatile area, and the heat was vicious, but it was beautiful in its isolation. The dark, icy swell of Downstairs, and the fluctuating climate of London Upstairs, could never compare.

'I thought you knew,' his father said.

'Me? Why would I know?'

'This was a request from the Home Secretary, so I assumed Ms Samson was a politician.'

'Oh,' Gerald frowned, thinking. There had been a lot of

cabinet reshuffles in the wake of the Sir Alastair dossier, so he hadn't kept up with the local parliamentary roster. He made a mental note to chase this up later.

'Was there a reason given for this request?'

'No. Which makes me think it's politically motivated.'

'Ah.'

Government ministers loved omitting the reasons for their requests, often to absolve themselves of guilt. They assumed the Reapers would always assassinate indiscriminately and they would have their enemies eliminated without a second thought. It was the first sign of a person desperate to have their request fulfilled quickly. He could imagine that the Sir Alastair fallout would encourage others to hide their own reasons in the future in case a Reaper failed to complete a request before certain truths could be hidden. It made Gerald glad to know the elites were scrambling to keep their corruption secret.

'Well,' Gerald said, 'I'll look into this before accepting. I just have to meet with Mr Crow to discuss the prom thing.'

'Oh, well you mustn't miss the opportunity to let your hair down. Death is a burden, Gerald. It can weigh heavy.'

'So I see.'

'Cheer up, son. Just don't repeat the mistake.'

'Thanks, Dad.'

Gerald felt lighter after he hung up, but he still took time to contemplate the events of the afternoon. When he felt slightly better about himself, he journeyed to Lex Crow's office to discuss the upcoming prom. Tyrell Bane had just lost his executives – the prom might be the perfect opportunity for his retaliation.

CHAPTER FIVE

Amy

The previous two days had been a blur. On the night of the fire, after all the statements and questions, Amy crashed and burned on the bed Gerald provided for her. She had imprisoned herself in the room ever since, flickering between sleep and wakefulness in a cocoon of silk paisley sheets, a lamb's wool mattress, and down feather pillows. The nightmares had been the worst: constant images of the house bursting into flames; a shadow of her grandmother imprinted on brick and plaster; the wailing of her spirit as her beloved treasures fell apart into ash. Amy should have been more careful – she knew they were being watched and followed. She had grown arrogant in Gerald's impenetrable defence.

The room he gifted her was mocking in its opulence. Bedposts of varnished bocote converged into a four-pointed star above her head. Thick velvet curtains protected her from the piercing sunrise coming from a wall of windows that overlooked the King's Cross skyline. When she finally gathered herself to get a wash, her feet graced a wool rug that was feathery in its softness. She forced herself to look at her reflection after not wanting to acknowledge her own existence for two days. Puffy eyes, a sallow complexion, and hair that was matted and dry because her bonnets were all burned to shea butter crisps in Streatham. She sighed and went to the en suite bathroom.

The floorboards were warm, and the turquoise tiles that covered the walls and ceiling were so shiny she could see her reflection in them. A free-standing copper bath faced another floor-length window from its place in the centre of the room. She stared at it, wishing for water that was so hot it would burn the stench of ash and soot from her skin.

The drain stopper snapped itself shut and water burst from the taps. She jumped backwards, staring at the bath.

'Okay . . . all right. I'm guessing you heard me?'

Not quite. I read desires. The voice was light and serene. She felt it more than heard it – a twinge in the middle of her head, something like a dizzy spell or the first signs of migraine.

'Well, thanks,' she said. She slipped out of her clothes and tested the water with one wary foot, then the ankle, and before long she was neck-deep in water. She closed her eyes and rested her head against the rim of the bath. From the steam, she could smell mint and tea tree.

'What's your name?' she asked the bath.

Copper is fine.

'I'm Amy.'

Pleased to meet you.

'I needed this,' she whispered.

She plunged her head under the water. When she resurfaced, there was a tray of As I Am Curl Clarity Shampoo, as well as oils and butters to moisturise her hair. She tapped Copper appreciatively, and then began looking after herself again.

When Gerald returned later that evening, he looked surprised to see her on the sofa in the living room. His relief was a sharp, intense feeling. She watched him, smiling at his elation. 'Can't mope around forever.'

'But you're well within your rights to do so,' Gerald said.

'I suppose.'

Gerald shrugged off his coat and sat opposite her. He rolled up his sleeves. She noticed that he automatically checked his gloves to make sure they were tightly secured.

'Have the police contacted you at all?' he asked.

'Yeah. They wanted to go over a few things, but honestly, we both know they won't find the culprits. Not when magic's involved. They're already saying shit about accidental gas leaks and whatnot.'

'True,' Gerald said it slowly. He was avoiding her gaze. 'Blythe found the culprits. They're in prison.'

'*What?*'

'And I killed some of them.'

'Gerald!' Amy staggered to her feet, demanding an explanation.

When Gerald told her what had transpired in the London Bridge prison, she flopped back in the chair. Damask cushions rolled to the floor around her. She was annoyed that Blythe of all people had found her arsonists, and she was shocked that Gerald had killed four of them. She felt numb, stuck between satisfaction, anger, and the pain of so much loss.

'Bane?' she asked.

'Nothing yet. But they disclosed the possible locations of his hideouts. Blythe's sent two of his men on a search. Bane's elusive, as we kind of saw from his room in the den. But he's clearly making moves now. We just need to pin him down.'

'That bastard. I did nothing to him.'

'I know.'

'Why'd he get them to burn my grandma's house?'

Gerald shrugged helplessly. His aura was a whirlwind of half-formed ideas.

'This is what I get for following a little princess around. What will you do to make it up to me?'

'Whatever you want?'

She had been joking, slightly, but his guilt was so potent, it made her feel sorry for him.

'You don't have to feel that bad,' she said quietly. 'I get it. You're an assassin. You're in all sorts, and I chose to follow you. He's a coward. I don't see him going after Blythe's house. Or *this* place. He'd know not to.'

'Hmm. I think they hold humans in contempt. You've seen before, with Megan and Clover, how some creatures are disdainful towards the non-supernatural world. And it's easy for those types to get overly conceited; they have so many humans at their beck and call, promising them something as ridiculous as magic powers if they do as they're told. You're all collateral to Downers like that.'

'Well, why don't they come out of the shadows? Start living in the open if they don't care about us?' Amy folded her arms, cussing them repeatedly in her head. The sofa depressed beside her as Gerald sat down. She felt better now that he was more at ease, but there was a sense of danger overriding her otherwise calmer thoughts. She was now heavily involved in this world and her face would be known by Downers all over the city, both friend and enemy. Even if she wanted to leave it all behind and return to the normal land of Upstairs, she would be a target for someone. Megan's shocked, somewhat envious words came back to her now – hundreds of Downers would kill to be in her position. She wondered whether the witch had meant this literally.

Gerald cleared his throat, pulling her away from the depths of her thoughts. 'Would you like dinner? I can take you somewhere out to eat. I'm guessing, based on the loungewear that you've got on now, that you've seen the wardrobes?'

'Yeah. Thanks for getting me so many clothes so quickly.'

'You're welcome. Honestly, it's not even the least I could do. There's a restaurant next door that's quite nice – the Midland Grand. I thought it best to keep things local and not wander around London too much, considering what's happened.'

'Sure, I don't mind. I guess we should discuss the big prom night tomorrow while we're at it?'

Gerald paused. 'You don't have to do it if you don't want to.'

'Nah. Staying here will get me depressed. Anyway, I think it'd be interesting to see how magic kids get down.'

'You'd be surprised.'

Once Amy was changed and ready for the evening, she said, 'Any chance I'll get to see these wastemen who burned up my grandma's house? You know, the ones still alive?'

'We can visit them anytime.'

'Great.'

Gerald radiated peace, and it soothed her. The Reaper treated Amy to a meal of great expense, and she relished the sliver of luxury amid the charred ruins of her life. When their evening drew to a close, she felt at ease, but an unnatural weightlessness disturbed her body. The destruction of Nan's house had severed something within her, and she had to face yet another loss.

CHAPTER SIX
Gerald

At midnight, the significance of Gerald's prior behaviour weighed on his shoulders. He forsook sleep and approached the tapestry beside his bed. It was the entrance to a private arboretum, the door of which could only be opened by a Grimtongue command. He promptly sealed the door behind him in case Amy could feel the devastation of the space, and he was wary of disturbing her.

Inside, a ceiling of dazzling light bulbs pelted energy onto exotic trees and wildlife, and the ground was soft with fresh earth, a self-manicuring lawn, and an expansive flower bed. The air was thick with the peppery scent of pollen and the sickly sweetness of nectar. It was a solemn occasion to visit the arboretum, and he walked in purposeful silence among the flower bushes, staring straight ahead at the small rock shrine as it rose from an untouched pond. He stripped before the shrine, unsheathing his gloves first and removing his socks last, then he plunged into the icy water. The cold was startling, but he ignored it to stand directly before the grey stone of the shrine.

The rectangular stele was like a tombstone. Its face was engraved with the Grimscript names of hundreds of Reapers that came before him. The script was crudely written, as if gouged from the stone with talons. These Reapers were failures, their actions forever written in the stele. Unlike their lauded counterparts whose souls were sealed into stars that lovingly caressed newly Awakened Reapers with their powers, the arboretum names patrolled the boundary of chaos – a warning against succumbing to bloodlust. They had grown drunk on Death's Vengeance and killed unapologetically outside of their requests: unrepentant murderers basking in the curse on their hands. After failed meetings and tireless mediations that led nowhere, the failures were executed by the Tribe heads of their respective eras, by which time they were babbling spectres, lost to ecstatic violence. It had been two hundred years since the last Reaper execution.

Gerald dipped his head in the water, rubbed his face with his bare hands, then broke the surface with a gasp. The names of the failures began to bleed in response. Great globs of blood swelled in every joint and curve of the engraved names, then ran into the pond. Gerald dipped his head again. When he re-emerged, the shrine wept. When he dipped a third time, the pond was dyed red, and the face of the stele was scarlet and sticky and wet. He saw his reflection in the surface of the pond – his eyes were the same colour as the shrine now, and glowing.

He wanted to speak to Armageddon again, to ask if he was at risk of becoming a failure and destroying everyone's expectations of him. If Gerald succumbed to his bloodlust, it would mean his Tribespeople would lose faith in the light that baptised him when he was born and it would imply Armageddon was a lie – that Gerald, as Death's Medium, had been wrongly chosen.

Unbeknown to Amy, something else existed within him, something that marred his personal history in blood-soaked sand and a crowd of frightened Tribal faces. His Wall was his only defence against it. Now, he felt that presence move, pulsing angrily against its stone prison, desperate for release.

Gerald blinked, and bloody tears fell copiously down his face. Trembling with the shock of it all, he clasped his hands together as if in prayer, bowed his head, and asked for forgiveness in the Grimtongue. His body ached, and he hoped that somewhere, Armageddon was listening to his pleas.

CHAPTER SEVEN

Gerald

'Son.'

'Hello, Dad.'

'How are things going with you?'

'Much better, thank you. I did the cleansing.'

'That's clear. Your voice isn't so heavy. Have you seen the news? Upstairs, I mean.'

'No?' Gerald automatically checked the fresh pile of papers Zis had left on the coffee table. There was still much discussion about the Sir Alastair dossier, as well as news of the suicide of one Mike Carrington.

'Imogen Carrington's husband?' he asked.

'Yes. I don't know if you remember, but Michael was from humble beginnings and married Imogen as a come-up, even taking her surname to get him into places. They didn't get on well, and everyone said he felt emasculated working as a mere security guard at Belmarsh.'

'Well, it is his father-in-law's company. He could have left if he didn't like it.'

'Not if he was hoping to get inheritance from it. It must have pained him to put on that uniform every day.'

'Dad' – Gerald flicked through *The Times*, scanning for more information about the dossier fallout – 'you're not saying he killed himself in despair? He wouldn't do *that*.'

'Of course he wouldn't.'

Gerald paused. 'Murder?'

'It's a matter of technicality. The first coroner called it undetermined, the second classed it as suicide. Someone was paid off. Read *The Guardian*'s report – you won't get enough information from *The Times*.'

Gerald did as he was told, his frown increasing the more he learned of the situation. Mike and Imogen had been separated for several months before his death and he had been a security guard stationed at the home of Henry Butler, the senior MP named over eighty times in Sir Alastair's dossier. Henry Butler was an ally of the Carringtons but an ominous paragraph in *The Guardian* suggested that Mike Carrington could have been an informant, providing evidence against Butler for Sir Alastair's damning report. It would have been a fruitful revenge against his estranged wife to contribute to the downfall of this long-time partner of the Carrington empire. Butler had done many things for them, including securing major contracts for their flagship enterprise WCT Security.

'Well, if they had the means to kill people themselves, why bother making a request to us for Sir Alastair?' Gerald asked. He promptly folded the paper and tossed it on the table.

'We were just a way to declutter their schedule, it seems.' Father said it with humour, but Gerald could hear the irritation in his voice.

'Should we refuse their next request?'

'Oh, of course. Let them manage their own affairs for a little while. Anyway, enough gossip, are you prepared for tonight?'

'Yes. A good old prom.'

'And will the human be in attendance?'

'Amy? Yes, Dad, she will.'

'Hmph.'

'My behaviour the other day was all my own; nothing to do with her.'

'If you say so.'

Gerald gripped the phone. A breeze crackled down the receiver, but it sounded cold. Harsh flecks of sand peppered the air, almost beating against his ear. The silence that remained was of the wind only, no chimes, no bells, no spoon against porcelain, no patter of running tea.

'I have to go. Speak to you later,' Gerald said. He ended the call and rested the phone on the table. The screen remained blank: one plain rectangular void offering a silent accusation.

CHAPTER EIGHT

Amy

Sunset spilled through the clocktower window of Gerald's living room. Donning a rose silk dress with spaghetti straps, Amy packed her hair in a pineapple bun. The shoes Gerald had gifted her waited beside the front door. He appeared on the spiral staircase from his own room shortly afterwards. The simple skinny-fit suit he wore – all black – made him look much older than usual. He had on a pair of skin-tight leather gloves, and his fade was fresh.

'I feel like we're going to a movie premiere or something,' Amy said once her hair was done. 'And what kind of school prom *starts* at ten? You lot really are without morals.'

'Well, it *is* a Friday. The party normally goes on well after midnight. Some of the older teens even have after-parties. Everyone loves prom.'

'I bet they do.'

'You look nice, by the way.'

'Thanks. So do you.' Gerald smiled at her.

She had been worried before; his aura had been thick with annoyance for most of the day. It read *I'm tired of everyone right now* and she had been too considerate to ask why.

'Are you feeling better now?' she asked as he flopped on the sofa beside her.

Gerald raised his brows in surprise before answering, 'I'm okay. Was I in a mood earlier?'

'Kind of.'

'I'm sorry.' He rubbed his temples, then plunged his hand into his abdomen to get his Grim Book. 'Just the usual Reaper fare. And there's someone else on my list that I need to look into before assassinating. I haven't accepted yet.'

Despite her misgivings about the Book, Amy shuffled beside him to read the name. 'Nadine Samson? *That* Nadine Samson?'

'Oh? Someone you know?'

'You *don't?*' Amy grabbed for her phone, then quickly searched the name. As expected, the image of a young beautiful Black woman appeared on her screen. The woman was often photographed in the all-black attire of an American revolutionary, but she was British, and well-known in activist circles. She was the leader of Kill Blue Meadow, which was in reference to an infamous detention centre. Blue Meadow was a prison in which those without state and unmoored from their distant homes were punished for their vulnerability. Nadine Samson coordinated die-ins at airports across the country to block unfair deportations and had organised an upcoming peace march around Blue Meadow for supposed human rights violations. Even as she briefly scanned Samson's biography, Amy smiled in admiration.

'*That's* her?' Gerald frowned in confusion.

'Yeah. Who the fuck asked you to kill her?'

'The Home Secretary.'

They stared at each other.

'Gerald!' said Amy. 'You better not!'

He appeared to weigh her words, and the waves of his aura lapped with uncertainty. At last, he nodded. 'Okay. I won't. But it's quite a big thing for someone of that status to ask my Tribe for an assassination. Is a local activist really such a big threat?'

'Maybe the Home Secretary doesn't want a lil' Black woman coming along and messing up the deportations. Let me look a bit more.'

As she scrolled the most recent news about Nadine Samson, a notification appeared across the screen that almost made her scream. She gripped her phone, tilted it to read the foreign letters from another angle in case she had lost her mind and was seeing nonsense, then expanded it, her heart thumping in her chest. Beside her, Gerald craned his neck to read it.

'Ah, great,' he said. 'You've been paid.'

Amy turned to him. 'By *whomst*?'

'My family. This has been a busy month so far, so there's a backlog. But this is what you're owed for being my partner. We split the assassination fee now.'

'Oh my God.' Amy flicked though her Natwest app again. A quarter of a million pounds was just sitting there in her bank account.

Gerald sighed. 'I know it's not a lot, considering—'

'Shut up, just stop being overly rich for a minute. Are you *sure* about this? I haven't even gone with you on all of them!'

'It's more than enough, Amy. Your house is gone. In London, that's not even enough for you to buy it back.'

He became enshrouded in a potent deluge of guilt. The pain of it was vicious, a bitingly cold watermark on her skin. She rested her hands on his shoulders to look at him properly.

'Thank you,' she said. 'It's enough, honestly. Is this the kind of money you normally get paid? Because I could fully leave my library job for this.'

'I hope you do.'

Amy paused. It had crossed her mind once before, but

now that her house was gone, her job was the final artefact of her life with Nan. It was more than a government building – the library was her second home. 'Well, I'll think about it.' She said it playfully, not wanting to cause Gerald more worry.

He snorted in response.

As they left the apartment, Amy slipped on her shoes. 'I'm kinda looking forward to this prom after all!'

Gerald glanced at her. 'So I see.'

They quickly left the Renaissance Hotel. Gerald whisked them across the street to the lifts in the adjoining block of flats. Carole scrutinised Amy, her aura spiked with jealousy, and she muttered to herself as she made the cerasee tea. Amy ignored her. Nothing could ruin tonight, not even the bitter tea or the vendetta that the Warden family seemed to have against her.

Carole deposited them on the street next to the Crow residence. All around, the teenagers of the Downstairs social elite bundled into hired carriages in their best gowns and suits, all on their way to prom. Several Downers shot curious glances at Amy and Gerald, most likely wondering why two grown adults had decided to outdress school children at their own event. They picked up the pace on the path leading to the Crows' front door. Although Peaches had planned to be fashionably late, there was no point if she missed her cue.

Peaches flounced out of her home in a wave of silk magnolia, her face expectant for Gerald's verdict.

'Wonderful,' he said. Amy trailed behind them and was the last to be seated in the waiting carriage. They rolled across the cobbles through the city centre, taking the long way to Greymalkin's to ensure every Downer possible could witness Peaches Crow's debut. The onlookers acquiesced, waving at the glossed windows and shouting raucous well-wishes. The swell of jubilation was dizzyingly high, and a flush of sweltering rose filled the confines of the carriage. Amy observed Peaches, her shining eyes and flushed cheeks, and the way her smile tightened, as if trying to lock tears away. Her hands were held firm in her lap, fingers laced together as if in prayer, and her knees trembled, a slight vibration that assimilated into the sway and shudder of their journey. Amy reached forward and placed a tentative hand over Peaches'. The mage flinched and stared at Amy with well-contained shock.

'You look great,' she said. 'It'll be a fun night.'

Peaches nodded. When she blinked, the glassy sheen in her eyes evaporated. She returned her gaze to the window, flashed a smile, and finally offered the crowd a wave in return.

They stopped at the purple carpet of Greymalkin's. A growing crowd of younger students, barred from the event, lined the entrance with their camera phones held aloft.

'Mr Reaper, you must escort me to the door,' said Peaches.

'Oh? Oh.'

'Go on, *Mr Reaper*,' said Amy. 'Make her night memorable.'

Gerald refused to look at Amy, but he held a cordial expression, exiting the carriage first to gallantly help Peaches down the swaying steps. A chorus of breathless gasps rose from the crowd, like the whisper of endless rain, and the real cameras appeared now as lightning flashes, blinding Amy as she squirmed in her corner of the carriage. She watched Peaches dominate the carpet before her adoring fans. She and Gerald planned to stay outside and patrol the event at regular intervals, but when Gerald emerged from the interior of the school, he looked troubled.

'What's up?' asked Amy.

'A text from Blythe. Looks like they've made some

interesting discoveries in the hideouts: Bane's definitely been in them, but they've all been ransacked so far. He's covering his bases and seems frantic.'

'Is that a good or a bad thing?'

'Depends. Sometimes people make stupid mistakes when they panic. Or they grow more violent.'

'True . . .' She paused because the crowds thinned outside. Peaches had fulfilled her desire to be fashionably late as the last pupil of note to arrive at the prom. As the prickly adolescent auras dispersed, and the general milieu of excitable Downers slipped into the wind, there was nothing to mask the aura that Amy recognised. There was a sharp, acrid stain on the air, so faint as to be almost unnoticeable, but it was now burned into Amy's skin and seared on the insides of her skull. Like the ashes of Nan's house, it had left a noticeable mark in her mind.

'Bane's here,' she whispered. Gerald froze, staring at her.

'What did you—'

'Or . . . he's not *here*. He was close. A few roads down. I can . . .' Amy concentrated, shutting away Gerald's powerful presence and ignoring the furore inside the school. She could feel Tyrell Bane slipping away, but a thin line connected her to his location. 'Can we take this carriage down there?' she said, pointing back towards the city. 'It's weird. He was Downstairs earlier. That's what it feels like anyway. His aura's so faint now . . . fuck.'

Gerald leaned over the window and made a command to the carriage. It moved on its own. He said nothing as Amy parsed, watching her anxiously. She held herself, her body numb with the tension of finding him here, meandering Downstairs, so flagrant and carefree. The carriage swayed ominously, disturbing her equilibrium. The creaking wood of their transport was like the groan of an old boat. Outside, a sea of Downers parted for them, and all the while, the glinting, mocking pulse of Tyrell Bane remained. Amy told Gerald what she felt, and he talked to the carriage, and eventually, they rested on Whitehall at the base of the mayor's office in City Hall.

The pair scrambled out of the carriage with Amy leading the way. Then she stopped because the aura did.

'What? What's happened?' asked Gerald.

'Gone,' she said.

The building was in darkness. Only the vestiges of City Hall's staff remained inside, as everyone else had returned home. She felt a wave of power beside her, and watched with keen interest as Gerald scrutinised the building's interior, his irises illuminated by scarlet, his face firm in concentration.

'No one's in there,' he said. 'Mr Crow's Upstairs with his wife, keeping a low profile. They have a third home they've hidden in for the time being. I can't see Bane in here.'

'It feels like he just vanished here on this spot,' said Amy. She remembered the chase in South Kensington: how Gerald had transferred his Hammerspace to the ground, and how Bane had allowed his executive to escape them by the same method. 'Can you use a Hammerspace tunnel to get Upstairs from here?'

'No. That's not allowed and it's impossible. He would have come Downstairs using the lift, but he has access to brilliant disguises, ones that can even bypass the Wardens' detection. Mr Crow was right to be concerned; Bane really was after him next. It's all but confirmed that he knows Crow made a request for him now.'

'And it would've been the perfect time to kill him or whatever,' said Amy. 'Everyone's focused on the prom, you're helping Peaches, *Gardien*'s running around looking for his hideouts. No one would've known until tomorrow!'

Gerald tapped at his phone. 'I'm calling Blythe. If Bane came here and left, we'll have to talk to the Wardens.'

Amy waited in fractured patience. Bane's aura continued to disperse, unspooling into the distance. They only had a little time to find him before whatever essence he left around London vanished completely. Gerald and Blythe's conversation was brief.

'Let's go to the Mason residence,' he said. Afterwards, they flitted to Nightingale.

INTERLUDE: THE WITCH

The grapevine of rumours was unbearably thick of late, so it was difficult to decipher Tyrell's movements. Melanie had exerted most of her energy scrying through the ether for a glimpse of him, aching to find out where he was. When he was not in his usual hideout, she grew restless and desperate, worried he had been arrested or killed.

Two weeks ago, she had peered into her cauldron and found herself watching Megan's bedroom. She now knew it had been an instinctive decision, seeking the wisdom of her older sister during a time of crisis, but instead of recoiling from the image and searching elsewhere, Melanie had stayed. She kept watch, taking in the lilac walls and cramped shelves, the wilting vines and overripe mandrakes, and remembered when they were living in Willow Drive in the streak of tar that was their childhood home.

The *Nightly Moon* had branded Melanie as a parricidal cancer. At one point, it was implied she had led Tyrell astray, that she was a domineering mastermind, fatal to males both human and Downer. But enough people were aware of her family, its abuse and dysfunction, to know the truth. The Willow Drive witches were callous and unrelenting to residents that discarded the unspoken social codes of the neighbourhood, and so, even though they were aware of

Melanie's plight, they did nothing to help, and relegated the Lavenders to the enclaves of pariahdom.

Grettan and Argot Lavender had clung onto their cottage in a sleepy witch idyll by winning the lottery when most had hoped for an eventual Cruickstown relocation. Friendless and isolated, the Lavender parents spoke only to each other: acrid words that burned through the walls and left a stink outside.

Tonight, Melanie steeped bay leaves in hot water, reeling from the shadows of her childhood. She added one dried honeycomb, some cloves, a splash of vodka, and little white shards of cracked pixie bone taken from the wing joints. Her special ingredients were running dangerously low now, and she had not the time nor luxury to barter on the illegal market for supplies. Once again, desperation drove her, and she waited for the potion to cool, where it turned a sickly peach hue and thickened to the consistency of polenta. As she stirred the mixture, she caught a glimpse of scarring around her wrist, the faint crocodile prints of a rope tied too tightly, and was gifted with the assault of a memory she wanted to abandon.

Whenever loneliness and fear overwhelmed her, and she was trapped in the molasses of self-doubt, she would remember Grettan tying her to his bedpost while Argot pretended to cook something in the kitchen. Grettan's temper tended to flare against Melanie often, and she would be beaten and verbally hounded until she was a weeping wreck, a burn stain on the wall. Her father always did this when Megan was out at work, but one time, the elder sister came home early, and she hexed Grettan until he cowered beside the mantlepiece. Afterwards, she moved Melanie into her bedroom.

Megan was good with hexes, which is why, when Melanie had stumbled across her room during her thoughtless scrying session, and Megan saw the baleful eyes of her little sister glowing in her bedroom window, she made a sign with such precision as to appear as a sleight of hand. There was a quiver of her fingers for a passing moment, and then Melanie was dragged away from the scrying surface and fell off her chair. She had felt her skin burn and she ran to her mirror to see Megan's work. She was now marked with a permanent curse that forced her to stay hidden from the Lads. Melanie's current self-exile in the Duck Island Cottage, at first a refuge by choice, was now an inconvenient necessity.

As the witch pasted the freshly made concoction on her skin, running it over the scars on her wrist, she wondered if there was more to Megan's behaviour. That night, when her older sister had saved her from Grettan, they had turned the lights off and sank onto the bed together. In the dark solitariness of Megan's room, they made plans to escape the house once they had saved up enough money. Then they would travel and see the other hidden magic cities all over the world. Megan didn't know that Melanie had already met Tyrell by that point, and that he had already saved her, and proposed a way to rid the world of Grettan, and his passive enabler Argot, for good.

Had she betrayed Megan? She paused now, watching the peach potion rest discomfortingly atop the cursed skin of her forearm. A raw anger pulsed in her stomach and she bit her lip until blood pooled in her mouth. No, Megan had betrayed *her*. How realistic was it, really, given all of Melanie's bruises, reddened cheeks, tender steps, and harrowed expressions, for Megan to remain unaware for so long?

Megan was just like Argot: ignoring what she did not

understand and feigning ignorance so she could enjoy a life of pitiful aspiration, modifying her clothes from the vintage emporiums to match the latest trends, wearing the same straw hats as the other witches, and dyeing her hair stupid colours. She carried paintbrushes and notepads in her fake leather satchel, complained about the science boys in Greymalkin's postgraduate department, and purposely came home late after the beatings had long since ended.

Megan was just like their father, who hobbled resentfully in the matriarchal morgue that was his house because his lack of talent excluded him from the Warlock's Workshop, so he had cloaked himself in pity and sorrow. He became the victim of the family, grinding them down until they had no choice but to appease and pamper him. Megan was the smart sister, the one who stood a chance to redeem the Lavenders' social standing, so all it took was a harrowing sigh, a loud musing about what life could be like if only she could attend such-and-such a party or audition for whatever art class or theatre troupe passed through their neighbourhood, and her parents would adhere to her every shameless demand. The only one who understood Melanie was Tyrell.

Melanie almost tipped her cauldron over. She shot to her feet and paced the dusty ground, then without thinking, slid the window open to get some air. She saw the night sky looming above her, and the stars shining against the side of the slumbering pink pelican of St James's Park, and the distant lights of the city shimmering between the trees, and her underling staring back at her from the windowpane.

The witch hissed and slammed the window shut, reactivating the concealing enchantment on the cottage. She was too late; a moment of emotional weakness had disarmed her, and now, a human – one of her own – had seen her. Now he knew his boss was not a human.

A tentative knock on the door stilled her once more. She swore under her breath, then turned to let him in. She only opened the door a crack, but the underling – Ennis – swept into the cottage with unbecoming force. He spun in the darkness to gape at her and her strangely coloured skin, then he scanned her dwellings with a look of wonder, noting the cauldron and the herbs and the supernatural paraphernalia.

'What are you doing here?' she asked. 'How did you even know where I was?'

Ennis did not answer immediately. He continued to note all the oddities of the cottage, then shoved his hands in his pockets, his smirk sly and knowing. It made Melanie wonder how long her Lads had suspected her of being supernatural. Ennis rested his weight on one leg as he at last refocused on her. 'I . . . I have ways of knowing, boss.'

Melanie grimaced. This was not the demeanour of an underling. Ennis thought himself on equal footing now, having uncovered her secret. His eyes shone with the darkness of extortion. The witch relaxed, watching him closely.

'And why'd you come?' she asked.

Ennis nodded. It was an acknowledgement of joint collusion. He quirked a smile at her, quite clearly satisfied. Presently, he unfolded an envelope from his inner jacket and placed it on the nearby table. Before, he would have presented it to her hands. Ennis pointed at the document with his chin.

'I would've sent these to you directly, but if you got hacked in any way, it would've been bad. And I did try to call you, but your phone kept going to unavailable. I can see why.' He snorted, looked at her once more, and shook his head in wonder. 'Boss, what are you?'

Melanie ignored him. She stalked over to the envelope and scanned its contents. Here was a list of all of Darkhouse's businesses, which were now at risk thanks to the Channel controversy. This was fantastic intel: she could buy these back as leverage and offer her services to Tyrell for a price. He needed her help. She wanted to give it.

'Well done, Ennis,' said Melanie. 'I'm a witch, by the way.'

She turned to Ennis directly. He was much taller than Melanie, but she held his gaze with such intensity that he looked away from her with a husky laugh.

'A witch, yeah? Broomsticks and that?'

'Broomsticks and that. Look.'

She gestured to the vodka bottle beside her cauldron, and it lifted from the wood. A quick gesture, like the sharp tugging of stubborn blinds, cracked the bottle into thick, jagged shards. Melanie beckoned to the largest shard and sent it shooting towards Ennis. It sank into his chest and punctured his heart. He staggered backwards, staring dumbly at his wound and the swell of blood that rapidly drenched his polo shirt and jacket, and a spray of crimson gushed from his mouth. He crumpled to the ground, staring at her with eyes of bewildered pain. Melanie crouched beside him, watching his gaping mouth, and how freely it filled with blood, how the blood spilled over and swamped him, caressing his head as a velvet cushion, giving him a glimpse of luxury in death. She met his eyes again, all but forcing him to look at her as he died, and only when he stopped pitifully gurgling did she stand upright.

Melanie snatched up the envelope again. She stepped over

Ennis and settled into a nearby chair, making notes on the easiest of Tyrell's businesses to purchase first.

'Very well done, Ennis,' she muttered. Behind her, Ennis stared unblinkingly at the ceiling.

With this information, she would find Tyrell. When she found Tyrell, everything would make sense again.

PART THREE

Pursuit

Magic Practitioners: Witches and Warlocks

Creatures born with the ability to harness the natural magic from the earth. Magic practitioners have long lifespans, superstrength, and possess more durable bodies than humans. They are split into categories dependent on their skill and manifestation of magic.

Witches

Channel magic via nature (flora and fauna, animals, blood) and can conjure spells out of thin air. Potions and Familiarcraft (animal companions) are their specialties. The Grand Coven et Familiaris is their governing body. Downstairs, witches primarily live in Willow Drive and the Nile Valley. Usually female presenting.

Warlocks

Channel magic via nature (flora and fauna, animals). Unlike witches, they ground their magic into powder. These spells are then stored in breakable phials. Hammerspace manipulation is their speciality. The Warlock Workshop is their governing body. Usually male presenting.

CHAPTER ONE

Amy

The mansion was packed. It was the first time Amy had seen it as such. Instead of the usual smoke-stained office, Archer led the pair to a large dining room. The shine of the marble floor tiles and the film of dust on the shell-coloured piano denoted a room in a state of regular disuse. Blythe watched his guests behind steepled fingers, his demeanour irritable. Amy glanced around the table at the strange assortment of people she would come to know as the agents of *Gardien*, Blythe's private secret service.

A witch with long braids watched Blythe attentively beside her *Gardien* partner, a pale vampire with shoulder-length hair dyed neon green. The vampire's totally black eyes were like blocks of coal amid his chalk-white face. He was totally disinterested, staring straight ahead at the candle chandelier that hung precariously over the dining table.

Amy recognised Josh, the wraith from South Kensington, sitting opposite the witch and vampire. Beside Josh was a werewolf with an unusually calm aura, the heat of his magic pulsing like the warmth of a log fire. His hazel eyes were shrewd, and thick chestnut brown hair fell in coordinated waves around his face. He wrote quickly in a leather notebook as Blythe spoke; staves of elegant cursive ran across the page.

Directly opposite Amy and Gerald was a mage. His staff,

that he rested on the chair beside him, was enshrouded with a power that made Lex Crow look juvenile in comparison. His skin was a deep russet brown. Thick, free-form locs framed a narrow face.

Three empty chairs remained for the agents who were seemingly away on other business.

The group had been in an urgent discussion, but when Amy and Gerald took their seats, all conversation ceased. The witch straightened in her chair and her vampire companion looked mildly curious. The werewolf dropped his pen, and the mage stared at Gerald with reverential intensity. Only Josh was ebullient. He waved at them both, frantically, and his colleagues shot him horrified looks.

Archer appeared with a tray of refreshments in the hot silence. Blythe took the time to help himself to a generous serving of alcohol.

'Good evening, everyone,' said Gerald. 'You've passed on our news, Blythe?'

'No. We were going over our own plans. Dagwood and Brian are staking out Clapham in case Bane makes an appearance there. They've accosted two of his members, but these are lower-level, not aware of Downstairs.'

'The fuckers saw Brian's face,' said the vampire with green hair.

'Oh dear! That must have been a fright. What happens now?' asked Gerald.

'Wraith to the rescue,' said Josh. He dragged the werewolf with him as he stood. 'I'll wipe their memories, it's fine. Also!' He abruptly turned to his partner and slapped him on the shoulder. 'This is Ulrich, Amy! The pissy werewolf I was talking to you about before. It's a full moon tonight, so more stress for me, I guess?'

'I beg your pardon?'

'Both of you get out and do your jobs,' said Blythe.

They left shortly after. Josh had a burst of glee, and Ulrich was sweltering with anger. Amy waved at Josh, trying her best not to laugh at his werewolf partner's expense. She had many questions about their conversation. The most pressing was the mystery of the agent called Brian, and the supposed horrors of his face, but she held the queries in her head with the plan to question Gerald later.

'Right, well, I suppose I should explain what happened earlier?' Gerald asked. When Blythe only shrugged, he faced the others. 'Bane was Downstairs.'

An exclaimed chorus rose from the assembly. The room was spiked with determined rage, and Gerald had to raise his hands, conciliatory, to quieten them. He promptly turned to Amy, which in turn forced the others to acknowledge her. She flushed beneath their gazes, self-conscious to explain the revelations on Whitehall.

'I felt his aura,' she said. Her words were followed by a confused silence.

The mage took a chance, leaning forward in his seat to watch her closely. When he spoke, she noticed his bottom teeth and canines were silver. 'And how do you know what his aura feels like?'

Amy glanced at Gerald before answering. 'We went to his old den and I parsed his stuff. I can sense him from a distance now.'

The mage quirked a sceptical brow, to which Amy said, 'It's the reason I traced him all the way to City Hall.'

'Where did you feel him first?' the mage asked.

'A couple of roads down from Greymalkin's. Then he went through the city centre, down Whitehall, and vanished on the steps of the mayor's office. I'd say he was here about an hour, two hours ago? Not long.'

It was the witch's turn to speak. She marvelled as she regarded Amy. 'You can . . . detect auras from the air? As in, someone can walk through a place, and you can follow them simply based on the vestiges they leave behind?'

'Like a fucking cadaver dog?' said the vampire.

Gerald spoke before she could respond. 'It's how we met. Amy felt my presence on a random street in Camden and followed me all the way to St Pancras through parsing alone. Virtually turned up at my doorstep.'

In the silence, Amy felt the cooling of tension. The diffusion gave way to a panicked awe. They stared at her as if she were an oddity, but their attention was without malice. There was something anthropological about the atmosphere, and she wanted to laugh at the absurdity of it, imagining this group of elite Downers observing her in private and making notes about her abilities. Up to this point, she had been a source of scorn for their kind, and at last she had received acknowledgement. Not since Nan had anyone regarded her as such, and she allowed herself to accept their feelings towards her. In this world, she was the one to be observed and written about; Amy was not inferior to them.

'Well, I'm convinced,' said the witch. 'Dani, by the way. Very impressed.'

'I'm Shaun,' the mage said. His smile was easy as he reclined in his chair. 'And same. I hope you know that's not normal.'

'Is it fuck,' said the vampire. 'Felix.'

Gerald swelled with pride beside her. Blythe's aura warred against it, bitter with frost. Amy tipped her head at their compliments, and they took her gesture with good humour.

'We suspect Bane was trying to confront Mr Crow, based

on his request to me,' said Gerald, returning to business. 'But as his office is closed . . .'

'Bane's just pissed off somewhere, yeah,' said Felix. 'But if you're saying he went like an hour ago, and probably left Downstairs completely, we've missed him, ain't we? Not like we can follow him now.'

'We can,' said Blythe. He still exuded despondence as he addressed them. 'I spoke to the Wardens as soon as Gerald raised the alarm. A lone Downer took the lift to Dalston Kingsland an hour and a half ago. That he was unrecognisable to the Warden stationed there – as well as anyone else in the city – most likely means he was in disguise. In fact, he probably timed it perfectly: the five-year-old was on Warden duty for Dalston.'

'Dalston Kingsland?' said Dani. 'That means he's headed to one of the bases those executives mentioned.'

'Either the shop by Voodoo Rays or Sitton Road,' said Shaun, nodding his agreement.

'As such, I'm splitting you up,' said Blythe. 'Dani will head to Voodoo Rays. Shaun and Felix to Sitton Road. Hollow's patrolling near there so I'll tell him to go with you. I feel it's more likely he's at Sitton Road as it's the last location for us to find on our list. A mage and two vampires makes a suitable team to confront him.'

The group nodded their assent and rose from their chairs. They gathered their belongings to leave.

'Can Amy and I accompany the Sitton Road party? It might provide some clues for my assignment,' said Gerald. The room halted.

'You do what you want. I don't employ you.'

'But you realise that if I see someone on my list tonight, I might have to kill them?'

'Do what you want. I don't employ you.'

Gerald beamed at him. 'Well, as long as I have your blessing.'

'*Do what you want.* All of you, get out of my house. Now. Right now.'

Gerald led the charge to the Mason lawn outside. As he walked, his suit transformed, fluttering away into black petals that disappeared in the wind, and a moment later, he was enshrouded in the spare cloak and veil that he stored in his Hammerspace.

'What about my outfit?' Amy asked. 'I can't really go out on a crime-fighting spree wearing this little thing.'

'Of course!' Gerald plunged his hand into his stomach. 'I have a few more outfits in here. Actually, why don't you step inside? Then you can change with dignity.'

'You can fit someone into your Hammerspace?' asked Dani.

'He's the Reaper. Of course he can,' said Shaun, his staff looking like a scythe on his back. 'Good luck. Let me know if you need any backup.'

Dani saluted. The silvery drawer of her Hammerspace appeared out of thin air. She snatched a broomstick from its confines and departed in an instant, shooting upwards, flying far above the raucous crowds of the city.

Amy turned away from the curiously prying eyes of the others as Gerald cast his Hammerspace on the ground. She had made a spectacle at the *Gardien* meeting, and even though she had been proud to show them just how strong her abilities were, the sobriety of the outside lawn had humbled her a little, and now, all Amy could think about was the inevitable danger she was about to walk into.

When she stepped into the familiar emerald room, Amy could hear muffled conversation outside. She quickly undressed, located a wardrobe of spare clothes, and got changed into something more comfortable. Afterwards, she knocked on the table loudly. The world twisted in a rush of wind, and she was back on Blythe's lawn.

'Wasn't so bad, was it?' Gerald asked quietly.

The group promptly made their way to the nearest lift, continuing a discussion about their next course of action that Amy had missed while getting changed.

'I've texted Hollow where to meet us,' said Felix once they were inside. This lift was manned by Clover. She didn't look at Amy or anyone else as she took them to Dalston. 'Let me say, Mr Reaper. I'm gassed to be working with you, mate. I didn't think this would ever happen. Kinda mad, right, Shaun?'

'Yeah, it is. Pleasure to be working with you tonight. And you, Amy.'

'Yeah, Amy! Sorry about not believing in you before,' said Felix. 'What a team we've got tonight, eh?'

'Oh, please don't expect too much from me,' said Gerald. 'I'll try my best not to get in your way.'

'As if that could ever happen!'

Outside was colder than expected, but surprisingly welcome for Amy. The tension had been so suffocating in Blythe's mansion that the Upstairs atmosphere had a refreshing, healing effect on her body. She could feel the others relax beside her as if someone had loosened their limbs.

They were hidden behind the Dalston market. Empty stalls with tarpaulin covers swayed in the breeze. Plastic carrier bags floated above pavement that was wet with fish scales and blood from butcher shops. A random clue from the hectivity of the daily trade would reveal itself in some way: a lone breadfruit beside a lamp post, a box of rotten Julie mangoes left out for foxes and pigeons to eat, a discarded wig, a disembowelled box of chicken and chips with its fried contents all spilled out on the ground around it.

'Hollow said he'll meet us down at the Sitton Road bus stop,' said Felix. 'All good to go, you lot?'

'I'm good,' said Shaun. 'See ya.' He tapped his staff on the ground and shot into the air. Amy staggered backwards, watching as the mage's outer coat flushed obsidian, unfurling like leather bat wings to carry him unseen into the night.

'Cheater,' said Felix. 'In a bit, you two.'

He darted away from the empty market, leaving behind imprints in the tarmac. His speed rendered him a green smudge on the air.

'They are a lively bunch, aren't they?' said Gerald.

'Makes me wonder what they're doing working for Blythe.'

'I hear the salary is very persuasive.'

Amy considered this, and her own new-found wealth. 'I hear that. I guess we should hurry along too?'

'Right.' Gerald grasped Amy's hand and flitted towards the Sitton Road bus stop. Not to be surpassed, the Reaper made sure he was the first one there.

CHAPTER TWO

Amy

The Sitton Road area was a quiet, hidden neighbourhood in an otherwise frantic and unpredictable district of London. It was comprised of four-storey terraced houses with ivy-adorned pillars on either side of polished front doors, and basements used for wine cellars, man caves, and home offices slumbered beneath them. The number three bus stop, where the strangely assorted *Gardien* assembled, overlooked a corner shop, a chippy, and an antique furniture warehouse. It was now close to midnight and the area was deserted. The silence made Amy nervous. She tried searching for nearby auras but the thrum of humanity slumbered within the confines of their homes.

Something hit the roof of the bus stop and she instinctively ducked away from it. A shadow detached itself from the night sky above and stood amid the group. It was a tall male of athletic build with pearl-white skin and jet back hair that fell to his tail bone. Amy knew he was a vampire before he turned around to reveal his black eyes and angular, handsome face. He offered a pleasant smile to his colleagues.

'All right, Hollow?' Shaun drew him into a side hug.

Hollow's eyes rested on Gerald. 'Wow. The Reaper. Great to have you with us, mate.'

'No problem at all.'

When he saw Amy, his expression hardened. He scrutinised her in wonder, as if she were a rare archaeological discovery. His aura transformed, plunging Amy into a thicket of bloodlust, where a dark mist encircled her, and she was helpless against him. All her thin threats of confronting vampires melted before Hollow. The heat of his irrational desires rested on her skin. The vampire rubbed his neck, and she felt the desert barrenness of his thirst in her own mouth, turning her throat into cement – rough terrain torched by drought. By this point, the rest of the group was looking at him as if he had lost his mind.

'Great,' he said to no one. 'I didn't know someone like this would be here.'

'Someone like what?' asked Amy.

'Ugh, please don't say anything. Makes it worse.'

'Excuse you?'

'Oh, I know what it is!' Felix turned to the bewildered assembly. 'She's his disposition.'

The others nodded as realisation settled. Felix's answer had satisfied them enough to drop the issue completely, leaving Amy in the dark.

'I'm his *what*?' she asked, looking around helplessly.

'Oh, vampires tend to crave the blood type they had when they were human,' Gerald said. 'They can drink any type of blood, but the blood type they favour is the one that gives them more strength. They call that a vampire's disposition. Unless I'm mistaken, Felix?'

'Nah, you got it.'

'Sorry,' Hollow said thickly. He shot an apologetic grimace at Amy before glancing at the others. 'S'gonna be a bit of a distraction for me, not gonna lie.'

'Hollow.' Felix stretched his own arms wide in invitation. 'You can always take some of mine. Come here, Bartholomew.'

Hollow eyed him warily. 'Yeah . . . yeah, okay. Thanks.' His voice was a strangled whisper.

He pinned Felix to the steel shutters of the corner shop. With one arm resting above Felix's head, and the other gripping the front of his jumper, Hollow desperately drank from his fellow vampire's exposed throat. Felix sighed as their bodies pressed together. He crushed the back of his free hand against his mouth. Shuddering, the hand soon slipped away, slapping onto the shutters behind. Felix's eyes were closed, and he breathed heavily into Hollow's ear. Only Amy could feel the heat of their shared arousal, and Hollow's sated bloodlust towards her.

She turned away from them, as did everyone else.

Shaun looked at both Gerald and Amy for help. 'What the fuck?'

'Should we make a plan?' tried Gerald. 'Do you know the layout of this area?'

'Yeah,' said Shaun. He shook his head as if to remove the image of the vampires from his mind. His expression grew sheepish. 'I've heard a little bit about your Awakening. It's something all us mages are interested in. Is it true you have omnipresence now?'

'Yes, in a way,' said Gerald. 'I can project my consciousness to see things from a bird's-eye view. And as long as there's no smokescreen or barrier, I can see through things as well. Although, I'm still new to this so my capabilities are limited. What do you need me to do?'

Shaun nodded slowly before answering. His eyes lingered on Gerald for a long time. As Amy read his aura, she was overcome with Shaun's sense of reverence. At last, the mage unfixed his gaze. Using the narrow end of his staff, he drew in the air, and the silver outline of a circle akin to a

Hammerspace door shimmered before them. Afterwards, Shaun turned to Gerald.

'I make maps,' he said. 'If I'm in an area, I can get a rough outline of our surroundings to show the safest routes for Downers to travel, away from human eyes. I'll draw a map in here.' He nodded towards the floating circle, and its interior was flushed with a silver topography of lines, street signs, and the roads of their immediate area. 'That should give us a good route to the house we're after.' He nodded at the brightly lit Sitton Road on the map. Adjacent roads glistened red, indicating their human traffic. 'But, if possible, I'd like you to provide a layout of the house itself so we're not surprised by anything in there.'

'Got it,' said Gerald. His eyes flashed scarlet and Amy grew tense as she watched him. She steadied herself against the endlessness of his presence as he used a more potent iteration of his omnipresence than what she had witnessed outside City Hall. He raised an arm to draw a pattern on the air, and Shaun's circle was immediately filled with an intricate network of gold lines. The pattern grew more complicated, transforming into a moving diagram of a four-storey detached house with a disused loft at the top and an empty basement at the bottom.

It took Shaun a moment to recover from Gerald's display. As the fluctuation of the Reaper's aura dimmed to normal levels, Amy refocused. She parsed the layers of the neighbourhood, extending her reach as far as she could go. Eventually, she felt the cutting spark of Tyrell Bane in the air, but like Downstairs, it was worryingly faint.

'That's odd,' said Gerald. 'I can't see anyone in the house. It appears to be completely abandoned.'

Amy took that opportunity to vocalise her own concerns.

Shaun stared at the map and the empty house that hovered before him with a frown.

'We should still head in there. Could find some clues, at least.' He tapped his staff on the ground and the enchantment dispersed on the wind.

Hollow had already broken away from Felix's neck, but he held the vampire against the shop shutters, lightly rubbing his tongue over the jugular wound to seal it. Once he was properly upright again, he licked his lips, mopping up the last of a thick black liquid. 'Thanks.'

'Anytime, bro!' said Felix, slapping Hollow's shoulder.

'I guess you heard all that?' Shaun asked them.

''Course,' they said in unison.

Amy wanted to avoid Hollow entirely. She felt his satisfaction after such a long feed, but beneath his amiable feelings was a spark of strained desire. He maintained a troubled wave of emotion, and a shadow hovered beneath the surface of his self. It was the threat of thinning time, an allusion to a fragile constitution, and the knowledge that a short trigger would be enough to dispel his countenance. To his credit, the vampire appeared to be avoiding her too. She shuffled closer to Gerald just in case.

'I'm not sure if there's anything you'd like to do, Mr Reaper?' asked Shaun.

'No, I'll leave it all to you. Amy and I are just random guests after all; I would hate to impose.'

He was met with cries of, 'Of course not!'

'Well, I suppose I can help gather any items if needed, but for a scouting mission, Amy's far more suitable than I am.'

Her chest fluttered at his compliment. She felt the buzz of blood around her body and was glad for the cool night air to diffuse any flush to her cheeks. Amy was overwhelmed by everyone's affirmations this evening. As she departed the bus stop with *Gardien*, she felt confident enough in her purpose that Hollow's potential threat became miniscule.

Everything was still on Sitton Road. The wind was silent, and the houses were all impenetrable and black. There were no signs of life: no blue glow of televisions, no static hum of radios, no parents yelling for children to sleep, no rumbling bass of a teenager's stereo. It felt as though no one had lived on Sitton Road for years. Amy was so curious that she parsed every house they saw, but she felt no warmth of humanity. She frowned at the vacantness.

The aura of Tyrell Bane grew stronger the closer they advanced towards their desired house. Sitton Road had clearly been his first destination upon failing to confront Lex Crow, but he had since departed the area.

At the targeted house, the *Gardien* team assembled themselves in hidden alcoves away from the view of the windows. For the second time, Gerald scanned its interior with his omnipresence. When he saw nothing and vocalised as such, Shaun drew a sign in the air with his staff. An invisible shockwave of heat rocked the house, eclipsing it in a flash of light, and then it dimmed again.

'No enchantments,' he said. 'Still, though. We'll do the normal formation: vamps in front. I'll take up the rear.'

Felix charged first. He kicked in the door and disappeared into the darkness of the house, followed shortly afterwards by Hollow. Gerald held onto Amy's wrist as he took her inside, and Shaun was the last to enter. He jabbed his staff at the felled door and it reassembled itself to seal the house.

The darkness was heavy and dry. The glow of street lamps illuminated the ridges and angles of a living room still occupied, frozen in the midst of family activity: injured photographs of hidden contents dangled from black walls, the cotton mounds of sofas were worn and depressed from regular use, and there was a distinct warmth, the absence of central heating, that rested on Amy's shoulders. But she could feel no auras at all.

The group crept around the living room, but Amy stayed by the door. The Reaper's eyes were illuminated, the vampires had keen senses, and Shaun was a mage, but without her ability to parse the auras of the house, the empath was blind and deaf.

'Something's not right,' she said. Her voice was overloud in the quietness. 'People recently lived here but I can't feel them. Their auras are being concealed.'

Her heart hammered in her chest as she considered what this meant. Gerald could conceal his aura. She had wrongly assumed that he was the only person with the ability. When she and Gerald wasted time chasing Bane's Darkhouse executive around South Kensington, the gang took that opportunity to torch her house. What would happen this time?

The atmosphere was too heavy, too unknown, and it closed in around her. She scanned the darkness, annoyed that no one considered her during their inane search, no one thought to at least turn the lights on so she could be part of the proceedings.

She pressed her hands against the walls that framed the front door, slid her palms across the smooth wallpaper, and sighed in relief when she felt the cool ridge of plastic, the dip of a metal screw, and the slope of a light switch. She snapped it on.

'Shit!' said Hollow.

A blinding light blared into the living room. She was knocked to the ground by a cold, unseen force. Everything was doused in bleach white, a pulsing ferocity that made her eyes ache. A guttural, animalistic expletive hissed from Felix's throat as he fled, an emerald blur of movement, into the adjoining unlit passageway. When Amy's eyes adjusted, she saw Gerald a few feet away, already recovered from the glare, and stalking towards her. Shaun was beside the gaping fireplace, his expression and aura saturated with severe concern.

A shadow rested against Amy. It was cold. A pitiful noise, like a keening mammal, erupted from within it.

Hollow shielded her. His body was tented, a triangle to give her space, both his arms pinned on either side of her head, nails digging trenches in the wooden floorboards. His face was crumpled in agony, his energy receding. Amy squinted, her eyes aching by the assault. As her vision cleared, she saw a pestilent redness snake around Hollow's arms. The light bulbs had been set at an impossible brightness that doused everything in a piercing, colourless glare, and the vampire suffered because of it, and his skin reacted to the bulbs as if the sun had been cast into the room with them.

'Fuck, Hollow!' said Shaun. He darted towards him, dragged the vampire away from Amy, and all but carried him into the passageway. Gerald dropped to her side.

'Are you okay?' he said.

'Y-yeah . . .'

When she sat upright, her body turned to ice. An axe head slept in the ground, stolidly bifurcating a floorboard. Amy had been standing there moments prior. Hollow had saved her.

Gerald helped her stand. She automatically darted to the passageway to check on Hollow, and found him slumped against the main staircase of the house, curled into Felix's chest. He drank desperately from his fellow vampire's neck, his hand burrowed deep in the electric green shards of Felix's hair. Alongside the methodical beat of gulping, the burns on Hollow's arms receded, seeped into the blank whiteness of his skin. Amy backed away from them, removed herself from their cloud of unmitigated longing, and hid herself in an alcove of the living room, her body hot with shame.

'I'm sorry,' she said to Gerald and Shaun.

'Not at all, Amy.'

'Nah, it's our fault,' said Shaun. 'We should've been mindful that you can't see. Hollow's a big boy, he'll be fine.'

Their words did nothing to console her. She only partly listened when Gerald asked, 'I thought there were no enchantments?'

'There aren't any. Prick's gone and booby-trapped the place. Human-style.'

At this, Amy came to attention. 'But I should be able to feel them. How's he hiding everything so well?'

As soon as she spoke, a ripple distressed the air. In its wake was a swell of malice, the cool calculating presence of subterfuge, and a mechanical twang that made her body tremble with static. At the sensation, Gerald snapped his head upwards. He stared at the ceiling with crimson bewilderment. A moment later, four trapdoors came loose from the ceiling. Amy only saw the sheen of metal, and a wink of some acute danger, before she realised they were being attacked by a volley of harpoons.

CHAPTER THREE

Amy

There was no impact. A thick, heavy drumming reverberated through the room with such force that the ground trembled. Amy uncoiled from the foetal panic she had been reduced to. She stumbled to her feet and looked around the room, noted the awestruck expression on Shaun's face, and the curious indifference of Gerald's.

A glass cavern, red and translucent, protected them. It was sharp and angular, like a ruby, and totally impenetrable. After the onslaught of at least a dozen barbs of shrapnel, it stood firm. A final weapon's trajectory was halted by the cavern, and it rolled off the side and clattered to the ground. The ruby was without an aura, but it held a familiarity that was unmistakably Gerald's.

'And what's this?' she asked.

'Something, something, Awakening.' Gerald tapped the glass. It made a dull noise. 'I didn't even know I could do this. I assume it happened instinctively.'

'Well, you better learn to use it! This is useful.'

'Absolutely insane,' Shaun muttered. He approached the nearest wall of the ruby with the intention to touch it, but he recoiled, instead stuffing his hands firmly in his pockets. Amy saw his frown and she felt the sombre foreboding that seeped into his aura. There was something about this power that gave him cause for concern, and Amy was curious to know the reason for his anxiety.

Gerald unsheathed his gloves and touched the cavern with his bare fingers. It shattered instantly, falling to the ground in chunks of red before dissipating in the air.

When the ruby vanished, Amy was overcome by a tsunami of sorrow. It unbalanced her. The room twisted with the force of it. Gerald and Shaun and Felix and Hollow melted into nothing. The swell of the tide weighed on her shoulders, a pressure that was as nonsensical as it was frightening. It came from every direction of the house; the walls oozed with it and the ceiling leaked it and the homes on either side swayed and rocked tempestuously with its force. The worst of it came from below. A basement lurked beneath their feet, putrid with the stagnant water of despair.

'Oh my God,' she breathed. 'All the auras are back. Something's in the basement!'

Shaun left first. As Gerald held onto her wrist again to steady her, his face was a mask of worry. His hold was firm, the only reassurance she could feel. They passed the vampires as they followed Shaun to the basement on the reverse side of the stairs. Hollow was weakened, but his skin was without any burns. He rested in Felix's embrace. Felix tapped rapidly into his phone, likely relaying the incident to Blythe, and nodded desultorily when he saw them.

The basement gaped open. She heard voices. Words in languages she could not identify. Shaun edged down the stairs that led to an empty dimness. A click of a light switch later, and he cursed under his breath. Amy followed closely behind Gerald. She froze at the lip of the basement. The stench was unfathomable, but the sight made her retch.

At least twenty men, women, and children huddled together in a dank and destitute room. Their clothes were rotten and their bodies, once flushed with olive beauty, were marred with dirt and grime and unknown substances. The haunted emptiness of their eyes was known to Amy; she had seen identical expressions peeping out from the shadow of ship containers smuggled across the Channel. The executives had been wrong: Bane used more than one property on Sitton Road as a hideout. Every house on the road was drenched in the desperate horror of betrayed refugees. Whatever human cargo Bane had salvaged from his failed Channel enterprise had been imprisoned here. Amy was too stunned to cry.

'Fucking hell,' said Shaun. His arms hung uselessly at his sides.

Amy grabbed onto Gerald's nearest arm for support. 'What do we do?' she whispered.

She turned to him and froze. His expression was disturbingly neutral as he watched the prisoners, and his aura betrayed no horror, no acknowledgement of the magnitude of their find. Amy parsed, eager to find something reasonable within him. The Wall stood firm, and Gerald's shoulders twitched in response to her mental nudge, but he did not acknowledge her. The steam of evaporation rested upon his aura, and a nick of ice was melted away. It dribbled to nowhere, but Amy was rewarded with a gentle tremor of pity, a slow bite of annoyance, from the sensation. She returned her gaze to the now-babbling refugees, trying to decipher their most immediate need.

One brave man staggered to his feet. The others watched him, their hope in him evident in their demeanours. He appeared to search for English words to say, but at last, he was ready. As he began his speech, a deluge of blood streamed from his open mouth. Shaun leapt away from him. Amy fell on her step. The refugees screamed hysterically, which brought Felix and Hollow to the doorway. The man crumpled to the ground and died. The woman closest to him suffered the same fate. One by one, the refugees followed the first, their bodies reduced to streams of blood. They died slowly, felling like battered trees, and were motionless in the aftermath. It took less than a minute for the room to die. An agonised hole rent the air as all the houses on Sitton Road became mausoleums. The atmosphere was drenched in the iron and rust of red mist.

'Fucking bastard,' said Felix.

On the damp wall of the basement, written haphazardly in red paint, a warning made itself known. The words glistened in the dimness. At last, Gerald's aura was spiked with rage as he read Tyrell Bane's words, so perfectly timed with his act of barbarity. Amy read it once, then stumbled away from the basement entrance, crawling past Felix and Hollow, her vision blurred with the weight of so much death and anguish. When she closed her eyes, the words were scorched into her eyelids.

> *FOLLOW-FOLLOW FRIENDS. KEEP STALKING ME AND I'LL JUST GIVE YOU MORE SHIT TO CLEAN*

The house was flushed with the sensation of magic, and a series of Hammerspace doors appeared in the walls. Six Downers marched onto the scene. They were dressed in black overalls, sturdy leather boots, and wore square military caps, most of them turned backwards. The first to emerge was a mage – a white man of a tanned complexion and playful brown eyes. His staff was strapped to his back like a shotgun. His lapels were illustriously decorated, with a label reading Supt Murphy. Behind him, a Black woman, also a mage, with an afro that threatened to unseat her cap, entered the room. According to her label, she was Supt Johnson. The remaining four mages were all Chief Inspectors, meaning that they had knowledge of *Gardien* and were most likely dispatched to maintain the secrecy of Blythe's organisation from the rest of Downstairs. They liaised with Felix and Hollow as the vampires relayed the night's events.

Superintendent Murphy detached himself from the throng to saunter over to Shaun, who stood watch behind the sofa that Amy and Gerald now occupied.

'You good?' he asked Shaun.

'Bro? That was mad.'

'Hmm.' Murphy tapped his staff and a case file comprised of glowing electrical lines appeared in the air. Amy watched as the Downey Met officers gingerly gathered evidence, mopped up blood samples, and zipped away shrapnel pieces in magic bags. Every now and then one would appear to ask Gerald a question about the evening, and he would answer with stoic professionalism. Amy was too numb to speak.

'Everyone shut up!' said Murphy.

The room went silent as the officer narrowed his eyes, keenly listening for something happening outside. All business, he extracted a piece of wood from an indent in his staff. What emerged was something the size of a magic wand, perfectly polished and tipped with ivory at one end. He flicked the wand, and the windows were doused in a pitch-black substance. The road outside disappeared, and it felt like they had been spirited away elsewhere. It contained the same empty magic presence as Gerald's Hammerspace room.

'There were humans approaching,' he said to everyone. 'As you were. Hurry up.'

Shaun glanced out at the windows. 'How many humans you reckon you heard out there?'

'About four. This place will be swarming with them come morning. We did a quick run around before we came here. I put the other houses in a smokescreen, too, but people still live nearby, you know. Like, there's houses all over this area. We don't know how many of the neighbours knew about these refugees. Concealment Act's gone to shit, mate.'

'Eh, we'll help if we can.' Shaun patted him on the shoulder.

'That's what you said last time. You tell that short man to pay us extra if he wants us to clean up you lot's fuckery.'

Amy looked out at the darkened windows. 'So that's what a smokescreen looks like,' she said quietly.

Gerald followed her gaze and nodded. 'Alex is good with them, and he has the keenest senses I've ever witnessed in a person, barring you.'

'I never even sensed anyone out there.' Amy sighed. 'I think I'm still in shock.'

'You know what? We're done here. Perhaps we haven't got Bane, not yet. But we'll get him. We have no choice if he's going to be pulling stunts like that. There's far too much at stake now. But you've seen enough. Let's go home. I'll make you some purple Gecko tea. It will help you sleep, I promise.'

She averted her gaze from the shadow of the passageway where the remaining Met officers braced themselves before going down to the basement.

'Fine,' she said. She wanted to forget the night's events. 'What madness. Everything was just fine a couple of hours ago. Who the fuck does stuff like *that*? And for what?'

'Because he's desperate and angry and wants to keep forcing us into a corner, or forcing Mr Crow into a corner until he withdraws his request, presumably,' said Gerald. 'Someone like that isn't worth wasting mental energy trying to decipher. Your thoughts would be better spent on his victims.' He stared at her with uncertainty, but a hardness in his eyes conveyed the anger he felt towards Bane and his desire to kill him. Gerald's bloodlust rumbled beneath his words. Amy averted her gaze, inevitably seeking the darkness of the passageway. Gerald's emotions were misplaced, a confusing mix of inappropriateness, and she was without the means to explain to him why.

They said their goodbyes to the team and slipped through Alex Murphy's smokescreen upon the mage's permission. When they were outside, Gerald whisked Amy away from everything – Sitton Road receded behind them, and the bloody night slipped away into the darkness of the smokescreen. But the memories and the scarlet stench and the unresolved pain would stay with Amy for a long time.

CHAPTER FOUR
Blythe

When Blythe's brougham rolled down the streets of Cruickstown on its way to Regalia Park, the locals scattered like startled herring. He promptly ignored them, focusing instead on the small alleys and alcoves that had once been a hallowed retreat during his school days. He had never appreciated how mortified the warlock must have felt the first time Blythe had asked Tyrell if he could visit his house, and when Blythe had asked to visit again after a successful first time, Tyrell had only sighed with sceptical resignation. The residents of Cruickstown, and later Bloodwood, never accepted Blythe Mason. He was met with hostile indifference, and he often imagined the streets bursting into celebration as soon as he travelled back to Nightingale. But Tyrell had indulged his sincerity. Their friendship, however, had cooled after the visit was exchanged.

Even now, Blythe remembered the expression that overcame Tyrell the moment he entered the Mason residence. It was at once awe-stricken and acrid, and was exacerbated by the condescension from Blythe's mother, the way she utilised the chipped and aged plates for dinner, and how she so poorly masked her efforts to hide expensive ornaments as they lay discarded around the house. In his embarrassment, Blythe cut the visit short and apologised, but the damage had been done. He wondered how annoyed Tyrell would have been had he known that Blythe was now looking after his parents, and smiled wryly at the thought.

St Olave's hid among a thicket of blackened tree stumps on the outskirts of Regalia Park. A pebbled driveway led to a three-storied stately home with a façade of black ivy. Previously closed to visitors, Blythe had been requested by the Banes, and feeling cornered and a little embarrassed, he obliged. Beside him on the velvet seat was a bouquet of daffodils from Upstairs. He wore his dungarees and a plain jumper, feeling comfortable as the denim hems bunched around his ankles. Archer opened the carriage door and he walked the rest of the distance alone. Despite his foreboding, he was grateful for this meeting; it meant he could enquire about the Downey Gang.

Inside, he listened in disdainful silence as the therapist rabbited on about the Banes' progress, shooting hopeful looks at Blythe as she suggested how much better everyone's treatment would be with a new wing and updated facilities. She finally deposited him outside the family meeting room and he slammed the door during a sudden passionate tirade against service cuts. Blythe sat on the cushion with great irritation. He patted his pockets to confirm there was an available cigar for the journey back, then reclined. He didn't want to admit it, but he was nervous. It had been over five years since he last saw Tyrell's parents.

A witch opened the door on the other side of the meeting room. She edged out to see him fully. Great puffs of black hair clouded around her head, streaked with wiry shades of grey that she had tried to dye with henna, leaving behind a slight ginger tinge that complemented her dark skin. She was still unnaturally thin, but there was a plumpness to her face that was absent before, and her eyes were less sunken, puffier with age. The smile she offered him was tight, fraught with the self-consciousness of missing teeth. She wore a wool dress and stepped lightly in silk slippers.

'Where's your husband?' Blythe asked, tossing the daffodils on the table before her.

'Sick. He's annoyed he couldn't see you. Maybe next time.'

'Hmm.'

Sylvia Bane stared at the wall ahead when she said, 'He's guilty, then?'

'Quite obviously.'

With a little nod, she blinked, and tears streamed down her face.

'You remember when you lot did that school project? What was it again?'

'Self-building bricks.'

'That's the one. That coulda made him some money, don't you think?'

'Probably.'

Sylvia wiped her face. 'Well? What happened to those days, then. You two were tight, no?'

Blythe shifted in his seat. 'It's been many years since his school project days. He's now grooming children to be gang leaders.'

'Watch your mouth.'

'I'm being honest.'

'What about that witch? How d'you know Ty's the one doing all this refugee shit?'

'Let's not be silly, now.'

'Well, where is she?'

'I'd like to ask you that exact question.'

'I don't have a clue.'

'And what of *his* whereabouts?'

Sylvia blinked. She reclined in the chair to watch him. 'I ain't seen him for ages.'

'But do you know where he *could* be? I'm only asking this out of desperation. Last night, dozens of refugees were killed by his hand, and it's clear he's working with someone else now. Most likely Lavender herself. I need you to overcome your delusion and wrack your brains a bit.'

'You really have a rotten mouth.'

The wraith said nothing as he leaned on his lap, staring at Sylvia unblinkingly. When she realised he was going nowhere, and that she would be trapped in this room with him until she at least tried to be helpful, she sighed, and shook her head. Blythe waited, inwardly impatient, and ready to commit her words to memory.

'Right.' Sylvia rubbed her eyes roughly with the sleeve of her dress. It made her eyebrows messy. Blythe made a gesture, miming an arching motion over his own brows, and she quickly smoothed hers over. 'He used to love Upstairs. I think he felt free there. He liked going to the parks.'

'Narrow your scope.'

'Well, they're all nice, aren't they? St James's,' she said at last, sighing, rising her arms with resignation, then letting them fall with a pitiful slap on her thighs. She scowled at the wilting daffodils, and Blythe knew from her body language that she told the truth, and that it was a truth of heavy weight. He made a mental note to message a suitable *Gardien* agent for the task of checking St James's Park for hiding places, relieved for the light of progress.

'Is it true he's on the Reaper's list?'

'Yes. A double request, in fact.'

'What happens now then? If he dies, he won't see me better.'

Blythe regarded Sylvia, his scarlet eyes boring into her brown ones. 'Well now you get better for yourself,' he said. 'And leave the ghost of the past behind you.'

She looked away from him, staring at the wall for a long time. Eventually, she gave a curt nod. It was almost invisible, only noted because her soft, ethereal hair flounced around her head in response. He tutted, fished the cigar case from his pocket, and opened and closed the lid absently. The snapping and clicking was the only noise in the room.

'You can't smoke in here,' said Sylvia.

'Pity,' said Blythe.

He returned the case to his pocket.

CHAPTER FIVE
Gerald

The *Nightly Moon*'s sensational leading story described Bane's latest act in much detail. Gerald grimaced as he read the paper over breakfast, nodding his thanks to Zis when a pot of tea floated to rest beside his toast and jam. Thanks to Alex Murphy, Patricia Johnson, and the rest of the Downey Met squad that cleaned up the area, the secret mission of *Gardien* and its members was omitted, but Gerald's presence had been noted as a bystander. He turned the paper over and finished his breakfast in deep thought. Unaccustomed to inefficiency, he felt the discomforting itch of stalled work. His hands flexed instinctively.

In the Upstairs papers, the mysterious deaths of Sir Alastair and Mike Carrington were being linked with Stephen Walters's untimely death in Gray's Inn. According to several reports, Walters's boss, Owain Chambers, was so distressed by all the bloodshed that he had taken an extended leave of absence. Gerald snorted at this news. According to more truthful sources, the barrister had left for the Maldives with his mistress, keeping a low profile to avoid suspicion.

A bleary-eyed Amy entered the kitchen. Flopping onto the stool opposite, she smiled at Zis when a teacup was presented to her. Amy frowned when she poured the deep purple tea.

'What's this?' she asked.

'Hibiscus.'

'Hmm.'

They sat in an uncomfortable silence.

'Are you okay?' Gerald asked eventually.

She shrugged. 'I couldn't get that basement out of my head. What are we saying about Bane? Any news?'

'Maybe. Blythe asked me to come Downstairs. There's a meeting happening in a couple of hours. You can come if you want.'

'Yeah. If I stay in here, I'll be getting flashbacks every minute.'

'Would you like some toast?'

Amy nodded. Gerald stood, took a plate from the cupboard, and made Amy breakfast, shooting a self-conscious glance at Zis as he did so. Afterwards, he checked for any additions to the Grim Book, then paused over Nadine Samson's name. Since Amy's identification of her, Gerald had researched more about the young activist with keen interest. She had planned a massive protest at Blue Meadow on May Day weekend. Online forums were split between hailing her as a modern-day Boudicca and a race-baiting troublemaker. He rejected the assassination request, using the other end of his fountain pen to erase her name. The space returned to its blank creaminess, as if Nadine Samson had never graced the interior of the Book.

When they eventually left the apartment, it was after midday. He anticipated Blythe's latest updates with both excitement and trepidation.

The streets of Downstairs were littered with stray newspapers about the Sitton Road incident. Downers chatted excitedly in the cafés, rickshaws, and supermarkets. It was the biggest scandal since the formation of the Downey Gang in the first place, and various journalists raised the alarm of the slow movements of law enforcement. Bane, Lavender, and their associates had created most of Downstairs' problems, and as Gerald and Amy passed the communal news screens in the city centre, the sense of indignation from the public was palpable.

Their first stop was Voodoo Rays to return the house key to Megan. Jen the warlock greeted them with his usual ambivalence.

'She's . . . not here,' he said, tugging at his ear nervously. 'Took the day off. Press banging on her door and that.'

Beside him, Amy tutted her disproval.

'Anything we can do?' Gerald said.

'Probably not, but I can take that.' Jen nodded towards the key. 'Maybe don't visit her for a while. She's proper upset.'

'I understand.' Gerald handed over the key. 'Please send her our regards.'

Once they were outside, Amy shook her head in disgust. 'That's terrible,' she said.

'Yes. But understandable. I'm sure everyone wants to play armchair detective now and try to track Melanie down. They didn't care before, though.'

'Megan mentioned something like that last time,' Amy said with a frown. 'About how she's not a Mason or whatever.'

'There are a lot of prestigious families down here that hold significant public interest,' Gerald said as he hailed the rickshaw to the meeting place. 'If such a scandalous murder happened in any of those families, you can imagine it would be the Downey Met's highest priority. It would never leave the papers. The public would never stop talking about it.

Unknowns like the Lavenders and the Banes, for that matter, just slip through the net.'

'And produce gang members.'

'Correct.'

They squashed onto the back of the rickshaw and Gerald gave the address to their rider.

'We're not going to Blythe's house?'

'No. He said he's been out and about doing his own research, so we'll be meeting at Ulrich and Josh's house.'

They soon arrived at 13 Juniper Close, a four-storey Georgian terrace in a pleasant neighbourhood. The row of houses curved into a crescent overlooking a gargoyle fountain. Blackened petals from the nearby upside-down beech tree floated like lily pads on the water's surface. It was peacefully quiet, as most of the Close's residents were werewolves that were resting after the full moon. When Gerald buzzed for flat three on the third floor, Josh appeared behind the entrance door shortly afterwards, quickly escorting the pair to the modern home he shared with Ulrich.

'We're in the bedroom,' Josh said, rolling his eyes. 'Would you like some tea? Water?'

'Water will be fine, thanks,' said Gerald.

'Great. And you, Amy?'

'Any juice, please.'

'Sure. Just straight ahead. The others are in there.'

When Gerald opened the door, he found Ulrich the werewolf tucked firmly beneath a duvet. His previously elegant waves hung limp over puffy eyes. His skin was pale and waxy, and he stared at everyone with utter scorn. When he saw Gerald, he attempted a professional demeanour until the Reaper gestured for him to remain resting. He had never seen a werewolf during their post-transformation sickness, so it was a disarming image. Clearly the other members were accustomed to the sight, as they didn't pay any attention to it while they discussed the previous night's events passionately among themselves.

Hollow sat on the windowsill, his back resting against the arched design, frowning warily when he saw Amy in tow. Felix was at the foot of the bed with Dani opposite. Shaun lounged on the floor encased in a gate of silver circles, each one inscribed with its own map that he scrutinised carefully. He mumbled to himself as if making mental notes of all the places they still needed to search.

Dagwood Somme, a talented warlock, balanced himself on the pouf chair by the dresser. A thick auburn beard framed his pale face. Brian Salem stood sentinel beside the wardrobe. Brian was a basilisk, and as such, he was completely covered in rich emerald scales. Dagwood and Brian had been absent during the meeting at Blythe's house the previous evening, and Gerald was glad to see them both doing well.

A single mobile phone rested on Ulrich's tightly bound body. An irritated voice rasped on the other end, pausing every so often to smoke.

'Good afternoon, Blythe,' said Gerald, which drew everyone's attention.

Blythe said nothing.

'Mr Reaper,' said Felix. 'We were just going over a plan to check the Dalston area again.'

'Oh really?'

'I've got some intel,' Blythe's disembodied voice crackled from the phone. 'One informant indicated St James's Park, which Josh looked into earlier, and found evidence of witch activity in the Duck Island Cottage. We can assume Lavender was based there, but the place has been thoroughly scoured. Either way, it's a good starting point. Moving on from that, my informants Upstairs have said there's been an influx of irregular humans around Dalston. Snooping. As we all know, there are several establishments over there that are popular among Downers, so random groups of humans suddenly taking an interest will obviously cause suspicion.'

'What kind of people are they?' Gerald asked the room.

'Big, burly men, apparently,' said Felix with a smirk.

'My informants have taken note of each one's appearance. Everything points to them belonging to Darkhouse. They seem to be searching for their lost executives – the ones Gerald killed. Once this is all cleared up, I'll have them apprehended and their memories wiped, like we did with the other two last night. We need to clean up all these contraventions to our Concealment Act quickly.'

'Agreed,' said Gerald.

'So what's the plan?' asked Josh, sliding into the room with a tray of drinks for Amy and Gerald.

'Stake out Dalston,' said Blythe. 'If you see anything untoward, do something about it. Last night did not yield any results. I do not wish to hear of any more massacres going forward.'

The *Gardien* team looked decidedly embarrassed.

'I promise we're more organised than this,' Ulrich said, his voice thick and gravelly.

'I think you're very organised,' Gerald reassured them. 'I worry that I caused some distraction last night. I apologise if my intrusion brought you any problems.'

The room erupted into a chorus of, 'No, no, don't be silly!'

But Gerald held up a placating hand. He heard Amy snort beside him, most likely making fun of how reluctant they all were to offend him. He nudged her in the ribs in response, trying his best to hide his growing smile.

'Quite,' said Blythe. 'I've done my part, even though I shouldn't have had to. Give me results. Do not contact me unless it's to say Bane has been apprehended or that you've found his protector.'

And with that, the call disconnected.

'Tough boss,' said Amy. The comment dispelled the tense atmosphere immediately. Even Hollow smiled, a small twitching at the corners of his mouth that he tried to hide as he stared out the window.

'So lads, how we gonna run this?' Felix asked as he scanned the room.

'First of all, we need good surveillance,' Shaun said, gesturing to the floating maps around him and then glancing at Gerald. 'I was kind of inspired by your omnipresence. It's a useful skill, but as you said, you're new to it. And I doubt you'd be able to just scan all over London to look for two people, not even knowing what kind of disguises they're using. That'd take ages. So I made my own version of your ability. It's not perfect, but it will definitely help in future missions.'

A stunned silence followed Shaun's words, but he shrugged amiably before gesturing to the floating maps with his nearby staff.

The maps within the circles shifted until they bore the street names of the Dalston and Hackney areas. As before, the reddish lines denoted roads overpopulated by humans, and the silver ones showed routes that were safer for Downers to travel. The maps became more detailed as they changed colour. Green, brown, and grey splodges appeared within the circles, blooming further into the centres like ink spreading through cloth. Objects began to move until they looked like shimmering paintings. After a few moments, the group was staring at what could only be described as moving CCTV images. The live footage hovered above ground, each circle displaying a different location through a translucent filter. Gerald heard Amy gasp beside him, and he observed the awestruck expressions of Shaun's colleagues. He was excited by it. Shaun possessed renowned magic abilities, and it was something he had been aching to see for himself.

Downey society suffered the same issues of inequality as Upstairs, with various families dominating politics and culture. The Masons, the Wardens, and the Reapers were included in the super-elite, but dozens of lower families of formidable reputation proved to be equally influential. Shaun Forbes, heir to an arms and metal mining dynasty which forged the unparalleled Forbesteel, was the rogue of his family, having spent most of his youth creating his own weapons outside the family business. He sold dangerous items to the worst of Downey's criminals for personal profit, and splurged his ill-gained money on women, exclusive carriages, and decadent properties around the city.

One of Gerald's first assassination requests came from a widow seeking revenge. Her oil magnate husband had been found murdered by a weapon that looked like a knife, but upon contact with skin, would leak silver into the bloodstream until the body was poisoned stiff with metal. The assassination request had been for the murderer as well as the person who made the weapon – Shaun Forbes. Unbeknown to the mage, Gerald rejected the request, and Shaun lived to create magic like this display today. The Reaper had considered Shaun's talent, and his obvious potential, and made a subtle suggestion to Blythe. The appointment to

Gardien had raised brows among his fellow agents, but Blythe also knew what Shaun was capable of. With *Gardien*, the mage could make as many weapons as he wanted, away from the judgement of the Forbes family.

Gerald stepped forward, observing the live footage within each of the circles. With an educated guess, he assumed Shaun had pre-prepared transmitters that would provide an image of a small area, then feedback the footage to a bank of mobile receivers that he could conjure on demand.

'This is amazing,' he said, peering around one of the receivers to look at Shaun directly.

'Thank you.'

'Bloody hell, Shaun!' said Dagwood. He sprung to his feet to examine the receivers. 'How long did this take to do?'

'Quicker than you think.'

'And this is *live* live?' asked Dani.

'Yeah, but with a seven-second delay.'

'Oh yikes, look at that.'

The group directed their attention to Brian the basilisk as he pointed to a receiver that showed an image of Sitton Road. It was cordoned off by police tape, and human journalists reported to a bank of cameras, their expressions both stern and guarded.

'Oh God,' said Josh. He was perched beside a now-slumbering Ulrich, the werewolf's head lolling across his shoulder. Josh held him there, absently stroking his deflated hair. 'We all knew this was coming.'

'Yeah, Alex told me they found eighty bodies altogether across all those houses,' said Shaun as he scrutinised the screen. 'Now I need to get sound on these. It would be good to know what the humans are speculating. The Concealment Act really *has* gone to shit.'

'Bodies found in basements, mass suicide cult,' Amy said, reading from her phone.

'Oh, they went *that* route, did they?' asked Dani with a frown.

Amy nodded. 'They're saying there were loads of suicide notes in the bedrooms, strange prayers pinned to the walls with instructions of how to see heaven . . . some fundamentalist Christian group . . .' She then looked around the room sceptically. 'These notes were all planted by those police officers, right?'

'I assume so,' said Shaun. 'They stayed long after we'd all left to forge documents and stage the victims. I get why they didn't keep the refugee angle; if Upstairs digs any deeper into this Channel thing, we might as well just invite them all down here to help us find Bane themselves. Fucking hell.'

'I didn't see any bodies when I examined the houses from the outside,' Gerald said with a frown. It was the overriding mystery of Sitton Road. Bane had concealed human snares, human bodies, and a host of other traps within the houses. His own powers of omnipresence had meant nothing, and they had found themselves at the mercy of the unknown. He turned to Amy for an explanation, doubly curious about why she had been unable to feel Bane's aura. She shrugged, her expression equally bewildered.

'I didn't sense anything,' she said. 'How's that possible?'

'Dunno, Hammerspace door?' Shaun asked the room.

'I would have seen it,' said Gerald. 'And Amy would have felt it.'

'Velvet Coffin,' said Dani. When confused silence followed her words, she smiled at her colleagues mockingly. 'I spoke to Rochelle last night and she sent me some samples from the house – it all leads to that. A Velvet Coffin is blood magic, and it's how witches used to hide from burning trials back in the day. They're complex and dangerous, but it means you can hide some*thing* or some*one* in a location that's even deeper than Hammerspace. And it totally wipes them off the map: no aura, no magic trace, no thermal outlines. It's like they don't exist. There's usually a time limit on the spell. You just happened to be there when the time ran out. He was obviously waiting for you to find it.'

'But that's witch magic,' said Gerald. 'So how did Bane get a hold of that?'

'Gotta be Lavender,' said Dani. 'Most witches avoid using Velvet Coffins. They need a blood sacrifice. Like if I was to make one for myself, I'd use a small animal, like a rat. These were multiple families. That needs a body or two.'

'And she's already killed someone. Some people,' said Shaun. 'What if she drained the blood from her parents after murdering them? I bet she had it in her mind she'd need to use something like this if she's part of the most infamous gang we've had down here for years.'

'Sad to say I wouldn't put it past her,' Dani said with a sigh. 'Everything about that girl is a messy tragedy.'

'But what about the schism between Lavender and Bane?' The room went silent again to watch Hollow as he continued to stare out the window. 'If Bane used a Velvet Coffin to hide those humans and Lavender helped him . . . is the schism still happening or what?'

'We'll look into it.' Felix gestured to Hollow and the slumbering Ulrich. 'We won't be able to join you in the daytime Upstairs, so leave that with us. Blythe ain't the only one with informants.'

'Great,' said Shaun.

'Oh, what a mess,' said Dagwood. 'I don't envy Lex Crow.

He's just watched his daughter have a fantastic debut and now he has all this to sort out. Or maybe he'll be forced to go back to Blythe. The Masons are good friends with the British royal family, aren't they? Perhaps Blythe can use his influence with them to do something about all this . . . we don't want to draw any more attention to Downstairs.'

Gerald didn't hear the rest of the conversation. His focus was captured by an image of Kingsland High Street, where a woman walked decisively down the road, weaving in and out of the Saturday afternoon foot traffic. Despite her attempts to look like everyone else, her demeanour dripped with the delicate flavour of affluence. It was the uncertainty of her steps, and the uncomfortable glances she threw towards the crowds, as if she was worried someone would bump into her or notice the subtle label on her designer bag. She wore pearls around her neck, and a garish emerald brooch glinted in the afternoon sunshine, pinned to a light wool cardigan. Her blonde hair was tucked into a neat bun, and her sunglasses obscured most of her face, but she looked too familiar to ignore. She quickly disappeared into Voodoo Rays, where she remained for some time.

'There's a seven-second delay?' Gerald asked, silencing the room immediately.

'Yeah,' said Shaun. 'You want me to play something back?'

'This one.' Gerald pointed to the Kingsland transmission. Shaun set the image to run in reverse. 'Stop there, please,' he said once the blonde woman was back in view.

They all waited for Gerald to speak again. It didn't take him long before he tutted as the memory came back. 'Mrs Carrington.'

'Carrington? Why does that sound familiar?' asked Dani.

'Ah! I know!' said Josh, all but jumping on the bed. He

quickly steadied Ulrich's head before it rolled off his shoulder. A look of unease crossed his features, and he stared unblinkingly at Gerald. Before the others could question his abrupt behaviour, he whispered, 'There's a wild, wild story about her, Dani. She's the widow of the security guard. Haven't you lot been following Upstairs news? There's been some crazy shit going on up there for months. All about some Dolphin Square scandal, paedo politicians – a total mess! Loads of important civil servants have died, just dropping like flies, no explanation.'

The room refocused on the Reaper as they linked his involvement to the deaths. Gerald ignored them. 'What's she doing there of all places?' he muttered. 'Can you continue the tape again, Shaun?'

The others watched as Mrs Carrington slipped into Voodoo Rays, the popular Downer haunt, unbeknown to the poor human who managed it.

'So she knows about Downers, because she's the one who made the direct request to my Tribe to kill Sir Alastair. And now she's going into Voodoo Rays . . .'

'Oh fuck me,' said Shaun, ignoring his usual formalities around the Reaper.

Mrs Carrington left the restaurant accompanied by another person. He was tall and brown, face glinting in the shadows of a dishevelled hoodie. As he lumbered down the street, the contours of his face changed imperceptibly, and he became someone new within a few paces. This new man was the warlock Tyrell Bane.

'Josh, go,' Shaun said. '*Now*, Josh.'

'Here.' Dani quickly snatched a handheld mirror from her Hammerspace and threw it to the wraith. 'I'll follow you by scrying; wouldn't want anyone to trace you from a phone signal.'

'Cool,' he said, stowing it away in the front of his denim jacket. He carefully repositioned Ulrich on the bed, then vanished into thin air as soon as the werewolf was tucked beneath his duvet.

'What's next?' asked Gerald. He felt the rise of bloodlust in his body as his desire to kill Bane consumed his thoughts. He had expected to go with Josh, but his promise to Blythe remained: he would delay the assassination as much as he could until *Gardien's* investigation was completed. Sighing, he breathed deeply, and focused on what was important. He needed to trust *Gardien* right now and believe that they would receive the answers about the Downey Gang's true leadership, factions permitted, and arrest those responsible. The refugees had died with their secrets. He could not afford a repeat of this error.

'You good?' whispered Amy.

Gerald turned to her. Her large brown eyes were full of concern. *Did she feel my inner conflict?* As soon as he focused on her gaze, as innocently understanding as it was, he felt his desire to kill slip away from him.

'I am,' he said.

'I guess now we wait,' Amy said, inclining her head towards Dani's twin mirror.

'Yes. Now we wait,' said Gerald. He rested his head against the wall and forced himself to relax.

CHAPTER SIX
Amy

They watched Shaun's surveillance footage with bated breath until the scope of his radius weakened. Josh vanished and reappeared on various rooftops, among parked cars, and upon street corners, his expression determined as he followed Tyrell Bane and the elusive Imogen Carrington down the high street. The pair entered a black car parked near Dalston Kingsland station. The images grew grainy, infected with salt and pepper static, then shimmered with the faint silver outline of Shaun's magic, until they were once again staring at the bare bones of a floating map, all street names and red lines, with nothing tangible to tell them of the trio's whereabouts.

'I gotta put more transmitters out there. Dunno how long it will take, but I'd like to have covered most of London by the end of the year.'

'You did well, Shaun,' said Dagwood, patting him on the shoulder.

Amy waited until Gerald calmed down. She had only felt his anger – his true, unfiltered emotion – once before, and that was at Sitton Road. This aura was different. He was both anxious and annoyed, but at the base of it was a desire to kill. Bloodlust wasn't new to her: she used to trawl around London looking for Otherworldlies to observe, and vampires in the throes of desire were a common occurrence.

They nurtured a base, primal feeling, and gave the impression of wildlife: foxes stalking suburban gardens or snakes tracking prey behind desert brush. Gerald's desire was deeper; it felt indiscriminate, as if any one of them at 13 Juniper Close was in danger if they said the wrong thing. The thought froze her mind, and her heart hammered against her chest when she felt it, but she had willed her mouth to speak, if only to calm him. When she asked if he was okay, he returned to his normal self, but the undercurrent of unease was still there, fighting to break through.

'Why do you think the Carrington lady's with Bane, then? That's a weird connection, innit?' she asked.

Gerald shrugged against the wall. 'I honestly don't know.'

'And she's not a Downer?' asked Dani.

'No, definitely human. From a very well-to-do family.'

'So what's her connection to the political scandal? A shame Josh isn't here. It seems like he's been following it avidly.' Dani offered a wry smile. 'Is it anything to do with Downstairs?'

Gerald returned the smile before explaining. 'Sir Alastair sends *The Times* a dossier of an alleged Westminster paedophile ring. Henry Butler MP is one of the named suspects. Mike Carrington is an ally of Sir Alastair. It's suspected that Mike leaked information to Sir Alastair regarding Henry. Imogen' – Gerald nodded towards the floating maps – 'asks my Tribe to assassinate Sir Alastair to prevent the dossier from going public. Her husband Mike dies by mysterious circumstances weeks later.'

'Wasn't Mike Carrington your target, too?' asked Dani.

Gerald shook his head. 'Imogen only requested the assassination of Sir Alastair. I believe she hired someone else to kill Mike.'

'Why would she do that?' asked Amy.

Dani flicked through her phone, frowning at reams of news stories. 'Hah. A committee was due to submit evidence for the refugee scandal inquiry that week. When Mr Reaper assassinated Sir Alastair, all news of the inquiry disappeared from the press. Sir Alastair's death was the bigger distraction.'

A wave of fury descended on the room. Amy turned to Gerald askance, noticing that an intense heat radiated from him, rolling in great, ashen waves to the far corners of the room. It dwarfed everyone else's presence and his anger was so potent that the other Downers watched him with unease. She expected his eyes to flash scarlet, but thankfully they remained brown, which she hoped meant he had some control over his anger.

'Wanna tell us what's wrong?' she asked.

'I take my job very seriously. I don't like being used in that way. If she's communicating with Bane, it means he put her up to the request in the first place.' He turned to Dani, his eyes black with rage. 'Where is Josh now?'

Dani wasted no time fishing the mirror from her pocket. She hissed at it, and a bright, crimson eye flashed on the surface.

'You lot won't believe what's going on,' Josh said in a voice as clear as if he was in the room with them. Without explaining, he angled his half of Dani's mirror towards an industrial estate which Amy knew was in Tottenham, as it was close to an ice rink that she had visited for an end-of-year trip at school. A Mercedes was parked beside a shipping container, poorly shielding Tyrell and Imogen as they fucked against an adjoining wall. Tyrell had Imogen pinned against the wet moss and old brick of a warehouse. Two pale, stubby legs were wrapped around his waist. Josh flashed the mirror back to himself. Amy caught a glimpse of his outraged grin. 'Are you *seeing* this?'

'Send the location,' said Gerald. Josh read out the address, then repeated it to make sure everyone had remembered it correctly.

'Come quick!' he said. 'I can't watch this alone.'

'Thank you, Josh,' said Dani before stowing the mirror away.

'Right. Let's get this started,' said Shaun. 'It's the middle of the day so we need to do this carefully. I think Dagwood and Brian should go with Mr Reaper and Amy. Me and Dani will stay as backup.'

'Sounds good to me,' said Dani.

'We'll let you know how we get on,' said Dagwood. He then flashed an excited smile at Gerald. The group promptly left Juniper Close.

When the lift doors opened, a tall Warden with shrewd, penetrating eyes greeted them. Her hair was styled in elaborate Ghana braids. She nodded to Brian first, then offered a short curtsey to Gerald before ignoring everyone else.

'Hi Chris,' said Brian.

'Hello Christelle,' said Gerald. To Amy's relief, his tone and demeanour had softened since leaving Juniper Close, and whatever anger he had felt towards Bane's audacity was rumbling beneath his usual pleasant air, restrained and caged deep within his aura. The warlock named Dagwood made the request for Tottenham Hale. Brian, who Gerald explained was a basilisk, changed into human-friendly attire. He snapped a pair of tinted goggles over his eyes and tied a leather mask to the bottom half of his face. A black hoodie that enshrouded him in shadow finished the look. His aura was thick and peaceful but hid a depth that was reminiscent of a swamp. He dwarfed everyone else in the lift, a hulking mass that threatened the already-cramped confines. Amy smiled at him.

'Very cool,' she said, grinning harder when she saw the basilisk's shoulders tremble with quiet laughter.

The lift took them to a tower block that overlooked the busy streets of Tottenham. In the far distance, Amy saw the outline of what was once Allied Carpets, a building that had been immortalised in the news as a crumbling inferno during riots that felt like a lifetime ago. Nowadays, Tottenham was the same chaotic North London town that everyone remembered, and the dark shadow of gentrification loomed over the streets with icy slowness.

As soon as they were out of the building, Dagwood and Brian immediately disappeared among the crowd, not walking together, making their own journey to the desolate road leading to the currently closed industrial estate.

Gerald and Amy promptly followed. She felt a tremor of anxiety clawing up her spine. Dagwood and Brian were seasoned professionals, but she was totally new to everything pertaining to Downstairs, and the dread of last night weighed heavy on her mind. As if sensing her concern, Gerald shuffled closer beside her as they walked. He easily floated through the high street crowds, masked and attired in casual black day clothes.

'Are you okay?' Gerald asked her.

'Kind of. A bit nervous, really, especially after last night. I can't believe we've finally got him. What if I get in the way?'

'I won't let anything happen to you.'

'Seriously, you better not. How stupid is he? It almost feels like he's doing this to draw you out. You planning to kill him?'

Gerald's eyes wandered as he thought. 'I'm honestly not

sure. I . . . it's been a long time since it's taken so long to do an assassination. I'm sure you've noticed that I often pop out during the day and evening, getting things done. Bane has really sent me round the houses. And who knows where Lavender is . . .'

'But maybe this is a good thing.' She smiled sadly at him as he watched her enquiringly. 'Sometimes when you get anxious, your aura turns sour. It makes me uneasy, like you'll go and do what happened with the prisoners again. You need to learn how to endure things like this, otherwise you'll just start killing everybody.'

'I understand.' His tone was morose.

'I don't mean anything by it,' she said quietly.

She refused to say anything more, reluctant to admit that she had heard him wailing in his sleep the night he killed the four prisoners. His turmoil had awoken her, and she scrambled out of bed and ran to his loft. The door to his room was locked, so she had pressed her ear against the cold wood, listening as Gerald pleaded to no one in sorrowful Grimtongue. The grogginess in his voice was thick with sleep, but the emotion that hung on his words was that of someone fully awake and alert to the sins of themselves. As she had clutched at the cold wood of the Reaper's bedroom entrance, she wished she had the ability not to feel so acutely, to become submerged in the tsunami of another's turmoil. She did not want to hear him agonising in his sleep again. The memory of that night made her shudder.

'No, I'm glad you said it. I need to remember that. It's important. Especially with my Awakening. Ah, looks like we're here.'

Gerald pointed to the intersection ahead of them, across which Dagwood and Brian had reunited, walking determinedly towards a deserted area guarded with the tall metal fences of an industrial estate. The pair followed suit, weaving between the crowds until they had joined the others.

Impenetrable steel panels stretched the length of the complex on White Hart Lane. It was heavily fortified, infested with CCTV, and silent from the other side. The main door was padlocked, and seen from between the grills of the gate, rusted shipping containers, warehouses, and transit vans awaited the working week ahead. Something clicked loudly from the padlocked door, and Josh's mischievous face appeared behind the entrance. The quartet slipped through the gate in silence.

'They've stopped shagging,' Josh said. He then indicated the path directly ahead. 'They're literally just down there. I've turned the cameras on that path in the opposite direction.' He pointed at the row of CCTV cameras outside each of the buildings. Instead of focusing on the path and the areas immediately around them, they were all face down as if in shame.

'How should we do this?' Josh asked. 'You wanna lead, Daggy? Get us over there and we can ambush 'em. If he's all flustered and surprised, it'll be easier to capture him, I think.'

'Sounds good!' Dagwood said. He splayed his hands towards the ground to conjure the outline of a Hammerspace trapdoor.

'Excellent,' said Gerald, turning to Amy. 'Few people can make Hammerspace tunnels as well as Dagwood.'

Dagwood's face reddened. He turned from Gerald, to Brian, to Amy, to Josh, then back to Gerald, his eyes glistening. 'Well, Mr Reaper, I—'

'No time for gushing, Dagwood,' said Brian, tapping him firmly on the back. 'Let us in.'

A flustered Dagwood opened the trapdoor to reveal a gaping blackness into which he and his *Gardien* colleagues slipped without hesitation. Amy could feel there was nothing untoward from the tunnel, but the impenetrable darkness was intimidating. Gerald gripped her wrist tighter, stepping into the space and pulling her along with him. She inhaled as cold air reached up to meet her, then exhaled sharply once they were on the ground. The trapdoor closed above them, encasing them in a winding tunnel that was tiled with sandstone. Fire torches lined the walls. The ground was cement and cold. The *Gardien* trio darted ahead of them, their black figures almost disappearing into the gloom.

As he ran after the others, Gerald glanced at her from over his shoulder. 'Find a place to hide when it's safe to do so.'

'Gladly.'

At the end of the tunnel, a silver square phased into view on the ceiling above. Gerald narrowed his eyes at the ceiling, and the scarlet flash indicated he was staring through their confines to the industrial estate above. The *Gardien* agents, and Amy, stilled in the darkness to watch him. His hurricane of magic encased her.

'There's a collection of wheelie bins a few yards away from where Bane's car is parked,' he said. 'Please head there as soon as you can, Amy.'

Amy nodded dumbly, and she stared at the ceiling in hopes that she could peer through the pavement herself. She barely had a chance to prepare when Gerald gently linked his arm with hers. He shot upwards, crashing through the Hammerspace opening.

The world rushed all around her. Amy heard a shrill scream; she felt scraps of metal and plastic rain into her hair. The stench of fresh leather, Cool Water aftershave, and semen filled her nose, and the arousing moist aura of lust vanished in favour of fear, horror, fright; it was like the sudden gravitational jolt felt during the plunge of a roller coaster or the tremor of a heart skipping at the news of a sudden, unexpected death in the family. The aura transformation was quick and strong, and it was all coming from Imogen Carrington, who screamed as Gerald and Amy crashed through the base of her car, ripping it in half at the impact, and hurling her across to the other side of the path to flounder against a shipping container. She was still attached to her seat. The second aura that was unnaturally calm and frosty with rage came from Tyrell Bane.

The warlock quickly flipped over the car wreckage, crouching into a low, threatening stance as Dagwood, Brian, and Josh came to stand in front of Gerald, while Amy used the furore to flee to the warehouse behind them. She pressed herself behind the row of wheelie bins, watching the quartet confront Bane. Great chunks of the expensive Mercedes were strewn across the path between them like black glaciers, their polished surfaces all but glistening in the sun.

From her hiding place, Amy still had a clear view of the warlock's unpleasantness. Skin that could have been rich and golden with youth was pale like butter, and deep circles marred cruel eyes. His clothes were dishevelled, but he hid it well: rolling the sleeves of his hoodie to his elbows to hide the frayed cuffs; wearing longer jeans than was necessary so that the grime of his Converses couldn't be seen. And that defiant, desperate presence punctuated his otherwise aggressively aloof aura. He was the leader of a formidable gang, and in control of many people, but he had still fallen on hard times. Becoming romantically involved with a woman of Imogen Carrington's status was smart for him, and absolutely foolish for her. The warlock glanced at her now. She was still strapped to her seat, and her screams were shrill. A frown marred his features further, and a deep unease drenched his aura.

He returned to his adversaries with an unconvincing sneer. 'Dagwood. You're looking well.'

Dagwood bristled, but before he had a chance to respond, Gerald had conjured a scythe from his Hammerspace. He marched forwards, and it was then that Bane fully realised who was in this group. His eyes widened in disbelief at Gerald. The Reaper took the moment of confusion to advance upon him. Bane conjured a steel staff of his own with a speed that surprised everyone, blocking the sharp blade of the scythe.

'So, you're actually here, Reaper?' he said.

'Are you really that desperate to provoke me?' Gerald's voice was flat with irritation.

'What? You not used to that? We ain't all scared of you, you know. And I know you only do *that thing* in certain circumstances, so I reckon I'm good.'

The others in the vicinity flinched at the mention of *that thing*, and it triggered an uncharacteristic aggression in Gerald. The Reaper applied more pressure. The noise of metal grating on metal pierced the air. Amy saw Josh running over to the still-hysterical Imogen Carrington while Bane and Gerald fought. Bane's eyes glanced at Imogen once more, but the slight distraction was enough for Gerald to sweep him off his feet. As the warlock rolled on the ground, dodging Gerald's indiscriminate swipes, Brian lay in wait, anticipating a chance to petrify the warlock. Dagwood joined the offensive. He made a sign in the air, and an arch of black phials appeared in a puff of smoke above his head. He sent the phials whizzing towards Bane with another hand sign. They exploded upon impact, but Bane nullified the worst of it by conjuring an arsenal of green phials of his own.

Gerald was painfully restraining himself, making every attempt to incapacitate Bane without killing him as the warlock danced around the estate, looking increasingly exhausted, his clothes singed by Dagwood's attack. He kept looking at Imogen as he fought, as if hoping to grab her and escape. His aura eventually succumbed to the inevitable, and Amy felt the annoyed resignation crash within him as he decided to abandon his lover.

'Fuck it,' he hissed. A Hammerspace trapdoor opened beside him. He jumped inside. His eyes met Amy's before he disappeared, and a confused expression crossed his face.

Dagwood, Brian, and Gerald launched themselves at the trapdoor and ended up crashing into each other. Brian swore loudly and Dagwood sighed, balling a disappointed hand on his hips. Gerald shook his head, returned the scythe to his Hammerspace, and glanced backwards at Amy. When he exhaled, his body hung with deflation. The burn of irritation returned to his aura. Amy grimaced, then jogged up to rejoin the group.

'Sorry guys,' she muttered.

'Fucking annoying,' Brian said. He fiddled with the side of his goggles to slide the tints back over his eyes.

'All's not lost,' Gerald said. He was staring at the inconsolable Imogen Carrington as she failed to escape from Josh. 'She'll lead us to him.'

The others followed his gaze, and Amy felt the shift from despondency to determination in the air. Returning to the heiress provided a comical sight. She tried to run away from Josh while still restrained by her seat belt, and any attempt

Josh made to help resulted in a louder scream, more aggressive but pitiful punches, and a fresh wave of tears.

'Oh dear!' said Dagwood.

'Let's put them both out of their misery,' said Brian. 'Dagwood, do something about these?' He gestured to the car debris.

'Right,' said Dagwood. He got to work sending the ruins of the Mercedes into a series of Hammerspace tunnels. What he would do with them afterwards was beyond Amy's comprehension, but she appreciated watching him clean up the wreckage. It was the bizarre banality that she needed after such an intense fight. Dagwood's clean-up gave her a chance to calm her nerves, to breathe normally again, and for the adrenaline to reduce to a low simmer. She only felt satisfied when the pounding in her ears abated.

But there was one thing she couldn't ignore: Bane's eyes as they bore into hers, and the way they looked like a warning. She hoped it was a misread, that the sunlight had made him squint, that him managing to locate her amid all that frenzy was a coincidence. She would keep hoping. The thought of him marking her as a target was too frightening to consider.

CHAPTER SEVEN
Amy

Imogen had refused to cooperate unless she was given a representative. After the *Gardien* agents had freed her the day before, the heiress had been taken into private human custody to await questioning, which eventually led to Gerald and Amy being invited to the Ritz Hotel using a direct lift from Downstairs in the morning. Blythe, with his royal connections, accompanied them, much to the disappointment of Josh, who would have loved to attend and get the latest gossip.

For this meeting, Gerald wore an outer cloak over his everyday clothes. It was made from black crushed velvet and pooled around his feet. The wide hood cast a shadow over his face. His veil was impenetrable. Beside him, Blythe wore his best black suit, abandoning his usual oversized loungewear. Dark sunglasses obscured his eyes. Amy kept her attire formal, but she was too curious about the upcoming events to care what she looked like. It was Sunday, and their meeting was booked for ten a.m. prompt.

At half nine, the lift doors opened into an elaborately decorated room on the third floor of the hotel. The carpet was soft and plush, and golden filigree artwork adorned pearl walls. A single rose-varnished table surrounded by velvet chairs awaited them. There was a silverware set already left on the table with an assortment of teabags and continental breakfast pastries. Because she was hungry, Amy helped herself to a croissant and poured some English breakfast tea.

'Want some?' she asked them.

'Why are you even here?' asked Blythe.

'Gerald said I could come.'

The wraith swivelled to face Gerald. Even behind his glasses, the look of loathing was obvious. Amy shivered in the coldness of his anger, quickly shrugging it off in indignation.

'I'm his partner,' she said. 'I should know what's going on.'

'She's right, Blythe,' Gerald said lightly. 'Let's all sit down. Amy' – he turned to her, and it was impossible to read his expression with so much of his face covered – 'what you're about to witness is a rare open meeting between human and Downer executives. With the Concealment Act, we try to avoid each other if we can, but this is an unusual situation. And I can only think of a handful of times when a Reaper has had to directly confront a human that's made a request, but I don't think Imogen will understand the severity of her involvement with Bane until she sees me in person.'

'And that's why you're hiding your face even more than usual.'

'Yes. Can't have any of them knowing what I look like.'

She refocused when the door opened and a mature white man in a suit entered with Imogen in tow. She looked every part the damsel: eyes still puffy and pink from a night of crying, hair down to brush against her shoulders in a state of static dishevelment, and not a lick of make-up. But there were some things she still couldn't do without: a glimmer of diamond earrings poked through the blonde curtains of her hair, and an emerald brooch was pinned to a cashmere jumper, lightly clinking against the pearl beads that hung low from her neck.

In lieu of a greeting, Gerald unsheathed his gloves out of view and brought his bare hands to rest on the tabletop. Both humans baulked at the sight temporarily, but quickly recovered, settling down in the chairs opposite.

'Viscount Brighton,' said Gerald to the man. Amy frowned. This wasn't his normal voice. It came with the lilt of an accent she could not identify, but there was something almost French about it.

'Sir Gethsemane,' the Viscount said. 'And Mr Mason.'

'Brighton.' Blythe nodded.

The men turned to Imogen.

She drew into herself defensively. 'Gentlemen,' she sniffed, then looked away at the far wall.

Amy sipped some tea to mask her smile. There was an unmistakable essence of prejudice enshrouding both the guests, but it was tinged with aristocratic politeness. The man called Viscount Brighton was racked with an anthropological curiosity as he observed the Reaper in all his foreignness and the equally African-descended wraith beside him. Imogen's was accompanied by a note of fetish, as if she was comparing both Gerald and Blythe to Tyrell Bane and trying to figure out which was the better-looking one. Racism always had so many different tones to it, but this was the first time Amy had the chance to parse the auras of anyone of such elite status. She was a Black woman from Streatham; she doubted anyone of the landed gentry even knew it existed. So accustomed was she to the heavy notes of people from her own part of London, as hot and irritating as the bristling heat of werewolves, that this new aura, with its cunning unctuousness, was a novel sensation.

'Well, there's no need to pussyfoot around the issue,'

Blythe said to Imogen. 'We all know why we're here. What is your connection to Tyrell Bane?'

'We are business partners.'

'That's not how it was told to me.'

'Well, we *are* just acquaintances.'

'Acquaintances with benefits?' asked Blythe with a sneer. He leaned over the table, removing his glasses to stare at Imogen with scarlet animosity. She flinched. Her eyes shimmered with tears, and she turned to Viscount Brighton with a pleading expression.

'I think honesty is best here,' said the Viscount. He glanced at Gerald's exposed hands as they rested atop the rosewood. Imogen followed his gaze, then nodded sullenly.

'Good,' said Blythe. 'So how did this all come about?'

'I'm keeping the peace,' she said. 'This is a delicate situation.'

Amy felt the surge of humiliation rise from within Imogen's aura. She was curious now and decided to give full details to Josh when she next saw him.

When Imogen prolonged her silence, Blythe hissed his annoyance. He stared at her piercingly.

'So, Bane knows your father, obviously, and it appears they've worked together, on and off, for a few years. I can imagine the situation at the Channel would have been disastrous for anyone even tangentially connected to Darkhouse, let alone a regular collaborator. Does Walter Carrington fund Tyrell Bane?'

'No, not at all!' Imogen drew backwards, as if she had been slapped. Her cheeks flushed crimson. A raw indignation flavoured her aura, and she stared at the wraith evenly as she finally offered information.

'Yes, Tyrell has done business with my father. Thanks to the Whitehall death' – she glanced at Gerald – 'my father has been able to keep a low profile. But there's always still the threat of an investigation into his . . . into our family business, especially with the Butler connection. I'm just trying to ensure nothing untoward happens between either of them.'

'So where is Bane now?' asked Gerald.

Imogen avoided his gaze. 'I don't know.'

'She's lying,' said Amy. The room turned to her, then refocused on Imogen. The heiress only had eyes for Amy as she shot her a venomous glare.

'Where is Bane now?' Gerald repeated. 'I'm sure I don't have to go into detail about how serious this situation is, Mrs Carrington.'

Imogen fiddled with a strap on her bag as she spoke. 'Well, I don't know the full location. He has a hideout on Cromwell Road in South Kensington. I haven't been to it myself, not directly. But he tends to take me to restaurants around that area. That's where he disappears to. I know nothing other than that. Seriously.' She said the last word directly to Amy.

Gerald and Blythe waited for Amy to confirm Imogen's honesty. When she nodded, they visibly relaxed.

'How long has your father been working with Bane?' asked Blythe.

'For about three years, since the rise of his gang, really. We've always known about Tyrell Bane. A few people in our circles have at least heard of him, but not all of them know he's not human. They just suspect his criminality. But he's genuinely charismatic. I mean, you don't reach those heights without some manipulative skill, so no one cares to pry too deeply into his affairs. That's how he's kept a safe profile within high society. But the only person who knows that he was the main organiser of the refugee situation is my father. The people arrested in the case are some of Bane's gang members, who my father also knows. But they're human, and they're of low rank, so they don't know they've been working for a warlock all this time. All the senior executives who knew his full identity mysteriously vanished.' She scrutinised Blythe with scepticism.

'Yes, yes, very mysterious,' said Blythe.

'Are you aware of Melanie Lavender?' Gerald asked.

'Little witch?'

When Gerald nodded, she continued. 'They were together once, apparently. She has a bit of an obsession with men in power. But he doesn't care about her like *that*. She's another one, easily manipulated, and always ready to be used.'

Gerald and Blythe grew tense, their auras thickening with anticipation.

'When did they last make contact?' the Reaper asked.

'She reached out when the smuggling business got exposed. After his executives went missing, Tyrell grew desperate. Lavender agreed to take over some of his load and assist with a few jobs here and there. At the moment, they have a truce, but no one else in the business knows. They still think it's Darkhouse versus the Lads. Not even my father knows this. Just me.'

Blythe reclined in his chair. Amy could feel the iron in his resolve. She could only imagine the reams of thought unravelling in his mind as he calculated his next move with *Gardien*. Gerald was mildly satisfied, according to his aura. There was a chance that his assassination would go smoother now that Bane and Lavender were working together again. As everyone disappeared into their thoughts, Viscount Brighton cleared his throat.

'Are there . . . any more questions?' he asked the room.

'None for now,' said Gerald, turning to Blythe.

'No,' said Blythe. 'But we might need to meet again. I'll let you know.'

At this, Imogen's aura was spiked with anxiety, but she hid it well.

'I wonder if Bane knows of the secret entrance to Kensington Palace?' Blythe asked. He slid his sunglasses back on his face, smirking cruelly when Imogen looked at him in horror. 'Oh, was I supposed to keep quiet about that?'

Viscount Brighton frowned at the reddening Imogen. 'Did the warlock visit you in Kensington Palace?' When no answer arrived, he sighed deeply. 'You have been sent there because you're in custody. Do not allow that man to enter royal grounds again.'

'Yes, of course,' she said absently, but from parsing her aura, Amy knew this was a lie.

'This has been helpful. Thank you both,' said Gerald. The two aristocrats nodded stiffly, then left the room. The hallway behind the door was flushed with their relief. Amy snorted with bemusement. It must have been a bizarre experience to meet with Gerald and Blythe of all people.

'Well, we're getting somewhere,' Gerald said, nudging Blythe playfully. The wraith squirmed away from him before coming to a stand.

'Obviously.'

Satisfied and determined, the trio entered the awaiting lift.

On Bank Holiday Monday, Amy and Gerald split their time between St Pancras and Juniper Close, where *Gardien* had established their base of operations. Shaun had set up a series of transmitters around the South Kensington area to observe Cromwell Road specifically, while the other members took turns to patrol the area. Just a few days earlier, Amy, Gerald, and Josh had sat on the steps of the Victoria and Albert Museum, unaware that Tyrell Bane was only a few feet away in his hideout the whole time.

In the early afternoon, they separated. Gerald carried out an assassination on the other side of the city alone. At the Renaissance Hotel, Amy took to the mezzanine floor of the apartment. She ran tentative fingers along the spines of black leather books, pausing every now and then to chance a perusal. Many of the pages were written by hand, often in the distinct cuneiform of Grimscript, and others were sealed shut by an enchantment. Those in English detailed expressive poetry honouring the Death King Armageddon or telling the story of the Disaster Quartet that Gerald had mentioned prior. Conquest was always disparaged in the texts, but no explanation was provided for the great schism that made him an enemy of Death. There was another name, however, that often accompanied Armageddon – the angel Golgotha. She tried to search the name on her phone, but it offered no tangible results, just referrals to Christian sites.

Her scrolling was interrupted by a notification from her banking app. Her portion of Gerald's assassination fee had been transferred into her account. She watched the screen with an increasing sense of unease. Her new-found fortune was most welcome, but it was blood money, and she was still nervous to spend it.

A flash of a news item appeared on her screen as another distraction. After hearing that the Home Secretary had requested Nadine Samson's assassination, Amy had set up alerts for anything relating to the anti-deportation movement. She was increasingly impressed with Nadine's activity:

at only twenty-one, she had staged ten die-ins at Heathrow Airport, had raised thousands of pounds in legal fees for detained Caribbean-British citizens, and re-centred the humanity of Britain's abandoned refugees.

Today, Nadine declared a massive march on Whitehall, followed by a Peace Camp to be set up outside Blue Meadow Detention Centre in Bexley. According to the Kill Blue Meadow website, Nadine had some major news to reveal about a slew of alleged human rights offences taking place within the facility, many committed by the guards hired by WCT Security.

'WCT Security?' she murmured, frowning at the familiarity. She began to search the name of the company and was horrified by what she found.

CHAPTER EIGHT
Gerald

When Gerald returned from his assassination, he heard Amy fussing about in her room, only to rush down the stairs shortly afterwards dressed for war. Two braids ran down both sides of her head, phasing into a pair of neat plaits that curled on her shoulders. She wore all black, including lipstick.

'Get into your civilian gear,' she said. 'We're going to Bexley. The coach leaves in an hour and we need to get a good seat.'

'Okay? And this is for?' Gerald asked, complying with her demands by removing his mask.

'WCT Security!' Amy rushed towards him, her eyes wild with excitement. 'The Carringtons' company runs Blue Meadow. All the refugees in this whole Channel scandal were found in WCT boats and shipping containers. They're involved with Bane's human smuggling ring! Nadine Samson said she's got a bad boy piece of information about them and she's gonna reveal it tonight outside the centre. We *have* to go. It'll give us clues about Bane... we don't know who else might be there. If a major protest was happening right outside one of your bases of operation, would you not send someone to scope it out for you?'

'Wow. Okay, wow. I hear you.' Gerald increased his pace. There was no spare clothing in his Hammerspace for him to transform into, so he rushed up the stairs and returned to the living room in his black civilian clothes, wearing thick rubber gloves instead of his usual leather. He messaged Blythe as he got ready to inform him of these developments, making sure to mention it was all a result of Amy's investigation. When they finally left the apartment, he flitted across to central London.

Every road outside the Palace of Westminster was packed with people, and the traffic had been diverted to avoid the protest. Britons from all walks of life hurled abuse at Parliament's gilded, impenetrable walls. Protestors clambered up Winston Churchill's statue with smoke flares. Garlands of slogans hung from every plinth in Parliament Square. Whitehall was jammed in a sea of black as people marched up the road to Trafalgar Square, which was then flanked by a row of nondescript coaches to take people to Blue Meadow on a first come, first served basis. Using his superspeed, Gerald ensured he and Amy were the first to embark on one of the coaches. They both decided to forego Gerald's abilities to travel, realising the potential to gather intel from the protestors on the journey.

As they crammed into their seats, he felt his stomach flutter with the daringness of this operation. He rarely went to protests, and making unpredictable decisions like this was against his nature. His day was dictated by the Grim Book, and the cycle of his conversations with his father, and the movements of Downstairs. For a being of great supernatural power, his life was relatively repetitive. He watched Amy askance as she scrolled through her phone relentlessly, trying to bring him up to speed with all the information he had missed over the past few months, and marvelled at her ability to follow the wiles of her heart so confidently. He reclined in his seat to listen properly, committing her intel about Blue Meadow to memory.

The cavalcade of coaches began to move, rumbling away from Trafalgar Square, and the protestors cheered enthusiastically in response. All around him, young people in black tracksuits ran up and down the aisle to speak to friends and fellow activists. Seasoned protestors, their faces marked with the scars of their struggles, took the time to give oral histories of the last time they marched to Blue Meadow, or joined in the 2011 riots, or fought against the police in the eighties, or how their parents and grandparents, great aunts and cousins took part in the Battle of Cable Street. He smiled with polite scepticism as some of the stories became more fantastical and diverted from the written account.

Gerald watched the world outside, peering over Amy's shoulder to see the zoetrope of faces that regarded the coach, some with the unmistakable disdain he had grown accustomed to in Britain, and a few with the hopeful, tight smiles of British-flavoured encouragement.

'Do you know the Home Secretary?' asked Amy. 'Deportations are her remit, right? She might be involved, too.'

Gerald frowned. 'Vaguely,' he said. 'She's not a Carrington. She's from the Adamson family. The current patriarch is the . . .' he narrowed his eyes in thought. 'Marquis of Exeter. He's around the same age as Walter Carrington. Might be a connection there. I'll look into it. I'll probably have to ask my father.'

'Sure,' Amy said, then continued her search. 'Nadine's had a few death threats, not surprising with all the stuff she knows. Looks like she's made a few hints here and there that she's got a whistle-blower in Blue Meadow. I think that's the bad boy piece of—'

'What does that mean?' Gerald asked. 'Bad boy . . . ?'

Amy hid her mocking grin very poorly. 'You're like an old man. Like, I can't believe I'm two years older than you. It doesn't make sense.' Looking back out the window, she said, 'It means she's got something mad incriminating, that's what it means. Maybe something to send people to prison.'

'I'm looking forward to *that*,' Gerald said, ignoring her teasing.

'I signed up to the mailing list. I think I know what she's gonna do.'

'What's that?' Gerald glanced at her.

'She's probably set up a message to go out to everyone who signs up to the mailing list with all the info she has. It's the smartest thing to do if people in the government want her dead. Oh, my days, imagine if she does a Sir Alastair and sends things to the press? Oh, that will be a madness.'

'You sound so excited.'

'Of course I am! This is a *good* cause, Gerald. This country has no right deporting people like this after all it's done to the world! My grandma came here on a fake dream. She worked her arse off, wasn't allowed to take out a bank loan to buy a house, wasn't allowed to rent because of those stupid signs on the doors. She got spat at, called a nigger and a wog and all that shit. You think she *wanted* to stay here that long? Nah, nah. Burn it all to the ground.'

Gerald paused in thought, mesmerised by the way Amy's passion covered her cheeks. It froze his tongue, and he was lost in the storm of her indignation. He had not experienced such fervour for another person before, but a chord quivered within him, and strange thoughts invaded his head – thoughts that contained the burden of justice.

'I hear you,' he said eventually.

They exchanged ideas all the way to Bexley. By the time they disembarked outside the detention centre, the sun had begun to slip towards the horizon, and the warm orange hue bled into the darkness of the coming night.

The sense of camaraderie was contagious as they marched up the desolate slope towards Blue Meadow. When they rounded on the flatter Meadow Road, the protestors grew silent. In the darkening evening, the vast open space of empty field on either side of the road was unsettling even for Gerald. It was as if the fields stretched for miles without end, and not even the smallest members of English wildlife graced the area.

'What can you feel?' he murmured to Amy.

When she didn't answer, he looked at her and faltered. Her eyes were wide and glassy, lips slightly parted as she stared ahead at the plain metal gates at the end of the road which marked the entrance to the detention centre. He also watched the gates, marvelled at how plain they were, how they revealed nothing about the people inside.

'Amy,' he prompted, more urgently this time.

'Death,' she whispered.

He held onto her wrist as a precaution, not wanting her to faint among the crowd. His heart thumped along with the heavy beating of her pulse. He lightly rubbed his thumb along the soft skin inside her wrist, hoping that it was enough to encourage her. On Sitton Road, he had been too distracted by Bane's audacity to focus on Amy, but this time, she looked haunted. He felt a displaced anger churn in his stomach. Amy had been thrust into countless dangers since partnering with him. He was a failure. This is not what he had wanted, and he was sure her place in his life as Armageddon's promised outlier should have had mutual benefits. What had he offered her since their partnership? Had he been of any use to her at all?

'Please tell me, Amy. Where is the death? In the centre?'

She nodded.

'Who's dead?'

'Women. And some men. They're getting killed in there. And people have been beaten. I can almost feel the bruises on my skin there's so much of it. And everyone's scared because ... it feels like something's been taken. Someone. Some people. They're trafficking people out of there, smuggling people in, for money ...'

Her hands balled into tight fists. He felt her arms tremble. He had not seen this expression on her before, and her distressed, shaken demeanour burned something within him. The resolve of his Wall wept at her terror. He had not properly considered the exhaustion, and the abject turmoil, of being assaulted with the gift of empathy.

'Okay, don't say anything else,' said Gerald, gripping her wrist tighter. He steadied his breathing, but Amy's erratic pulse disturbed him. The roiling mass of his stomach flared again. His body felt weightless. He was struggling to control himself.

In the heightening silence and the increasing dark, a young woman emerged from the front of the crowd. She stood above the assembled protestors, brandishing a megaphone. Her eyes were covered by sunglasses, and her braids swung low over her back. They swayed in the light breeze coming from the fields. She was surprisingly small, but something about her demeanour was intimidating in its defiance. Nadine Samson was beautiful to look at. She clicked on the megaphone, and her soft, disembodied voice crackled with static.

'Three . . . two . . . one. Everyone, check your mail.'

The buzz of hundreds of vibrating phones sounded like a locust storm, and an eerie, robotic chorus of various ringtones cut through the silence in distorted harmonies. And then, the human voices as they looked: short little gasps, screams of shock, angered yells, strings of swear words.

Gerald fished Amy's phone from her pocket, forcing eye contact with her for permission. She gave him a slight nod, but her glazed focus was fixed on the empty gates of the detention centre. When Gerald saw the images on the email, his hand gripped the phone tightly.

There were dozens of photos of naked people, beaten children of various ages, women in insulting positions bent over bed frames, some already assaulted and visibly unconscious. Most of the photos had a grinning WCT Security guard posing beside the abused, flashing peace signs, middle fingers, thumbs-ups. An attachment of documents revealed the names of missing children that had been sold to the centre from the Channel refugees, and bank statements showed the mutual exchange of people and goods between WCT Security and another unregistered organisation called Waterfront, which Gerald assumed was an alias for Darkhouse. Tyrell Bane, his elusive enemy, danced tauntingly out of reach. Gerald should have killed him in Tottenham. He wanted Bane's name out of the Grim Book, crossed over with the finality of his death. Gerald grabbed at the air with his free hand, almost mimicking the feel of pulped flesh, an image of Tyrell Bane in grey mortification solidifying as a potent desire in his mind.

'Now we're gonna stay here all night if we have to,' said Nadine. She gestured to the camera lenses all around her, nodding to the superior equipment that must have belonged to local and national news. 'Until someone comes out of there and gives us answers. Until our prime minister steps down. Until this government is gone. Until this trashy prison is burned up and all the refugees are free!'

The resultant roar of support rumbled in Gerald's ears. He put the phone on sleep and stared at the gate and its mocking simplicity. Without thinking, he slipped into the darkness of himself, calling upon the hands of unknown powers that had wormed into his body on the night of his Awakening. Amy flinched beside him, but he held onto her anyway. He could see inside the facility now, but due to his powers still being weak, he was restricted to the outer wings, the ones that were closest to the Meadow Road. It looked normal enough, just like a prison. Small families huddled in communal rooms and slept in bunkers; lone women were followed between floors by WCT guards. The guards also stood sentinel by the immediate entrance, in the lower ground floors, the staff room, the toilets.

The mundane nature of the evening workings of Blue Meadow calmed him a little until he saw a guard kick what looked like a teenage girl down the last of a flight of stairs, sending her tray of food clattering to the floor, dousing her in gravy and yoghurt. The guards in the area looked up from their tables and then returned to their prior activities, uncaring. Other guards who saw the incident simply stared at the girl and watched as she tried to clean up the mess she didn't cause. Gerald submerged himself in his feelings. He gave himself up to his rage. He was desperate to kill something, anything.

'*Laanah morthexis*,' he murmured.

At least fifty silver threads floated towards him from the banal façade of Blue Meadow. With all the commotion around him, and the stamping feet, and the push and sway of protestors as they threatened to knock the gates down, he was able to concentrate on his own task, watching as the insignificant spools of life, fragile like spiderwebs, calmly floated above the crowd, attaching themselves to all the guards he could see with his omnipresence.

'Gerald,' Amy whispered beside him.

He ignored her.

Sever.

The threads snapped with a musical pinging, tearing apart and floating away into the evening sky. Gerald steadied his breathing and closed his eyes, sending the powers away again with strained gratitude. The heat swelled within him once more, but this time he basked in it. When he opened his eyes again, Amy was staring at him in horror, but there was something pitiful about her expression, as if she understood what he had just done and why he did it, and that a part of her wondered whether she would do the same thing if she had powers like him, too. He trembled as the realisation of what he had just done dawned on him. He considered the repercussions, the shock of his family, the bleeding shrine, and the chastisement of his ancestors as they would inevitably visit him at night. But he couldn't force himself to care. His body flushed with violent heat. He had to fight away the cold smile that tugged at the corners of his mouth.

He was doused with a warm presence. Amy latched onto him, squeezing him into a hug until he felt he couldn't breathe anymore, the soft curls of her plaited hair rubbing against his cheek. He refused to reciprocate her touch, unable to trust his hands or what they would do, so he pushed her away. Panic flashed across her face at whatever expression she saw on his. With a vestige of dignity, he turned away from her, not wanting her to see him, and worried that she could feel it anyway.

As he walked away, a siren wailed through the air. Distant screams echoed from the Blue Meadow building.

In the silence of his bedroom, he made the phone call. It was quiet on the other side. No running sand, no tinkle of green tea, no wind chimes. Just a wall of hollowness. The atmosphere down the phone belonged to the Deep Arboretum, a place only permitted to the heads of the family. At last, Gerald heard a haggard sigh down the phone.

'I'm disappointed, Gethsemane,' said his father. And the call ended.

CHAPTER NINE

Amy

She called in sick the next day. By Wednesday morning, Amy told her manager, Vilma, that she was so unwell it was unlikely she would come in for the rest of the week, then after a lot of placating *I'm fine*'s, she hung up the phone with much guilt. When she felt the harrowing aura from upstairs, she knew she had done the right thing.

Gerald had not left his room since coming home on Monday evening. She left him alone at first, and then the chill of death awoke her from sleep, all but pushed her out of bed, and sent her running down the hallway to Gerald's room. After banging on the locked door and calling his name, she waited helplessly until the cold dissipated, giving way to a wave of grief that drowned her. She had stood vigil all Tuesday, listening as the Reaper groaned in his sleep, then went deadly silent, fighting with something that caused him great anguish. On Tuesday evening, she took a duvet and pillow downstairs because the aura was too cold and the pain within him was making her physically sick.

Her ill feelings were only exacerbated by the news that she read religiously. The UK threat level had been raised and citizens were advised to be vigilant at large gatherings. An intense operation was conducted at all prisons and government buildings, with most civil servants advised to work from home. Thanks to the Downey Met, the Upstairs public believed this was a new form of terrorist attack, but the tiny population of high society would have most likely suspected the Reaper family, and as such, assassination requests dropped dramatically in fear. Every day, Amy forced herself to flip open the latest page of the Grim Book only to be met with an earnest whiteness.

She understood their fear – in a setting where no one truly knew who was privy to the truth of Downstairs, suspicion would only grow wild within the aristocratic community. This anxious silence was what Gerald had called the culture of subterfuge: feign ignorance and assume everyone is an enemy. Who could you trust? And with whom could you discuss assassination? What if they were also watching the news in horror, believing that one of their number had requested the Blue Meadow deaths without thinking about the potential repercussions of exposing Downstairs? The only option would be to endure whatever irritant crossed their paths until it was safe to start killing again.

The deaths in Blue Meadow threatened to bury the revelations of the human rights violations from the same facility, but there were various late-night newsreaders that made it their mission to report on the newly opened inquiry into the matter. The photo of Walter Carrington was plastered all over the news. He was an ordinary man with age spots on a bald, wrinkled head, and dark eyes that were keen with intellect. The Home Secretary, revealed to be the grand-niece of Walter Carrington by marriage, resigned in the wake of the scandal, having been accused of overlooking the smuggling ring due to her family ties. So far, there was not enough evidence to conclude that Walter Carrington was the benefactor of the Downey Gang.

In all the upheaval, there was no news from any *Gardien*

members regarding Tyrell Bane's whereabouts, but a cursory glance at Gerald's notifications told her that Shaun surveilled the area twenty-four seven, and the rest of the team went out in twos or threes in twelve-hour rotations to locate the hideout in South Kensington. They tested the waters by releasing the two fugitives from Blythe's prison after wiping their memories, then following them around London to see if Bane would try to contact them again as his only remaining executives, but so far, they had been left alone. Now they waited to see if Melanie Lavender would make her move instead.

On Thursday morning, Blythe rang Gerald's phone. It rattled pathetically against the side table by the front door, having been firmly abandoned on May Day evening. After hesitating, Amy answered. When he heard her voice, the wraith went dead silent.

'Where is he?' Blythe asked at last.

'He's here. He's here. But he's not feeling too good.' She blinked and two droplets of water fell on the table in front of her. She balled her free hand into a fist and wiped her eyes aggressively. She hated that her voice wavered, but there was no way to hide it. She was scared and upset. 'He's been locked up in his room ever since Monday. He's not coming out. I don't know what to do.'

'I'll be up in a moment,' said Blythe before promptly ending the call.

He appeared at the hotel quicker than she expected. When the doorbell rang, she jumped in surprise, then rushed over to the door. Blythe was wearing his sunglasses, a beige trench coat, and fitted dark overalls. He offered her a curt nod, then made his own way up the stairs without looking at her.

'You want a drink?' Amy called up after him.

'No.'

She listened. Shortly afterwards came the resounding click of a lock, the creak of old hinges, and the echoing finality of a closing door. Amy collapsed against the stairs, allowing herself to cry more freely, and hoped that Blythe would help the Reaper get back on his feet.

CHAPTER TEN

Blythe

The wraith stowed the spare key to Gerald's bedroom in his Hammerspace and padded barefoot across the carpet, having left his shoes outside the door as habit. The room was reduced to velvet shadows and the bed was unmade and unslept in. The desk was untidy, sticky with spilled ink. Scraps of parchment paper fluttered across the draughty floor like ghostly tumbleweed. The sour scent of an unwashed body – like ammonia and sweat – was strong in the air. Blythe wrinkled his nose, then went straight towards the thick tapestry that hung on the wall beside the queen-sized bed. He let himself into the open arboretum. It was one of the few times since their initial meeting that Blythe was reminded of Gerald's vulnerability.

Their introduction had been typical for the future heads of two very important Downer families. Gerald had been seventeen at the time, and Blythe twenty. The Masons hosted the Reapers for dinner Upstairs at the Dorchester. His family had wanted to make a good impression, hiring a private suite on the top floor to give the Reapers a view of London, something markedly different to all that heat and sand in the Sahara, with hardly anything to see apart from the occasional camel and travelling merchant. Even now, Blythe cringed when he recalled his mother's ignorant speech about their homeland. But one thing he appreciated was the gracefulness in which it was received. The Reapers only smiled kindly, agreed that London really was interesting and unique, and that they were so excited for Gerald to begin his work in the city.

The meetings became more frequent the closer Gerald got to his full appointment to London. It was during one of these latter events that Blythe finally grew bored of it all and went into the garden to get away. He smoked cigarettes back then, and he enjoyed rolling the small menthol tip between his fingers, watching as the chalk-white filter turned a tarry brown within moments. He was so lost in thought that he never heard Gerald approaching until the Reaper was sitting beside him, crouching low to watch the koi pond with great interest.

'It's a lot of fuss, isn't it?' Gerald had said. 'I didn't know so many dinners were needed to establish a connection. We're not getting married, are we?'

'If it was up to my mother . . .'

Gerald snorted. He looked up at Blythe with the doe eyes of absolute innocence, his hair thick and unruly, his rounded face pokable and childish. Blythe frowned at him, all confidence lost in the so-called heir of the lauded Reapers.

'I'm Gerald, by the way,' said Gerald.

'I know who you are.'

'Hmm. What's your name?'

'You know my name.'

'Yes, but I want you to say it,' said Gerald. 'We haven't introduced ourselves properly at all.'

'What are you talking about? We met last year at the Dorchester. We were introduced.'

'By our families.' Gerald smiled at him. 'We never got a chance to talk.'

'Blythe. Obliged.'

'Glad to meet you, Blythe. I hope we can become great friends.'

'Not necessary,' said Blythe. 'You know how these things go. It's a business transaction, Gerald.'

'Doesn't have to be. I know, I'll come to your house tomorrow for lunch?'

'No.'

'Would you like to come to mine?'

'Not at all.'

Gerald smiled, then he started to chuckle to himself. Before long, he was all but rolling on the ground, cackling with laughter. Blythe watched it all with distaste, wondering whether there had been a mix-up at the birth, and the giggling child before him was really a changeling planted to mock the Reaper name. At long last, Gerald rose to stand, wiped his eyes with gloved hands, and brushed the grass from his knees.

'Well, I'll see you later, Blythe!' he said, turning on his heel to go back inside.

'Why did you even come out here?' Blythe said.

'Oh.' Gerald turned to watch him askance, his expression playfully confused. 'We're both lonely, aren't we? Doesn't that kind of thing just gnaw at your insides? Sometimes I feel like I can't stand it.' He flashed Blythe another grin and left him in the garden. Blythe shook his head, almost to rid himself of the entire conversation, and lit another cigarette.

Right now, Gerald floated face-up in a pond of blood with two scarlet track marks of old crusted tears lining either side of his face. His blank expression didn't change when he saw Blythe standing by the pond. His eyes moved to follow the wraith as he sat down on the rocks around the perimeter.

They stared at each other for so long that a fresh wave of tears ran down Gerald's face. The Reaper sniffed, then stared up at the artificial sky again, with its pulsing brightness imitating a volatile sun. Blythe removed his sunglasses anyway, squinted at the resultant light assault, then blinked rapidly to adjust.

'Why are you so upset?' he said.

'I did something bad, Blythe.' Gerald's voice was barely a whisper.

'Explain what you did.'

'Haven't you heard? You must have heard. I'm sure all of Downstairs is talking about it. Gethsemane the mass murderer. Killing humans left and right.'

'Everyone's talking about it, yes. But not out of horror, if that's what you're worried about. They don't expect anything less from you. You're a Reaper. They just assume it was a massive request that you undertook. You're the only one having an existential crisis about it.'

'Because it's worth one.'

'Well, if you were going to feel like this, why do it in the first place?' Blythe patted his coat down for a cigar, then glanced around at the untainted wildlife, and with an annoyed sigh, decided not to smoke.

'I wasn't thinking. Amy tried to stop me. I just couldn't. Something came over me and all these feelings just rushed out before I could do anything.'

'According to the news, all sorts of atrocities were happening in there. Who wouldn't want to kill those people after witnessing that?'

'It's not the right thing to do. It was classless; lacking elegance. I'm not supposed to succumb to my emotions and kill people because of them. Don't you think it was wrong?'

'I don't think about right or wrong. I look at outcomes. If we all considered the rightness and wrongness of things before doing them, nothing would get done. Arguments of morality are often used to avoid doing anything at all.'

'But Blythe—'

'Are you saying you were just going to look at those photographs, see children being abused in a government facility, ingest the information that the guards were working with Bane to traffic vulnerable people, and then turn around and go home?'

When Gerald didn't say anything, Blythe sighed again, removing his coat because it was too hot now.

'You don't know he did this, but your father explained your training to me when I first met him,' he said. 'Apparently, Reapers aren't allowed to experience emotions properly. You all purposely inhibit yourselves when you feel too happy or sad and tuck it behind that Wall or whatever. But you're the *special one*, so he raised you with even more emotional restriction because your Awakening was always going to be the most powerful and dangerous if not kept in check. Is all that correct?'

'That's correct.'

'And the reason your training was especially brutal is because of what happened in the desert that day.'

Gerald flinched in the water, and he appeared to chew his lip to stop himself from talking. Blythe knew this was beneath him, and his hands felt stained with the rot of decayed fruit, but he persevered, because he was the only one to whom Gerald had fully revealed that event: that day when he had lost control, succumbed to the entity that prowled behind his Wall, and was found by his Tribe leaders surrounded by the bloody entrails of another. It floored him that the Tribe's response was to torture their heir to stoicism instead of examining the circumstances that had triggered his behaviour. And because Gerald was the only Reaper with direct contact with that blasted Armageddon, the Tribe relied heavily on their millennia-old traditions to resolve the issue. The Death King had a lot to answer for.

'If anyone's to blame for this, it's your father.'

Gerald finally looked at him. His brows knitted in offence.

'That man deifies you and it's not healthy,' said Blythe. 'Fuck it,' he growled, grabbing a cigar from his pocket, and lighting it decisively. 'What happened on Monday is the result of poor training. You Reapers are cursed for various reasons, and one of them is the fear you all have of your own powers, inventing all these new rules and customs to make life harder for yourselves. You did what you did and you can't take it back. The most you can do to make amends is finish the job by getting Bane and Lavender, the ones who put you in all this mess.'

'Are you just saying this because you want to close the case?'

'Of course I am. But I say it for you also.' He took a long draw from the cigar, relishing in the welcome tarry cloud that surrounded him afterwards. 'You are not yet finished. There are two Downers just waiting for this all to die down so that they can pick up the fallen pieces and resume their criminal activity. And there is an unknown person looking after them, probably funding them, giving them amnesty. Don't you want all of that to come to an end?'

Gerald shrugged and the water rippled around him. 'I used to say with confidence that I'm not a hero and that Reapers are impartial. We just do what we do because we must, nothing to do with wrongness or rightness. I think I said all of that because I never allowed myself to feel anything. But Blythe, can't you see that my not feeling anything is what enables me to do my job? If I caved into the feelings of my heart all the time, things would get complicated. Like now. I don't want to relish the taste of destruction.'

'And I'm saying you need to do both. Find a healthy balance between feeling and unfeeling, otherwise you will always be cursed.'

'I *will* always be cursed.' Gerald held his arms aloft until his hands were directly above him. He squinted as the skylights caught his eyes. Bloody water dripped from his grey, polished bones, and splashed on this face. He closed his eyes as if to feel the beads of blood roll down his skin and rejoin the water in the pond.

'I mean a curse of the mind,' said Blythe. 'If you keep trying not to feel anything at all, you will go insane. And next time, you won't just kill the bad ones.'

'Hmm.'

'And you know what else?' Blythe stubbed the cigar on a nearby stone. 'Your father told me to look after you during that conversation. He said you would one day get into some trouble because it happens to all Reapers eventually. Because the strain of the curse and the restrictions on your emotions lead to destruction. At the time, I thought he was exaggerating. Today I wonder, if these wild outbursts are so well known, why have the Reapers not tried to change their methods? Perhaps considered other ways to navigate this curse of yours? And now, their golden child is in a full-blown meltdown because of his own family's stupidity, and here *I* am, keeping a silly promise and indulging you all. What a cursed family.'

'You're on a roll today, Blythe.'

Blythe stood and looked down his nose to watch Gerald before he slid on his glasses.

'Hurry up and get better. You can only get better by trying again. We *will* find Bane eventually. You have a job to complete when we do.'

He turned and left Gerald in the pool. He heard the slosh of water as the Reaper heaved himself onto the rocks.

By the time Gerald said, 'Thank you,' Blythe had already slammed the door shut.

CHAPTER ELEVEN

Amy

When Blythe had descended the stairs, he pulled an envelope from his Hammerspace and tossed it on the office desk without looking at her, then left. As annoyed as she was, the difference in the aura upstairs was instantaneous. It was still unpredictable, like an unsettled storm, but she could sense the abating of the tempest winds that had wreaked havoc with Gerald's psyche for the best part of a week.

Out of curiosity, she checked the envelope and discovered field notes from *Gardien* from their patrols around Cromwell Road and the surrounding areas. Some light reconnaissance work had been performed around Dalston, with a few informants offering information about the disused shop — now totally stripped of all potential evidence by Bane — beside Voodoo Rays. Shaun and Dani had tapped into the neighbouring restaurant's CCTV footage for any further Bane sightings, but besides his latest venture with Imogen Carrington, the warlock was nowhere to be found.

There was also information pertaining to their resident heiress, who had been moved to a more secure location in Kensington Palace after an attempted break-in from Bane. Imogen had been visibly shaken, claiming that all the warlock had achieved was stealing back the emerald brooch he had gifted her as a means to reclaim the last of his riches, but she was still unaware of his whereabouts afterwards. Her father's arrest had been traumatic for her, but the notes concluded that Walter Carrington was not the protector of the Downey Gang.

Interestingly, the notes also explained in more detail the reconciliation between Lads and Darkhouse after the latter's dissolution. Following Bane's supposed disappearance and the deaths of his top executives, the remaining members of Darkhouse melted into everyday London delinquent activity, searching for another criminal group to claim as family. The more stable Lads appeared to have returned to Bane's control.

There was a question of Lavender's whereabouts. The witch was still nowhere to be found, but evidence of her loyalty was seen in the sudden clean-up of businesses that formerly belonged to Darkhouse, and the appearance of a new unregistered company – Gardens Construction – among the list of shareholders that bought the dregs of the fallen WCT Security firm. Based on her elusiveness, it was concluded by *Gardien* that Lavender had kept her status as a witch secret from her faction, with which Amy agreed.

Sometimes it was hard to believe Melanie Lavender was only eighteen. She moved with a shadowy expertise, a seasoned finesse belonging to someone twice her age. She had saved her former partner, used her potent magic to aid in his latest desperate endeavours, and remained unseen and untouchable in the process. Amy could not place her motives. At this point, the witch was as big a mystery as the unknown gang protector. But despite Lavender's skill, she was a child traversing the world of adults. Whatever grooming the witch had endured had created a maelstrom of violence. Amy nursed an uncomfortable pity towards her. She wanted to meet her, if only to understand the thoughts in her head.

*

On Friday, she awoke with a sense of relief as the coldness from Gerald's room finally vanished. She went shopping around the area to gather some snacks and supplies for the house, browsing the artisan bakeries and independent clothing shops at Coal Drops Yard, getting lost within the glittering light display at the flagship Tom Dixon store, and resting beside the pattering water feature that ran the length of Pancras Square.

At the Renaissance Hotel, she caught up on whatever television shows were trending on her phone. On Saturday, she slept in her room and enjoyed a perfectly unbroken sleep for the first time in a week. On Sunday morning, she awoke to a warm aura coming from downstairs. When she checked the kitchen, she saw a room revived: steaming teapots whistled with enthusiasm, saucepans bubbled on the stove, the oven flared with life as fresh bread swelled within it. There was much clattering from cutlery as lamb sausages were chopped on the counter by an invisible hand, and oranges were crushed in the nearby juicer.

It was at this point that she felt it: an electrical charge, something hot and welcoming. It ran down the length of her back. Amy darted from the kitchen and found Gerald sprawled on the sofa, making notes across the *Gardien* papers. He was in loungewear: thick grey jogging bottoms and a matching T-shirt. His leather gloves were fitted, making his bony fingers look long and elegant as they held the pen. It was as if he had been there all morning and all week, like nothing untoward had happened. His eyes met hers and he smiled. He was consumed by an aura that felt like a meadow.

Amy ran to him, collapsing into his chest. Gerald gasped, then ran a tentative hand through her bushy hair. He was unaccustomed to touching her with his hands. His fingers got stuck a few times before he stopped altogether with an awkward laugh and opted to pat her on the shoulders instead.

When she drew away from him, he smiled sadly. 'Sorry for worrying you.'

'It's fine,' she said. 'Sorry about what happened.'

'It's not your fault.'

'Maybe it wasn't a good idea to go to the protest after all . . .'

Gerald frowned. 'I hope that's not been bothering you. Neither of us knew what was going to happen that day. I've made peace with it. Well, kind of. I think I've learned something about myself. I want to be better.'

'Mmhmm. Me too.'

'Oh?' Gerald raised his brows. 'Any killing sprees I should know about?'

'Loads.'

They laughed. Out of habit, Amy parsed his aura, sinking deeply into the marrow of it until she arrived at the Wall. With a stifled gasp, she felt a subtle steam wafting from its surface, and something like melting ice oozing down the face of it. As if sensing her presence, the Wall became solid again, harsher than before. A biting gale dispelled the warmth and the steam, and it was fortified by the thickest sheet of ice yet. It felt like it had doubled its defence, even, and the cold was so sharp and shocking that she quickly drew away, her heart pounding against her ribs.

Gerald rose and placed the *Gardien* notes on the coffee table. He glanced over his shoulder to look at her. 'Amy,' he said. 'Believe me, you don't want to know what's behind it.'

Then he turned away into the kitchen, and she felt a distance lengthen between them.

CHAPTER TWELVE

Amy

On Monday, Amy returned to reality. She got ready early and went to the clocktower window to watch London unfold below her. Pressing her forehead against the cool glass, she could feel the vestiges of auras, a mixture of human and non-human. She belonged to both worlds now, and for the past month and a half, the latter had consumed every minute of her life. She thought back to that strange night in March, and how it had taken her on an unthinkable journey that led all the way to the May Bank Holiday massacre. The secrets of the supernatural world she now knew weighed heavy on her shoulders. There was also the realisation that Downers knew her too. Gerald was no hidden member of the supernatural community, and as his partner, she was uncomfortably conspicuous. It was with this in mind that she made the decision to leave her job.

Gerald appeared at the top of the spiral staircase, his aura calm and settled. Amy turned to watch him and tracked his slow descent. Once he was beside her, the Reaper smiled lightly, then he stared out at the windows as if trying to feel and understand what she had moments before.

'Are you sure about leaving?' he asked, not looking at her.

Amy refocused on the distant roads and clotted traffic, the shimmering ants of Londoners below. She shrugged and felt a pang in her stomach.

'I don't have much choice,' she said.

'It's my fault. I'm sorry.'

'Don't be dumb.'

Gerald rested against the desk, bracing his body weight with his fists. They both stared at his gloved hands and the leather that stretched taut across his knuckles. Amy could feel their aberrant aura, still eerily noticeable within the draughty fortress that comprised the Reaper. She was no longer nervous around his hands, but their presence was unsettling, a physical mark of her new life in this hotel, living with the most important supernatural creature in London.

'I've caused you a lot of upheaval,' said Gerald. 'You've had to change a lot of things, have lost many more. I don't take that lightly.'

He turned to her and leaned his back against the desk this time. When he folded his arms, his gloves crunched. Gerald stared at Amy with such focus that she looked away from him, determined to focus on the pad of flesh above his clavicle. He was right; everything had changed, and she had not recovered from the loss of Nan's house. A pile of letters awaited her by the table beside the front door, urging her to write statements and complete insurance forms, and the stress of it all swelled inside her head, pounding beneath her temples. Despite the trauma, she did not regret seeking Gerald out that night in March, and she was grateful to be here with him. She wondered if he felt the same.

'How's it been for you?' she asked quietly. A tentative warmth swirled into Gerald's aura and at last Amy met his gaze. He smiled at her – a soft expression that made her smile in turn.

'I'm happy we met. It's not what I was expecting when I . . . well.'

'Broke into my house like a stalker?'

'I think it's clear we were stalking each other.'

Amy snorted, then swivelled around and rested beside him, glad for the sound of his responsive laughter and the bubbling relief that flooded his aura. 'You don't regret it?'

'No,' Gerald brushed the back of his closest hand against her forearm. It was a glancing movement that left a trail of successive goosebumps on her skin. His aura fluctuated then, and Amy felt a heavier presence, a swelling cloud containing something unsaid. She waited, hoping he would vocalise it, anxious to hear the things he withheld from her. Instead, Gerald stood upright, his expression implacable, and made his way to the kitchen.

Without thinking, Amy blurted, 'Why did you stay?'

Gerald halted. He turned to watch her over his shoulder, his brows raised enquiringly.

'The night we first met ... you were planning to leave, right? I freaked you out a bit, but when I asked you to stay, you did. Why?'

The Reaper's aura seeped away, sinking deeply into nothing, and Amy was confronted with a gaping hole in the air. She frowned, searching his body language for clues, but only saw the perfect veneer of a seasoned killer.

'I'm not entirely sure,' he said. 'Still working it out.'

He didn't give her a chance to press further; Gerald seemingly decided against going to the kitchen. Instead, he scaled the stairs and departed towards his room. His aura remained a mystery for the rest of the morning.

On the bus to Mornington Crescent, Amy considered the notice letter she had drafted, how informal and inconsequential it was, and how its delivery signalled the end of her old life. She planned to finish her morning shift to ease herself into the day and send the letter to her boss, Vilma, just before lunch, after which she could go outside and commiserate in a nearby café. All around her, human auras wafted and waned, and the world outside the bus melted into a mass of presences, lapping like storm waves against the cool metal and rubber.

For years, Amy had clung to the library despite Nan's disapproving comments of selling herself short, and after Nan's death, the long journey from Streatham to Camden had provided a welcome distraction. For an hour and a half, Amy could cave into herself, listen to music, and watch the city pass by. It made her feel both anonymous and part of something big, squashed onto a packed bus as it chugged along congested roads. The commuters became her unofficial family, and the library had been her cocoon: somewhere quiet and purposeful, a final act of good-natured defiance against her grandmother. Whenever she ended her shifts, she could pretend that a pot of brown stew chicken, boiled yam and sweet potato were waiting for her, and that when she opened the front door, the terse string of patois cusses about her far-away job would cut through the air towards her.

But the house was gone now. Nan had been dead for five years. It was time for Amy to put the delusion to rest.

'Feeling better?'

In the staff room, Cordory flopped onto the sofa opposite her. She was everything one would expect of a Camden millennial: choppy blonde hair streaked with electric pink highlights, ragged Converses with laces that were chewed up and muddy, and washed-out jeans that were custom-ripped by the owner. She was friendly and cheerful and unproblematic, but the aura that surrounded her was turbulent. The first time they met, Cordory had a permanent grin affixed to her face, but as Amy had taken her through the orientation, she was overwhelmed by her new colleague's depressive aura. As the years went by, Amy parsed through the layers of a Yorkshire runaway hiding a secret, estranged from her family, and constantly engaging in illicit activities to tide her over until payday, because working full time at a public library would never provide enough to live, and Amy had lived more than humbly until her recent windfall. When she found out that Cordory was an alias, she decided to stop probing her aura out of respect.

'I am, thanks,' Amy said. 'How's it been since I was away?'

'Same ole same ole.' Cordory shrugged. 'We have a new stapler.'

She was at the enquiries desk for the start of her shift. Amy observed the customers who came in accidentally, seeking the public services offered by the Crowndale Centre in the other half of the building, and then the others: stray wanderers needing somewhere warm to sit, jobseekers making use of the free internet, teenage introverts, and new parents embarking on a rite of passage with their infant readers. When she first started working at the library, she was constantly on her feet, but the visitors slowly dissipated with the public service cuts, and now a large portion of her day was spent looking for something to do.

She frowned inwardly as she left the desk to restack some of the shelves in the biographies section, remembering how often Nan had made throwaway comments about the progress of her peers: the completed master's programmes and the lucrative internships, and all the various neighbours who had gone to work in Europe or America only to quickly become tech moguls and little stars of inspiration for their fellow Black inner-city Londoners. But she had always liked the library, and she liked the calming atmosphere, where auras were serene and manageable. With such strong empath abilities like hers, the only other option for a headache-free life was the funeral home. She tried not to focus on her peers because they were not her friends. Detached, compulsory invitations to secondary school reunions were transferred to junk mail. She had no desire to revisit the trauma of her teenage years.

The town hall clock chimed at twelve. It reverberated down her spine. Amy inhaled, steeling herself for the difficult conversation with Vilma, and made her way to the admin office. She loved the library. It hurt to part from it.

As she passed the entrance of the staffroom toilet, a damp chill flushed her body. Amy paused, sensing a draft but unsure of its origin. She scanned the corridor, her heart fluttering with unease. It felt like the supernatural coldness of a Hammerspace door.

CHAPTER THIRTEEN
Gerald

Earlier that day, Carole's demeanour had been kind when she saw Gerald in the lift at King's Cross and St Pancras. She folded her hood back, gave a cursory glance, and then brightened. Gerald smiled.

'No need for the cauldron today, Carole.'

'Good. It is a bit long having to make that tea. I wish there was a way to keep it in a flask for her, but it needs to be done fresh every time.'

'Well, I appreciate your efforts.'

'Thank you. How are you feeling? That was a big kill the other day at that protest.'

'Better, I think.'

'That's good.' The lift shuddered to a halt on Blythe's road. 'Have a good morning, Mr Gerald.'

Inside the main office of the Mason residence, Gerald presented the *Gardien* field notes to Blythe. The wraith glanced at the envelope, scanned Gerald's additional notes with the information he had gathered about the Carrington family's link to the Blue Meadow situation, and nodded. He then reached for the decanter of whisky before Gerald stopped his hand.

'Isn't it too early for alcohol, Blythe?'

After a silence saturated with one-sided irritation, Blythe reluctantly poured some herbal tea into the whisky glass instead, sneering at Gerald with a toasting gesture.

'Is that all?' he asked, tapping the notes.

'Yes, I think so,' said Gerald. 'I'm about to meet with Mr Crow to update him on everything that's happened so far, but I'll let you know how it goes afterwards.'

'Mmhmm.'

Gerald stood, sliding his chair beneath the table before he left.

'Are you better?' Blythe asked his back.

Gerald paused with his hand on the doorknob. He looked at Blythe from over his shoulder. 'I am,' he said.

Blythe drew from his cigar, enshrouding his own face in smoke. A small brown hand emerged from the tar, shooing Gerald away. With a polite nod of gratitude, the Reaper left the mansion.

Despite Blythe's assurances to the contrary, Gerald could sense the unease that followed him as he journeyed through the city centre. The only person who had ever consistently noticed the wariness that surrounded him was Amy. He was accustomed to it: ever since his first time Downstairs, Downers treated him with fear, reverence, and quiet animosity. It was as if they expected him to descend into a murderous rage all the time, and because the legends that surrounded his family persevered on both sides of the ground, it was always difficult to form meaningful relationships, or at least to assuage anyone's fear. His behaviour at Blue Meadow did nothing to reassure anyone. It was hard not to feel a little sad at the averted gazes, tight smiles, and apologetic gestures whenever he caught the eye of someone he knew. In the end, he faced forwards, settled into the hailed rickshaw, and focused on other things until he arrived at City Hall.

The bubbly mage at the reception desk was equally stiff in his presence, but Gerald noticed with some concern that her eyes shone with infatuation as she regarded him. She promptly led the way to Lex Crow's office, flicking her thick ginger hair away from her face, and blushed when Gerald thanked her. That was a notably common reaction to his daily job that he would never understand.

The Downey mayor sat behind his desk, watching Gerald, his arms clasped over his chest. It was such a contrast to the shaded elegance of the Mason residence. Crow's office was a plain room with dusty floors, pale walls, ceiling tiles that were near to crumbling, and a chipped desk pocked with coffee rings. The mayor's staff rested against the wall beside his coat rack, upon which hung various official robes in need of dry cleaning. The brightness of the lights made Gerald squint, having become accustomed to the dim shadows of Blythe's house. Worst of all was the mayor himself, who feigned an air of authority, but failed to hide the trembling in his fingers as he steepled them. Eventually he released his stance, coughed unconvincingly, then rose to fiddle with the water cooler.

'A drink?' he asked.

'Yes, thank you.'

Lex Crow poured some water into a polystyrene cup and handed it over to Gerald. Gerald took a polite sip before resting the cup on the already marred office desk.

'I owe you an apology,' said Gerald, meeting Lex's gaze evenly. 'My behaviour last Monday was unbecoming, and it could have led to a breach of the Concealment Act. If you need me to make any statements or help clear up any discrepancies in the official Upstairs narrative, I'd be more than happy to.'

The mayor's eyes widened in surprise at Gerald's confession. 'No, it's fine,' he said stiffly. 'I see that a lot happened with the Carrington business, and how the company was tied into Bane's affairs. Anyone would be upset at that. And you did help to protect my Peaches. Is there . . . any news, or ETA about the assassinations? I'm still reeling from the knowledge that he was here, potentially lying in wait.'

'I understand. I've narrowed down his base of operations,' Gerald lied, remembering to hide his heavy involvement with Blythe. 'Lavender is another matter, but it seems as though she's most likely wherever Bane is.'

Lex Crow froze, his eyes wide in shock. 'What? Together, you say?'

'Oh yes. She's created a company to buy up some of the shares from WCT Security, and she already consolidated most of Bane's spare members. According to my very reliable source Upstairs, they've called a truce and are back on good terms. The Lads and Darkhouse split is no more.'

'Right. Right. Well, that's dangerous.' His eyes wandered and beads of sweat bloomed across his forehead. Lex sighed deeply, finally focusing on the photo of his wife and daughter on the bookshelf. An uncertain finger glanced off the glass. He dropped his hand to his side. 'This is a mess.'

'Not to worry, Mr Crow,' said Gerald. 'I'm aware this is a dangerous time for your family, but Bane and Lavender don't appear to be focused on you at this moment. I'm sure they're aware of the request in my Grim Book, which explains why Bane was so brazen with me when I confronted him the other day.'

'You confronted him?'

'Yes. He was hiding in Tottenham. When I gave chase, he disappeared through a Hammerspace tunnel.'

'So you almost had him, and you let him go?'

Gerald said nothing. He stared at Lex Crow without expression, tilting his head in wait.

'I'm sorry,' Lex said after a pause. 'Forgive me. Totally out of turn.'

'Noted.' Gerald stood, his eyes still fixed on the mayor. 'Anything else?'

'No. Um. Have you had any special intel today, or . . . ?'

'I'm afraid not. Good day, Mr Crow.'

Gerald heard the deflated exhale from the other side of the door once he had closed it behind him. Afterwards, he decided to go back home to Zis, have breakfast, and then see Amy at work. She was handing in her notice today, much to his excitement. He hoped she would appreciate the surprise. The rest of his morning was leisurely. At twelve, he started his journey to Camden Town Library.

The Crowndale Centre was on Eversholt Road in North London, just a short walk away from the pandemonium that was Camden Town. It housed government services, boasting floors of municipal offices where council workers sat behind desks to decline housing assistance, rolled their eyes at regular service users, and tersely redirected residents to other offices, and other buildings, and other people that were far away from the Crowndale Centre itself. The ground floor was home to the Camden Town Library, but after spending several frustrating hours with the council, members of the public were too annoyed and too tired to browse bookshelves. And so, the library languished in a city during a time where such services were sacred and few. Gerald observed the almost-empty building, which he had expected to be much busier on a Monday afternoon, and smiled wistfully at the waste.

No one was at the enquires desk, but sometimes a library user would hesitate beside it, look around with a perplexed expression, and then leave. Gerald sat on the reading chairs closest to the desk, expecting someone to arrive, but after several people tried to wait patiently for assistance only to be met with the stale air of the desk, he called Amy's phone. There was a notification for a missed call from his father which he promptly ignored. His attempt to get through to Amy failed. He hung up without leaving a message and waited a little longer.

A frenzied woman rushed behind the desk, making a big show of logging onto the computer, sighing loudly as she looked around for another colleague. Her hair was pale blonde with pink highlights. Gerald took a chance and went over to her. She froze momentarily, eyes raking his body. Gerald looked at himself. He wore civilian clothes, which were black jeans, black Doc Martens, and a black jumper. The jumper was fitted. He couldn't help but frown, feeling slightly self-conscious beneath the librarian's gaze.

'Hello,' he tried. 'Does Amy work here? Is she on break?'

The librarian sighed. 'Well, she's supposed to work here! But she's suddenly disappeared and now *I'm* in trouble. How does *that* work?'

'She . . . disappeared?'

'Yeah! Just heard her phone ringing in her locker.'

Gerald's heart pounded in his chest. He glanced around the library, trying to look for anyone that seemed suspicious. One of the library users detached herself from a nearby shelf with a pile of books tucked beneath her arm. Her friendly manner, and the way in which she greeted the librarian behind the desk, and the frayed library card that swung from a lanyard around her neck, all revealed her to be a regular customer. She grinned when she neared Gerald before plopping the pile of books on the enquiries desk.

'Amy? Oh, she ran off with her boyfriend,' she said.

'Oh yeah?' The librarian rested her head in her palms, eyebrows raised suggestively.

'Yep. Tall man. Light skin.' She rolled her eyes at Gerald.

The library spun. Gerald steadied himself by placing a gloved hand on the desk. He turned to the woman with as calm a face as he could muster, not betraying the dread that threatened to overwhelm his body. 'Did you see where they went?'

The woman shrugged. 'Nah, last I saw, they were just out in the corridor over there, but it wasn't my business, so I left them to it. It was like an hour ago, though.'

'Thanks.' He made his way to the door before either woman could ask him anything else.

Outside the Crowndale Centre, he was lost. He looked around the area for any sign of an abduction. He was desperate for some clue of the supernatural to appear before him, but none came. With nothing else to do, he called Blythe. The wraith answered on the first ring.

'Bane's got Amy.'

'Come Downstairs.'

He departed in an instant.

INTERLUDE: THE WITCH

Melanie was out of the cottage and back where she belonged — that is what she told herself. She sat at an oak table with a small vase of yellow chrysanthemums. They were wilted and dying, and the vase was dry and crusted with limescale. She resolved to buy some more.

Brown water oozed from the terracotta walls and pooled into the far corner of the room. Crested with moss, she remembered peering through the same puddle just a month and a half before when she was yearning and desperate and wanted to feel the coolness of Tyrell Bane on her skin once more. She touched her fingertips along her forearms. Bruises flowered there. Tyrell had not been happy to see her at first and had made it known. But it was Imogen Carrington's fault, that heiress with the loose mouth, and Gethsemane Reaper's fault, and Blythe Mason's fault.

Mostly, the blame lay with the empath Amethyst St Clair, a human of no consequence who was hard to track, but Melanie had found where she lived. Because of Melanie, everything Amy had was destroyed, and the commotion enabled Tyrell to transfer his refugees to Sitton Road. She saw her clay decanter hobbled on the nearby shelf, its bloody contents reduced to brown crusts. She had saved that blood from her parents for so long, hoping to use it as an escape for herself one day. Instead, her prudence had been wasted on random humans in a basement just so Tyrell could taunt *Gardien* and the Reaper. All she had left was a single talisman that could conceal auras from a distance. Such items took months to make and required bundles of tropical plants. The last one she loaned was with one of Bane's Darkhouse executives, the sycophant known only as Gary, but he could have been anywhere.

Melanie had done much more and helped Tyrell in whatever way she could ever since he went on the run. She had tied up all of Darkhouse's loose ends and now that she had bought some of Tyrell's businesses, they would not be bankrupt anymore. She saved him. So why was she sitting here, bruised and trembling with pain?

There was another man who had said he loved her, that's why. And Melanie drank the words that oozed from that man's mouth, grew intoxicated, and for over a year, turned her back on Tyrell. She had been defiant, flaunting the Lads in his face, acting like she was a person of worth and stature, and Tyrell had given her grace, left her alone, allowed her to do it all. She should be grateful, really, that he was so forgiving now, that he took her back in after everything that had happened, that he hadn't gloated when she admitted that she had been betrayed by her other man, her old lover. She deserved this.

Empty footsteps drummed the ground and the door opened. Tyrell. He nodded at her, and she stood, waiting until he was seated before sitting down again.

'Got her,' he said. 'She's down the way.'

'That's good.' When he said nothing else, she added, 'What d'you want to do with her?'

'She's bait.'

'Yeah, makes sense.'

She searched his face as he refused to look at her. His eyes were narrowed into slits, reading something on his phone, some update from the Carrington woman maybe, or a snippet of unwanted news. The office was cold. His demeanour was arctic. Melanie reached for his nearest arm and he snatched it away.

'What?'

'Well . . .' she said. 'You ever thought . . . this is all getting a bit long, innit? You haven't been yourself for a while. You're not happy. I'm not happy, either, you know. With the money I have, we could just leave. If we're really on the Reaper's list, we'll never survive, not in London. We don't have to stay here. We can go anywhere!'

'The fuck you on?'

This was a new expression. Not anger, not indifference. It was rabid. His eyes were piercing. His skin was burning rock. Tyrell rose slowly, towering over her, casting his shadow on her body. She shivered in its wake.

'I'm sorry,' she said.

'Just . . . go and do something, Mel. Just *something*. Make dinner. Be useful.'

He waited until she left. On the other side of the door, she exhaled, and her breath was acrid and painful in her throat. The scar around her neck throbbed again. Her whole body was scalded. Perhaps this was a mistake. Perhaps this was the best thing for her. Perhaps they could win. Or they would lose everything.

PART FOUR
Prisoners

Magic Practitioners Continued: Mages

Mages

The most powerful of the three main classes. They use the source of all magic (aether). In other words, witches and warlocks call upon the 'thunder' of magic, and mages use the 'lightning'. They require a medium to channel this energy, so rowan staffs are often their weapons of choice. A mage without a staff or other medium can only perform basic spells, and attempts at more extravagant spells risk immolation or bodily combustion. Typical mage spells include smokescreens, which obscure the interiors of buildings from the outside, and barriers, which prevent outsiders from infiltrating an area using Hammerspace. The Mage Guild is their governing body. Gender presentation seems to have no significance.

   A mage is typically appointed as the Saint of the Guilds, a senior government position that oversees the politics and customs of the three magic practitioner communities and their respective governing bodies.

CHAPTER ONE

Amy

She awoke, bound by nylon ties, in a cold and damp chamber. From somewhere far above, human auras were spiced with the scent of evening revelry. There was a faint imprint of previous auras underlying these current ones, and she parsed these layers, frowning at the multitudinous footfall that had dispersed not long before. It made Amy feel so lonely, knowing she was within parsing distance, and totally bound and unable to join the rest of humanity. Not for the first time, she considered her precarious position as a human among Downers: waiting prey, a lost child. After everything that had happened, she had hoped for a slower return to normality. This was the last thing she needed.

Her sojourn to Vilma's office had been intercepted by the errant gale of a Hammerspace opening. So different from the cool dryness belonging to Gerald's, this intrusion had been damp and cloying, and before long she had been engulfed in a sharp anger, an anger that left her breathless and lightheaded. With no time to think, she had been thrown into a Hammerspace tunnel that pressed against her skin with its vanta-blackness. The void suffocated her, reduced her throat to a rawness so that she could not scream, and in the dark, an arm dragged her with the forceful disdain of a person desperate to discard trash. The arm threw her on the ground of this dungeon, bound her with supernatural speed, and left her squirming at the feet of Tyrell Bane. That all felt like hours ago, and her heart pounded as she tried to consider what would happen now, and what he planned to do with her. His silence weighed heavy on her shoulders.

She heard footsteps coming from the corridor opposite and she straightened. Someone other than Bane was making their way towards her, their steps light and fleeting. A hot, crackling aura filled the vicinity, imprinting shards of molten ore on Amy's spine. What emerged was a short, petite witch, whose pretty face was almost completely hidden by a curtain of thick black hair that appeared to glimmer in the subtle glow of the dungeon. Despite the weightlessness of her footsteps, she approached Amy with a self-assured swagger, her face a mask of disdain as she looked upon her.

So accustomed was Amy to the madness of Downstairs that it took her a while to notice that the witch's skin was purple. Taken aback, the empath parsed her captor, delving further into Melanie's being. This was her chance to get a proper read of the elusive leader, and she wanted to know if her concerns had been warranted. Beneath the heat Melanie had previously encased herself with, an unmistakable tremor of fearful disappointment reverberated through her aura, and as Amy observed the witch more closely, she could see an inventory of dubious marks: crocodile keloids that braceleted her wrists and haystacks of scars that were scattered along her arms. Amy pondered their meaning and origin, and considered their usefulness in her captivity.

'Dinner,' Melanie said, dropping a plastic container of food that Amy had no interest in eating. She made to return to the corridor, but Amy stared with such intensity that the witch halted mid-turn. 'You good?'

Amy exhaled, strangely thankful for the contact. She ignored the tears of sweat that coursed gently along her hairline, and hoped that her expression was placid enough to not garner Melanie's mockery.

'I can't exactly eat with my hands tied,' she said, nodding at the container. She saw two hard dumplings and something that thought it was oxtail, but looked more like dog food. It was no tragedy that the food would remain uneaten, but she needed an opening for conversation.

Melanie shrugged. 'You can work it out.'

'Why bring it then?' Amy performed a struggle, exaggerating the motion of shuffling over to the container. She wiggled her wrists against the nylon ties and winced – the motion genuinely stung, but she was committed to making as much noise as possible. Melanie's shoulders twitched at her pain, and a frozen panic pierced the uneven surface of her aura, but it passed quickly, and she recovered enough to resume a stolid countenance.

'It really ain't my business. I don't care.'

The witch spun on her heel and stalked out of the cavern, but her steps were unsteady this time, no longer light and surreptitious. This was the heavy plodding of a drunkard, of someone desperate to get away, and the aura that followed was disturbed and bewildered. Amy had done the right thing to emphasise her wrist injury: a deep trauma was melded into Melanie's mind. The empath would have to utilise this evidence if she planned to escape with her life.

Time passed achingly. She could feel the weight of the night on her shoulders. A heavy pressure in the atmosphere and the slow, tranquil auras around her meant that it was late, and whatever shop above that had enjoyed a lot of business earlier was now closed until morning. She must have been in

Bane's secret lair in South Kensington. Harrods and Harvey Nichols were options, but so were the three huge museums further down Cromwell Road. Yawning, she turned on her side, propping against a corner between the wall and the floor, and allowed her eyes to brim over. When she wiped her face afterwards, it came with a sharp sting from around her wrists. She had to fight to stop herself from crying all over again.

The discomfort of her sleep was made worse by the returning image of the refugees on Sitton Road. It was something she would never heal from, and a sense of gratitude washed over her that she hadn't seen the deaths in Blue Meadow, but the gaping auras had been enough to scar her for a lifetime. Dozens of holes had scorched the atmosphere like cigarette burns and rapidly grew, limned with fire. They had expanded and converged together, melting into an emptiness above the detention centre, black as tar and as expansive as space. Just the memory of that wall of death made her shiver. She had never experienced something like that before, and she had no plans to endure it again.

A rainfall of footsteps echoed down the corridor. One set was heavier than the other. Bane came into view first. Melanie appeared behind, her eyes set straight ahead, not looking at Amy or anything else.

Amy rolled into a sitting position again. She raised her chin to stare Bane in his eyes. She was starving and exhausted, and the loss of the auras upstairs had removed the sense of comfort she had been relying on – even if it had made her lonelier. It was near silent in this prison, and above was only a vacant space where souls had once mingled and resided. All that was left was the residue of their existence, the flutter of birds' wings, and the echo of stray rats that trawled the city.

Bane's expression was calm, but the deepness of his eyes betrayed his frustration. Amy considered the power he wielded now: his rival was back on his side, and the remainder of the human gang members would most likely consolidate back into his control. He had Imogen Carrington to provide money and connections to the country's super-elite. The only person more powerful than him was Gerald. And Amy was his weakness.

'You want to kill Gerald,' she said.

Bane only stared at her, but Melanie's tightened expression spoke volumes.

'You can't kill Gerald.' Amy tried to stifle a delirious laugh. 'He's . . . the Reaper.'

Bane crouched in front of her; examined the details of her face. 'You don't know this world. You don't know how things work. Reapers fail all the time. They get things wrong. They think they're too powerful. And with that arrogance comes mistakes.'

'Gerald's not like that. He's the most reasonable person I've ever met.'

At this, Lavender scoffed. 'The guy who just killed fifty random people Upstairs?'

When Amy didn't respond, the witch snickered, bowing her head as her shoulders trembled mockingly, her black hair falling thick over her body. 'Well, if he's so great, why is he so reckless?' she said.

'Yeah, yeah, all right,' said Amy. 'What would you know?'

Melanie's nose flared in anger. She swooped towards Amy, and Bane shifted to allow her space. He watched the witch with a bemused expression, entertained by her behaviour.

'*You're* a human! *You* don't talk to me like that!'

'And you're a child, Melanie. Give it a rest.'

The witch recoiled at Amy's familiarity. An untamed anger boiled within her, and the air spat with heated fury.

'It's funny you've got so much confidence in the Reaper. If he's so great, how come he can't even see—'

She never finished because Bane backhanded her across the face, and the force of it was so strong that the witch rolled over onto her side. When she faced him again, her chin was marred with the grime of the floor, and her mouth bled onto her teeth. She spat, staring at Bane with a stunned expression.

'What the fuck have I told you about your mouth? You talk too much. Get out.'

The witch scrambled to her feet and left the cavern in embarrassed anger, her aura on full display for Amy to feel the heat of her humiliation. Amy quickly parsed through the treacherous waves of Melanie's being to get a sense of the witch's mind. She felt longing, and desperation, and a strong presence of love towards Bane, but these feelings were marred with doubt, dissatisfaction, and fear.

'Oi.' Bane gripped her jaw, pulling her to meet his face. Amy stared at him, and the warlock returned her glare. He looked as if he was deciding what to do with her, whether it was worth keeping her alive after all, and the thought scared Amy into submission until her expression must have changed enough to satisfy him. He waited until she understood her situation, then let go of her face. When he finally left her alone, she exhaled slowly. In the silence, Amy shook the tiredness away from her body. She made plans for an escape.

Her underground cavern was wide, with one corridor that led to Bane and Melanie's quarters, a ceiling that allowed her to feel auras potently, and walls that were thin enough to feel the draft coming from outside. When it was totally silent, the distant murmur of cars rumbled through the wind. A part of her cavern also stretched to the outside streets, and this is where she needed to aim if she was to find a way out. With considerable effort, she could move around by pivoting her bottom and sliding across the floor to get a better sense of the space. There could have been another corridor hidden behind a crevice or a trapdoor. She swivelled again, squirming across the ground pathetically, resting every few feet to catch her breath. When she was sure she had completed the cavern's perimeter, she leaned against the wall, panting. Her priority now was the restraints that had rendered her limbs heavy with numbness.

Another patter of footsteps sounded from the corridor. They were accompanied by a wounded aura. Amy froze. Melanie entered the cavern again with another container of food. Bane had given her a beating. Her purple face was swollen, and the slick sheen of fresh blood swelled in the corner of her mouth. It was amazing that Melanie had done so much alone and had controlled so many ventures when she was the leader of the Lads, only to succumb to docility as soon as she was back within Bane's orbit. She moved gingerly now, and crouched beside the untouched meal to place the second beside it. She frowned at both, her eyes wandering over the contents, as if contemplating their purpose. After deciding something within herself, she dragged herself upright. Her mouth was pulled into a tight frown, and her aura swelled with the agony of her injuries.

'I can't eat that one either,' said Amy, tipping her head towards the pair of containers. Her head was heavy and her neck ached, but she persevered through the discomfort. 'Are you just doing whatever he tells you even if it makes no sense?'

'I told you not to talk to me,' said Melanie. She spoke to the wall behind Amy and turned for the exit once more.

'Has he tied you up like this before?' asked Amy. The words tumbled out of her mouth in a desperate, breathless muddle, but Melanie froze, inches away from the open corridor. Her aura was thrown by a tempest. 'Has he . . . imprisoned you or something? Are you imprisoned now? Doesn't seem like you're up to this.'

Melanie rested her shoulder against the damp wall. She stared out at the corridor ahead, not looking at Amy or anything behind her. 'I'm gonna need you to shut the fuck up,' she said. And she shuffled out of the cavern.

CHAPTER TWO
Gerald

In Blythe's peach dining room, the *Gardien* assembly waited in anxious silence. Shaun, brows knitted, was gated by a circle of surveillance screens, rewinding footage when necessary. Felix and Dani sat opposite Dagwood and Brian, then Josh followed with a newly recovered Ulrich. Hollow sat alone without a partner. Gerald and Blythe occupied both ends. After mulling over the events of the morning leading up to Amy's disappearance, they narrowed down Bane's hideout to the area between the Victoria and Albert and the Natural History Museums. They would need to split into two groups and examine both buildings until they found Bane's Hammerspace door.

It had taken several hours of combing through Shaun's footage, watching where Bane miraculously emerged among hundreds of tourists and commuters, following him as he ran errands, met with countless suspicious humans, and then returned to Cromwell Road, where he would disappear within the jostle of bodies between the two museums. By the time they had finished mulling over their plans and confirming the hideout location, it was night-time, and Shaun's surveillance screens were less defined, giving way to blue-black outlines of unidentifiable bodies, sprinkles of starlight on windows, the sheen of cabs as they hovered beneath LED street lamps, and the glare of red traffic lights on car windscreens.

'It's all right, we know enough,' said Felix. 'Who wants to go to the V&A?'

'We can go,' said Ulrich, gesturing to Josh.

'I'll go with you lot,' said Shaun.

'So, we'll be at the Natural History then,' Felix nodded at Dani.

'I'll join you,' said Hollow.

'Well, with two vampires on the Natural History team, Brian and I can go to the V&A, too,' said Dagwood.

They then turned to Gerald. 'I already have a feeling that Bane's put a smokescreen around the area, but I'll try to see if I can look around first as I usually do. If not, I'll go with my gut when we get there.'

The group promptly gathered their belongings and left, but Gerald lingered. Blythe had said nothing during the meeting, merely dragged on his cigar at regular intervals, staring straight ahead at something no one else could see. He ignored Gerald as the Reaper stared at him to get his attention, then finally sighed loudly, turning to face him. His scarlet eyes were narrowed, and full of irritation.

'What?'

'I'm going to kill him tonight after all, Blythe.'

There was a pause. Blythe reached for his nearby decanter. He poured whisky into a glass, and it fell over the ice ball in the centre. They both stared at the alcohol, and at how sweetly the ball danced in its golden bath.

'Why are you telling me? Isn't that your job?' asked Blythe.

'Are you sure you have nothing to say to him? No questions to ask? I could try to bring him back here, but he may escape.'

'No. Kill him.'

'You won't get another chance.'

'Kill him.'

'Okay.' Gerald nodded. He rose from his chair, locking eyes with Blythe as he did so. The wraith's expression was unreadable. 'I'll talk you to later, Blythe. Take care.'

He left Blythe at the table, forcing himself to look forwards.

CHAPTER THREE

Amy

She was lost to the dark incomprehension of the cavern and had no sense of time. It was a disconcerting experience, a shipwreck of nonsense. Amy was stranded, and she recounted the madness of her recent life and wondered whether it had been worth it after all. Her only consolation was Gerald – knowing that both Melanie Lavender and Tyrell Bane were his targets, and that the Reaper had a stubborn principle of seeing his requests to their end. At some point, he would have to find her. She could not consider anything else.

Melanie dominated her thoughts. Bane's last assault had bloated the young witch's face, and it had allowed Amy to see the childish roundness of her features. It was a stark contrast to Megan's waif elegance. Melanie wore her vulnerability openly, but she could not imagine that it had always been this way. Bane's presence had quelled whatever power she once had. He had been leading, controlling, and pressuring Melanie all along.

The damaged footsteps returned, as did the bruised aura, and Melanie entered the cavern. She stared only at the two containers. She smelt of spiced herbs, and her movements were more fluid than before, if not slower. She swept towards the uneaten meals and bundled them in her arms, then turned away from Amy once more, focusing pointedly on her exit route.

'I'm not trying to be funny,' said Amy, 'but my wrists are *really* hurting right now.' And she meant it. The nylon ties had become burning rings. Her fingertips prickled hot and cold. 'Can't you do anything? Loosen them a bit?'

Melanie halted. She threw the containers to the ground, and they exploded into chunks of congealed gravy and rubber dough. The witch whipped around and stormed towards her. Amy's heart leapt into her mouth and she scuttled backwards, sending daggers of pain shooting up both arms, but petrified enough to ignore the sensation. She struggled against her fear until there was nowhere left to go, and the cold wall, weeping moss and limescale, dampened her clothes. Melanie swooped downwards until her face was inches from Amy's. They stared at each other in deathly silence.

'What are you playing at?' asked Melanie.

'Nothing.'

'You're trying something. Empath shit.'

Amy snorted. It was involuntary, and she was delirious with pain, but the recognisable venom gave her the relief of familiarity. She ignored Melanie's angered glare so she could explain herself 'Your sister said the same thing.'

Melanie drew backwards. She searched Amy's face, eyes scanning every ridge and slope, and then she staggered to her feet. 'Sister?'

'Megan.'

The heat of Melanie's aura vanished, and was instead assaulted with the needles of ice rain, long shards that punctured gaping holes in her psyche, drowned her, pierced her solid façade. All the while, her expression remained neutral, offering Amy a Gerald-level disguise, but unlike Gerald, the witch was still young and inexperienced, and she bit her lip and folded her arms tightly around her body, mirroring the anxious behaviour of her elder sister.

Melanie nodded. She said nothing, but continued to stand there, staring down at Amy, as if waiting for more information. A curious tremor vibrated through her: the smoke of regret.

'She has a shop now. A restaurant,' Amy tried. 'Seems to be doing all right.'

Melanie nodded again.

'She's angry at you . . .'

'Obviously.'

Melanie spread her arms mockingly, presenting her body, and gestured at the deep purple skin that marked her.

'*She* did that?' Amy frowned. It was an unexpected revelation. With horror, she wondered whether she had misjudged Melanie's injuries. 'Did she . . . was it *Megan* who imprisoned you?' she asked, and the question was spiked with incredulity. 'She made those marks on your arms?'

'Stop talking about things you don't understand. It wasn't her, so just shut up about them.'

The deceit was absent from Melanie's aura, but the layers of familiarity that enshrouded her words implied someone with considerable proximity had abused her in the past. If Megan was innocent, that left Tyrell, or the parents she had murdered in apparent cold blood. Her body went numb at this possibility – an unwanted interruption she had not considered before. She knew Melanie would not relay any more information about this, and so she dropped the issue, but she yearned to know more.

'Okay, okay,' she said. 'I understand some things. Things that you wouldn't get because you're too young.' She recounted the conversation with Imogen Carrington and the heiress's mocking assessment of Melanie. The witch most likely did not know about the affair, and that Bane had enjoyed a romantic release during her hard work to consolidate his assets. She noted Melanie's sceptical brow, but took courage in the still tumultuous storm of her aura. 'You're too young to know that Tyrell Bane's a piece of shit. And that he's just using you. He's having an affair.'

It was the wrong thing to say. The fury warred against the rain within Melanie, and her expression soured. The witch turned on her heel and left, still holding onto her body, her arms folded tightly as an unmoveable shield.

INTERLUDE: THE WITCH

The dining room felt impossibly small, and the walls pressed against her. Unlike the empath's dungeon, which was dark and draughty, this space was now hot with overbearing wall sconces, cramped with junk on the shelves, and littered with evidence of Tyrell's feelings towards her. A shattered bowl beneath the table was smeared with her own blood, but he had only thrown it at her because he was frustrated, and understandably so after everything that had happened. The overturned chair on the opposite side of the dining table had been her own fault because she had almost revealed their benefactor to the blasted empath, and that revelation would have ruined all that Tyrell had been building and rebuilding after losing everything. She rubbed her wrists and stared at the dark knots in the wooden table. It was imperative that she remembered everything Tyrell Bane had done for her. He had listened when no one else wanted to, and gave her a chance to vent, to cry. He offered protection. He had been a real father, a real lover.

She paused now and frowned. Those were opposing occupations. They did not belong together. What did it mean that Tyrell was both?

All the while, the empath's gloating, earnest gaze seared her memories. Those acidic, abusive words she had just spoken, accusing Tyrell of being trash, and by extension, accusing

Melanie of liking it. Of course Tyrell was having an affair, but it was a fake one. The Carrington bitch was the one being used. Tyrell needed Melanie; there were plenty of human heiresses for him to choose from, but only one Melanie Lavender. Imogen and her decrepit father were nothing special.

It did hurt, though. Seeing him flick through his phone and pause, for just a breath of a moment, when her pale milky face flashed on the screen. Her smile had been self-assured, and she had been accompanied by a Tyrell that Melanie had not seen before: at ease, at rest, as if he had found solace in her company.

It could have all been an act, a persona he needed to convince the Carringtons. Tyrell was good at disguises, and his gift of speech had bewitched many others before.

It could have all been an act, him being with her, assuring her that there was solitude in his arms, that staying by his side would bring her freedom and redeem her past.

It could have all been an act, her belief in him, and perhaps now, she could no longer lie to herself.

PART FIVE
Liberation

Magical Minorities #1: Basilisks

Bipedal reptiles that can petrify others upon eye contact. This is a controlled power and not automatic as some legends state. Some basilisks can turn internal organs into stone. The most prominent basilisks are the Warden family, who gained the ability to shapeshift into human form many centuries ago.

   N.B. The Warden family also possesses the mysterious and extraordinary gift of travel, which was instrumental in forming Downstairs. As the only creatures in the supernatural world with this ability, the Wardens guard the secret cities in various countries all over the globe. They are an invaluable resource for magical creatures and therefore enjoy much infamy and prestige.

Haunted Creatures #2: Werewolves

Former humans who were infected when a werewolf's saliva entered their blood, usually through a bite. A human infected by werewolf saliva can be saved within a short window, but as the cure is often difficult to access, these cases are rare. Like vampires, werewolves have extreme regenerative abilities and superstrength. They suffer from pre- and post-transformation sickness, which is typified by fever, nausea, and fatigue. Werewolves can utilise a partial bipedal transformation at will, and shift into full wolf forms during the full moon. Werewolves who spend too much time in wolf form are at risk of developing Feral Syndrome, where they lose their sense of self.

    N.B. The werewolf who infected Ulrich Dagger was feral.

CHAPTER ONE
Brian

The Victoria and Albert group split in two, with Ulrich and Josh breaking through the roof to search the top floors, and the latter three taking the bottom. The V&A was massive, and a feeling of time sensitivity made the group anxious to finish the job quickly. It was eerie at night, with vacant corridors that loomed into blackness, the silhouettes of artefacts casting distorted shadows against tapestry walls. Dagwood, Brian, and Shaun crept between the stone sculptures on the ground floor that overlooked the gardens. Security cameras that would have normally tracked them were distorted by Shaun's magic, creating enchanted footage that removed the trio from view. With his keen eyesight and sense of smell, Brian took the lead.

He had his face uncovered so he could hear better. Most movement came from spiders idling beside the double-glazed windows of the gardens, and the occasional moth, and the comforting hum of the air filtration system that protected the humidity of the museum. The silence was very much like Brian's own house Downstairs on Rockdale Drive, a mountainous enclave a mile away from Greymalkin's, and home to the London basilisk community.

Basilisks were quiet and secretive by nature, so their commune was one of metamorphic foreboding, but they nursed a pride towards the Warden family, the integral guardians of

Downstairs. Sometimes Brian wondered, with the heat of embarrassment, if the only reason he joined Blythe's secret service was because of his wish to unsheathe himself from his inferiority complex.

The first day he was partnered with Dagwood and completed his first successful mission, he stood in front of his mirror, examining himself, his feet sunken into the crinkly reams of freshly moulted scales, and hoped that his previous anxieties had been discarded with them. There were times that he felt as if he could do anything, and other times he felt helplessly small.

'Well aren't you lost in thought?'

Brian smiled at Dagwood, then shrugged. 'Nothing wrong with thinking.'

'Right, you should practise that a bit more, Daggy,' said Shaun and then continued, ignoring Dagwood's indignant muttering, 'You know what would be easier? If we had a little help. Hold on.'

He dragged the wider end of his staff on the floor, and for the first time, Brian noticed that he had reinforced both ends of his staff with Forbesteel, the special substance the Forbes family was renowned for. Brian revelled in the sound the metal made as it crunched against the stone. It reminded him of walking barefoot in the rock pools near his home, or the sound his scales made after shedding: a melodious crackle that betrayed just how formidable and impenetrable his outer skin was.

Without warning, the sculptures closest to the trio began to move, slowly at first, as if stretching after a long nap, and then, as they grew accustomed to movement, became more fluid and confident. Dagwood yelped and the noise bounced off the naked walls around them. Unperturbed, the sculptures encircled them. Brian could see their vacant expressions, how their sightless eyes watched Shaun in mock anticipation. Dagwood shuffled closer to Brian. The basilisk could hear the frantic beat of Dagwood's heart, and the rush of blood as it crashed through his body. *For such a talented warlock, he certainly frightens easily.*

'Right, I need you lot to let me know if you feel a Hammerspace door,' Shaun said to the statues. 'Or any sense of warlock magic – not from him,' he added when the sculptures automatically turned to Dagwood. They all nodded their comprehension, then marched away in different directions to search the museum for traces of Bane.

'It really is a treat to see you at work, Shaun!' said Dagwood. 'I'm glad you came along with us.'

'Ah, it's nothing. I prefer being with you two, anyway. Last time you weren't around, the vampires got weird.'

'Oh?'

'Yeah!' Shaun grimaced as he turned to Dagwood more fully. 'Like, all licking each other's necks and shit.'

'Oh dear.'

Brian snorted. 'It's how they are, Shaun.'

'Well I don't wanna *see* that shit!'

They resumed their journey between the remaining sculptures. This time, Brian could hear the heavy, measured footsteps of their stone assistants on the floors all around them. He sighed with relaxation as he listened to them.

'But speaking of impressive skills,' Dagwood continued, 'isn't Amy an interesting person?' He directed his question to Brian.

'Yeah.' Brian nodded. 'She did well at Sitton Road. Better than a normal human would, given the circumstances.'

'And that aura reading of hers . . .' Dagwood frowned in

thought. 'I mean, sure, my fellow warlocks and I can read auras a little bit – not as well as witches, I guess – but I've never seen anything like *that*, you know? Being able to *read* the *intentions* within the aura and even follow an aura across vast distances.'

'Empaths do more than read auras, though, that's the point,' said Shaun. 'Granted, her ability is the maddest I've witnessed in anyone.'

'Are we sure she's fully human?' Dagwood asked the room.

'Well, her family's from St Thomas, apparently,' said Brian, 'but she's definitely human. I can tell you that as a basilisk. It's kind of our job to sense humans since we can petrify them longer than Downers.'

'St Thomas?' asked Dagwood. 'St Thomas's hospital?'

'Jamaica, you idiot.'

'Oh, so what's so special about that?'

'Obeah,' said Shaun.

Brian was content with the silence that followed as they left the sculpture room and entered the main atrium, but Dagwood fidgeted, waiting for Shaun to continue.

'Well go on then! What's Obeah?'

'Ah, vodun, I guess. There's a lot to it. My family's from Grenada so I know about it a bit.'

'Oh, I know about Grenada! The nutmeg people!'

Shaun glanced at Dagwood with contempt.

'Maybe some of the supernatural vibes of St Thomas contributes to her gift. We'll never know,' said Brian, surreptitiously coming between the pair as they walked. 'I mean, there are some humans in the developing world who know about supernatural things, aren't there? Like the Tuareg people.'

Dagwood and Shaun both stared at Brian. He glanced down

at them from his impressive vantage point and frowned. 'Didn't you guys ever do History of World Magic at Greymalkin's?'

'Oh no, that's an applied course, and you need distinctions for that,' said Dagwood. 'I *wish* I had those grades.'

'And I'm a school dropout,' said Shaun.

'Utter disgrace,' Brian muttered, but playfully. 'How did you guys get anywhere in life?'

'Please tell us about the ancient magic peoples of the world, great teacher,' said Shaun.

'Ha! Well, if you must know, we learned about the Grim Tribe on that course—'

'Ooh,' said Dagwood.

'Yep. As you know, they're from the Sahara in Africa, but they share the desert with loads of human ethnic groups, like the Tuareg. They're nomads too. So, they've encountered the Grim Tribe quite a bit, and they're not scared of the Reapers even though they know what they can do. It's probably how they've been able to survive for so long in such volatile conditions. They know the land and the magic that comes with it. Honestly, it's a really interesting history.'

'Imagine that, ordinary humans in regular contact with the Reapers, and not even scared, while Downers can barely look in Mr Reaper's eyes!' said Dagwood.

'Speak for yourself,' said Brian.

He could hear their stone helpers as they crouched beneath artefacts and pressed their cemented ears against walls, and he trained his own senses to feel for the acute draft that could only come from a Hammerspace door, but found nothing.

The trio had transitioned into the fashions exhibit, creeping past displays of elaborate Tudor dresses and the floral wool work of ancient coats from the Far East. Their reflections were stretched and distorted against the glass displays, and Brian realised how out of place he was in such a delicate space, his hulking frame standing in stark contrast to the filigree artworks that he could never imagine wearing.

'Amy's not scared of him,' he said at last.

'She don't know him,' said Shaun. 'She doesn't understand.'

'Not yet,' Brian tried.

'Hmm.'

'Should we try the floor above then?' asked Dagwood. 'It's clear there's no entrance here. I'm starting to worry that they're all next door in the Natural History Museum instead.'

'Wouldn't that be the best outcome?' asked Shaun. 'To be honest, I'm not feeling like getting into another long fight, not after what happened at Sitton Road. D'you know how hard I've been grinding these past few days, anyway? And not a single titty in sight.'

'Excuse you?' said Dagwood.

'What? For comfort, I mean. I haven't been out anywhere for ages.'

'Are you a baby?'

'We'll take the stairs,' said Brian. He was lost in thought as they ascended to the upper floor. His first time meeting Amy, she had pilfered through the layers of his aura so impolitely, like a curious child searching for their favourite toy. Basilisks were reclusive because the legends around them made everyone else wary, and it was unsettling to see bipedal lizard people walking with the muted poise that they exuded, with thick scales as sharp as iron, and eyes that were penetratingly soulful. No basilisk would ever randomly petrify people for the sake of it, but everyone acted like an attack was always just around the corner. That kind of suspicion wore on you.

It was refreshing to meet Amy, devoid of the fear he had grown accustomed to.

'It doesn't matter,' he said in response to nothing. When his companions only watched him, he directed his attention to Shaun. 'Amy,' he said. 'I don't think it will matter when she sees what Mr Reaper is, in his full sense. I don't think she'll care.'

Shaun narrowed his gaze. 'Why d'you say that?'

'Basilisk intuition.'

They watched each other silently as they climbed the stairs. Dagwood kept his distance.

'Yeah?' said Shaun.

'Yeah.'

They stopped once they were on their desired floor.

'I hope you're right,' Shaun said. 'I want her to accept him.'

'Why?' Brian frowned. He hadn't expected that.

'Because . . .' Shaun's attention was taken by one of the sculptures across the walkway. The black marble figure tapped a nearby wall, then rested its ear against it to check for an opening. When it saw Shaun, it tipped its head, and Shaun offered a lazy salute in return. When he looked back at Brian, the basilisk noticed the sadness in his expression. 'Reapers are lonely, man.'

In ponderous silence, Shaun led the way in the opposite direction of the black marble helper. Brian considered his words. He wondered if he had more in common with Gerald than he realised.

CHAPTER TWO

Amy

The return of Melanie's soft footfall was unexpected but welcome. Amy straightened, parsing the air, and was comforted by the unsettled nature of the witch's aura. Her previous words had stung, but their impact had left an impression. She would have to be smarter this time.

Melanie paused by the entrance. Her expression was guarded. She leaned against the wall, her eyes watchful. The arms were still tightly folded, and her shoulders were raised with tension. She was waiting for Amy to say something.

'I wasn't lying about the affair. I saw him in the act. Fucking some white woman right on top of a crate.'

Melanie nodded. Her gaze refocused on the ground, at some untethered space beside Amy's numb feet. 'Yeah. I know.'

Amy's mouth went dry at the admission, and the soft way in which it had been spoken. For some ridiculous reason, her throat ached with the threat of incoming tears, and she swallowed, annoyed at herself. 'Do you need help to escape?'

Melanie flinched. She stared at Amy, her eyes wide, the blackness of her irises a vast, overwhelming galaxy of fractured hope.

'Because . . .' Amy continued, 'because you've been put in Gerald's Grim Book. You know that, right? Which is why Bane wants to kill him first, I'm guessing. But Gerald has this annoying principle, like he always carries his requests through.'

'Yeah, yeah, human, we all know about that. The Reaper always completes a job once he's accepted them. We're told about the Reapers in school; save your lecture.'

'Okay, well, fine. But I'm an empath. If I speak to him, I might be able to convince him.'

'Ah.' Melanie released her arms. She seemed to be reasoning with herself, nodding as if in conversation with another person, and then she took a decided step backwards. 'Another liar.' A cloud of disappointment cast a grey shadow over her aura.

'No, I'm not lying! I'm telling you I'll talk to him. I swear. If you get me out of here, I'll do everything in my power, absolutely everything, to convince him. I can't guarantee. But I'll try. Either way, keeping me here as a hostage isn't doing shit. You're just . . . imprisoning yourself further. If we leave together, you have a better chance of living, of escaping everything.'

'And what then?'

Amy frowned, confused. 'What do you—'

'What *then*?' Melanie did not look at Amy, and instead demanded answers from the damp space before her. 'If the Reaper was mad enough to let me live, what do I do? Where do I go? I'm still a fugitive. People in the other supernatural cities know my name, they know who I am. I can't just go waltzing around the place, can I? I'll still be trapped.'

Amy swallowed. She had nothing to say to this. She opened and closed her mouth, desperate to offer something meaningful, some inspirational word that would convince Melanie to let her go and leave Bane behind, but the witch's shoulders were taut and stiff, and her body looked unassailable. She was still the former leader of the Lads, still a stubborn, determined Downer, accustomed to relying on her own misfortune and the bloody reality of her life. It was an existence that Amy could not fathom, despite her empathy, and as she felt the waves of apprehension and worry and fatigue washing against the confines of her prison, she was lost, flailing with her inability to provide something more comforting than a chance.

Melanie continued to burn questions into the mottled ground. Eventually, her posture loosened, and her aura fluttered with a nascent hope. She parted her lips once more to speak, but a noise in the corridor alerted them both, and Melanie darted away from the cavern with panicked urgency. When she was gone, Amy groaned. She flopped against the wall, and this time, she wept silently. She needed to get out of here – Melanie was taking too long.

With a wilting strength, Amy shuffled along the floor, groaning at the damp that seeped into her clothes, gritting her teeth to distract herself from the swollen moss and the stench coming from the algae on the walls. She floundered and knew she looked ridiculous, trying to find an exit in a closed cavern when it was clear the only true exits were where Melanie and Tyrell kept disappearing to, but she tried anyway. She couldn't forget the threat in Bane's eyes, how his gaze had burrowed deep into her skull. Desperation like that could drive someone to to make frightening decisions – her life was not safe.

A piercing flame engulfed her arms and she hissed. She could go no further; the nylon ties were pulled too tightly, her legs folded at an uncomfortable angle. She inhaled deeply and exhaled, fighting against the urge to cry again. Gerald was out there somewhere, searching for her. When they first partnered up, she had been naïve and childish, clinging to memories of Nan and hoping to reconcile the scepticism of her own past. Since then, she had seen the Reaper at his most impressive and at his worst. Like Bane, he was a killer. He could be cold and cruel and enjoy the thrill of violence, a stark contrast to the galaxy of magic that had stunned her to silence just a month and a half ago. She was at constant risk as his partner, thrust so brazenly into a world she only barely understood, but even with all his contradictions and the danger he posed, Amy trusted him. Gerald had proved that even if he struggled to understand the value of a life, he had placed much importance in hers. There were so many things she still had to teach him. She did not want her journey to end here.

Amy braced herself again. She steadied her breathing. Once more, she scanned the cavern, and searched for a means of escape.

CHAPTER THREE
Ulrich

Shifting without a full moon was always painful, and Ulrich was limited to his bipedal transformation. He grunted as he scaled the posterior wall of the museum with Josh on his back, then unceremoniously rolled him off his shoulders once they were on the roof, facing the domed glass skylight that overlooked the highest floor. Sighing, he stretched, wishing for nothing more than a hot bath, some chamomile tea, and a foot massage. As Josh surveyed the vacant landscape of the roof, Ulrich glanced at the dark sky longingly. The night was without clouds, and the light pollution from one of London's busiest districts had taken the stars away. It was easy during such times to ponder his first transformation fifteen years ago, when he was a weedy teenager, an Oxford implant to Twickenham, unceremoniously dragged into the secret darkness beneath the capital.

Josh beckoned to him enthusiastically from the glass dome of the roof. Once Ulrich was beside him, the wraith disappeared and reappeared on the other side of the glass, far below on the walkway inside the museum. Ulrich marvelled at the silent whirlwind his partner created around himself and how he used the soles of his feet to surf the current upwards, all the while staring at Ulrich through the glass. Once he was directly beneath the dome, Josh began unscrewing fixtures to open the windows.

As he worked, his hands assured and confident, Ulrich bit his lip, remembering how Josh was the first person to befriend him after he passed into Downstairs society. As a young man newly infected, Ulrich had tried to live normally with his parents, begged them not to go to the police, and took some time off school as he was wracked with fevers. Then his first full moon came, and his body was doused with flames. He ran out of the house on instinct to look for deer in his nearby Richmond Park.

Instead of dinner, he found a boy dressed in a black cloak standing above the body of a creature that was neither deer nor man. Ulrich recognised the werewolf's prone body by scent. That stench would always bring back the horror of jagged teeth – an attack that had rendered him a feverish, bestial mess. The boy flinched, observing Ulrich with scarlet eyes. He pulled his hood back to reveal a stunning face of aquiline intensity. Glossy black hair fell in thick curtains around his face. He gripped a crossbow, and was about to raise it towards Ulrich, when something about Ulrich's expression apparently made him falter, and he lowered it again. Upon closer inspection, Ulrich realised that he and the boy were around the same age, and even though he had been aching with hunger before, something about the scent this boy exuded quelled the sensation instantly.

The now-grown Joshua Rivers-Lee grinned at Ulrich from the slab of open window he had created.

'Hurry down, partner!' he said.

'Let me ride your back.'

Josh raised a brow before pivoting. Ulrich climbed through the panel and perched himself on the offered seat, pressing his chest against Josh's shoulder blades as he secured himself for the descent.

'What's made *you* all touchy-feely?' Josh asked once they were on the walkway below.

'Memories.'

Ulrich trained his ears to listen for anything untoward. He could hear the other trio several floors below. Dagwood was moaning about something while Brian and Shaun were in a heated debate about the virtues of succubae. Curiously, a low grating sound rumbled through the museum like background static. With his heightened senses, he could feel no other heat downstairs besides his companions. It almost felt like the other presences were made from stone. Assuming it to be a mage trick, he refocused on his own floor, and the body heat he could feel emanating from an unknown entity in one of the adjoining rooms.

'Stay close to me,' he said.

They edged through the dark ceramics corridor in silence, past cabinets of decorative pottery from ancient and modern eras, and delicate multicoloured jewellery made from precious clay. As they progressed through the displays, the heat became more potent. Ulrich crouched low, his mane bristling instinctively, then pounced upon what he assumed to be Tyrell Bane or Melanie Lavender.

He fell to the floor on top of an overgrown rat instead. It squealed in his arms, biting hands that were thicker than leather. Ulrich hissed in annoyance, gripping it by the neck until he felt the resounding snap, then gestured for Josh to open his Hammerspace so he could stow it away.

'Disgusting. Vile. Atrocious,' said Josh, backing away onto the adjacent wall once it was gone.

'It's not like I'm going to eat it raw.'

'Oh, I'm sorry! How will you eat it, honey?'

Ulrich thought a moment. The more he pictured it, the

hungrier he became. 'I'll roast it. Add some rosemary potatoes in goose fat. Red wine jus. And I'll fry the heart with some crispy onions to make a crumb.'

'Ugh!' Josh helped Ulrich to his feet. 'I don't get *how* you lot eat that.'

'It's a werewolf delicacy.' Ulrich smiled wryly. 'I keep saying you should try it.'

'Sounds grim. No thanks.'

'Honestly, it tastes just like pidg—' Ulrich hissed in pain. He collapsed on the ground, cradling his ankle, where a pulsating fire was slowly spreading through his skin, into his blood, and up his leg.

'Ricky!' Josh fell beside him. He ripped Ulrich's trousers, and Ulrich squinted downwards to see the circular end of a silver bullet slowly seeping into his skin. 'I don't think so!' Josh's hand disappeared and he scooped the bullet out of the injured leg. Ulrich shivered as a coolness enveloped his ankle, and a strange tickling sensation indicated Josh's fingers were carefully avoiding any veins. The ordeal felt like it lasted an hour, but after only a few moments, the bullet was on the ground, rolling away from them across the mosaic.

The human who fired the gun – silencer attached – was frozen in fear on the other end of the corridor. His hands trembled as he held the gun aloft. An old WCT Security uniform clung to his sweaty, misshapen body. The silvery sheen of a heat-resistant blanket surrounded his feet. In one swift movement, Josh darted towards the security guard, who had tried a little too late to flee.

Slumping against a nearby wall, Ulrich was weakened. The pain had subsided from his ankle, but he felt feverish and slow. It had done the intended damage; they were handicapped now. Before him, the stunned security guard struggled beneath Josh's restraint. The wraith pressed the guard's face into the floor, his knee firmly between his shoulder blades, arms pinned tightly behind the tail bone. The guard gasped, and Josh loosened his hold. Ulrich looked at the silver bullet warily.

'Now what's a human doing with something like this?' Josh asked the guard.

'I'm sorry, I'm sorry!'

'Don't just say *sorry*. Who gave you this?'

'A man!'

'Narrow it down.'

'I can't remember his—' He wailed as Josh crunched his knee deeper into his back. 'Okay, fucking *hell*! Thomas! Thomas Banton! You know him? He's one of you lot!'

Ulrich and Josh exchanged a sceptical glance at the alias.

'And why would *he* give you this?' Ulrich asked. The wall was nice and cool against his back as he rubbed his ankle. 'What kind of patrol are you doing here?'

'Honestly, I don't know, I swear.' The guard's eyes brimmed with tears. 'I'm telling you the truth. But look at me – if a guy doing all sorts of crazy tricks just comes out of nowhere and tells you to use this on any intruders, you're gonna do it, right? I wasn't gonna die for no one!'

'What else did he tell you?' asked Ulrich.

'That if I don't do what I'm told, he'll send a witch to come kill me.'

'Just how many people does he intend to tell about us?' Josh asked the ceiling. 'Well, there's no need for you to get into this,' he said to the security guard. Once again, his hands disappeared, but his arms hovered above the man's head. Ulrich saw the security guard's eyes roll backwards, and he panted in short gasps through an open, dribbling mouth. His body went slack beneath Josh, and then the creases in his face vanished as he entered a deep sleep. Josh's memory-altering abilities proved useful whenever they needed to remove their existence from a human who saw too much. Even now, the last two executives of Darkhouse were still walking around without any recollection that they ever knew a warlock called Tyrell Bane.

Ulrich closed his eyes to focus on healing his internal wound. He felt Josh's body press against his. He rested his head on Josh's shoulder, sighing as he felt the resultant forehead kiss.

'You okay?' Josh's voice was a soft rumble against his ear.

'I will be. I'm guessing this means our foes are next door.'

'Yeah. No way would a scared little security guard be enough to guard Bane's hideout if it was in here.'

'Well, I'm glad. I'm starving now. Can't wait for the rat.'

'I'll cook it for you when we get home.'

'How gallant.'

Josh chuckled. At the other end of the corridor, pale light streamed through the glass ceiling to cast cubic shapes on the ground. It was a mock imitation of moonlight – just some nearby LED lamps reflecting off the glass, but it made him nostalgic, and he longed for a full moon.

'You should get a crossbow again,' Ulrich said. 'You're a talented archer.'

'Oh yeah?'

'Mmhmm.' Ulrich closed his eyes again. After a little while, he slipped into a comfortable slumber, revisiting the long, impenetrable grass of Richmond Park, and the piercing eyes of the hunter boy who saved his life.

CHAPTER FOUR

Amy

Amy jolted awake. Her dank little dungeon was bitingly cold now, her bottom was numb, and when she tried to wiggle her arms and legs, they were stiff and achy. But none of that mattered, because it was not the cold nor the discomfort that woke her up, but the cool trickle that ran down the length of her spine. Normally, a vampire's aura would have been a foreboding sign, but tonight, Amy relished its soothing surety. Alongside the twin fountains of Felix and Hollow was the warmth of Dani's witch aura, so comfortingly different to Melanie's prickling heat. Knowing that her friends were so close, Amy started stretching her limbs as far as they could go. She remembered a video she watched on how to release oneself from nylon ties, and although her previous attempts had been painfully unsuccessful, the presence of *Gardien* gave her renewed inspiration.

Before she got a chance to start, Melanie marched into the room, her eyes narrowed in irritation.

'Get up,' she said. 'I'm moving you.'

'No.'

Melanie rolled her eyes. She made a sign in the air, and Amy was lifted from the ground by some vine-like plant. She struggled hopelessly in mid-air, swearing as she did so.

'Do you even realise what's going on?' Amy asked

breathlessly, having given up on fighting against the supernatural. 'Gerald's near.'

'We haven't seen him anywhere.'

'He's near.' Amy stared into Melanie's eyes, searching for a soul, some evidence that a real person existed beneath her unconvincing, callous exterior. 'He's near. Melanie, listen to me. I can convince him to let you go. Or, at least let me try to.'

Melanie glanced behind her shoulder nervously, as if to confirm that Bane wasn't nearby.

'What kind of life d'you think you'll even have?' Amy pressed. 'Just constantly on the run from a fucking *Reaper*? With a man who doesn't love you? Bane's some . . . crusty, dusty warlock. You don't mean anything to him! Why die for someone like that?'

Melanie took a tentative step towards Amy. 'Are you sure he'll spare me?' she whispered.

Amy saw the shimmer in the witch's eyes. She felt the pained hope that coursed through her aura, and she found she did not want to mislead her, to follow the path of everyone else who had caused her harm. 'I can't promise anything. But I'll try to make him listen.'

The witch made another sign and Amy was lowered to the ground. She then held out two fists, twisted an invisible rope – one twist forward, another back – and the nylon ties snapped and fell from Amy's limbs. She sighed in gratitude, trembling, as her wrists finally had some reprieve. They were raw and red, and still bleeding, and the throbbing pain in her legs indicated similar injuries around her ankles.

'I won't be able to do anything without some kind of relief here,' she said, holding out her wrists for Melanie to see. 'You got anything for this? Ibuprofen?'

Melanie started, her eyes widening at the wounds. She conjured a Hammerspace satchel, its silvery outline almost glowing in the dimness of the dungeon. A small purple phial appeared from the Hammerspace and she quickly shared its contents with Amy's wrists. Two drops each was all it needed before the wounds knitted together. The pain subsided.

'Don't push it,' Melanie said as she did the ankles. 'They can still open if you do too much.'

'Sure.'

Once she was healed, the two women stared at each other with uncertainty. Amy could feel Melanie's suspicion, but it was a multilayered sensation, an indication of a difficult life populated with complex and harmful people. She had so many questions to ask the witch. She was also worried that Gerald would reject her request, but she had no time to think about it. Getting outside to safety was her priority.

Melanie led her to the wall beside the main passage. She pressed her hands against the stone and a tunnel of total darkness opened before them. Its gaping hole wailed in the draft, permeated by a stale, damp smell. Melanie retrieved a candle lamp from her Hammerspace, saying nothing else as she entered the blackness. When Amy followed behind, the entrance closed, and they were sealed inside. She desperately parsed her surroundings, ensuring that there were no other presences in the tunnel.

Her eyes were focused on the lamp as they twisted in various directions. Sometimes the tunnel was draughty, other times it was uncomfortably humid. She could feel the auras of Hollow, Felix, and Dani slipping in and out of focus as they searched for her. Their directions were erratic and unfocused, but there was a methodical determination within the madness.

'Where are we?' she asked at last.

Melanie didn't answer. She stopped, and Amy saw that their journey was blocked by another empty wall. The witch pressed one hand against it, and the way opened into a barren passage. When she was fully outside, Amy took in her surroundings, frowning at the walls, decorated elaborately with terracotta tiles and ancient stone fixtures. The mosaic floor that stretched into the distance was limned with glass cases of dinosaur bones and fossils. It took her ages to realise that they were in the Natural History Museum, a place she hadn't visited since she was in primary school.

'That's why it was so busy,' she said.

'We'll go straight ahead,' said Melanie. 'I know this place better than Ty; he never cared about directions much. He'll know that I've taken you soon if he hasn't already clocked it.'

'And then what? We go outside?'

'Are you mad? He's put a barrier around this place; it's how he knew *Gardien* got through. That's why he sent me to get you.'

'So how're we leaving . . .'

'Hopefully' – Melanie quickly scanned the corridor, then gestured for Amy to follow – 'your *Gardien* pals will get to Ty first. I don't want any trouble. If that don't work, we'll go to *Gardien* instead. Then I'll take down the barrier, but only if they promise they won't kill me.'

Amy shrugged, sighing inwardly at what seemed to be another long operation she had got herself tangled up in.

'It's a plan, I'll give you that,' she said.

Melanie inhaled deeply, then let out a haggard sigh. In the light of the open corridor, Amy could see the lines of premature ageing on her face and the harrowing darkness of her eyes. As if to steel herself, she tied her hair up into a bun and fastened her cardigan.

In the underground dungeon, Amy hadn't noticed the necklace Melanie wore. It was an emerald brooch, identical to the one worn by Imogen Carrington. She scoffed at Bane's recycled gift before noticing that this brooch was slightly different. The plain, oval stone encrusted with pearls was what she had seen pinned to Imogen's cardigan, but now, the brooch had been affixed to another item, like a green amulet, quietly beautiful, surrounded by its own serene aura. Amy reached out to touch the necklace.

'I've seen this before,' Amy said. She felt her heart pounding in her temples. She met Melanie's gaze, baulking when she saw the knowing, almost mischievous grin in response to her shock. 'This was in Lex Crow's office.'

'Mmhmm. It's a pair.'

'Melanie, why do you have—'

The witch snatched the necklace away, stowing it beneath her cardigan. As she beckoned for Amy to follow, she shrugged absently. 'It's true what you said about old dusty men, and how they leave you when you've served your purpose,' said Melanie. 'Only with *this* one, he went and made an assassination request to make sure I couldn't kiss and tell.'

As if she hadn't just shared earth-shattering news, Melanie ran down the corridor, her steps light and skilful. Amy followed in a stupor, not believing that the protector of the Downey Gang had just been identified.

CHAPTER FIVE
Hollow

Thanks to Dani's Hammerspace door, getting into the Natural History Museum was easy. The trio walked carefully through the entrance, then stopped in the Hintze Hall to take in the impressive atrium that welcomed thousands of visitors a day. The large space was dominated by the skeleton of a blue whale that hung from the ceiling using invisible cables, providing a disconcerting sensation that the whale was alive, floating by its own means, and ready to sail elsewhere at a moment's notice. Hollow walked further into the hall, stopping once he was directly beneath the skeleton to examine it. As he lifted his chin, he caught the scent of Amy's blood, and his throat ached.

'She's in here,' he said. The others froze.

'What?' said Felix.

'I can smell her.' As he spoke, his mouth began to water. He had fed before the mission, but his stomach emptied as soon as he realised Amy was nearby – near enough to taste the sweetness of her blood in the air. He felt a pang of hunger, and he swallowed to get rid of the lump in his throat. He had taken a chance, hoping that she was in the other building, but now he would be tortured, driven close to frenzy to find her, only to not be rewarded with her blood at the end of it.

A firm hand gripped his shoulder. 'Bartholomew.'

He turned to see Felix looking at him behind lowered eyelids, presenting his neck in the vampire custom.

It was a misconception that vampires were totally devoid of blood. What had been drained during transformation was replaced by a thick black substance that was pumped around their body by a tiny section of the aorta. It was the only part of their hearts that was alive, and coincidentally, the one area of their body that provided a fatal weakness. The *lichid noir* never depleted, was rich in minerals, and was the only replacement for their disposition that a vampire had. In vampire bars across Downstairs, barrels of the substance could be bought cheaply to help those in need. It was invaluable for the vampires that craved rare blood types, and for those like Hollow who were unable to feed from their disposition for whatever reason. He was never in need of his blood type, but Amy's gave off a scent that was unlike anything he had experienced before. He could only assume it was the purity of her empath abilities, and he hated how desperate it made him feel.

He launched himself towards Felix's neck, puncturing the jugular with his canines. The treacly liquid flushed into his mouth, and as he gulped, he felt his strength returning. Felix's heart pounded in his head, and he heard the echo of the other vampire's pleasured groans. Hollow gripped the back of Felix's neck, rubbing his thumb in delicate circles along the base of his skull. The resultant goosebumps, and the strangled gasp from Felix, made him drink more forcefully. The deeper the arousal, the sweeter the *lichid*, and before he could do or say anything else, his mind slipped away into scarlet heat, and all he could feel was the pounding of Felix's pulse beneath his own chest.

Hollow forced himself away. They breathed in sync. Felix

held onto Hollow's shoulder to steady himself, and Hollow rested his hands on his knees.

'Thanks,' Hollow said.

'Nah, thank you.' Felix grinned at him.

Hollow was dimly aware of Dani, who sat cross-legged several feet away from them. She waved her hands mystically above a brass cauldron, her eyes clouded over in concentration as she scried the museum. When Hollow stood beside her, peering over her shoulder to get a look, all he could see was an opaline liquid in the cauldron that rippled by some unseen force, but Dani appeared to read something within the surface.

'Glad you're all done,' she said just as Felix took her other side. 'There are loads of windows in this museum, perfect to get a look at all the different rooms they could be hiding her in.'

'See anything?' asked Felix.

'Not yet.'

'What about her scent?' Felix asked Hollow.

Hollow sniffed, this time more confidently now that his bloodlust was satisfied. Amy's scent was faint, but it came from the direction of the main dinosaur exhibit on the ground floor, which was only two corridors away. It could potentially take a long time to track her down by scent alone, but at least it was a rough direction.

'Shame about the smokescreen,' Dani said after Hollow vocalised his assessment. 'It would be so much faster if Mr Reaper could just look inside for us.'

Hollow glanced towards the way they had come. On the other side of the vast entrance doors, Gerald stood watch, hovering outside the barrier that Bane had created to lock him out. If they could get to Bane first, they could force him to remove the barrier, thus making the Reaper's job easier.

'Let's split,' he said. 'I'll go for Amy. You two look for Bane. They're not together; I know his smell anywhere.'

'You sure?' asked Felix, eyeing him warily.

Hollow nodded. He swallowed, embarrassed at the thought of stalling the operation. He was determined to control himself. 'My sense of smell would be better for finding her.'

'What about Lavender?' asked Dani.

'Dunno,' he said, frowning. 'I can't get a trace of that one.'

'She's far too good at concealing her presence for her age,' Dani muttered, 'but all right. We'll trust you with Amy's retrieval. If she's separated from Lavender and Bane, it's probably because she's escaped, or at least tried to. I'm sure she could do with your help.'

'Right.'

'Let's go, Felix,' Dani said, rising with the cauldron floating beside her. 'We'll try Bane. Be mindful of traps, boys.'

Hollow darted towards the dinosaur exhibit, kicking open the oak doors that sealed the room in the museum's Blue Zone. The room was cavernous and dark, with a winding path that would take visitors on a journey through the Jurassic, showcasing an array of fossils, dinosaur bones, and interactive fact sheets. A metal walkway above was framed by the hanging fossilised bones of dinosaurs of varying shapes and sizes. Hollow was only faintly aware of his surroundings as he ran down the winding path, noting that Amy's scent grew stronger the further he advanced.

He whizzed around the corner where the now-still, animatronic T-rex watched him with bewildered eyes. As he ran past it, he slammed into Melanie Lavender.

The witch flew backwards, tumbling over herself in mid-air, and crashed into the wall behind. Amy squatted on the floor, her eyes wide and fearful. Hollow grabbed her by the arm and pushed her behind him, crouching into a defensive stance as Melanie quickly recovered.

'You came up much faster than I thought you would,' Amy said, her smile sheepish. 'I didn't even get a chance to warn her.'

'*Warn* her?'

Hollow watched as Melanie reluctantly held her hands outwards in a sign of defeat. She stumbled towards him, her expression totally uncertain.

'She's on our side now,' said Amy. 'She wants to get away from Bane.'

Hollow straightened, not at all convinced. He folded his arms, scrutinising the witch with a look he hoped was cruel. 'Does she now?' he scoffed, and he phoned Felix.

CHAPTER SIX
Gerald

It was a credit to the efficiency of the Downey Gang that Gerald was currently trapped outside such a massive barrier. Even more impressive was the smokescreen that clouded the interiors of the buildings. When Gerald and *Gardien* arrived on the scene, he immediately attempted to scan the insides of both museums only to be met with a curtain of black tar. The smokescreen had burned his eyes and he was forced to retreat, mopping up the resultant tears. Smokescreens were mage magic. He knew that Bane was a talented man, but Gerald would not have expected him to be capable of so much. This whole operation was a clear provocation: Bane wanted to antagonise him, and it had worked.

After trying to destroy the barrier, Gerald relented, trusting the Downers hired by Blythe to complete the mission given to them. All he could do was observe the two buildings from a good vantage point, cloaked within the darkness of the night, his face obscured by his veil. He was angry with himself the most. When Amy told him she was going into work, he gave little thought to the dangers around her. Even now, he tried to think of what he could have done differently without looking like an over-controlling taskmaster, or an annoyingly chivalrous suitor, stalking her around London, keeping track of her lunch breaks, and fending off any supernatural interferences. Amy had survived this long without him, so there was no reason to doubt her now.

A little while after he had left Camden Town that afternoon, he received a call from Amy's manager to enquire about her whereabouts. The confusion passed quickly as he realised that Amy had made him her next of kin. With a heaviness in his voice, he had promised to keep her informed. That was hours ago now; if he didn't want the Upstairs Met to get involved, he would have to save her quickly.

A weight he hadn't noticed slowly evaporated from his shoulders, and the world was flooded with colour. Without warning, the sooty mist that enveloped the V&A and the Natural History Museum blew away into the wind. He peered forward and saw Hollow and Felix speaking with Amy in the Hintze Hall of the latter building. Dani stood nearby with Melanie Lavender. The younger witch was bound with a bronze chord, her gaze downcast, as if she had resigned herself to her imprisonment. Gerald flitted to the entrance and passed through using Hammerspace. He headed straight for Amy, not looking at the others. She turned to him, and he could see the moisture in her eyes threatening to break through. Gerald hugged her and held her head on his shoulder, pretending that he didn't see her tearful expression. She wrapped her arms around his waist. She was warm in his arms.

'I'm sorry,' he said. 'I should have—'

She pulled away from him with a look of reproach. 'It is what it is. Not your fault. Don't start that up again.'

'If you say so.'

He quickly remembered where he was. Dani and the vampires looked decidedly uncomfortable, but he smiled at the room. 'Thank you, everyone.' Then he loosened his gloves and stalked towards Melanie. The witch yelped and backed away.

'Wait, Gerald!' said Amy, standing between them. 'You can't kill her.'

'I . . . beg your pardon?'

'The only reason why the barrier's broken right now is because she lifted it, even if it would upset Bane. She's helping us.'

'And she's on my list.'

'Yeah. I get that.'

'Step aside, Amy.'

'You can't. I *promised* her. That's why she's helping us!'

Gerald turned to the witch. She trembled beneath his gaze.

'Are you in a position to negotiate with anyone?' he asked her.

Melanie shook her head rapidly, thick hair flaying about her head. 'But I can help you!' She looked around at the other *Gardien* members. 'I promise. I can tell you anything you need to know.'

'Like what?' asked Felix, crossing his arms over his chest. 'You're guilty. You've served your purpose.'

'Not to Blythe Mason, I haven't!'

At this, Gerald paused. He stared at her until she continued.

'I know that Mason's been after us for years. D'you know how I know? Because our boss told me. Our boss helps us out. He makes it so we're always one step ahead of Blythe and your little group here. He always leaks info to us, you know. Or he used to before things went sour. And Blythe's been searching for *him* for years, too. Trying to find out who's really protecting us.'

'Oh fuck off,' said Felix. 'The lies of a rabbit at the fox house.'

'It's true! Tell them!' Melanie turned to Amy, her anger palpable in the air.

'She's telling the truth,' Amy said. 'I don't even need to parse her aura. Look at her necklace.'

Gerald and the others directed their attention to the emerald brooch around Melanie's neck. The Reaper noticed the garish item as formerly belonging to Imogen Carrington, but this time, it was fitted into another outer case. He faintly recognised it but could not remember from where.

'Speak,' he said.

Melanie sighed in relief, shooting a grateful look at Amy before continuing. Gerald watched as she fidgeted with her restraints, fighting some internal battle to prepare for what she was about to say. Her eyes darted back and forth, as if expecting Tyrell Bane to jump out at any moment.

Melanie exhaled slowly, ridding herself of whatever hold her boyfriend had placed her in. She stood to her full height to face Gerald evenly.

'Your mayor. Lex Crow,' she said.

The room erupted into outraged gasps.

'Fucking liar!' Felix said as he stormed towards her.

'I'm not!' She brandished the necklace. 'He gave this part to me – it was a pair! We were together for a little while, and he used to buy me things all the time!'

'She's not lying,' said Amy, which helped to calm the room, but only a little. 'I saw that amulet at Crow's office. And her aura's legit.'

Dani crouched until her eyes were level with the younger witch's. 'This is a massive accusation, you know,' she said. 'You better be correct.'

'I am.'

'You need to tell us the full story, and it needs to be

convincing,' said Hollow. 'I get it, Amy's an empath, but it's us you need to convince, not her.'

Gerald was too stunned to speak. Lex Crow was a name that hadn't even registered for him. The skittish, weaselly mayor did not have the conviction to associate with an organised criminal network, and Amy had met him several times and never detected anything.

Gerald had met his family and had countless meetings with Lex. There had never been any indication that he was hiding anything. Even in the mayor's office, everything was transparent: from the Viagra blister packs he absently left in his bin, to the food-stained robes on his coat rack, and the betting slips he kept pinned to his noticeboard. And yet, some loose threads that he had chosen to ignore began to knit themselves together.

'Explain,' he said quietly.

'The Crow family's broke, but the only one who knows that is Lex himself. He's always relied on the Masons to fund his campaigns, and the Geckos to sponsor the running of his office, but who's paying for his lifestyle? Can you imagine, a big man like that, running to little Blythe or madman Gecko to ask for spending money so he and his wife and bratty kid can go galivanting off to the Bahamas or something? *We've* been giving him money this whole time!' Melanie grinned, relishing the salaciousness of these revelations. 'He came to us years ago when the gang started making big deals Upstairs. Said if we sponsored him, he would let us off the hook and make it hard for the Downey Met to find us. All that time, we paid for his Kensington house, we paid for his daughter's carriage that she takes to school, we paid for the housekeeper and his suits. Everything. And he protects us. He makes sure we don't get caught, so that he can keep getting his slice of our money.'

Amy turned to Gerald. 'I'll be honest, I never felt anything dishonest in his aura.'

'Oh, he has ways to hide all of that,' Melanie said. 'You ever notice how he keeps his staff hanging up somewhere? If he was to hold it, he'd cancel my concealing spell. Took me ages to make that for him: it's the reason why he keeps winning elections and why he even managed to get a partnership with the Masons and all these high-flyers, even though he's obviously a bit dry. Got his own special little cloud of charisma hiding up his true, ugly self.'

'Okay, okay, hold on,' said Hollow. 'Tell us about the schism. Was that all in his plan too?'

'No.' Melanie shook her head for emphasis. 'Lex caused it, though. Basically, Ty wanted Lex to legitimise us. He doesn't just want protection to get away with our crimes anymore, but a job. That's how the human mafia works, right? And loads of drug lords Upstairs operate like that – they're friends with politicians and then they can get cushy little jobs in cabinet and start making proper, global moves. Ty wanted to plant me in Lex's government, but Lex said no, and Ty used that as an excuse for extortion.

'So we were split. I liked how things were. I mean, look at me. I'd never be able to show my face around Downstairs after that thing with my parents . . .'

'By *thing* you mean when you hacked them to death?' asked Felix with a raised brow.

'Ty wanted more power,' Melanie continued without acknowledging him. 'Look how he operates, all his Upstairs connections, the whole partnership with Carrington and them. He's ambitious and greedy. So when Lex turned him down, he got hostile. Threatening Peaches, sending ransom letters, defunding his lifestyle – whatever it took to get the mayor's attention. He tried to abduct him on the night of the Greymalkin's prom, but Lex wasn't there so he just decided to kill the refugees instead. He was hoping for you guys to find the bodies, but didn't think you'd come to his hideout so quick. Ty's mad and he'll do anything to get in someone's head. Even the smuggling thing was just to add pressure on Lex. I'm laidback, I didn't care. I like Lex. He was always there for me when things got funny with Ty . . .' Her eyes shone with the threat of tears. 'I literally walked away from the love of my life for Lex, and was prepared to make Ty my enemy for him. But he still sent out for my assassination anyway. I guess I know too much.'

Gerald's mind unravelled as he thought about the mayor's recent skittishness: the desperation to get this case resolved that went beyond reasonable behaviour, hiding the assassination request from Blythe, and trying his very best to separate Gerald's operations from Gardien. Even the request was questionable, opting to go straight to Gerald instead of consulting Blythe first, knowing full well that the wraith was investigating the Downey Gang so devotedly. During their last meeting, Lex had been horrified to hear that Melanie and Tyrell had reunited. Now he knew why. Gerald had been so focused on the killing aspect of his job that he never paused to ask why the gang was suddenly so obsessed with their mayor, and why the mayor was so anxious to have them killed.

'It makes sense,' he said simply, looking at the others and finally shrugging his defeat at Amy.

Melanie sighed in relief. She offered a determined smile, and then her jaw exploded. Bones and blood burst into the air, and reams of purple skin fell like strips of rotten cabbage on the floor. The group ducked instinctively as Melanie fell.

She grabbed the gaping, mottled mess of her face and screamed, rolling from side to side. It was an eerie, sickening sound. Gerald saw Amy crouch beside her, eyes wide and fearful, and Dani stood guard, conjuring twin daggers in either hand from her Hammerspace, brandishing them at the unseen enemy. The vampires both hissed and looked around for the source of the attack, but Gerald could see him travelling below.

The Reaper leapt into the air just as Tyrell Bane emerged from a Hammerspace trapdoor brandishing a silver revolver. He looked irritated that Gerald had seen through his surprise so easily.

'Wagwan, Reaper?' he said.

Gerald brandished his bare hands as a warning. 'Hello,' he replied.

CHAPTER SEVEN

Gerald

The Reaper conjured a scythe from his Hammerspace and darted towards Bane. He slashed the scythe in a downwards arc towards Bane's head, but the warlock dodged just in time, firing his revolver. Gerald ducked and swung his scythe at the gun, reducing it to shards of metal. The warlock snarled, backed away, and conjured twin handguns instead. Gerald mirrored him by conjuring a second scythe. He seemed surprised by this action, which filled Gerald with satisfaction. The Reaper wanted to relish this fight. Tyrell did not deserve a quick exit, not after what he had put Amy through.

He glanced over to the far corner of the hall, where Amy crouched beside the near-comatose Melanie Lavander. Dani knelt by Lavender's head and poured an emerald tincture over her injuries from a miniature cauldron. Gerald narrowed his eyes, watching the trembling flutter of the younger witch's chest as she tried to remain conscious, and felt his heart pound uncomfortably beneath his ribs. He did not want Melanie to pass away by herself, not when she was within his reach. He felt compelled to conjure her life thread and felt the pulsing warmth of desire coalesce behind his navel, but then Amy flinched, and whipped around to stare at him. Her eyes were wide and haunted. Her mouth was set in a pleading, yet disapproving frown. There was an unnatural stiffness that entered her posture just then – defensive.

Gerald swallowed, turned away, and ignored Amy and the witches altogether. *Just focus on Bane. Make him suffer.*

A brown phial appeared overhead and exploded by itself. In response to the spell, the ground rippled, becoming a moving sea of mosaic. Great waves of hard stone sloshed around Gerald, crashing over his head, then ebbing to the outer limits of the hall. He slashed at the waves with his scythes, then advanced on the retreating Bane who had used the furore to escape to the walkway above the hall.

The mosaic sea became more tempestuous. Gerald was detained as he tried to quell them. He heard the vampires swearing amid the roar, punching the stone as it threatened to overwhelm them. The waves shattered at the impact in an explosion of tiles and cement. He briefly saw Hollow kick at the arches that supported a section of the surrounding walkway. The disruption returned Bane to ground level, but then the warlock levitated until he was back upstairs.

The sea settled to an abrupt halt. An incoherent noise filled the silence: the dry twang of snapping strings, like a guitar tuned too tightly.

'Gerald!' Felix and Hollow yelled in unison.

The Reaper looked upwards to see the skeleton of Hope the blue whale falling towards him in a roar of wind, having been released from her invisible cables. Before impact, she miraculously stopped inches above his head. An elaborate network of silver strings held the whale in place, connecting it to the ceiling once more. Gerald, Hollow, and Felix turned towards the museum entrance, and at the panting Shaun, staff aloft, his locs askew.

'Maaate!' said Felix.

'The fuck?' said Shaun.

'Where're the others?' Hollow turned towards him.

'Helping Ulrich. He was shot.'

Gerald was only faintly aware of their conversation, watching as Bane ran the length of the first-floor walkway. He had a massive arsenal in his Hammerspace for difficult Downers, and as he saw the warlock fleeing for his life, the sweetness of bloodlust rumbled within him. He felt the mantle of death rest on his shoulders and knew that his eyes had changed, helping him to see all the different paths that Bane could potentially use to escape.

'Bring him down,' he said. The vampires immediately hammered their fists into the two pillars directly below Bane, and that part of the walkway crumbled into powdered stone. Bane crashed to the ground once more. Gerald ran towards him again, scythes aloft.

Bane conjured a metal staff to block the scythes, and the grating sound of metal on metal wailed through the hall. Gerald maintained eye contact between the resultant sparks, staring menacingly until he felt the warlock's resolve weaken. Behind him, Shaun secured the whale skeleton to its rightful place, and the vampires skittered away as Gerald pushed against Bane more forcefully. Just as Gerald was about to touch him with his bare hands, the warlock disappeared through a Hammerspace trapdoor, repeating his escape at the industrial estate in Tottenham.

A moment later, and the warlock was back in the room, directly behind him. Gerald whipped around, slashing the air with his scythes. Bane disappeared again only to reappear mere feet away. The warlock looked around in confusion, first shooting an enquiring look at the injured Melanie, then at Dani, who seemed too preoccupied to acknowledge the fight.

'You ain't the only one who can make a barrier,' said Shaun. The group turned to the sound of his voice. He sat above them on the lower jaw of the whale, his legs dangling leisurely, staff in hand. Outside, the windows were flushed with the pitch-blackness of a smokescreen, encasing the group within the confines of the battle once more. 'And I'm a mage,' Shaun continued. 'Mine's better than yours. You stay in here until the Reaper deals with you.'

'Fuck you, Forbes!'

Bane desperately fired a rapid stream of bullets towards Gerald, then hissed in pain as both guns were shattered by the twin scythes. Levitating himself again, he ran to the entrance stairs, past the statue of Charles Darwin, and pelted down the remaining walkway in the direction of an artefact room. Gerald conjured four more scythes. They were joined together by a metal chain, and they fanned out behind him as he flew towards Bane. The scythes moved of their own will, propelling him forward like extra legs, their chains jangling together, creating a shrill chime that Gerald hoped was within Bane's earshot – it would be no fun if he took the warlock by surprise. He crashed down the gallery walkway, shattering the glass cages of ancient relics and fossils that were beyond monetary value.

The walkway led to the space and science exhibits of the Red Zone. False rock formations covered the walls, encasing Gerald in a plaster cocoon. One of the rocks shifted beside him and he ducked. By the time he was upright again, the walls had started to close in. The chains of his scythes grew taut as they scattered in all directions, cutting the rocks away with ease. Gerald swung his own twin scythes indiscriminately, and great chunks of foam and plaster rained down around him, littering his hair with debris and falling into his eyes. He narrowed his vision as he advanced through the assault course.

Bane waited for him at the other end of the room. A circle of daggers surrounded the warlock, all pointing at Gerald. The Reaper could see the heavy rise and fall of Bane's shoulders, the sweat that frosted his forehead, and the slight tremble of his fingers as he held them in a magic sign in front of his chest, willing the circle of daggers to remain aloft.

'It looks like you really thought you could kill me,' Gerald said. 'Why?'

'Why not? Is this the first time someone's stood up to you or something?'

'No. People fight for their lives when faced with death all the time. It's natural. Instinct. But none of them fight me like they can win.'

'Arrogant little *shit*.'

The daggers flew towards Gerald faster than he thought they would. He did what his father had taught him years ago: expanding his Hammerspace and shifting it around to make his body porous enough for the daggers to pass through him. Three slipped through his blind spot, puncturing his left shoulder and thigh and grazing the flesh above his ribs on the same side. He hissed in pain as Bane vanished again. When Gerald stepped forward to follow, he sank into the warlock's Hammerspace trapdoor – a snare that had slipped his notice. The space was pitch black. It contained the buoyant resistance of water. Gerald held his breath on instinct, a precaution in case the oceanic atmosphere was poisonous, and swam in what he hoped was a forward direction. He had no vision here, and the smokescreen was thick.

A distinct whipping noise cut through the Hammerspace. One of Gerald's scythes became animated by his command, whacking away the dagger that Bane had sent to kill him.

Again and again, a dagger would whizz towards him and he would knock it away, sending it back in the same direction. He realised there were probably hundreds of these daggers waiting for him, so he splayed his hands outward, willing his scythes to shatter them to mechanical debris. Unbeknown to him at the time, they had encircled him in a tight balloon.

The sea rushed around his body, propelling him upwards. With a resounding *pop*, Gerald broke the surface of Bane's Hammerspace, re-emerging in the Hintze Hall. He offered Shaun a brief smile in gratitude for his barrier. He was dry but disconcerted, and immediately used his omnipresence to find Bane.

An abnormal bruise swelled behind the Darwin statue. Gerald threw a scythe towards the marble, sending great iceberg chunks into the air on impact. Bane fell out from his haphazard Hammerspace curtain, his energy receding. With a reserve of strength, he advanced towards Gerald, his expression firm and venomous.

Gerald countered. He rammed Bane into the wall with the handle of one of his scythes. Bane gritted his teeth, trying to push back. Just as Gerald swiped at him with a bare hand, the warlock once again dipped into a trapdoor.

He appeared directly behind Gerald, so close that Gerald could feel his breath on the back of his neck, the coldness of a gun barrel as it sunk into his hair, and the hatred that rolled off him in waves. It was the worst thing he could have done. The Reaper pivoted easily, right palm exposed, and grabbed Bane by the neck. The warlock's eyes widened. They dimmed. Gerald felt him go slack, arms and legs loosening until they were all but swinging above ground. He watched the blankness of Bane's eyes, the paling skin. He listened to the whisper of strangled breath as it oozed out of his body. He imagined the lungs inside squeezing their last and could almost feel the slowing of blood from the jugular vein that stretched taut beneath his fingers. Gerald had been desperate for this after everything that had happened in recent weeks. It was glorious.

He released his hold on Bane's neck, watching as the body fell to the ground, then toppled over itself down the stairs. It rolled to a halt beneath Hope the blue whale where Shaun was still perched, watching it with a look of distaste. With a wave of his staff, the mage released his barrier, but the windows of the museum remained black with a protective smokescreen.

Exhaling, Gerald walked down the steps, stopping when he was beside Tyrell Bane. He crouched over the warlock, took out his Grim Book, and made his final notes. Shaun and Felix didn't approach him until his hands were covered again.

'You missed something massive,' he heard Felix say to Shaun.

'More massive than what I just saw?'

'Yeah, mate . . .' The vampire then explained Melanie Lavender's revelations about Lex Crow. It was then that Gerald remembered she had been badly injured. He quickly stowed the Grim Book away and went to join Amy and Dani's vigil. Hollow hesitated beside them, leaning against one of the damaged pillars nearby, his expression stony. Amy was tight-lipped when Gerald crouched beside her. He noticed her eyes were red and raw. Dani was equally morose, but maintained the professional stoicism as befitting her station. Lavender herself was glassy-eyed and alive, her breaths guttural as they hissed from beneath the ragged flesh of her throat. Gerald loosened one of his gloves, but Amy grabbed his arm.

'Let her go on her own,' she said, not looking at him.

Gerald hesitated. He was about to go two-for-two. The satisfaction of a fully completed mission, after everything that had happened, was within touching distance. As soon as this thought came to him, he was overtaken by an unusual emotion. He frowned, trying to place it, flicking through the pages of himself to see if it had ever emerged within him before. Ever since mercilessly killing the executives in Blythe's prison, he had struggled with his behaviour, and the Blue Meadow incident almost broke him for good. But he had just experienced an exhilarating kill. Why should he feel this way now? Amy glanced towards him, offering a small smile. If he wasn't mistaken, she was looking at him with pity. Was he feeling regret right now? Or guilt? Guilty for what? Wasn't this a legitimate kill too?

He stared at the dying witch, taking her in properly. He listened to the wet whistle of her ragged breaths, observed the sheen of sweat on her cursed, purple skin. The shadow of her lover and groomer was cold behind him. A grotesque, complicated life.

Backing away, he observed the destruction of his final fight with Tyrell Bane. Three broken walkways, a shattered statue, hundreds of fossils and exhibition displays destroyed, and the near destruction of the priceless Hope, who was hanging none-the-wiser from the roof of the Hintze Hall. He was satisfied that Bane was finally dead, but it was a fleeting sensation. The operation had been messy and without elegance. It was not the precise, subtle movements of a Reaper.

A moist, rustling noise took his attention, and surprised gasps rose from the tight vigil around Melanie Lavender. Hollow and Felix assumed battle stances and Shaun and

Dani sprang into action. The witch, still leaking thick globs of blood, backed away with a speed that surprised them all, and conjured a burst of purple cloud from her Hammerspace. Gerald darted forward, using his omnipresence to see as she scaled a nearby pillar using some thick, vine-like plant, and disappeared over the balcony.

'Fucking cockroach!' said Felix.

The other Downers turned to Gerald, waiting for his command: Lavender was his kill, his responsibility, and he could see the wariness on their expressions, a fear that he would lose his temper and end them all, the knowledge of Blue Meadow hovering like frozen mist above the museum.

Amy scrambled to her feet, her arms splayed pleadingly. She tugged at his arm, and he refused to look at her, determined to watch as the witch hobbled to a fruitless escape with whatever remained of her strength. A command tingled his tongue, like the pungent seeds of a Scotch bonnet. He had the power to call it, to conjure her life thread, to pull it and snap it and kill her, complete his job and purpose.

'Gerald. Please.'

He forced himself to see Amy. Her eyes were all-encompassing. The heat left his mouth, and he sighed. 'No one follow me.'

They did not need to be told. Gerald pulled himself away from Amy's grasp and mounted the vine conjured by Lavender, its great emerald leaves depressing languidly beneath his weight. He leapt onto the balcony and flitted down the adjoining corridor, and at the sound of his presence, Lavender yelped and staggered away.

The Reaper was behind her instantly. He grabbed her by the waist with one arm, tipped her in a moribund dance. They froze in this position, locked in the final stance of a death waltz. He stared at her frenzied eyes, the gaping flesh of her mouth and the rattling wail of her breath. She was determined to live. Gerald bit off the glove from his free hand, and the witch turned to stone in his grasp. Fresh tears coursed down her face. He hovered his curse before her, made patterns in the air with his skeletal fingers, threatening her to silence.

'I so badly want to kill you,' he said. 'It would be permissible. Within my law.'

She gurgled something nonsensical.

'I always stick to my word. I have never reneged on a request before. It's unbecoming.'

The witch keened louder. The pitiful noises contradicted all her previous bravado. The leader of such a powerful gang had been a helpless child all along. It was stupid.

'Be quiet,' said Gerald. 'I won't. I won't do it. It will make her sad. Just . . . be quiet.'

Lavender's expression softened. There was an infuriating knowingness in her eyes, as if she believed herself to be a kindred spirit of his. He recoiled, and it took everything in his power to swallow the cry of his bloodlust.

Still holding tightly onto the witch, Gerald fished his phone from his cloak pocket. A familiar voice crooned down the phone.

'Hi,' said Gerald. 'I hope I haven't disturbed you. I need a favour, please.'

When he returned to the Hall, the assembly appeared to be in their same positions, actively waiting for his verdict. He noted that Shaun and Dani both turned to Amy first, confirming whether Melanie Lavender was dead. The empath's gaze turned glassy and unfocused as she parsed the air, frowning, watching, before meeting his gaze. Gerald faced her evenly. He knew what she had felt: the opening of his Hammerspace and the presence of someone she did not recognise, who then vanished with Melanie Lavender in their arms.

'She's gone,' Gerald said, his eyes still on Amy.

Amy nodded, and the others relaxed, although Shaun offered a final, lingering look in their direction, at the unspoken oath cast between Reaper and empath. Amy would not expose Gerald's act of weakness, and Gerald would not elaborate on Lavender's location. But she was alive.

CHAPTER EIGHT

Amy

Shortly afterwards, Shaun made a phone call for clean-up and the silvery outlines of a dozen Hammerspace doors appeared around the walls of the Hintze Hall. Downers of all shapes and sizes flooded into the room. The Downey Met, in their black elegance, quickly examined the area. One crew disposed of Bane, zipping him in a body bag, then magicking the bag away. It sank into the ground and disappeared soundlessly. Another crew was dispatched to the upper floors. Gerald was in his own corner speaking to the Commissioner, a stern-looking witch with a tawny complexion named Afua Addo, while Amy watched it all from beneath the remaining walkway. Hollow stood sentinel beside her.

Felix, Shaun, and Dani answered questions from their own respective officers, most likely creating an elaborate yet coherent story that would avoid exposing their *Gardien* membership.

'You okay?'

Amy turned to Hollow. He was looking at her with concern, and any trace of bloodlust that she had felt on him before was absent, giving way to an empathy that she found unexpected.

'Kind of.'

'You're a good person.'

'Am I?'

'Yeah. That witch fully hurt you, helped to get you abducted, and almost ruined your life for a bit. But you had compassion for her.'

'I'm an empath.'

'Nah, it's more than that.' Hollow smiled at her. 'I think that's why Mr Reaper likes having you around.'

She contemplated this. Gerald had pretended to kill Melanie to maintain his standing with the other Downers. He had spirited her away with a person that contained a galaxy of power within them. Amy had not considered that another person in London could rival Gerald's aura, and the thought lanced her skin with cold pressure. Melanie Lavender was not dead. The witch had been given a second chance. Gerald had broken his personal principle for Amy. She wanted to cry, so relieved and hopeful for the new life Melanie could lead, far away from abusive men.

'That's nice of you to say,' she said eventually. 'And thank you, by the way. You really put your neck out for me the other day, but I was too shocked to say anything.'

'No problem.'

'This is nice. You're okay to talk to, Hollow. Makes a difference from all the dribbling.'

'Give me a break. If you could only smell yourself—'

'Hollow!'

They were distracted by a tall, muscular vampire with skin the colour of rich cedar. His black eyes were bright with mischief, and long thick locs trailed down his back, swinging below his tail bone. Judging by the symbol on his blazer, he was of a higher rank, which meant that he was aware of *Gardien* and its members.

'All right, Faust?' Hollow said, acknowledging the vampire kindly.

The vampire called Faust drew close to Hollow with a thunderous expression. 'Don't *all right* me. I thought you didn't work with Dani?'

Hollow sighed. 'I don't. It's a coincidence, I swear. There's no romance here – right, Amy?'

Amy nodded, not impressed by how she was dragged into the conversation. 'Yeah,' she said with little enthusiasm. 'All professional.' She frowned as she parsed the atmosphere between Faust and Hollow; the latter was flushed with an inexplicable reverence, and the former's was of a depth that contradicted his playful air.

Just then, a mage approached the trio with the measured steps of austere competence, a total contrast to the slouching nonchalance of Faust. The mage's glossy hair was cut into a neat bob and the label on her epaulette read *Insp. Ali*. She gave an enquiring glance to Amy before addressing her superior.

'We've restored the building, sir.'

Amy blinked, looking around in surprise. She had been so distracted about Melanie that she hadn't noticed that the walkways, the glass cases on the galleries above, and Darwin were all back to their former glory. It was as if nothing untoward had happened, that a warlock hadn't died on the cool mosaic floors, and that a human hadn't been held captive in an underground cellar beneath it.

'Cool,' said Faust, 'and the CCTV?'

'Altered.' She then turned to Hollow. 'What on earth were you lot doing here?'

Hollow bit his lip in discomfort while Faust balled his hands on his hips with an expectant smirk, as if anticipating a ridiculous story. Amy, too, watched with interest, wondering if he had had time to corroborate an excuse with the others.

'Me and Felix had a fight,' he said.

'A fight?' Inspector Ali's expression was incredulous.

'Yep,' said Hollow, 'just vampire things.'

'Vampire things,' Faust said to Inspector Ali. 'You wouldn't understand, Asmina.'

'Okay,' the mage said slowly. 'And Bane? Lavender? The Reaper just informed me he disposed of her body, even. Sounds like it was a bloodbath.'

'Oh, all a coincidence,' Hollow said with more confidence. 'We stumbled upon their little hideout during the battle, then found the empath here.' He gestured at Amy with a smile.

Inspector Ali raised a brow, but did not press it further. 'Well, next time you lot are doing your little ... vampire things, can you confine it to one room? And maybe choose one that's *not* a national attraction?'

'Of course, definitely. But this isn't all our fault, so we can't take all the blame,' said Hollow.

Inspector Ali frowned. 'Then who—'

'There's your culprit.' Faust nodded towards Gerald, who was still in deep conversation with Commissioner Addo. Inspector Ali froze, then averted her gaze.

'What? Nothing to say now?' Faust asked. The inspector rolled her eyes, and then stalked away from him. 'Anyway,' he said, turning to Amy, 'what was your name again?' Even without Amy reading his aura, the vampire's intentions were transparently lecherous.

'And this is why Dani dumped your arse,' said Hollow.

'Oi.' Faust pressed a hand on his chest in mock indignation before refocusing on Amy. 'Stay away from this one, love. Hollow the Ho, we call him.'

'Commander!' Commissioner Addo called to Faust, beckoning him over to her audience with Gerald. Faust grinned at

Hollow, walking away backwards so he could continue to taunt him.

'I'll remember that next time you're knocking on my door at midnight, starving for a drink,' Hollow said.

Two middle fingers were Faust's only reply.

'What do you think happens now?' Amy asked. The hall started to clear as the officers removed the final traces of magic in the area. They were impressive in their efficiency. So far, *Gardien* had caused a lot of mess in various parts of the city, leaving behind bodies and unexplained upheaval. The Downey Met had painstakingly cleaned up behind them at every step, expertly maintaining the secret of their underground city.

Hollow shrugged. 'Honestly, it's gonna be a bit of a mare going after Crow. We'll have to tread carefully now so he doesn't try to run away. I bet Blythe is *so* mad right now. I don't fancy being in his next meeting.'

'Is there evidence, though?'

'Now that we have a lead, we can work on it. Blythe's pretty persuasive, so if these officers keep their mouth shut as he's asked them to, it gives us all time to get the evidence. Bank accounts, photos, and other stuff. But gosh, I'm not jumping at the chance to arrest him. This is our *mayor*. He always seemed like such a sound person.'

Amy shrugged, thinking about the controversies surrounding the government Upstairs. 'Normally that's how it goes, right? The most unassuming ones are always hiding something. If they had nothing to hide, they wouldn't be politicians.'

Hollow barked a humourless laugh. 'You're right about that, can't lie.'

'But anyway,' she said, remembering something crucial, 'I

kind of need to leave a message on my boss's phone. I think she thinks I'm dead.'

She slipped away beneath one of the walkways. Using the phone that Gerald had borrowed for her, she left a brief message on her manager's phone, apologising profusely once again for her absence, and promising to return to work tomorrow. She would take annual leave for her notice period, she decided. There was no point going into work with so much risk. It was hard not to think about Nan – she might have been happy that Amy was no longer working at the library, but she never would have imagined what her granddaughter had got herself into.

Gerald approached her, his expression sheepish. 'Hi,' he said.

'Hi.'

'Well, we're good to go. Commissioner Addo has it all covered from here. Best not stay around too long.'

'You gonna tell me where she is?'

'No. She's somewhere safe. I promise you.'

'All right. Fine. Thank you.' She swallowed. He would never understand what this decision meant to her. Amy was grateful. She would not press it further; the magnitude of the Reaper allowing a target to live was not lost on her, and she was wary of saying the wrong thing, potentially weaving a fatally stubborn resolve in the Gerald of the future.

'Are you embarrassed by all the mess you've caused?' she asked instead.

'I'm sure you already know that.'

Amy grinned at him. His aura was red with the heat of humiliation. She had felt a range of new emotions on him this evening, and judging by his expression, these emotions had been new to him also. It was almost charming.

'You can't be the perfect Reaper all the time. I was a bit distracted to watch your fight properly, but it looks like Bane didn't just roll over and let you get away with things like always.'

Gerald rubbed the back of his neck absently, his cheeks flushing as they left the Hintze Hall. 'I would prefer for things to be much neater next time.'

'Oh, so you just want people to go out gently, do you? Ain't there a poem about that?'

'I see you're as sprightly as ever.'

'Maybe I am.'

They smiled at each other when they were at the entrance. It had been a difficult, torturous day, but knowing it was over – if only temporarily – brought about a sense of relief so strong, it was impossible not to be jubilant. Gerald held her hand. He spent a few moments watching their clasped fingers as they intertwined with one another, a sense of calm swirling into his aura, before he flitted back to St Pancras.

And for the first time since her house was destroyed, Amy felt like she was home.

CHAPTER NINE

The Reaper and the Empath

The city centre of Downstairs was packed. Chairs, tables, and benches were squashed into every available space. Food stalls selling various Downstairs delicacies introduced a strange smokiness to the proceedings, and for the first time, a queue of enthusiastic witches trailed out of the nearby Voodoo Rays. Everyone was irreverent as they watched the massive screens that floated before the brightly lit skyscrapers, outlined in the signature silver of Shaun's magic. He had worked hard to plant several more transmitters around London, which was why the whole of Downstairs had assembled to watch Lex Crow's arrest at Biggin Hill Airport.

It had been a week since the battle at Hintze Hall, and Blythe, Commander Faust Damari Xavier, Commissioner Afua Addo, and the rest of *Gardien* had worked almost without sleep to provide indisputable evidence of Lex Crow's involvement with the Downey Gang and its factions. When the alleged deaths of Melanie Lavender and Tyrell Bane were exposed, the initial celebrations were replaced by apprehension. The Downstairs public was aware that the witch–warlock duo had an accomplice, and a sense of the unfinished began to permeate the news. The Downers wanted answers, and some retribution to the anonymous protector that was indirectly responsible for the massacre at Sitton Road.

Blythe had planned it perfectly. After the evidence had

been gathered, he made Faust and the Commissioner hold a press conference, promising the public that the results of their investigations were pending, all to intimidate the mayor. Paid informants tracked his movements, tracing his phone calls to reveal his upcoming holiday. And, as a senior member of the magic community, he would inevitably travel from Biggin Hill, away from the prying human eyes at Heathrow, Gatwick, and the other busier airports around London. The unknowing staff of City Hall was surprised to hear he was taking annual leave during such a critical time, but assumed he was rewarding himself after a stressful season. It was only after discovering he was travelling alone that they grew suspicious.

On the morning of his arrest, during his frantic journey to Biggin Hill, the *Nightly Moon* published the explosive scoop of Lexton Crow's humble rise to mayorship thanks to the Mason purse, the financial struggles that plagued his life leading to his involvement with the Downey Gang, his subsequent affair with Melanie Lavender, the extortion, and his final act of revenge by making an assassination request to the Grim Tribe. Shaun's surveillance followed Crow's taxi as it tore down the streets of South London and into the green outskirts of Bromley. When his transport halted outside the airport with a screech, he was left to exit with his hands raised in surrender. The Downey Met surrounded the area, and Blythe Mason sat on the steps of a private jet, legs folded in mocking leisure.

A roar erupted from the spectators in the city square. Beer sloshed out of pint glasses and finger food spilled on tables. Beside Gerald, Amy looked around at the proceedings, clearly unimpressed, before taking a furtive sip from her own glass.

'It's not the football,' she told him once the crowd quietened to watch as Lex Crow was marched into a waiting transport. Gerald grinned at her.

His phone buzzed and he glanced at the screen. His father was calling him again. He hesitated, then stowed it away in his Hammerspace.

'You can't ignore him forever,' said Amy.

'Mmhmm,' Gerald said. He watched as Blythe walked purposefully to his own car. With his black trench coat that flapped around his ankles, and the thick sunglasses glinting in the early morning rays, and the way his curls appeared to bounce as he walked, Gerald thought he looked so cool. He would always admire Blythe, his first and oldest friend.

'I think some space is good – for both of us,' he told Amy. 'We'll talk when I'm ready to.'

The empath patted him on the shoulder. 'Fair enough. How d'you feel about Crow getting arrested? Mad that he was the one behind all of it, right?'

The Reaper sighed. 'Stranger things have happened.'

They toasted to that – Gerald with his cup of jasmine tea and Amy with her red plastic tumbler of rum and coke – and watched as the Downey Met packed up and went home. The party continued well into the afternoon. Downers of all kinds relished the swollen rancour of their society, performing their extraordinary commonness, and Amy coexisted with them, an observer and confidante. She snatched her phone from her pocket, scrolled through the apps, and instinctively went to her messages.

One profile picture of two pairs of sand-dusted feet stood as an icon for her mother, boasting a recent holiday with her husband to the contacts that she wished would care. The photo said *everything is fine*, and the last messages exchanged with her daughter were over a year ago. Her father's icon was of a car.

She scrolled onwards, saw Cordory's rainbow graphic and Vilma's photo of carnations on a windowsill. At last, she found the object of her search – a single slice of rum cake, glistening with stewed sultanas, haphazardly wrapped in cling film and poorly captured altogether: a too-bright flash with edges out of focus. Amy clicked on the icon, smiled at the last words she had exchanged with the baker of the rum cake, and started her new message. *Nan*, she said, *I have so much to tell you. It's mad.* And she wrote the story of her unfathomable, tumultuous spring.

EPILOGUE: DORCAS

Although small in stature, Dorcas held a presence that was impossible to ignore. It took her only a short while to get to Marrakech, a journey that was a day and a half by normal human standards. After buying some saffron and argan oil from the market, she returned towards the desert. Her black cloak fluttered in the warming weather, and she smiled at her attendant as he waited beside Ember, their camel transport, on the cusp of the mountains. Two lone desert wanderers would automatically alert tourists, to which the locals would only offer a cursory glance before muttering, 'Nomads.'

Are you sure you didn't want anything, Abrax? she asked her attendant in Grimtongue.

No ma'am.

She smiled again, securing her belongings with flesh and blood hands. Abrax, who was a member of the Tribe, but not a Reaper, had hands like hers. Sometimes she wondered how it would feel if her own husband had the ability to touch her without his leather gloves and the threat of her instant death. It was hard to forget her surprise when her firstborn emerged from the womb with stubby brown fingers. She had relished in his bubbling warmth and infant desperation, weak nails cloying at her vital, maternal body. But then she had to witness the death of his hands. Brown skin blackened and became flaky and shed away, and by the time he was five, he could no longer hold her.

Dorcas eventually arrived at the Point of No Return. It was a sandstorm that roared across the most volatile parts of the desert, and like the Grims, was never stationary, appearing and disappearing at various locations to solidify its illusion. Dorcas, Abrax, and Ember all headed straight towards the storm and vanished.

On the other side was a loud and bustling community of black-cloaked individuals. Merchants shouted from market stalls and an array of illustrious tents billowed in the desert breeze. Teenagers loitered outside cafés and children raced each other in swimming pools and men shouted and cursed around radios and women read newspapers and books within the cool serenity of the boutiques. A chorus of languages accompanied the frenzy: from Grimtongue to Bambara to Arabic to French to English and more.

When the Tribe saw Dorcas, they saluted before making way for her to pass. She would nod politely, offer a few pleasantries, and continue towards the mansion.

The Reaper residence was at the edge of the community. Made from shimmering glass and mosaic, it towered over the tents and was the only fixture that fell outside the Point of No Return, but was still hidden by a magic of its own. She thanked Abrax and headed inside.

'What is this?' she asked, spinning around the foyer and frowning at the pile of suitcases and outer cloaks that occupied most of it.

'It's your husband, ma'am,' said one of the younger maids, who gently placed two passports on the dresser beside the front door before skittering away. Dorcas breezed through the foyer and headed upstairs to the bedroom.

She found Faiz sitting on the edge of the bed, his eyes staring at something that only he could see, his gloved hands clasped together, fingers tightly laced. He had a handsome face that was ruddy and deep brown, with a dark beard that framed his jaw and fell in thick curls to his chest. Only a few wisps of silver denoted his age. He reminded her of those old Babylonian etchings, with his black hair and unmistakable power. He made the ruby-silk sheets and the violet flooring and the gold ornaments all look cheap in his presence.

Faiz, she said. He started, then looked at her. Briefly. *What's troubling you? And what's all this in the foyer?*

After a pause, he rose, and almost appeared to shake away his obvious anxiety, leaving it all in a shadow on the floor.

It's your son, he said at last. *He isn't answering my calls.*

'And?' she said in English. She felt her chest tighten for what she knew was coming next.

'And we're going to London. Your bags are already packed.'

Dorcas sighed, deflated. She rested against the door post for support. Her husband moved around the bedroom with new-found vigour, packing his things in a smaller travel bag and going to the adjoining bathroom for his toiletries.

'You ready?' he called, his voice echoing against the bathroom tiles.

'Well . . . I guess so,' she said, and helped him gather the last of their belongings.

Acknowledgements

Writing a book is a long and solitary process, but there are significant lights that illuminate the darkness of the journey. Thank you to everyone who has offered kind words, encouragement, a shoulder to lean on, professional care, and a space to vent through it all, from the querying trenches and beyond.

I am a proud alumnus of Penguin #WriteNow, a programme that shoved me through the heavy door of publishing and granted me my childhood dream of being an author. Entering that competition changed my life.

Thanks to Molly Jamieson, my agent, for seeing *The Reaper*'s potential and being a fantastic support. Thanks to everyone at team Del Rey and PRH for your tireless support, encouragement and patience: Sam Bradbury, Feranmi Ojutiku, Laura Burge, Rose Waddilove, Rachel Kennedy, Issie Levin, Rosie Grant and Aoifke France-McGuire – special thanks to Louisa Burden-Garabedian and Kasim Mohammed, without whom *The Reaper* would not have been published.

Thanks to everyone at Black Girl Writers, including my colleagues Osob, Moyette Gibbons and Marissa Asli Bangura; Nancy Adimora, Sarah-Jade Virtue, Juliet Mushens for her tireless support of my writing, Liza DeBlock for beating my query package into shape, and every mentor and mentee who has supported us over the past five years.

Thanks to Michael Curran at Tangerine Press, who was the first person to publish me in a professional capacity. Thank you to everyone at *Anime Feminist*, for giving me my first paid writing gig.

ACKNOWLEDGEMENTS

Thanks to Sheriff, Felipe, Ellesh, Calum, Joseph, Russell, Richard, Sbeya, Hichem, Michael, Mark, Phil, Julian, David and all my work colleagues for their enthusiasm and for taking an interest in my writing journey, asking for updates about 'the book' and offering to put copies in the office library.

Thanks also to my wonderful friends: Tobi Dawodu, Hakeem Forrest, Akil Henry, Shade Henry-Thompson, Nate Martin, Tamara Saffir, Amarah Flood and everyone in the Debut 2025 group. Special thanks to Dami Odelola, who saw the advert for #WriteNow and thought of me. If she hadn't encouraged me to enter, *The Reaper* would still be a dwindling, aimless draft, and I would likely still be querying.

Thank you to my beautiful family: Ras, Damien, Con, Rox and Dad. My husband, Solomon, and my son (who is three years old at the time of writing this and is only faintly aware of what I do).

And finally, my mum, Verona Veronica Jackson: the woman who instilled in me a love of books, who irresponsibly granted eight-year-old me unguarded access to her Stephen King and Shaun Hutson collection, who always read my rambling childhood stories and offered me feedback and advice. She passed away unexpectedly in April 2023, leaving an irreparable scar. Her death intensified the themes of loss and bereavement in this series, and I cannot write without thinking about her. I am so sad she will never hold this book in her hands, but I am sure she would have been proud of my success.

About the Author

Jackson P. Brown is a writer from London, an anime and manga enthusiast, and the founder of Black Girl Writers – a mentoring programme for aspiring Black writers. After winning Penguin Random House's #WriteNow competition in 2020, her London-based urban fantasy series, which begins with *The Reaper*, was acquired by Del Rey UK.